To Neil and Tom,
whose absurd idea it was

and in memory of
a little lilac-covered cottage
where I used to live

ROSE
DAUGHTER

CHAPTER

1

Her earliest memory was of waking from the dream. It was also her only clear memory of her mother. Her mother was beautiful, dashing, the toast of the town. Her youngest daughter remembered the blur of activity, friends and hangers-on, soothsayers and staff, the bad-tempered pet dragon on a leash—bad-tempered on account of the ocarunda leaves in his food, which prevented him from producing any more fire than might occasionally singe his wary handler, out which also upset his digestion—the constant glamour and motion which was her mother and her mother's world. She remembered peeping out at her mother from around various thresholds before various nurses and governesses (hired by her dull merchant father) snatched her away.

She remembered too, although she was too young to put it into words, the excitability, no, the restlessness of her mother's manner, a restlessness of a too-acute alertness in search of something that cannot be found. But such were the brightness and ardour of her mother's personality that those around her also were swept up into her search, not knowing it was a search, happy merely to be a part of such liveliness and gaiety.

The only thing that ever lingered was the sweet smell of her mother's perfume.

Her only memory of her mother's face was from the night she woke from the dream for the first time, crying in terror. In the dream she had been walking—she could barely walk yet in her waking life—toddling down a long dark corridor, only vaguely lit by a few candles set too far into their sconces, too high up in the walls. The shadows stretched everywhere round her, and that was terrible enough; and the silence was almost as dreadful as the darkness. But what was even worse was that she knew a wicked monster waited for her at the end of the corridor. It was the wickedest monster that had ever lived, and it was waiting just for her, and she was all alone.

She was still young enough to be sleeping in a crib with high barred sides; she remembered fastening her tiny fists round the wooden bars, whose square edges cut into her soft palms. She remembered the dream—she remembered crying—and she remembered her mother coming, and bending over her, and picking her up, whispering gently in her ear, holding her against her breast, softly stroking her back. Sitting down quietly on the nurse's stool and rocking her slowly till she fell asleep again.

She woke in her crib in the morning, just as usual. She asked her nurse where her mamma was; her nurse stared and did not believe her when she tried to tell her, in the few words she was old enough to use, that her mamma had come to her in the night when she had cried. "I'd've heard you if you yelled, miss," said the nurse stiffly. "And I slept quiet last night."

But she knew it was her mother, had to have been her mother. She remembered the sweet smell of her perfume, and no one but her mother ever wore that scent.

Her perfume smelt of flowers, but of no flowers the little girl ever found, neither in the dozens of overflowing vases set in nearly every room of their tall, magnificent town house nearly every day of the year, nor anywhere in the long scrolling curves of the flower-beds in the gardens be-. hind the house, nor in the straight, meticulous rows within the glasshouses and orangeries behind the garden.

She once confided to a new nurse her wish to find the flower that had produced her mother's scent. She was inspired to do so when the nurse introduced herself by saying, "Hello, little one. Your daddy has told me your name, but do you know mine? It's Pansy, just like the flower. I bet you have lots of pansies in your garden."

"Yes, we do," replied the little girl politely. "And they're my favourite—almost. My favourite is a flower I do not know. It is the flower that my mother's scent comes from. I keep hoping I will find it. Perhaps you will help me."

Pansy had laughed at her, but it was a friendly laugh. "What a funny little thing you are," she said. "Fancy at your age wanting to know about perfume. You'll be a heartbreaker in a few years, I guess."

The little girl had looked at her new nurse solemnly but had not troubled to explain further. She could tell Pansy meant to be kind. It was true that she had first become interested in gardens as something other than merely places her nurses sometimes took her, in the peremptory way of grown-ups, when she had made the connexion between perfume smells and flower smells. But she had very soon discovered that she simply liked gardens.

Her mother's world—her mother's house—was very exciting, but it was also rather scary. She liked plants. They were quiet, and they stayed in the same place, but they weren't boring, like a lot of the things she was supposed to be interested in were boring, such as dolls, which just lay there unless you picked them up and did things with them (and then the chief thing you were supposed to do with them, apparently, was to change their clothes, and could there be anything more awfully, deadly boring than changing anyone's clothes any more often than one was utterly obliged to?). Plants got on with making stems and leaves and flowers and fruit, whatever you did, and a lot of them were nice to the touch: the slight attractive furriness of rabbit's-ears and Cupid's-darts, the slick waxy surfaces of camellia leaves and ivy—and lots of them had beautiful flowers, which changed both shape and colour as they opened, and some of them smelt interesting, even if none of them smelt like her mother's perfume. And then there were things like apples and grapes, which were the best things in the world when you could break them off from the stem yourself and eat them right there.

From the nurses' point of view, the youngest girl was the least trouble of the three. She neither went out seeking mischief, the more perilous the better, the way the eldest did, nor answered impertinently (and with a vocabulary alarmingly beyond her age), the way the second did. Her one consistent misbehaviour, tiresome enough indeed as it was, and which no amount of punishment seemed able to break her of, was that of escaping into the garden the moment the nurse's eye was diverted, where she would later be found, digging little holes and planting things—discarded toys (especially dolls), half-eaten biscuits, dead leaves, and dry twigs—singing to herself, and covering her white pinafores and stockings with dirt. None of the nurses ever noticed that the twigs, were they left where she planted them, against all probability, grew. One old gardener noticed, and because he was old and considered rather silly, he had the time to spend making the little girl's acquaintance.

Nurses never lasted long. Despite the care taken and the warnings given to keep the nurses in the nurseries, eventually some accident of meeting occurred with the merchant's wife, and the latest nurse, immediately found to be too slow or too dowdy or too easily bewildered to suit, was fired. When Pansy came to say good-bye, she said, "I have to go away. Don't cry, lovey, it's just the way it is. But I wanted to tell you: It's roses your mum's perfume smells of. Roses. No, you don't have 'em here. It's generally only sorcerers who can get 'em to grow much. The village I was born in, we had a specially clever greenwitch, and she had one, just one, but it was heaven when it bloomed. That's how I know. But it takes barrels of petals to make perfume enough to fill a bottle the size of your littlest fingertip—that's why the sorcerers are interested, see, I never knew a sorcerer wasn't chiefly out to make money—your pa's paying a queen's ransom for it, I can tell you that."

When the youngest daughter was five years old, her mother died. She had bet one of her hunting friends she could leap a half-broken colt over a farm cart. She had lost the bet and broken her neck. The colt broke both forelegs and had to be shot.

The whole city mourned, her husband and two elder daughters most of all. The youngest one embarrassed her family at the funeral by repeating, over and over, "Where is my mamma? Where is my mamma?"

"She is too young to understand," said the grieving friends and acquaintances, and patted her head, and embraced the husband and the elder girls.

A well-meaning greenwitch offered the father a charm for his youngest daughter. "She'll work herself into a fever, poor little thing," the woman said, holding the little bag on its thin ribbon out to him. "You just hang it round her neck—I'd do it myself, but it'll work better coming from your hands—and she'll know her mamma's gone, but it won't hurt till she's a little more ready for it. It'll last three, four months if you don't let it get wet."

But the merchant knocked the small bundle out of the woman's hand with a cry of rage, and might have struck the greenwitch herself—despite the bad luck invariably attendant on any violence offered any magic practitioner—if those standing nearest had not held him back. The startled greenwitch was hustled away, someone explaining to her in an undertone that the merchant was a little beside himself, that grief had made him so unreasonable that he blamed his wife's soothsayers for not having warned her against her last, fatal recklessness, and had for the moment turned against all magic. Even her pet dragon had been given away.

The greenwitch allowed herself to be hustled. She was a kindly woman, but not at all grand—greenwitches rarely were—and had known the family at all only because she had twice or three times found the youngest daughter in a flowerbed in one of the city's municipal parks and returned her to her distracted nurse. She gave one little backward glance to that youngest daughter, who was still running from one mourner to the next and saying, "Where is my mamma? Where is my mamma?"

"I don't like to think of the little thing's dreams," murmured the greenwitch, but her escort had brought her to the cemetery gate and turned her loose, with some propelling force, and the greenwitch shook her head sadly but went her own way.

The night of her mother's funeral her youngest daughter had the dream for the second time. She was older in the dream just as she was in life; older and taller, she spoke in complete sentences and could run without falling down. None of this was of any use to her in the dream. The candles were still too high overhead to cast anything but shadows; she was still all alone, and the unseen monster waited, just for her.

After that she had the dream often.

At first, when she cried out for her mamma, the nurses were sympathetic, but as the months mounted up to a year since the funeral, and no more than a week ever passed before another midnight waking, another sobbing cry of "Mamma! Mamma!" the nurses grew short-tempered. The little girl learnt not to cry out, but she still had the dream.

And she eluded her protectresses more often than ever and crept out into the garden, where the old gardener (keeping a wary eye out for the descent of a shrieking harpy from the nursery) taught her how better to plant things, and which things to plant, and what to do to make them happy after they were planted.

She grew old enough to try to flee, and so discover that this did her no good in the dream; it was the same dark, silent, sinister corridor, without windows or doors, the same unknown, expectant monster, whichever way she turned. And then she discovered she had never really tried to run away at all, that she was determined to follow the corridor to its end, to face the monster. And that was the most terrifying thing of all.

She wondered, as they all three grew up, if it was the dream itself that made her so different from her sisters. They were all beautiful; all three took after their mother. But the eldest one was as brave as she had been, and her name was Lionheart; the second one was as clever as she had been, and her name was Jeweltongue. The youngest was called Beauty.

Beauty adopted the nerve-shattered horses, the dumbly confused and despairing dogs that Lionheart left in her wake. She found homes for them with quiet, timid, dull people—as well as homes for barn-loft kittens, canaries which wouldn't sing, parrots which wouldn't talk, and sphinxes which curled up into miserable little balls in the backs of their cages and refused to be goaded into fighting.

She brought cups of tea with her own hands to wounded swains bleeding from cries of "Coward!" and "Lackwit!" and offered her own handkerchiefs to maidservants and costumiers found weeping in corners after run-ins with Jeweltongue. She found tactful things to say to urgent young playwrights who wished to be invited to Jeweltongue's salons, and got rid of philanthropists who wished Jeweltongue to apply her notorious acuteness—and perhaps some of the family's money—to schemes towards the improvement of the general human lot.

She also kept an eye on the household accounts, to make sure that the calfbound set of modern philosophy Jeweltongue had ordered contained all the twenty volumes she was charged for, that all twenty sets of horseshoes the farrier included in his bill had indeed been nailed to the feet of Lionheart's carriage teams and hunters, and that the twenty brace of pheasant delivered for a dinner-party were all served to their guests.

On some days, when it seemed to her that everyone she met was either angry or unhappy, she would go out into the garden and hide. She had learned to avoid the army of gardeners, run by an ambitious head gardener who was as forceful and dominating as any general—or rather, she had never outgrown her child's instinct to drop quietly out of sight when a grown-up moving a little too purposefully was nearby. As soon as she stepped out onto the lawn, she felt tranquillity drift down over her like a veil; and almost as though it were a veil, or as if she had suddenly become a plant herself (a tidy, well-shaped, well-placed plant of a desirable colour and habit, for anything else would have drawn attention at once), she was rarely noticed by the gardeners, hurrying this way and that with military precision, even when they passed quite close to her.

The old gardener who had been kind to her when she was small had been pensioned off and lived in a cottage at some distance from their great house, on the outskirts of the city, where the farmlands began and where he had his own small garden for the first time in his long life. A few times a year she found half a day to go visit him—once with a convalescent puppy who had been stepped on by a carriage horse—but she missed having him in the garden.

Once she arranged the flowers for one of her sisters' balls. This was ordinarily the housekeeper's job. Her sisters felt that flower arranging was a pastime for servants or stupid people; Beauty felt that flowers belonged in the garden where they grew. But on the morning of this party the housekeeper had fallen downstairs and sprained her ankle, and was in too much pain to do anything but lie in a darkened room and run the legs off the maid assigned to attend her.

Beauty looked at the poor flowers standing in their buckets of cold water, and at the array of noble vases laid out for them, and began to arrange them, only half aware of what she was about, while her sisters were rushing around the house shouting (in Lionheart's case) or muttering savagely (in Jeweltongue's) while they attended to what should have been the housekeeper's other urgent duties on the day of an important party. Most of Beauty's mind was occupied with what the night's events would bring; she would much rather scrub a floor—not that she ever had scrubbed a floor, but she assumed it would be hard, dull, unpleasant work—than attend a ball, which was hard, dull, unpleasant work that didn't even have a clean floor to show for it afterwards.

Neither Lionheart nor Jeweltongue at best paid much attention to flowers, beyond the fact that one did of course have to have them, as one had place settings for seventy-five and a butler to cherish the wine; but when they came downstairs to have a final look at the front hall and the dining-room, even they were astonished by what Beauty had done.

"My saints!" said Lionheart. "If the conversation flags, we can look at the flowers!"

"The conversation will not flag," said Jeweltongue composedly, "but that is not to say that Beauty has not done miracles," and she patted her sister's shoulder absently, as one might pat a dog.

"I didn't know flowers could look like this!" roared Lionheart, and threw up her arms as if challenging an enemy to strike at her, and laughed. "If Miss Fuss-and-Bother could see this, perhaps it would quiet her nerves!" Miss Fuss-and-Bother was the name Lionheart had given to the governess least patient with the frequent necessity of fishing Beauty out of her latest muddy haven in the garden and bringing her indoors and dumping her in the bath. Lionheart had often been obliged to join her there after other, more dangerous adventures of her own.

But that ball was particularly successful, and her sisters teased Beauty that it was on account of her flowers and asked if she was keeping a greenwitch in her cupboard, who could work such charms. Beauty, distressed, tried to prevent any of this from reaching their father's ears, for he would not have taken even a joke about a greenwitch in their house in good part. The housekeeper, who did hear some of it as she hobbled around the house on a stick, was not pleased and contrived to snub "Miss Beauty" for a fortnight after. (She might also have denuded the garden of flowers in her efforts to have a grander show than Beauty's for the next party, but the head gardener was more than a match for her.) Beauty stayed out of her way till she had moved her ill will to another target; there was too much temper and spitefulness in the house already, and she thought she might forget her promise to herself never to add to it, and tell the housekeeper what a dreadful old woman she thought her.

Besides, she would probably then have to hire another housekeeper afterwards, and she could think of few things she less wanted to do.

The sisters' parties, over the course of several seasons, became famous as the finest in the city, as fine as their mother's had been. Perhaps not quite so grand as the mayor's, but perhaps more enjoyable; the mayor's daughters were, after all, rather plain.

Only the ill-natured—especially those whose own parties were slighted in favor of the sisters'—ever suggested that it was the work of any hired magician. Their father's attitude towards magic was well known. His sudden revulsion of feeling upon his wife's death had indeed been much talked of; but much more surprising was its result.

It was true that he was the wealthiest merchant in the city, but that was all he was; and if he had long had what seemed, were it not absurd to think so, an almost magical ability to seize what chance he wished when he wished to seize it, well, seers and soothsayers were always going on about how there was no such thing as luck, but that everyone possessed some seeds of magic within themselves, whether or not they ever found them or nursed them into growth. But no mere merchant, even the wealthiest merchant in the biggest city in the country, and whatever the origins of his business luck, should have been able to dislodge any magical practitioner who did not wish to be dislodged; but so it was in this case. Not only were all the magicians, astrologers, and soothsayers who had been members of his wife's entourage thrown out of his house—which ban was acceptably within his purview—but he saw them driven out of the city.

The sisters were forbidden to have anything to do with magic; the two elder girls still bought small street charms occasionally, and Beauty was good friends with the elderly salamander belonging to the retired sorcerer who lived near them; but none of them would ever hire any practitioner to do a personal spell.

It was no surprise to anyone who paid attention to such matters when Lionheart contracted an engagement with the Duke of Dauntless, who owned six thousand of the finest hunting acres in the entire country, and much else besides. Jeweltongue affianced herself to the Baron of Grandiloquence, who was even wealthier than the Duke, and had a bigger town house. They planned a double wedding; Beauty and the three sisters of the Duke and the four sisters of the Baron should be bridesmaids. It would be the finest wedding of the season, if not the century. Everyone would be there, admiring, envious, and beautifully dressed.

In all the bustle of preparations, no one, not even Beauty, noticed that the old merchant seemed unusually preoccupied.

He had hoped he could put off his business's ruin till after the wedding. He loved his daughters, but he felt his life had ended with his wife's death; he had been increasingly unable to concentrate on his business affairs in the years since. His greatest pain as he watched the impending storm approach was the thought that he had not been able to provide a husband for Beauty. It was true that she was not very noticeable in the company of her sisters, but she should have been able to find a suitable husband among all the young men who flocked to their house to court Lionheart and Jeweltongue.

He thought of hiring a good magician or a sorcerer to throw a few days' hold over the worst of the wreck, but his antipathy to all things magical since his wife's death meant not only had he lost all his contacts in the magical professions, but a sudden search now for a powerful practitioner was sure to raise gossip—and suspicion. He was not at all certain he would have been able to find one who would accept such a commission from him anyway. It had occurred to him, as the worst of the dull oppression of grief had lifted from his mind, to be surprised no magical practitioner had tried to win revenge for his turning half a dozen of them out of the city; perhaps they had known it was not necessary. The unnatural strength that had enabled him to perform that feat had taken most of his remaining vitality—and business acumen—with it.

The bills for the wedding itself he paid for in his last days as the wealthiest merchant in the city. He would not be able to fulfil the contracts for his daughters' dowries, but his two

elder daughters were in themselves reward enough for any
man. And her sisters would do something for Beauty.

It was ten days before the wedding when the news broke.
People were stunned. It was all anyone talked about for three
days—and then the next news came: The Duke of Dauntless
and the Baron of Grandiloquence had broken off the wedding.

The messengers from their fiancés brought the sisters' fate
to them on small squares of thick cream-laid paper, folded
and sealed with the heavy heirloom seals of their fiancés'
houses. Lionheart and Jeweltongue each replied with one
cold line written in her own firm hand; neither kept her
messenger waiting.

By the end of that day Lionheart and Jeweltongue and
Beauty and their father were alone in their great house; not
a servant remained to them, and many had stolen valuable
fittings and furniture as well, guessing correctly that their
ruined masters would not be able to order them returned,
nor punish them for theft.

As the twilight lengthened in their silent sitting-room,
Jeweltongue at last stood up from her chair and began to
light the lamps; Lionheart stirred in her corner and went
downstairs to the kitchens. Beauty remained where she was,
chafing her father's cold hands and fearing what the expression on his face might mean. Later she ate what Lionheart put in front of her, without noticing what it was, and
fed their father with a spoon, as if he were a child. Jeweltongue settled down with the housekeeper's book and began
to study it, making the occasional note.

For the first few days they did only small, immediate
things. Lionheart took over the kitchens and cooking; Jeweltongue took over the housekeeping. Beauty began going
through the boxes of papers that had been delivered from
what had been her father's office and dumped in a corner
of one of the drawing-rooms.

Lionheart could be heard two floors away from the kitchens, cursing and flinging things about, wielding knives and
mallets like swords and lances. Jeweltongue rarely spoke
aloud, but she swept floors and beat the laundry as pitilessly

as she had ever told off an underhousemaid for not blacking a grate sufficiently or a footman waiting at table for having a spot on his shirtfront.

Beauty read their father's correspondence, trying to discover the real state of their affairs and some gleam of guidance as to what they must do next. She wrote out necessary replies, while her father mumbled and moaned and rocked in his chair, and she held his trembling hand around the pen that he might write his signature when she had finished.

Even the garden could not soothe Beauty during that time. She went out into it occasionally, as she might have reached for a shawl if she were cold; but she would find herself standing nowhere she could remember going, staring blindly at whatever was before her, her thoughts spinning and spinning and spinning until she was dizzy with them. There were now no gardeners to hide from, but any relief she might have found in that was overbalanced by seeing how quickly the garden began to look shabby and neglected. She didn't much mind the indoors beginning to look shabby and neglected; furniture doesn't notice being dusty, corners don't notice cobwebs, cushions don't notice being unplumped. She told herself that plants didn't mind going undeadheaded and unpruned—and the weeds, of course, were much happier than they'd ever been before. But the plants in the garden were her friends; the house was just a building full of objects.

She had little appetite and barely noticed as Lionheart's lumpen messes began to evolve into recognizable dishes. She had never taken a great deal of interest in her own appearance and had minded the least of the three of them when they put their fine clothes away, for they had agreed among themselves that all their good things should go towards assuaging their father's creditors. She did not notice that Jeweltongue had an immediate gift for invisible darns, for making a bodice out of an old counterpane, a skirt of older curtains, and collar and cuffs of worn linen napkins with the stained bits cut out, and finishing with a pretty dress it was no penance to wear.

Nor could she sleep at night. She felt she would welcome

her old nightmare almost as solace, so dreadful had their
waking life become; but the dream stayed away. Since her
mother's death it had never left her alone for so long. She
found herself missing it; in its absence it became one more
security that had been torn away from her, a faithful companion who had deserted her. And it was not until now, with
their lives a wreck around them, that she realised she had
forgotten what her mother's face looked like. She could remember remembering, she could remember the long months
after her mother's death, waking from the dream crying,
"Mamma!" and knowing what face she hoped to see when
she opened her eyes, knowing her disappointment when it
was only the nurse's. When had she forgotten her mother's
face? Some unmarked moment in the last several years, as
childhood memories dimmed under the weight of adult responsibilities, or only now, one more casualty of their ruin?
She did not know and could not guess.

What unsettled her most of all was that her last fading
wisp of memory contained nothing of her mother's beauty,
but only kindness, kindness and peace, a sense of safe haven. And yet the first thing anyone who had known her
mother mentioned about her was her beauty, and while she
was praised for her vitality, her wit, and her courage, far
from any haven, her companionship was a dare, a challenge,
an exhilarating danger.

In among her father's papers Beauty discovered a lawyers' copy of a will, dated in May of the year she had turned
two, leaving the three sisters the possession of the little
house owned by the woman named. Beauty puzzled over
this for some time, as she knew all her father's relatives
(none of whom wanted to know him or his daughters anymore), and knew as well that her mother had had none; nor
did she know of any connexion whatsoever to anyone or
anything so far away from the city of the sisters' birth. But
there was no easy accounting for it, and Beauty had no time
for useless mysteries.

There was a lawyers' letter with the will, dated seven
years later, saying that the old woman had disappeared soon
after making the will, and in accordance with the law, the

woman had now been declared dead, and the house was theirs. It was called Rose Cottage. It lay many weeks' journey from the city, and it stood alone in rough country, at a little distance from the nearest town.

Even their father's creditors were not interested in it.

She wrote to the lawyers, asking if there was any further transaction necessary if they wished to take up residence, and received a prompt but curt note in reply saying that the business was no longer anything to do with them but that they supposed the house was still standing.

Rose Cottage, she thought. What a romantic name. I wonder what the woman who had it was like. I suppose it's like a lot of other house names—a timid family naming theirs Dragon Villa or city folk longing for the country calling theirs Broadmeadow. Perhaps—she almost didn't dare finish the thought—perhaps for us, just now, perhaps the name is a good omen.

Hesitantly she told her sisters about it. Lionheart said: "I wish to go so far away from this hateful city that no one round me even knows its name."

Jeweltongue said: "I would not stay here a day longer than I must, if they asked me to be mayor and my only alternative was to live in a hole in the ground."

It was teatime. Late-afternoon light slanted in through the long panes of their sitting-room. They no longer used any of the bigger rooms; their present sitting-room was a small antechamber that had formerly been used to keep not-very-welcome guests waiting long enough to let them know they were not very welcome. In here Jeweltongue saw that the surfaces were dust-free, the glass panes sparkling, and the cushions all plumped. But the view into the garden showed a lawn growing shaggy, and twigs and flower stems broken by rain or wind lay across the paths. It had been three weeks since the Duke and Baron sent their last messages.

Beauty sat staring out the window for a minute in the silence following her sisters' words. It was still strange to her how silent the house was; it had never been silent before. Even very late at night, very early in the morning, the bustle had only been subdued, not absent. Now silence lay, cold

and thick and paralysing as a heavy fall of snow. Beauty
shivered, and tucked her hands under her elbows. "I'll tell
Father, then, when he wakes. At least something is settled. . . ." Her voice tailed off. She rose stiffly to her feet.
"I have several more letters I should write tonight." She
turned to leave.

"Beauty—" Lionheart's voice. Beauty stopped by Jeweltongue's chair, which was nearest the door, and turned
back. "Thank you," said her eldest sister.

Jeweltongue reached suddenly up, and grasped Beauty's
hand, and laid the back of it against her cheek for a moment.
"I don't know what we would be doing without you," she
said, not looking up. "I still can't bear the thought of . . .
meeting any of the people we used to know. Every morning
I think, Today will be better—"

"And it isn't," said Lionheart.

Beauty went back to the desk in another little room she
had set up as an office. Quickly she began going through
various heaps of papers, setting a few aside. She had already
rebuffed suggestions of aid from businessmen she knew
only wished to gloat and gossip; uneasily she discarded
overtures from sorcerers declaring that their affairs could yet
be put right, all assistance to be extended on credit, terms
to be drawn up later upon the return of their just prosperity.
Now she drew a sheet of her father's writing-paper towards
her, picked up a pen, and began to write an acceptance, for
herself and her sisters, of the best, which was to say the
least humiliating, offer of the several auction houses that
had approached them, to dispose of their private belongings,
especially the valuable things that had come to them from
their mother, which their father had given his wife in better
days. Beauty had told no one that she was not sure even
this final desperate recourse would save their father from a
debtors' prison.

And in the next few days she made time wherever she
could to visit various of the people who had adopted her
animals. She learnt what she could, in haste and distress of
mind, of butter- and cheese-making from a woman who had
been a dairymaid before she married a town man, while her

cat, once a barn-loft kitten, played tag to rules of her own devising among their feet and the legs of furniture. She learnt bottling and beer-making from an old woman who had been a farm wife, while her ex-racing hound made a glossy, beer-coloured hump under the kitchen table. She took the legal papers she was not sure she understood to a man whose elegant, lame black mare had foaled all four of his undertaker son's best funeral carriage team. Another man, whose five cowardly hounds bayed tremendously at any knock at the front door from a vantage point under his bed, taught her how to harness a horse, how to check that its tack fitted, and the rudiments of how to drive it; and a friend of his saddled up his very fine retired hunter, the whites of whose eyes never showed anymore, and went to the big autumn horse fair to buy her a pair of pulling horses and a suitable waggon.

She came home from these small adventures with her head ringing with instructions and spent the evenings writing up notes, listening to the silence, trying not to be frightened, and wondering wearily what she was forgetting.

I can teach you to remember, the elderly salamander said to her.

"Oh—oh no," said Beauty. "Oh no, that won't do at all. But thank you."

Your other friends are giving you gifts, said the salamander, *gifts of things you need, things you ask them for, but sometimes things they know to offer you. Why may not I also?*

"It is very kind of you," said Beauty, "but I have no claim on you."

You have the claim of friendship, said the salamander. *My master, since he retired, is interested only in counting his money. I shall miss you, for you have been my friend. Let me give you something. It will be a small something, if you prefer, something smaller than memory.*

"I would rather forget how to smoke meat and brew beer and saw and nail if I might also begin to forget the last few weeks," said Beauty simply.

The salamander was silent, but she saw by the flicker in its cloudy eyes that it was thinking.

Pick me up, it said at last, *so that I may look into your eyes.*

Beauty picked it up gently, in a hand that shook only a very little.

This is more difficult than I expected. We salamanders rarely give gifts, and when we do, they are rarely small. It made a faint, dry, rattling sound Beauty recognised as salamander laughter. *This will have to do.*

Abruptly it opened its eyes very wide, and Beauty was staring into two pits of fire, and when she sucked in her breath in shock, the air tasted hot and acrid with burning. *Listen to me, my friend. I give you a small serenity. I would give you a large one, but I am uncertain of human capacity, and I furthermore believe you would not wish it. This is a serenity you can hold in the palms of your two hands—even smaller than I am.* And she heard the rustling laugh again, even through the thunder of the fire. *I think you may find it useful.* It hooded its eyes. *You may put me down.*

Beauty set it back down on the pillar where it spent its days watching the townsfolk and pretending to be a garden ornament. It turned suddenly, like the lizard it almost was, and touched her hand with its tongue. *I did not mean to frighten you,* it said, and its voice was tinny and distant, like the last reverberation of an echo. *Cup your hands and look into them now.*

Beauty did so and at once felt heat, as if she held a small glowing sun in her hands. She looked down and again saw fire, red and hot and bottomless. "It—it doesn't look very serene," she quavered.

Trust me, said the salamander, and curled up and became the statue of a salamander.

CHAPTER

2

In six weeks from the day the news was first heard that the wealthiest merchant in the city had resigned his post in disgrace, his daughters had packed up what few goods remained to them—including himself—and begun the long journey to their exile near a village with the outlandish name of Longchance.

Everyone knew the old man's health had broken with the ruin of his fortunes and that the girls were left to rescue themselves by what devices they could themselves contrive. While no one in the city was moved to offer them any financial assistance, there was a kind of cool ruthless pride in them that they had risen to the challenge. Beauty's negotiating skills had won, or been allowed to win, by the thinnest margin, the ultimate round, and their father was to be spared the final misery and disgrace of prison—not because she had anything very much to offer in exchange for the old man's meagre life but in recognition that her determination was absolute. And there was not, after all, any material gain to be had from letting the old man die in gaol. The price for this benevolence was a promise that the old merchant would do business in the city no more. It was a guarantee Beauty was happy to make for him.

They escaped only just before Lionheart's roaring ceased to compel delivery of their groceries.

None of the sisters had ever before ventured out of the city more than a few days' journey, and then only for some amusement at some great country seat. The old merchant had occasionally chosen to conduct his business in another city in person, but then he travelled by sea, always booking the most luxurious private cabin for the journey. Now they were on the road for weary week after weary week, with only such comforts as an ancient unsprung farm waggon and a pokey tent could offer. They had barely been able to pay for their place in a traders' convoy heading in the direction they wished to go; they would be travelling often through near wilderness, and banditry was common. But the traders did not welcome them, and they were made quickly aware that their leader's agreeing to take them on was not popular with the others and that they would receive no help if they found it difficult to keep up.

They did keep up. The merchant was ill and weak and wandered in his wits, but the three sisters did everything, as they had done everything since the Duke and the Baron had written a few words on two sheets of heavy, cream-laid paper and sealed them with their seals. Lionheart was tender to their two slow shaggy horses in a way Beauty had never seen her be tender with her high-couraged thoroughbreds, and Jeweltongue was gentle with their father in a way Beauty had never seen Jeweltongue be gentle with any human being less capable than she.

There was one bit of trouble early on, when one of the traders attempted to pay rough court to Jeweltongue; she had just bitten his hand when Lionheart hit him over the head with a horse-collar. The commotion brought some of the others. There was a brief, tense, ugly silence, when it might have gone either way, and then the traders decided they admired these soft city girls for defending themselves so resolutely. They dragged their colleague's unconscious body back to his own fireside, and their captain promised there would be no more such incidents. There were not.

Winter came early that year; the traders' convoy had to

take shelter in a village barely halfway to their goal. It might yet have gone hard for the three sisters but for Lionheart's ability to turn three wizened turnips into a feast for sixteen, Jeweltongue's ability to patch holes in shirts more hole than shirt out of a few discreet excisions from the hems, and Beauty's ability to say three kind words, as if at random, just before cold- and want-shortened tempers flared into fighting. By the time of the thaw, the traders were no longer sorry for their leader's bargain with the ruined merchant and his three beautiful daughters, and the fellow still bearing a knot on the back of his head from a blow from a horse-collar had mended a frost-cracked wheel for the sisters and refused any compensation, saying that companions of the road took no payment from one another.

The three sisters and their father went the last few miles alone. The lawyers' letter had described Rose Cottage as being at the end of the last track off the main way through the woods before Longchance's farmlands began. The traders knew the way to Longchance well, and while none of them knew anything of Rose Cottage, they knew which track the last one was—or what was left of it, for it had not been used in many years. It was just wide enough to take two small horses abreast, and just clear enough for an old farm cart laboriously to lumber down.

A surprising number of the traders came round individually to say good-bye to their travelling companions, and several mumbled something about maybe looking in t'see how they was doing, on the way home again. Then the traders went on the wider way. The three sisters and the old merchant went the narrow one.

The house too was recognisable from the description in the lawyers' letter. Small; thatched, now badly overdue for replacement; one storey, with a loft over half of it, the roof so peaked that the upstairs room would be only partly usable; stone chimney on either of the narrow sides of the house, the one on the loft side much the bigger; two small tumbledown sheds and some bits of broken fence; and a chestnut tree growing a little distance from the front door. The remains of an overgrown garden spilled out behind the house, but even Beauty was too bone-weary to explore it.

But the house was surprisingly tall for its small size, and this gave it a curious authority and a reassuring air of steadfastness. They all sat and stared while the horses, perceiving the end of the road and a lack of attention in the hands on their reins, dropped their heads and began to nose through the debris of winter for anything to eat.

It was earliest spring. The sky was blue, the birds sang, the chestnut tree was putting out its first sticky leafbuds, but the low coarse growth underfoot was matted weeds interspersed with bare muddy patches, the brown buds crouched on drearily empty branches, and the house had obviously been derelict for a long time. The clearing it sat in was reverting to woodland, with opportunistic saplings springing up everywhere; there was a bird's-nest built into a corner of the front door and an ominous crown of ragged twigs on one of the chimneys. The two sheds hadn't a sound wall between them; there was nowhere to keep the waggon or stable the horses. It was a cheerless homecoming.

Lionheart was the first to jump off the waggon, stride forward, and throw the unlatched door of the house open, spattering herself with shreds of broken bird's-nest and fighting off the maleficent embraces of the long thorny stems of an overgrown bush just beside the door. Jeweltongue and Beauty followed her slowly; their father sat dully in the cart. Beauty's heart sank when Lionheart opened the door so easily; she had feared the worst when the lawyers had sent her no key, but if the house had been open to weather and all depredations both animal and human. . . .

"No leaks," said Lionheart, looking towards the ceiling. She climbed the ladder and stuck her head through the trapdoor. "Nor any I can see up here," she said, her voice muffled.

"No rubbish in the corners," said Jeweltongue. She walked round the one big downstairs room, touching the walls. "It's not running with damp. It doesn't even smell of damp. Or of mice."

Beauty was standing in the middle of the floor, slowly turning in her place, half watching Jeweltongue touching the

walls, half looking round herself, thinking, It does not smell
of mice, nor of damp, but it does smell of something—I
don't know—but it's a friendly smell—not like a years-
closed-up house. Well, there may be horrors tomorrow—
birds'-nests in the chimneys, snakes in the cellar—but . . .
And her heart lifted for the second time since the Duke and
Baron had written those final lines, and she remembered that
the first time had been when she discovered the papers saying that they still possessed a little house called Rose Cottage. Rose Cottage. She had wanted the name to be a good
omen.

Lionheart came downstairs again, and the three sisters
looked at one another. "It's perhaps just a bit small," said
Lionheart.

"But it's ours," said Jeweltongue, and walked over to
Beauty and tucked her hand under her sister's arm.

"Those little leaded windows don't let in much light,"
said Lionheart.

"The ceiling is high enough to make the house seem
bright and airy," said Jeweltongue.

"None of our furniture will sit straight on this floor,"
said Lionheart.

"None of the wisps and remnants we now call our furniture is going to sit straight anywhere," said Jeweltongue,
"and we can invent a new parlour-game for winter evenings, rolling pennies across the slopes."

Lionheart laughed. "There's a baking oven," she said,
looking at the bigger chimney. "And think of the fun I'll
have learning where its hot spots are. The first loaves will
have slopes on them like the floor." She looked round again.
"And we'll never be lonesome because we'll always be under one another's feet. Not like—not like the last weeks in
the old house."

Beauty felt Jeweltongue shudder. "No. Never like that.
Never again."

They returned outdoors. Their father had made his way
down from the waggon and was standing under the tree near
the front door. "It's a chestnut," he said. "I've always
loved chestnut trees. I was a champion conker-player when

I was a boy. Chestnut trees are messy, though; they shed all year long. Aside from the sticks little boys throw up into them to dislodge the conkers." And he laughed. It was the first time they had heard him laugh since the blow fell, months ago in the city.

Jeweltongue, to her infinite disgust, found she could neither saw nor hammer straight; but Beauty could, and Lionheart learnt from Beauty. They rehung doors, patched broken flooring, rebuilt disintegrating shutters, filled in the gaps in the sills—mostly with planking salvaged from the tumble-down sheds. As their shabbiest dresses grew more and more ragged, they tied the skirts round their legs till it was almost as if they wore trousers; they wrapped themselves up in the old silver-polishing tunics that had once belonged to their major-domo; their hair they bound back severely, and Lion-heart threatened to cut hers off. "Long hair is a silly fashion for ladies who have nothing better to do with their time than pin it up and take it down," she said.

"I like my long hair," said Beauty.

"You have very beautiful hair," said Lionheart. "I used to think—before we shared a bedroom—I used to think it must shine in the dark, it has such a glow to it. Mine is just hair."

Their father was still frail and spent most of his days and evenings near the smaller fire, in the area which they used as their sitting-room. His was the one comfortable chair, but none of the three sisters ever sat still long enough to enjoy a comfortable chair—said Lionheart—so he might as well have it, or it would be wasted. As he began to grow a little stronger, he found a pen and a little ink and some bits of half-used paper, and began to write things down on them, and murmur to himself. But his eyes were now more often clear than they were not, and he recognised each of his daughters as herself and no one else, and they began to feel hopeful of his eventual recovery—as they had not for the long sad weary time just past—and went about their work with lighter hearts as a result.

Jeweltongue and Beauty at first were the only ones to venture to Longchance. "We don't all three need to go, and Father can't," said Lionheart, "and you two are much better at saying the right thing to the right person than I am—you know you are."

"What you mean is, we can come home and tell you who is going to vex you into shouting, so you can refuse to have anything to do with them and leave the work of it to us," said Jeweltongue.

Lionheart grinned, then sobered. "Yes, you're right—you nearly always are, it's one of your greatest faults—but, you know, we can't afford to . . . to annoy anyone here. I'll try to be polite, but when some buffoon is yammering away at me, my mind goes blank of anything but wanting to knock 'em down and sit on 'em."

So Jeweltongue and Beauty went alone to sell their horses and waggon, leaving Lionheart experimenting with lashing together an assortment of short whippy poles cut from the saplings they had begun clearing from round the house. There were still birds'-nests in one of the flues of the kitchen chimney, which they had thus far failed in reaching from either end, although Lionheart had managed to begrime herself thoroughly with soot, nest fragments, and bird droppings once already, with her last lot of lashed poles.

"You'll come home to two fully functioning chimneys," she promised, "or I'm going to drown myself in the well. Although if I succeed, I may inadvertently have drowned myself anyway, trying to rasp the feculence off me again."

"Couldn't we look for a greenwitch to sell us a charm for the chimney?" said Jeweltongue, dropping her voice after a quick glance at their father, who was chewing the end of his pen and scowling furiously at his scrap of paper.

"With what money?" said Lionheart, testing the whippiness of one of her poles with a muttered " 'Tis enough to try the patience of a saint."

"You wouldn't know," said Jeweltongue. "A witch's charm must be cheaper than having your body fouling our well."

"I will take pains not to drown myself," said Lionheart. "Now go away before I bite you."

Jeweltongue, while her sisters had been busy with repairs to the house, had spent her time cutting and sewing rough but sturdy shirts out of the several bolts of material they had found stowed in the back of the housekeeper's wardrobe. "What in sky or on earth did she want with such stuff?" said Lionheart on discovery.

"Perhaps her secret lover is a poacher. It would make a splendid poacher's jacket," said Jeweltongue.

"It would make an entire regiment of poachers splendid jackets," said Lionheart.

"Never mind," said Jeweltongue grimly. "The auction house won't want the stuff; whatever it is, we get to keep it. It'll wear like iron. I'll think of something to do with it." And so it had gone into the drab heap of bits and pieces they would take with them into exile.

Jeweltongue sewed till her fingers bled from the harshness of the fabric and the wiry strength of the thread; but the shirts (minus any pockets useful for poaching) would be as tough as she had predicted, and in the working community they now found themselves in, she was sure—she was almost sure—there would be buyers for them. Lionheart was right about their little remaining hoard of money: It would not last them their first year, and what they still needed for the house, plus a few chickens and a goat and somewhere to keep them, would take whatever they made on the sale of the horses and waggon.

Jeweltongue left her elder sister to her pole-lashing and went outdoors to find her younger one waiting for her. Beauty was sitting on the high rickety seat of the decrepit old waggon, singing to the horses, who were obviously listening to her. "And from her heart grew a red, red rose, and from his heart a briar. . . ."

"Oh dear!" said Jeweltongue. "Isn't there something more cheerful you could sing?"

Beauty stopped and looked surprised. "It has never occurred to me that that is not a cheerful song."

"I've never felt that lovers who failed to embrace while

they were alive were going to derive much joy out of plants embracing after they're dead," said Jeweltongue.

"Maybe you just don't understand about plants," said Beauty, smiling.

"No, I leave all that to you," said Jeweltongue. "I would rather make sailcloth shirts for the rest of my life than weed a flowerpot once. And I have absolutely no intention of making sailcloth shirts for the rest of my life." She climbed lightly up the side of the farm cart and settled herself delicately on the hard plank seat. "I shall not miss this cart in the least," she said.

"I will miss the horses," said Beauty a little wistfully.

"Perhaps you will become fond of the goat," said Jeweltongue. "Or even the chickens."

"Does one ever grow fond of chickens?" said Beauty dubiously. "Perhaps the goat."

"We will make an effort for a very nice goat," said Jeweltongue.

The two sisters were determined to be optimistic about their first meeting with the local townsfolk; but clinging to optimism left them little energy for anything else, and their conversation soon faltered. To prevent herself from thinking too much about their last experiences of townspeople, Beauty looked round the thinning woodland they were passing through and silently recited: Oak. Larch. Don't know what that is. Sycamore. Rowan. Wild cherry. More oak. Snowdrops, aren't they pretty! Truly spring is coming.

But when they arrived in Longchance, they discovered what else they had won by making aged turnips into feast dishes, and warm clothes out of rags, and cooperation from antagonism. When the traders' convoy had passed through, the only news of the new residents of Rose Cottage left behind was that they were a merchant's family, fallen on hard times. The traders had not so much as named the three sisters and had mentioned the old merchant's illness as if this were the central fact about the family. Most important of all, the traders left no sense of any mystery to be solved. The townsfolk were inquisitive—Rose Cottage had stood empty for a long time, and Longchance was small enough to be interested in any newcomers besides—but not agog; cautiously friendly, not suspicious.

And Longchance was a good-natured town. They gave the sisters good advice and a good price for the horses, if not for the rickety waggon. Beauty and Jeweltongue came home exhausted but content. They had credit to spend at the village shops, a promise of delivery via the carter from the sawyer and the smith, a basket of pullets peeping aggrievedly under the shawl tucked round them to keep them from leaping out, a bundle of fresh vegetables to enliven their stale end-of-winter stores, and a very nice goat indeed, following them thoughtfully on the end of a string tied round her neck. She was a silky brown and white goat with long eyelashes around her enigmatic slot-pupilled eyes, and the farmer's daughter had named her Lydia and wept at parting from her.

"Oh, fiddlesticks!" said Jeweltongue, shortly after they had turned off the main way onto the rutted little track to Rose Cottage. "I forgot to ask about a greenwitch! Fiddle, fiddle, *fiddlesticks.* If Lionheart hasn't got the chimney clear, there'll be no living with her. It's odd, though; I didn't see a signboard for a greenwitch, did you? I'd've expected her to be in the centre of town. Longchance is a little bigger than we expected, isn't it? Or more energetic, at least. I thought . . . well, never mind. I'm glad of it; I like it; it has a good air. But I'd've guessed it might almost support a seer or a small magician, and I didn't see hide nor hair of any of the professions. Well, a penny saved. And it will be much harder to sneak anything of that sort past Father in a house the size of Rose Cottage."

But they arrived home to discover Lionheart triumphant, if a little red from scrubbing, and two fully functional chimneys.

Spring advanced. Beauty and Lionheart were relieved to find that their awkward carpentry and inexperienced mends were holding firm and that, so far as they could tell, there was nothing terribly wrong with their little house. They hoped the thatch would keep the rain out one more year; perhaps next spring, somehow, they could find the money to have it redone. Meanwhile, their father slept in a truckle-bed by the warm banked kitchen fire downstairs, and the three sisters rigged a patchwork canopy—Jeweltongue took time out from making shirts to put together scraps from her mending basket—over the mattress they shared in the loft, so that the pattering rain of little many-legged creatures falling out of the thatch did not trouble them as they slept.

Beauty began to have strange, vivid dreams unlike any she had had before. Sometimes she saw great lordly rooms like those of a palace, though of nowhere she had ever herself been; sometimes she saw wild landscape, most often in moon- and starlight. Sometimes she saw her family: Jeweltongue speaking to a young man wearing a long apron, his hands covered with flour; Lionheart, with her hair cropped off so short that the back of her neck was bare, rubbing the ears of a horse whose nose was buried in her breast, while a man with a kind earnest face stood leaning against the horse's shoulder; her father, in a fine coat, reading aloud from pages he held in his hands, to an attentive audience.

And then one night her old dream came back. She had not had it in so long—and her life had changed so much meanwhile—she had almost forgotten it; or rather, when she remembered it, which she occasionally did, she thought of it as a part of her old life, gone forever. Its return was as abrupt and terrifying as a blow from a friend, and Beauty gave a convulsive lurch in bed, and a half-muffled shriek, and sat up as if she were throwing herself out of deep water.

"Oh, help!" said Jeweltongue, who lay next to her and was awakened by Beauty's violence. "My dear, whatever is the matter?" She sat up too, and put an arm round Beauty, rubbing her own eyes with her other hand. Beauty said nothing, and Jeweltongue began to pat her sister's arm and back in a desire to comfort them both. Beauty turned jerkily and put her head on her sister's shoulder. "Was it a bad dream?" said Jeweltongue.

"Yes," said Beauty. "Yes. It is a very old dream—I've

had it all my life—I thought it had gone—that I had left it behind in the city.''

''All your life?'' said Jeweltongue slowly. ''You have had this nightmare all your life and I never knew? I—''

But Beauty put her hand over her sister's mouth and said, ''Hush. We were different people in the city. It doesn't matter now.''

Jeweltongue kissed her sister's hand and then curled her own fingers tightly round it and held it in her lap. ''I swear you must be the nicest person ever born. If I didn't love you, I would hate you for it, I think.''

''Now you know how I feel the six hundred and twelfth time in a row you're right about something,'' said Lionheart sleepily from Jeweltongue's other side. ''What is happening?'' she said through an audible yawn. ''It's still dark. It's not morning already, is it, and I have forgotten to open my eyes?''

''No,'' said Jeweltongue. ''Beauty's had a nightmare.''

''Nightmares are hell,'' said Lionheart feelingly. ''I used to have them—'' She stopped abruptly. ''Not so much anymore,'' she said, ''except some nights, when the beetle and spider rain is bad, I start dreaming the thatch is leaking.''

''I'm all right now,'' said Beauty.

''No, you're not,'' said Jeweltongue. ''I can still feel your heart shaking your whole body. Whatever is your nightmare about? Can you tell us?''

Beauty tried to laugh. ''It sounds so silly. I'm walking down a dark corridor, with no doors or windows anywhere, and there's a monster waiting for me at the far end. I can't see it, but I know it's there. It's—it's . . . I suppose it's just that I haven't had it in so long. But it seems so—so much stronger than it used to. I mean . . . you always feel like you're in a nightmare when you're having it, don't you? Or it wouldn't be a nightmare. But tonight . . . just now, I was *there*.''

There was a little silence, and then Lionheart sat up as if to climb out of bed but stopped with one foot touching the floor. ''If Jeweltongue would remove herself so that she is no longer sitting on my nightgown, I will go brew us some chamomile tea. It's good for almost everything; it should be good for nightmares too. You stay here so we don't disturb Father.''

After that first time the dream came back often, but Beauty did not wake her sisters again. She grew accustomed—she forced herself to grow accustomed—to the feeling that she was there, that the only difference between her waking life and her life in the dream was that in the dream she did not know where she was.

She looked for details in her waking life that she would not be able to match in the dream, in some hope that such small exact trifles would orient her so firmly to the world of Rose Cottage and Longchance that the dream would distress her less when she found herself once again in that great dark not-quite-empty place, but this did not turn out as she wished. If she examined the wood grain in the walls of Rose Cottage one day, the next night she dreamed of examining the wallpaper in the corridor in the flickering light of the candles. If she touched the wall in reaction to the uncertainty of what she could see, or guessed she saw, she felt the slight roughness of the paper itself, the seams where the lengths met, and the slickness where the paint had been drawn on over the stencil.

She found that her dream had changed in another way. She had begun to pity the monster she approached.

She feared him no less for this; she did not even know why she felt pity and grew angry with herself for it. She would rush along the endless shadowy corridor with her head bowed and her arms crossed across her breast, feeling grief and pity and raging at herself, Why do I feel sorry for a monster who is going to eat me as soon as seen, like the Minotaur with his maidens? When she woke, she remembered how, when she was still only a child, she had realised that she did not seek to escape, but to come to the end of the corridor and get it over with—whatever it was going to be. And she remembered how sick and dizzy and helpless and wild—almost mad—that realisation had made her feel. It's only a dream, she had said to herself then, and she repeated it now, silently, in the peaceful darkness of Rose

Cottage, with the reassuring sound of her sisters' breathing by her side. It's only a dream. But why do I dream of a terrible monster waiting for me, only for me?

Jeweltongue gained her first commission to make fine shirts, for the family who held the Home Farm. "She bought two of my rough shirts for her husband a little while ago and said at the time that the work was far too good for farm clothes. Oh dear! It's just what I want to believe, you see."

"Home Farm?" said Lionheart. "Maybe the squire'll hear of you and order a dozen brocade waistcoats."

"Oh, don't!" said Jeweltongue. "I want it too badly. The squire has a big family, and they like good clothing. Mrs Bestcloth has already told me." Mrs Bestcloth was the draper's in Longchance. "She says they're the only reason Longchance even has a draper's and that someday one of them will be in when I am, and she'll introduce me." Jeweltongue buried herself in her task, sitting by the window while daylight lasted, drawing closer to the fire as dusk fell. Their one lamp lived at her elbow; Lionheart grumbled about cooking in the dark, but not very loudly. All three sisters resisted the temptation to stroke the good fabric Jeweltongue was working on and remember the old days.

But Lionheart had begun to grow restless. She had thrown herself into rebuilding the second shed to be marauder-proof, so they did not have to bring Lydia and the chickens indoors at night—"Just before I went mad," said Jeweltongue, who was the one of the three of them who minded most about a clean house and therefore did more than her fair share of the housework. Then Lionheart built them a new and magnificently weatherproof privy—"Please observe that all my joins join," she said—and finished clearing the meadow round the cottage so it was a meadow again. Beauty had helped with both shed and privy, but she was more and more absorbed in reclaiming the garden, which didn't interest Lionheart in the slightest; and Lionheart was, indeed, enjoying herself, although her hurling her materials round and swearing at her tools when she had not skill

enough to make them do what she wanted might have led
anyone who knew her less well than her sisters to believe
otherwise.

But there were no more major projects to plunge into and
grapple with. Lionheart trimmed the encroaching undergrowth back a little from the track that led from the main
way to their cottage; but after that she was reduced to chopping wood for their fires—and this late in the year they only
needed the one fire for cooking—and the cooking itself,
which was necessarily plain and simple and which she had
furthermore grown very efficient at. "Who wants to be indoors in spring anyway?" she muttered. "Maybe I'll ap-
prentice myself to a thatcher."

One morning she disappeared.

"Oh, my lords and ladies, what will she get up to?" said
Jeweltongue, but she had her sewing to attend to. Beauty
spent the day in the garden, refusing to think about anything
but earth and weeds and avoiding being torn to shreds by
the queer thorny bushes which there were so many of around
Rose Cottage.

Lionheart returned in time to have the last cup of tea,
very stewed, from the teapot, and to get supper. "Where
have you been?" said Jeweltongue.

"Hmm?" said Lionheart, her eyes refocusing from whatever distant mental picture she had been contemplating.
"Mmm. Don't you grow awfully bored just looking at one
stitch and then the next stitch and then the next? I have been
giving you something to distract you, by worrying where I
was," replied Lionheart, but, before Jeweltongue could say
anything else, added, "Have you met our local squire yet?
Or his sister? The sister is the one you want to put yourself
in the way of, I would say. She looks to be quite vain about
her dresses."

"Lionheart, you didn't!" said Jeweltongue in alarm.

"No, no, I didn't," said Lionheart. She dropped her voice
so their father, dozing in his chair by the fire, would not
hear her. "What would I say? 'Good day, sir, in the old
days my father wouldn't have let you black his boots, but
now my sister would be glad of a chance to make your

waistcoats? For a good price, sir, please, sir, our roof needs rethatching'?'' Lionheart's careless tone did not disguise her bitterness, nor did her sisters miss the glance she gave to her hands. In the old days they had all had lady's hands; even the calluses Lionheart had from riding were smooth, cushioned by the finest kid riding gloves, pumiced and lotioned by her maid. Lionheart raised her eyes and met Beauty's across the table. "I know that look," said Lionheart. "What sororal sedition are you nursing behind that misleadingly amiable stare?"

"I am wondering what you thought about the squire's sister's horse," said Beauty.

Lionheart laughed. "It's the right target, but your arrow is wide. The squire's sister drives a pair of ponies older and duller—although rather better kept—than those farm horses we brought here, and the squire himself rides a square cobby thing suitable to his age and girth. But if you had asked about the squire's eldest son's horse . . ."

"What?" said Jeweltongue. But Lionheart refused to be drawn. She stood up from the table and began to bang and clatter their few pots and pans, as if to drown out any further questions. Finally Jeweltongue said: "Have a little care. Mrs Oldhouse says the tinker will not be here again for months."

Their father woke up, stared bemusedly at the cup of now-cold tea sitting at his elbow, and went back to musing over his pen and scribbles. "May I make you some fresh tea, Father?" said Lionheart, guiltily caught mid-clash.

"No, no, my dear, I am not thirsty," he said absently; then he looked up. "You have been away, have you not? We missed you at lunch. Have you had an interesting day?"

A smile Lionheart looked as though she would repress if she could spread across her face. "Yes, Father, a very interesting day," she replied.

"Stop making those absurd grimaces," said Jeweltongue with asperity. "You look like you have bitten down on a mouthful of alum."

Lionheart was very thoughtful for the next few days, and while Jeweltongue tried a few times to wheedle something further out of her—with no success whatsoever—Beauty

felt that if Lionheart had decided to tell them nothing, then
nothing was what they would be told, and declined to help
wheedle. Furthermore, she was by now too preoccupied with
her garden to think long about anything else.

Beauty had not realised how much she had missed spending time in a garden, missed the smell and texture of earth,
the quiet and companionable presence of plants. It was a
wonderful spring that year, day after day of warmth and blue
skies and the lightest, freshest of breezes, and while the rain
fell as often as it needed to to keep the soil moist and work-
able and the streams full, it almost always fell tactfully after
dark.

There were a few little beds round the house—flowers
only, Beauty thought. Most of her attention was taken up by
the back garden, which was mostly vegetables and quite a
substantial plot for a house so small. Here she could more
easily trace the rows and blocks of old plantings. Near the
kitchen door, for example, was an herb patch. It had been laid
out in a circle, like a wheel with spokes; but some of the
wedge shapes were empty, and others had been colonised by
their neighbours. She picked leaves from the imperialists:
pungent, bitter, sharp, sweet. She knew the names of a few of
them: fennel, chervil, marjoram, mint.

Beauty had walked along what remained of the boundary
fence round the back garden, thinking that her first task must
be to replace it. (She had thought even then, while Lionheart
was still engaged upon rebuilding the privy, that she would
try to recruit Lionheart's assistance for the fence, though
she would not find it so interesting, because it would help
keep her out of mischief.) Once she started planting things,
she would want to keep the chickens from scratching up her
beds. Lydia was no problem; she was staked out each morning, helping to keep the newly reclaimed meadow a
meadow, and had shown no desire—at least not yet—to slip
her halter and go foraging for delicacies. But the woods ran
quite near them; deer, and who knew what else lived in the
wilds here, would eat anything the chickens missed. Except,
perhaps, strong-flavored herbs.

She stooped and broke off the tip of a dead vine. It still

bore small shrivelled pods of—something; Beauty wasn't
sure what. It was odd, when she thought about it, that the
garden didn't show more signs of the depredations of enterprising wildlife; it was no longer producing very much,
but—she rubbed the pods between her fingers—these would
have been edible the year they grew, and if they're growing
in a garden, presumably they *are* edible. Beauty dropped the
pods again. She had no more time now to puzzle over useless mysteries than she had had when she had been going
through her father's papers and discovered a will concerning
Rose Cottage.

If they had a successful garden, they would be able to put
up enough food that they would not have to fear the long
winter. The precariousness of their present life suddenly appeared to her as if she stood on the brink of a literal abyss,
staring into it till the impenetrable darkness made her dizzy.
She knelt heavily, feeling the cool dampness seep through
her skirts to chill her knees, and scooped up a little earth in
her hands, scrabbling at it, ending up with a handful of
earthworms and wild violet roots for her pains. But it made
her laugh—weeding with her fingernails—and the real
weight of the earth comforted her. A confused earthworm
thrust a translucent pink front end (or possibly rear; it was
difficult to tell with earthworms) out of her handful. She
knew this garden would do its best for her. It didn't matter
how she knew.

There were still cabbages growing, here and there, in er-
ratic little clumps, and those might be bean shoots, and
those, piranthus squash. And now, here, this was truly the
end. Beauty broke off a bit of the old fence, woven like
matting, and it crumbled in her hands.

She sighed and stood still. If they were going to have
food from the garden this year, she had to get busy. She
should already be busy. Next market-day she would ask
Jeweltongue to bring her seed—perhaps she should go herself and ask what grew most easily here—oh, but she
shouldn't waste a day; in weather like this the farmers' crops
would already be shooting, and she hadn't even cleared her
ground. She should be able to rig up some kind of scarecrow

till she figured out what to do about fencing; clothing suitable for scarecrows was perhaps the only thing they had
plenty of.

There was something plucking at the boundary of her
attention. She looked down at the fence shreds in her hand.
They looked like nothing at all and smelt both damp and
dusty, but . . . She shook them in her palm and then poked
them with a finger. A thread separated itself from the mis-
cellany: a green thread. She picked it up in her free hand
and held it under her nose. It smelt neither damp nor dusty;
it smelt . . . No, she couldn't say what it smelt of, but for a
moment she saw, as if she were dreaming it, a meadow
surrounded by a wood, and in it fawn-coloured cows grazed,
and the shadows from the trees fell strangely, some of them,
for they seemed to be silver rather than dark.

Her head cleared, and she looked at the bit of green thread
again. Greenwitch charms. There was a greenwitch in Longchance after all, and she had sold garden charms to whoever
had lived in Rose Cottage before them. Charms strong
enough to be working more than fifteen years after they had
been put into place. That was more like sorcerer's work, but
no sorcerer would stoop to making garden charms, certainly
not for anyone living in a place like Rose Cottage. Beauty
had already remarked that she'd never seen a chicken in the
back garden but had put it down to being still too unsettled
by her new life to notice everything that was happening
round her—even the things she meant to look out for.

Perhaps—perhaps if she took down and buried the remains of the old fence very carefully where it stood (and
before it finished falling down of its own initiative; obviously the charms had included no longevity spell for lathe
and reed), some of the old charm would persist. Whoever
the unknown greenwitch was, if she was this good, Beauty
couldn't possibly pay her for new charms.

She put the bit of string in her pocket. She felt curiously
reluctant to say anything about her discovery to her sisters.
Perhaps it was only her father's familiar ban on all magic
in their family that made her so uneasy, made her feel that
even her brief vision, with its unmistakable whiff of magic,

was a meddling in things too big for her. What did cows in a field have to do with a garden charm? Never mind. But if bits of green string would help to keep her garden whole, she would treat them politely. And she would as well put up a scarecrow and start at once on a new fence.

She had been staring at the musty little slivers of matting left in her hand and dropped them in relief. When she looked up again, she let her gaze wander down the length of the garden and was immediately distracted by her favourite mystery, the one she couldn't ignore, whether she had time for it or not. This one was, after all, quite an intrusive mystery. She wanted—she longed—to know what the deadly thorned shrubs that grew all over this garden were.

Lionheart, after her first few encounters with the dagger-furred ogre standing guardian by the front door (it was inevitably Lionheart who, flinging herself through the door at speed, had caught a superficial blow of the thorny branches across the forehead and come in with blood sheeting down her face), had wanted to have it and all its fellows out, as part of meadow clearance and garden ground preparation, and had offered herself "as the blood sacrifice," she said. "You can bury my flayed body under the doorstone to bring yourselves luck afterwards."

"Having failed to drown yourself in our well a few weeks ago?" enquired Jeweltongue. "You are such a life profligate. You'll be offering next to hurl yourself off the roof for—for—it escapes me what for, but I'm sure you'll think of something."

Beauty, who was the acknowledged gardener in the family, had declined this dubiously advantageous offer although she had immediately tied the chief offender firmly away from the front door and lopped off what couldn't be tied. She had already cut a hole in the truly astonishing climbing thorn-bush by the kitchen door. This had sent out so many long, uninhibited stems that it was now rioting over the entire rear wall of the house, nailing the kitchen door shut in the process as uncompromisingly as any carpenter could do it. It had climbed well up onto the roof also, no doubt considerably to the detriment of the thatch it clung to, and had

begun to curl itself round the kitchen chimney. Not even
the fact that this chimney was now in regular use again
seemed to discourage it.

Even Jeweltongue felt that Lionheart had the right idea,
if a little overexuberantly expressed, but Beauty said, "No.
They were planted; it's obvious they were planted deliberately. There must be a reason for them. I want to know what
it is."

After that she had to stand by her decision, but she none-
theless wondered if the game could possibly prove worth
the candle. Tied-in stems of these whatever-they-were had
a habit of working themselves loose, or suddenly growing
an extra half league, or turning themselves round where they
stood (Beauty knew that this was really only any plant's
desire to lean towards the sun, but quite often it seemed a
malign strategy) and grasping at passersby. There was also,
at each of the house's four corners, a lower, rounder shrub
with the same flexible stems covered with thorns. These
were almost more dangerous than the climbers, because they
were as wide as they were tall, and their arching branches
seemed to lie in wait for the unwary, suddenly uncoiling
themselves from round corners to ensnare their victim.

And in the very centre of the big back garden, where the
lengthwise central path met a shorter path running cross-
wise, there was another circular bed, like the herb wheel,
only much larger, and here grew more bushes like those
round the house, with long wicked stems studded with knife
points. While the herbs had merely colonised across their
spoke boundaries, these bushes had thrown an impassable
network of bristling stems higher than a man's head in all
directions, sprawling, manticore-tailed, across the paths
round them as well, so that forcing them back to within their
original bounds had been Beauty's first necessary operation
for reclaiming that part of the garden for other, more useful
purposes.

There was a statue at the heart of that great shapeless,
impenetrable morass, but it was so caught round with spiny
stems (and rank weeds bold enough to make their way
through) Beauty had not a notion of what it might be.

The stiletto bushes round the house were leafing out, big dark green leaves and surprising deep maroon ones. Many of the bushes in the centre wheel looked dead, their long, perversely floppy branches grey-green, almost furred, and nearly leafless. Some of them had the tiniest leafbuds showing, as if they were not sure of their welcome (that's true enough, thought Beauty). These in the centre bed were covered with the longest, toothiest thorns (many of them hooked like fangs, for greater purchase) of anything in the whole well-armed battalion. Beauty looked at them musingly every time she went into the garden. All the thorn-bushes were ugly, but these were the ugliest.

But it was this crazy tangle of them at the very centre of the garden which told her—even more clearly than the pernicious presence of their cousins by both doors of the house—just how loved these awful plants must have been. Very well, she would keep them—for this year.

CHAPTER
3

About three weeks after Lionheart's first disappearance, she disappeared again. She had gone into town a few times by herself meanwhile—always on some errand, carefully agreed upon beforehand—and had come home in each case looking frustrated, or amused, or pleased, in a manner that did not seem to relate to the errands she was ostensibly accomplishing. She came home sullen and discouraged the day she successfully arranged for a local farmer to deliver some of last year's manure-heap for Beauty's garden, and yet was jubilant and exhilarated the day she failed to find a suitable shaft to replace the handle of her favourite hammer, the accident that broke it having put her in a foul temper for the entire day.

Neither Jeweltongue nor Beauty saw Lionheart leave, but both saw her return. They had not immediately recognised her. A very handsome young man had burst into the house at early twilight, with the light behind him, and they had stared up in alarm at the intrusion. Lionheart looked at their frightened faces, and laughed, and pulled her hat off so they could see her face clearly; but her hair was gone, chopped raggedly across the forehead and up the back of the head as if she had sawn at it with a pocket-knife. And she was wearing breeches and a man's shirt and waistcoat.

Her sisters were speechless. Beauty, after a moment, recognised the clothing as having belonged to one of their
stablelads, which had thus far survived being turned to one
of Jeweltongue's purposes, but that did not explain what
Lionheart was doing pretending to be a boy.

"I have a job," she said, and laughed again, and tossed her
head, and her fine hair stood out round her face like a halo.
"They think I'm a young man, you see—well, they have to:
I'm the new stable-hand. At Oak Hall. But I won't be in the
muck-heap long because I made them dare me to ride Master
Jack's new colt—that's Squire Trueword's eldest son—this
colt's had every one of them off, you see. But I rode it. A few
of them hate me already, but the head lad likes me, and I can
see in his eye that the fellow who runs—that is, the master of
the horse—has plans for me. My saints, I ache; I haven't rid-
den in months, and that colt is a handful.

"Oh, and they say to get a decent haircut before I come
to work tomorrow; I'll have to bow to the squire, and to his
spoilt son, if I want to ride his horses."

Beauty trimmed her sister's hair and then swept the silky
tufts into a tiny pile of glinting individual hairs and saved
them.

The house was lonely at first, with Lionheart gone, but
she came home for a day every week, and baked all the
bread for the week to come, and, with her new wages,
bought butter and honey for the bread, and sugar and the
squashed fruit—chiefly the last of the winter apples—at the
bottom of the baskets at the end of market-days, and made
pies and jam. She had made friends with the butcher's boy,
who occasionally slipped her a few more beef knuckles for
the stew, a little extra lard in her measure; the butcher's boy
only knew that she had an ailing father and had recently
been taken on up at the Hall. He didn't know that the young
man he spoke to was also the sister who cooked the stew
and rolled the pastry.

Mrs Bestcloth was as good as her promise, and Jeweltongue's introduction to Miss Trueword was duly achieved.
And Jeweltongue was given a dinner dress to make. "From

a silly painted picture in a magazine, if you please! If a real person had ever tried to walk in that dress, she would be so fettered by the ridiculous skirts she would fall over after her first step. Fortunately Miss Trueword is a little more sensible than her manner.''

"Which is to say you talked her into being sensible,'' said Beauty, gently squeezing the small damp muslin pouch she hoped contained goat's cheese. Her last attempt had been more like goat's custard (as Lionheart mercilessly pointed out), but the texture this time was more promising.

"Mmm—well, I had a hard apprenticeship, you know, deflating that awful Mr Doolittle's opinions of himself. If he is a philosopher, I am a bale of hay. But that's all long ago now. And Miss Trueword is actually rather sweet. Here, let me hold that bowl for you. Don't fret, dear. It was excellent custard last time. Your only mistake was telling Lionheart it was supposed to be cheese.''

Miss Trueword's frock was a great success; Jeweltongue was commissioned for three frocks for her nieces and a coat for the squire. She also altered the stable-boy's uniform to fit Lionheart properly, using leftover bits from the squire's coat for strength. They were no longer using the money they had brought with them; a few times Jeweltongue or Lionheart even added pennies to the cracked cup in the back of the kitchen store-cupboard where they kept it. Beauty had hurdles for her fencing, and the scarecrow—or something— was working, for her seeds were sprouting unmolested.

Even their father was taking a little more notice of the world round him, and when he sat and scribbled, he scribbled more and dozed less. He came outdoors most days for a stroll in the sunlight, and he often smiled as he looked round him. He complimented Beauty on her garden and Jeweltongue on her sewing; he had been startled by Lionheart's new job—and even more by her new haircut—but had taken it quietly and made no attempt to forbid her to do something she had already thrown her heart into.

He still fell asleep early in the evenings and slept late into the mornings, while his daughters tiptoed round the kitchen end of the downstairs room getting breakfast and setting themselves up for the day. Each of the three of them caught the other two looking at him anxiously, heard the slightly strained note in the others' voices when they asked him how he did, to which he invariably replied gently, "I am doing very well, thank you."

"It is so hard to know if—if there is anything we should do," Jeweltongue said hesitatingly to Beauty. "He was never home when we lived in the city, was he? He was always at work. Or thinking of work. Even when Lionheart and I were little—when you were still a baby—he never seemed to notice anything but business, and Mamma. After Mamma died, we never saw him at all. Sometimes I think we only knew he existed because the next new governess, and the next one after that, came to us saying our father had hired her . . . you remember." She laughed a little, without humour. "Perhaps that's why we treated them so diabolically. Lionheart and I, that is; you were always the peacekeeper. And after we outgrew our governesses . . . I don't know what he was like before, you know? Other than abstracted. The way he is now, I suppose. But . . . I wish we could call in a greenwitch, or even a seer, and ask advice about him, but that's the one thing we do know, isn't it? No magic. And I keep forgetting to ask about it in Longchance—a greenwitch, I mean. It seems—" She paused, and there was a small frown on her face. "It seems almost peculiar, the way I keep not remembering. And the way it never comes up. Maybe it's different in the country. In the city which magician had just invented the best spell for this or that—champagne that stays fizzy even in a punch bowl, something to keep your lapdog from shedding hair on your dresses—"

"How to produce cheese instead of custard," murmured Beauty, watching Lydia's kid decide—again—not to enter the gate into the back garden, carelessly left open. Maybe he merely did not like narrow spaces.

"—was a chief source of gossip, nearly as good as who was seen leaving whose house at what o'clock at night. Don't you wonder what he's writing? He keeps it under his pillow at night and in his pocket all day."

Summer arrived. Beauty's runner beans ramped up their poles; the broad beans were so heavy with pods the crowns of the plants sank sideways to the earth. The lettuce and beetroot grew faster than they could eat it; there were so many early potatoes Lionheart made potato bread and potato pancakes and potato scones.

The thorn-bushes had all disappeared under their weight of leaves. Even the deadest-looking ones round the almost-invisible statue had not been dead at all, only slow to wake from winter. And then flower buds came, and Beauty watched them eagerly, surprised at her own excitement, wanting to see what would come. The weather turned cold for a week, and the buds stopped their progress like an army called to a halt; Beauty was half frantic with impatience. But the weather turned warm again, and the buds grew bigger and bigger and fatter and fatter, and there were dozens of them—hundreds. They began to crack and to show pink and white and deepest red-purple between the sepals.

One morning Beauty woke up thinking of her mother. She could not at first imagine why; she had not had the dream and had awoken happy, and thinking about her mother usually made her sad. But . . . she sniffed. There was something in the air, something that reminded her of her mother's perfume.

She hurried to the loft's one little window and knelt so she could see out. The thorn-bushes' buds had finally popped, and the scent was coming from the open flowers. Roses. These were roses. This was why their little house was called Rose Cottage.

She was the first awake; it was barely dawn. Her sisters would be stirring soon, and she wanted the first enchanted minutes of discovery to be hers alone. She wrapped the old coat she used as a dressing-gown round her—almost every morning at breakfast Jeweltongue promised to make her a real one *soon*—and went softly downstairs and into the garden, thoughtlessly barefoot, walked straight down the centre path to the big round bed in the middle of the back garden, the earth dawn-cool against her feet. The roses nodded at her as if giving her greeting; their merest motion blew their fragrance at her till she felt drunk with it.

Her sisters found her there a little while later, her hands cupping an enormous round flower head as if it were the face of her sweetheart. They stood openmouthed, breathing like runners after an exhilarating race; then Jeweltongue kissed her, and Lionheart reached out a hand and just stroked the silky petals of a pale pink rose with one finger. Neither said a word; slowly they went back indoors again and left Beauty alone with her new love.

At first she could not bear the thought of cutting them, even one, despite their profusion, but at last she chose just three—one white, one pink, one purple-red—and brought them indoors, found something to use as a vase, and knelt by their father's bed, holding them near his face. She saw him take a long breath in and smile, before he opened his eyes.

He murmured her mother's name, but gently, knowing she was gone but happy in the memory of her; then his eyes found Beauty's, and he smiled again. "Thank you," he said.

"They are beautiful, are they not?" said Beauty.

"Almost as beautiful as she was," he said.

Beauty said nothing.

For over two months the roses bloomed and bloomed and bloomed. Beauty had never been so happy, and for the third time in her life the dream went away. The monster was gone while her roses were in flower. She had to tear herself away from the contemplation of them to tend to the rest of her garden, to eat her meals, to sleep; she had never liked to do nothing, but she found now that if she could do nothing beside a rose-bush in full bloom, she was entirely happy.

Now that she knew what they were, she changed her mind at once about tending the bushes—however hazardous an operation this would be to herself personally. No longer were they in danger of being dug up and consigned to the bonfire as soon as she had time to spare. She trimmed and trained and painstakingly fixed and tied the bushes and climbers round the cottage. She groped gingerly into the very depths of the tangle of the round bed to take out all

the dead wood she could find and arrange the stems to arch
and fall most gracefully, the better to show off their radiant
burden of flowers. Every last spadeful of the remains of the
load of manure Farmer Goldfield had brought her went
round the base of the bushes, and she mourned the generous
hand she had used earlier in fertilising her vegetables. Next
year she would bargain for two loads of manure.

One mystery remained. She still could not decide what
the statue in the middle of the centre rose-bed represented.
In her valiant adventures pruning away the old wood and
scrabbling out the weeds, she had also made four of the
eight wheel-spoke paths navigable again, had therefore been
able to reach the hub and free the statue of its leafy con-
finement. But she still had no idea what it was supposed to
be. She almost thought it changed, from one day to the next,
because one day it would remind her of a dragon, the next
day a chimera, the third day a salamander, the fourth day a
unicorn. . . . "This is ridiculous," said Beauty, aloud, to the
unicorn. "You are not the least bit lizardy and snakelike,
and I know you have been lizardy and snakelike previously;
positively I have seen scales. Now stop it." After that it
only ever looked like some tall, elegant, but unknown beast,
its long sleek hair cascading over its round muscled limbs,
its great eyes peering sombrely out from beneath its mane.

"Now you are really very handsome," said Beauty.
"And much nicer than anything with scales. But I still wish
I knew what you were."

When the roses finally stopped blooming, Beauty felt as
if she had lost her dearest friend; but she gathered all the
fallen petals she could and put them in saucers and flat
bowls, and even after they dried, if she ran her fingers
through them, the scent awakened and made her happy.

She kept a little bowl of them by her pillow, where she
could reach them in the night, because as soon as the last
petal had dropped from the last rose in flower, the dream
returned. When it did, and she found herself safely restored
to her own bed but still shaken by the memory of the dark
corridor and the knowledge of the patient monster, she held
a cupped handful of rose-petals under her nose till the

warmth of her skin brought the scent out again, and then she drifted gently back to sleep.

The winter that year was long and hard, but the old merchant and his daughters were little troubled by it, except that Lionheart, two or three times, could not get home through the snow on her days off. Beauty's vegetables had surpassed all expectations, and the cold room under the house was full of sacks and bundles and bottles. The life that had been slowly returning to the old merchant had begun to grow strong; it was he who cleaned out the cellar, blocked the rat-holes, and borrowed the tools Lionheart considered hers to build the shelves to hold Beauty's produce.

"See that you take very good care of my hammer," said Lionheart. "I had a fiend of a time finding the right shaft for the new handle."

"I shall be very careful indeed not to hit it accidentally with any axes," said their father drily.

After the clean cold whiteness of winter, when spring's mud and naked brown branches and grey rain and smells of rot and waste came round again, they were only happy to know that summer was coming again—strangely content in their new life. There was never any longer an edge—except occasionally of laughter—to Jeweltongue's voice when she spoke to, or about, her clients. "I've decided judicious flattery is the greatest art of all," she said. "Forget philosophy." She hummed to herself as she drew up the dress patterns she delighted in creating.

Lionheart brought home the runt of the litter when the squire's favourite spaniel whelped, saying in outrage that the squire had planned to have it drowned. Once she came home still shaking in fury and told of thrashing some young lad who wanted to jump a frightened colt over a fence too big for it—"Just to show us what a big brave man he is. He won't last. Mr Horsewise won't have his kind near his horses."

The old merchant found a job doing sums for several of the small businesses in Longchance; he bought himself some clean sheets of paper and began copying some of the contents of his accumulation of scribblings onto them.

"Father, I am dying of curiosity," said Jeweltongue.

"I will tell you someday," he replied, smiling to himself.

Beauty's garden grew and bloomed, and bloomed, and the roses were even more spectacular this year than last. This second year Beauty took a deep, deep sigh, and cut many of her beloved roses, and worked them into wreaths and posies, and let them dry, and she went in with Jeweltongue one market-day to sell them, and they were gone by midmorning. She invested some of her little profit in ribbons, and wove them into bouquets with more of her roses, and raised her prices, and they, too, disappeared by midmorning at the next market-day she went to.

"Rose Cottage," the townspeople said, nodding wisely. "We all wondered if there was a one of you would wake 'em up again," and they looked at her thoughtfully. Several asked, hopefully but in some puzzlement, "Are you a—a greenwitch then? You don't look like a sorcerer."

"Oh, no!" said Beauty, shocked the first time she was asked. But eventually, as that question or one like it went on being repeated, and remembering Jeweltongue's puzzlement about the apparent lack of interest in Longchance in all the magical professions, she asked in her turn, "Why do you think so?"

But most of those addressed looked uneasy and gave her little answer. "The old woman was, you know," they muttered over their shoulders as they hastened away.

A very old memory returned to her: Pansy telling her that her mother's perfume smelt of roses. What she had forgotten was Pansy saying that it was generally only sorcerers who could get roses to grow. And she thought again of the green threads in the old fencing around Rose Cottage and how she had never seen any animal cross that boundary. Even their new puppy had to be let out the front door to do her business; she wouldn't go out the back.

But one woman lingered long enough to say a little more. She'd been listening, bright-eyed, to Beauty denying, once again, that she was a greenwitch, and the farm wife who received this news went off shaking her head. "There, there, Patience; we can't have everything, and that's a nice wreath you bought yourself.'' To Beauty she said: ''We all know Jeweltongue, and gettin' to be your father's pretty well known, that young scamp Salter, calls himself a wheel-wright, well, I guess nothing's wrong with his wheels, but he ain't never learnt nothing about running a business, and your father had him all tidied up in a sennight. And your firebrand brother, Lionheart, well, Mr Horsewise knows how to ride a high-mettled lad, too, and a good thing for both on 'em! But you're always home in your garden, ain't you? My cousin Sandy had a couple o'bottles of your pickled beets from your father last winter, which was sweet of him as she didn't expect no payment for what she done, but that's how we knew you're home working hard.

''My! Smell those roses! Don't it take me back! Funny how the house has stood empty this long, roses or no roses. It's a snug little place, even if it is a little far out of town for comfort. We knew when the old woman disappeared she'd left some kind of lawyers' instructions about it—but nobody came, and nobody sent word, and for a long time we just hoped she'd come back, because we was all fond of her, fond of her besides having a greenwitch in Longchance again, which we ain't had long before, nor since neither.'' She nodded once or twice and started to move away.

Then the greenwitch who had made the fence charms had *lived* in Rose Cottage! Then it was *she* who had left the house to them? But . . . Beauty reached out and caught the woman's sleeve. ''Oh, tell me more. Won't you—please?'' she begged. ''No one wants to talk about it, and I—I can't help being interested.''

''Not that much to tell, when all's said and done,'' said the woman, but she smiled at Beauty. ''Who is it you re-mind me of? Never mind, it'll come to me. We don't talk about magic much, here in Longchance, because we ain't got any. You have to go as far as Appleborough even to buy a charm to make mended pottery stay mended. We've had a few greenwitches try to settle around here—never at Rose Cottage, mind—but they never stayed. They said they had too many bad dreams. Dreams about monsters living in our woods. We've never had so much as a bad-tempered bear in our woods. In a hard winter the wolves come to Appleborough, but they don't come to Longchance. But dreams are important to greenwitches and so on, you know, so they leave.

"Miffs us, you know? Why not Longchance? We can't decide if it's because we're specialer than ordinary folk, or worse somehow, you know? But it'd be handy to have our own greenwitch again, and them roses ain't bloomed since the old woman left, and so we've been hoping, see?"

"The old woman—tell me about the greenwitch," said Beauty. "What was she like? How long did she live here? Did she build Rose Cottage, did she plant the roses?"

"You don't want much, do you?" said the woman, but she set her shopping basket down. Beauty hastened forward with the stand's only chair and herself sank down at the woman's feet. "That's kind of you, dear, and I like to talk. You want to know what the rest of us Longchancers don't want to talk about, you come to me—or if you want it in a parlour with a silver tea-service, you go to Mrs Oldhouse. Between us we know everything.

"No, our greenwitch didn't build Rose Cottage nor plant the roses, but there weren't much left of neither of 'em when she arrived. The roof had fallen in, and you couldn't see the rosebushes for the wildberry brambles and the hawthorn, and us in Longchance had wandered into the way of thinking that the roses were just a part of the old tale because no one had seen one in so long. It was funny, too, it was like she knew what she was looking for, like she was coming back to a familiar place, though no one round here had ever seen her before. I know this part of the story from my old dad, mind, I was a kiddie myself then.

"She came old, and when she disappeared, she disappeared old, though it was like she hadn't got any older in between, if you follow me, and she'd been here long enough to see babies born and grow up and have their own babies.

"She lived at Rose Cottage, and she made rose wreaths. That's another thing about her. She smelt of roses all year long, even in winter. She was an odd body generally—had a habit of taking in orphan hedgehogs and birds with broke wings and like that—took a child in once that way too, but when she grew up, she left here and never came back. A beauty, she was; stop a blind man dead in his tracks, I tell you.'' She stopped suddenly and gave Beauty a sharp look. ''My! It's prob'ly my mind wool-gathering, but it's that old woman's foundling you remind me of. It's prob'ly just the scent o' your roses, after all this time, confusing my thinking.

''Where was I? Well, the girl never came back, and no wonder, maybe, not to come back to this bit of nowhere, but it was a bit hard on the old woman, maybe. Not that she ever said anything. And when the old woman herself went off . . . As I say, we was fond of her, and if we'd known she was missing sooner, we might have gone looking. Maybe she went back to where she came from. If she died, I hope she went quick, just keeled over somewhere and never knew what happened.

''Rose Cottage has stood empty, ten years, fifteen, since she went. Not even the Gypsies camp there. She'd let it be known she was tying it up all legal in case anything happened to her. I suppose that should have told us we wouldn't be having her much longer, one way or another. We don't have much to do with lawyers round here; but most of us have family, and she didn't. Not that girl, who went off and left her and never sent no word back.

''But your sister—that Jeweltongue—she says you never knew the old woman. Never knew anything about it, except the will, and the house.''

Beauty thought of that last terrible time in the city, remembered again the lifting of the heart when she held the paper in her hands that told her they had somewhere to go, something that yet belonged to them: a little house, in a bit of nowhere, called Rose Cottage. ''Yes,'' said Beauty. ''That's right; we knew nothing about it till we saw the will. It had—it had been mislaid among my father's papers.''

''That's all right, dear,'' said the woman. ''I ain't prying . . . much; folks' troubles are their own, and we've all had 'em. But it's . . . interestin', isn't it? Like you said to begin, you can't help being interested. Because the point is, the old woman had to know something about you. And her roses—they ain't bloomed since she left. Till you came.

"And you're the one we've kind of been waiting for, see? Because you're the one always in the garden. All your family says so. 'That Beauty, you can't hardly get her indoors to have her meals.' And we maybe got our hopes up a bit. Ah, well, it's as I told Patience, we can't have everything, and I dunno but what your wreaths are even better'n the old woman's." She had picked up Beauty's last remaining wreath and was looking at it as she spoke. She hesitated and glanced at Beauty again. "D'you know why everyone wants a rose wreath, dear? Forgive me for insulting you by asking, but you look as if maybe you don't know."

"No-o," said Beauty. "Not because they're beautiful?"

The woman laughed with genuine amusement. "Bless you. Maybe it's no wonder they grow for you after all. You know—pansy for thoughtfulness, yew for sorrow, bay for glory, dock for tomorrow? Roses are for love. Not forget-me-not, honeysuckle, silly sweethearts' love but the love that makes you and keeps you whole, love that gets you through the worst your life'll give you and that pours out of you when you're given the best instead.

"There are a lot of the old wreaths from Rose Cottage around, not just over my door. There's an old folk-tale— maybe you never heard it in your city—that there aren't many roses around anymore because they need more love than people have to give 'em, to make 'em flower, and the only thing that'll stand in for love is magic, though it ain't as good, and you have to have a lot of magic, like a sorcerer, and I ain't never heard of a kind sorcerer, have you? And the bushes only started covering themselves with thorns when it got so it was only magic that ever made 'em grow. They were sad, like, and it came out in thorns. Maybe it was different when the world was younger, when people and roses were younger."

The woman stood up, and briskly took out her purse, and paid Beauty for her wreath, picked up her shopping basket, and turned to go; but she paused, frowning, as if she could not make up her mind either to say something or to leave it unsaid.

"I'd much rather know," said Beauty softly, and the woman looked at her again with her friendly smile.

"You may not, dear, but I'm thinking maybe you'd better. I've told you there's no magic hereabouts. There are tales about why, of course. I'd make one up meself if nobody'd taken care of the job before me. There was some kind of sorcerers' battle here, they say, long, long ago, no one knows rightly how long, and it ain't the kind of thing the squire puts down in his record book, is it? 'One sorcerers' battle. Very bad. Has taken all magic away from Longchance forever'—if we had a squire in those days, though Oak Hall is as old as anything around here, and sorcerers don't live in wilderness. But there's a curse tacked on to the end of it, like the sting on a manticore's tail. It don't rightly concern you, because the tally calls for three sisters, and there's only the two of you—"

"My . . . brother?" said Beauty faintly.

The woman laughed. "Oh, the menfolk don't count—like usual, eh? No, you want sorcery, you got to go to a man, but there's nothing anybody should want to have done a greenwitch can't do. . . . Now, now, don't go all wide-eyed and trembly on me like that. I shouldn't have mentioned it. There's nothing wrong with you and nothing wrong with Rose Cottage. And we're all glad of you; that Jeweltongue can almost outtalk *me* when she puts her mind to it, and you should see her wrapping that old Miss Trueword round her finger! That's a sight, that is.

"Pity you ain't a greenwitch then. We could use one. A greenwitch would make a good living here, you know. You could even afford a husband." And the woman winked. "Maybe you should talk to your roses about it, see if they'll tell you a few charms."

Ask her roses to tell her greenwitch charms? Beauty's astonishment and worry broke and were swept away on a tide of laughter, taking her questions about the curse, and about bad dreams about monsters in the forest, with it. The

woman took no offense but patted her hand, grinning, and
went away.

Jeweltongue returned even as Beauty was looking after
her, and said, "Beauty, if you've sold all your roses, maybe
you'll come lend me your eye? Mrs Bestcloth has a new
shipment in, and Miss Trueword says she will leave it up
to me, and I'm drowning in riches, I can't decide, I want to
use them all."

Over a late tea at home Jeweltongue said, "You and Mrs
Greendown were in close conversation for some while, were
you not? Did she tell you anything interesting? Mrs Tree-
worthy—she and her husband have the Home Farm, you
remember—says Mrs Greendown knows everything about
everything round here."

"Yes . . . oh . . . a bit. Not very," said Beauty, glancing
at their father, who had come home with them after a day
doing sums in Longchance, and now had his scribbles on
his knee, and was holding his teacup absentmindedly halfway to his mouth.

Jeweltongue knew what that glance meant and said
briskly, "Never mind. Help me remember what Miss Trueword's final decisions were, so I can write them down, my
head is still spinning"—help that Beauty knew perfectly
well her sister never needed.

By the time she and Jeweltongue were alone together, she
had decided to say nothing of the curse. She thought there
was a good chance that no one else in magic-shy Longchance would mention it to anyone else in her family; she
was the one who was supposed to be a greenwitch. What
did she herself think about the curse? She didn't know.
Curses were dangerous things; they tended to eat up their
casters and were therefore unpopular among magical practitioners, though they still happened occasionally. Most
likely Longchance's curse was some folk-tale that, in generations of retelling, had begun to be called a curse to give
it greater prestige.

Her first impulse was to attend the very next market-day,
find Mrs Greendown, and ask her to tell her explicitly just
what this curse was. But she had second thoughts almost at

once. She told herself that her interest might cause, well, reciprocal interest, and there was Lionheart's secret to protect. But she knew that wasn't the real reason for her change of heart. She didn't want to know because she didn't want to know. And she would set herself to forgetting that Mrs Greendown had ever so much as mentioned a curse. "There's nothing wrong with you and nothing wrong with Rose Cottage." She would leave it there.

Jeweltongue was fascinated by the story of the greenwitch who had left them Rose Cottage and appeared to harbour no suspicions that Beauty was holding anything back, and by the end of her revised history, Beauty had already half succeeded in forgetting what she had chosen not to tell.

"What a romantic story! At least we now know why we never found the Longchance greenwitch's signboard," said Jeweltongue. "All the way to Appleborough for a simple charm! I don't think I miss magic, do you? We have had little enough to do with it since Mamma died, but now it seems as if it's just one more thing we left behind in the city. It's not as though the cleverer practitioners ever came up with anything *really* useful, like self-peeling potatoes or needles that refuse to pierce human skin."

That night Beauty had the dream. Her first reaction to finding herself again in that dark corridor where the monster waited was of heart-sinking dismay, for her last roses were still blooming in the garden. No! she cried in her dream. Let me go! It is not your time! The light of the candle nearest her flickered, as if disturbed by the draught of her shout. But as she drew her breath in again, she discovered that the corridor was full of the smell of roses, a rich deep scent nothing like her mother's perfume and even more powerful and exciting than the scent of high summer in her garden. And she was not afraid.

CHAPTER

4

A second summer turned to autumn, to winter, and the third spring arrived. But this year was different. Spring was cold and bleak; the warmth of the turning year never came, and the rain never stopped. Summer arrived in seas of brown mud; the rivers overflowed and drowned the seed in the fields and more than a few calves and lambs. Everyone was still wearing coats and boots at midsummer; everyone was low and discouraged; everyone said they couldn't remember a year like this. . . .

And Beauty's roses never bloomed.

They tried. The bushes put out leaves, draggled as they were by the relentless rain, but the long, arching branches drooped under the weight of the water, the weight of the heavy dark sky. The climber over the kitchen door was torn out of its hold on the thatch, and Beauty spent a long dreary afternoon tying it away from the door so that she need not cut the long stems. She came indoors soaked to the skin and spent the next week sneezing and shivering and standing over bowls of hot water and mint oil with a towel round her head to keep in the steam.

The bushes all produced a few hopeful flower-buds, but the sun never came to open them. Those flowers too stubborn to know they were doomed turned as brown as the mud at their feet as soon as the sepals parted; a few Beauty rescued, half open, and brought indoors, where they sat dejectedly in a vase, too weary of the struggle to finish opening, their petals brown-edged and soon falling. Nor did they bear more than the faintest hint of their usual deep delicious scent.

Everyone grew bad-tempered. Jeweltongue's remarks had edges like knives; Lionheart shouted; their father withdrew again into dull silence. Beauty, who should have been spending most of her time in the garden, felt like a rat in a trap. She kept the house clean, mucked out the shed, fed Lydia and the chickens—who were too depressed by the weather to lay—cooked the meals, ran errands both real and imaginary just for something to do, and stared at the ankle-deep slop that should have been her garden. And, with some effort, kept her own temper . . . till Jeweltongue snarled and Lionheart bellowed at her too. Finally she shouted back, threw a plate across the room and heard it shatter as she ran upstairs—just before she burst into tears.

She buried her face in her pillow, so that no one downstairs should hear her. The puppy Lionheart had rescued a year ago, rejoicing in the name Tea-cosy for her diminutive size and the neat little hummock she made when she curled up for a nap, followed her, and burrowed under Beauty's trembling arm to lick her wet cheek.

The leak in the corner of the loft dripped sullenly into its pail. They had scratched enough money together at last to have their thatch replaced this spring; but not only could no thatcher work in a steady downpour, they now had to save the money to buy food for next winter—if they could. The farmers were all fighting the same weather that kept the thatchers indoors and ruined Beauty's garden; market-days at Longchance were a sad affair.

Beauty raised her head and gently pushed the cold nose and wet tongue away from her face. "You are a silly beast," said Beauty. "You know you can't climb down the ladder again yourself. What a good thing you never grew too large to carry."

Tea-cosy heard by the tone of Beauty's voice that she was succeeding in comforting her, whatever those particular words meant; the main thing, from her point of view, was that they did not contain the dreaded word *No*. She dodged Beauty's restraining hand, put her paws on Beauty's arm, and licked her face harder than ever, wagging her tail till her whole body shook. "Your generous sympathy is not all joy, you know," murmured Beauty through the onslaught.

She was just beginning to think she should go back down and sweep up the fragments and go on with dinner while Lionheart finished her week's baking when she heard footsteps on the loft ladder. Jeweltongue laid their dented little tea-tray down on the floor beside the mattress—the chipped saucers clattered in the dents, and the cups clattered in the mismatched saucers—sat down next to her sister, and began to rub her back gently. "I'm sorry. We're enough to try the patience of a saint, and even you're not a saint, are you? I don't think I could bear to live with a real saint."

Beauty gave a soggy little laugh, rolled up on an elbow, and caught her sister's hand. "Do you ever miss the city? You must think about it—as I do—but do you ever long for it?"

Jeweltongue sat quite still, with an odd, vacant expression on her face. "How strange you should ask that just now. I was only thinking about it this afternoon. Well, not so strange. It's the weather that does it, isn't it? The cottage grows very small when it's too wet to be out of doors. I hadn't realised how often I took my sewing outdoors, till this year, when I can't. And the cottage is smaller yet when Lionheart is here too, roaring away.

"I don't know if I miss it. . . . I miss some things. I sometimes think if I have to wear this ugly brown skirt one more day, I shall go mad. I still remember Mandy, who wore it first; do you remember her? Creeping round all day with eyes the size of dinner plates, waiting for me to say something cross to her. Oh! How many cross things I did say, to be sure! No, I don't long for that life. But I would like a new skirt."

"Do you miss the Baron?"

Jeweltongue laughed and picked up the teapot to pour. "I miss him least of all. Although I would have enjoyed re-decorating his town house. Drink this while it's hot. Lion-heart has sent you a piece of her shortbread, see? You have to eat it or her feelings will be hurt. She roars because she can't help herself, you know."

"I do not," said Lionheart's head, appearing through the trapdoor in the loft floor. "I roar because—because— If you let Tea-cosy eat that shortbread, Beauty, I really *shall* roar. And if you don't come downstairs soon, I will feed your supper to Lydia."

It was at the end of the summer that the letter came. Each spring and autumn since they had lived in Rose Cottage, one or two or three of the traders from the convoy that had brought them here stopped in on their journey past, to see how the old man who had once been the wealthiest merchant in the richest city in the country and his three beautiful daughters—with a good deal of joshing about the meta-morphosis of the eldest into a son, always accompanied by the promise not to give her away—did in their exile.

The leader of the original convoy seemed to take a pro-prietorial pleasure in their small successes and always no-ticed the improvements they had made since last he saw them: brighter eyes, plumper frames, clothing that not only fitted well (Jeweltongue would have nothing less round her) but which bore fewer visible darns and patches, chairs all of whose legs matched, enough butter and butter knives to go round when they had a fifth, or even a sixth, person to tea.

This visit was less cheerful than usual; the weather had been bad all over the country, and the traders suffered for it too. Lionheart, who was the best of the three sisters at pretending high spirits she did not feel, was not there, and Mr Strong was preoccupied. He was in a hurry; the convoy had lost so much time to the weather they were passing right through Longchance with barely a pause. "Mr Brownwag-gon and Mr Baggins send their regards and beg pardon for not coming round," he said. "But we'll be returning near here in a few days, before we head south again, and one of us will stop in if there is any reply we can take for you."

Reply? They glanced at one another, puzzled.

"I am very back to front today," Mr Strong said, groping in his breast-pocket. "Please forgive me. This rain gets into one's head and rots the intellect. I would have come anyway to say hello, but as it happens—" and he pulled out an envelope and laid it on the table.

Soon after, he said his good-byes and left them, but the echo of the door closing and the slog of his footsteps had long gone before anyone made a move toward the envelope. Jeweltongue, who had sat next to Mr Strong at tea, and was nearest, said, "It's addressed to you, Father," but her hands remained buried in the fabric on her lap. Beauty stood up and collected the tea-things, putting the bread and butter back in the cupboard with elaborate care, setting the dirty plates in the washing-up bowl as if the faintest rattle of crockery would awaken something terrible.

She had finished washing up, tipped the water down the pipe, pumped enough fresh water to refill the kettle and the water-jug, and begun to dry the tea-things and put them away when Jeweltongue abruptly leant forward, jerkily picked the letter up, and dropped it hastily in front of her father, as if she wanted to be rid of it as quickly as possible, as if she wanted to push it as far away from herself as she could, as if it were literally unpleasant to the touch.

Their father dragged his eyes away from the fire—hissing as the rain dripped into the chimney—and took it up. He held it for a long moment and looked back at the fire, as if tempted to toss it into the heart of the small blaze. With a sigh, he bowed his head and broke the seal.

One of his ships, presumed lost at sea, had returned, loaded with fine merchandise, worth a great deal of money. His best clerk—whose wife sent her regards, adding that she still prized her collection of once-silent canaries who now sang chorales finer than the cathedral choir, and whose rehabilitated sphinx was, she and her husband agreed, better than any watchdog they had ever had—had contrived to

have the ship impounded till his old master could arrive.
But he pleaded that he should come soon, for he himself
was only a clerk, and working for a new master, who took
a dark view of his new clerk working for another man.

"What he does not say is 'a man disgraced and driven
out of town,' " said the old merchant, having read the letter
aloud to his daughters. "I suppose I must go."

Silence fell. Beauty went on polishing and polishing the
dish in her hand; Jeweltongue stared blankly at the needle
she had just threaded. Tea-cosy, who had been hiding under
the table—her usual lair in anxious times—crept out, scut-
tled over to Beauty on her belly, and tried to press herself
between Beauty's feet, tucking her head and forequarters
under the hem of her skirt.

Beauty reached down absently with the hand still holding
the damp tea-towel, to pat the still-visible hindquarters.
"Wait at least till Lionheart comes home again," she said.

The old merchant appeared to rouse himself. "If I can.
But I must be prepared to leave when the convoy returns."

When Lionheart came home two days later, she hurtled
through the door as she had done every week since this
wretched year had begun, scowling, ready to shout at anything that displeased her, softening only to greet the ecstatic
Tea-cosy.

Her father's news stopped her. Bewilderment, and dismay, replaced the scowl. "Must you go? Surely—surely
you can ask Mr Lamb to dispose of the goods and—and
take a commission?"

"I could. But it would not be honourable." He lifted his
shoulders. "You do not know; there may be something left
at the—at the end." His daughters, Beauty particularly,
knew better than he did how many debts had been left to
pay after their house had been seized and their property
auctioned. There were legal papers saying these were to be
forgotten, but they would be remembered again as soon as
there was money to pay them. "What shall I bring you?"

Lionheart shook her head, and her scowl returned. "Yourself, home safe. Soon."

Their father smiled a little. "Jeweltongue?"

Jeweltongue smoothed the sleeve on her lap. It was silk, with lace insets, and the lace had gold threads in it that caught the light. It was much like one of the sleeves of a dress she had herself worn to the party when the Baron had taken her a little aside and proposed marriage to her, telling her that he cared for nothing but her and her beauty and brilliance and that if she agreed to marry him, he would be the happiest man on earth. She was to leave all her dresses and jewels to her sisters, for once she was his bride he would buy her a new wardrobe that would make the queen herself look dowdy; her father could provide her with a dowry or not, it was a matter of greatest indifference to him. She had always been fond of that dress, and when Miss Jane True-word had spoken of silken sleeves with lace insets, she had remembered it. "Nothing," she said. "Nothing at all. But that you come home again as quickly as you may."

"Beauty. There must be something I can bring you."

He looked so sad that Beauty cast her mind round for something she could suggest. He would know she did not mean it if she asked for jewels and pretty dresses. They had Tea-cosy and did not need another house pet, nor could they afford to feed and shelter anything beyond Lydia, her latest kid, and the chickens. Whatever it was, it needed to be something small, that would not burden him on the way. They really lacked for nothing at Rose Cottage—nothing but the sun—nothing, so long as they wished to stay here, and it seemed to her that they did wish to stay here.

Nothing but the sun. Her eyes moved to the windowsill, where an empty vase stood, and she gave a little laugh that was mostly a sob. "You could bring me a rose."

Her father nodded gravely, acknowledging the joke. And when the convoy returned, he went with them.

The winter the old merchant spent in the city he had been born in and lived in all his life till the last three years was sadder and emptier even than he had expected. His clerk had not succeeded in keeping the impoundment proof against raids from his old creditors; there was little enough left even by the time he arrived, and he saw none of it at all. Winter frosts came early, but no snow fell; the muddy, churned ground froze solid and into such rutted, tortured shapes that many of the roadways were impassable. He found himself stranded in the city week after week, with almost no money even to put food in his mouth; if the Lambs had not taken him in, he did not know what he would have done.

Yet he had to keep hidden even that kindness, for his clerk's new master disliked any expression of loyalty—or even human sympathy—to his old. The old merchant rather thought that Mr Lamb's new master had taken him on as a deliberate gesture of spite against himself, but he found he no longer cared. He lived in a tiny house called Rose Cottage, very far away from here, and as soon as the weather broke, he would return. He knew now that his daughters had been right, and he should never have come in the first place. Well, he had learnt his lesson.

But he was not able to wait for the weather. His old business rival discovered his clerk's, as he put it, duplicity, and declared that the clerk could choose between his job and sheltering a ruined man. Mr Lamb did not tell him this; the captain of the ship that had returned found out about it. The captain offered his own home as alternative, but the old merchant declined. He was bad luck in this city, and the sooner he left the better. Reluctantly he did accept the loan of a horse—or rather of a stout shaggy pony—from the captain, on the man's flatly refusing to let him leave town on any other terms. "It's winter out there, you old fool; you could die of it, and then where would your daughters be?"

My daughters would do very well without me, thought the old man, but he did not say the words aloud. Instead he admitted the pony would be useful and thanked the captain for his offer.

There was little traffic leaving the city. The old merchant found a few people to travel with; but he had to make a zigzag course from one town to the next, for no one (sensibly) was travelling very far, and some people turned back—or had to turn back—when they discovered the state of the roads. He was daily grateful for the pony, who, nose nearly at ground level and ears intently pricked, found her way carefully over and round the twisted furrows and rough channels where the frozen mud crests sometimes curled as high as her shoulder, and who seemed to have a sixth sense about which murky, polluted ice would hold her and which would not.

At long last he was within a few days of Longchance, and of Rose Cottage, and the weather was breaking at last. Spring was here—nearly. He had been gone the entire winter.

There was no one travelling in his direction, but he thought—so near to home—he could risk it alone. The track itself was easy to find; there were so few roads this far into the back of beyond it was hard to take a wrong one. And bandits usually stayed in the warmer, richer lands. He set out.

The first day was fine: blue and clear. He could not remember when he had last seen blue sky; he stared up till he was dizzy and had to cling to the pony's mane. Little soft airs moved round him, brushing his face and hands, toying as if in disbelief with the heavy, fraying edges of his winter cloak. When he made camp that evening, he was as near to being happy as he had been in the months since the letter had come. He was warm; he knew where he was; he would see his daughters soon. He thought of his secret work waiting for him and smiled; maybe sometime this year he would be ready to satisfy Jeweltongue's curiosity. . . . He wondered drowsily how many knots the sawyer and carter and wheelwright had got their accounting into in the last few months. He would sort them out soon enough. He fell asleep dreaming pleasantly of long straight columns of figures.

But the clouds rolled up while he slept, and the temperature began ominously to drop. When he woke, he found the pony lying beside him, her warm back against his, and there were snowflakes falling.

He saddled up, frightened, and turned the pony's nose to the road. But the flakes grew thicker and thicker, and the wind rose and howled round them, and soon the pony was going where she chose, because he no longer had any idea where they were and could not see the track for the drifting snow.

But the pony toiled on, showing no sign of wanting to stop; the old man was glad enough to hold on to the pommel and let her go, for he knew that to halt would be to freeze to death. He grew wearier and wearier and slumped lower and lower; once or twice he woke up just before he fell off. The pony's steps were growing slower. Soon he would have to get off and lead her. . . .

The snow stopped and the pony's hoofs struck bare ground at the same moment. She stopped, and he looked up in amazement, snow sluicing off his shoulders and back. They had come out of the woods into a clearing. The merchant, dazed with exhaustion and astonishment, at first could not make out what he was looking at. It was not merely that no snow was falling here now, no snow had fallen; the ground before him was green with grass. Immediately around them was a vast formal garden, laid out in low box mazes, dotted by small round pools with classical statues rising from their centres. The box looked freshly clipped, the pools quiet and untroubled by ice, and the paths were recently raked. This stretched as far as his tired eyes could see on either hand. Beyond the garden before him, at the end of a straight drive surfaced with small twinkling white pebbles, was the most magnificent palace he had ever seen, even in his days as the wealthiest merchant of the wealthiest city in the country.

The palace was perhaps only three storeys high, but each storey was twice the height of those in an ordinary house; the windows were as tall and wide as carriage-house gates. The facade was impressively handsome but forbiddingly plain, the heavy square pediments of the ranks of windows emphasising a glowering look, and all was made of a grey-white stone which glittered slightly, like the pebbles in the drive, and which made the building hard to look at for very long. It seemed to shimmer slightly, like an elaborate mirage.

The merchant blinked, but the garden and the palace remained. He looked down at himself. The snow was melting on his sleeves and along the pony's mane. He looked up. The sky overhead was iron grey, but he could not tell if it was twilight or cloud cover that made it so. But no snow fell from it. He was afraid to turn round; would he see wintry woods again, the blizzard that might have killed them? If this was a mirage, he wished to believe it was real till it was too late. . . . May kind fate preserve me, he thought. If it is not a mirage, this must be the dwelling of the greatest sorcerer that has ever lived. But where are his guardian beasts? His messenger spirits? Everything was wrapped in the deepest silence and stillness, deep as the snowbound stillness that follows a blizzard. When his pony bowed her head and blew, the sound unnerved him.

The merchant dismounted stiffly, took his pony's rein, and walked forward. His numbed face began to hurt, for the air here was warm. He stripped off his sodden gloves and loosened his cloak. The pony had come out of the blizzard and into this—this place at the head of the drive, as if she had been following a clear path. Perhaps she had. Their feet crunched on the pebbles; the sound was nothing like the squeak of feet on fresh-fallen snow.

The huge arched portico over the doorway into the palace was lit with hundreds of candles. There was not even so much wind as to make the candle flames flicker.

He stopped on the threshold, but only for a moment; he was too tired, and too precariously balanced between fear of what lay behind them and fear of what lay before, to risk any decision. His feet had decided for him; let them have their way. He took the pony through the archway too, partly for company, partly because he would not leave her behind after all they had been through together. She balked, briefly, when her hoofs touched carpeting, but she did not wish to be left alone either, so she crowded up close behind the merchant and pushed her face into his back.

They walked down a long corridor together; the old merchant was simply following the line of lit candles. He saw great dark doorways on either side of him, but he had no

urge to explore. The way they went was full of light, and
he went on hopefully, though he would not have wanted to
say precisely for what. He and his pony both needed sleep
and food as well as shelter, but it seemed ridiculous that
they should be wandering through an enchanted palace looking for these things.

He looked back once over his shoulder. Their passage was
leaving no muddy footprints, no dark damp patches of
melted snow. He did not look back again. He knew they
were caught up in some great magic, but this little reminder
of it was almost more frightening than the fact of the palace
itself. They walked here without trace; it was as if they were
invisible, insubstantial, as if they were ghosts. . . . He tried
to rally himself: Think of the row in an ordinarily grand
house if one such as I, and leading a dirty, shaggy pony as
well!, should be found indoors, and uninvited! Think of the
cries of outrage, the rush of servants with their buckets of
soapy water to scrub the carpet—think of the disdainful
footmen hustling us back to the door!

He remembered the passionate strength he had had in the
first weeks following his wife's death, when he had forbidden any magic or any practitioners of magic in his house
ever again. It was the only absolute law he could ever remember making. He would have laughed, now, had he the
strength, at what seemed to him suddenly the wild waste-
fulness of his younger self. For the truth was that he had no
wish now to spurn what appeared to be offered to him. He
was grateful to have his life, to be granted the hope that he
might, after all, see his daughters again.

But he wished someone would come and reassure him
they did know he was here. And he wished that whoever it
was that came might be more or less human. Or at least not
too large. There had been a sorcerer he had had mercantile
dealings with who had a hydra to answer his door. He'd had
to call on the sorcerer himself because his clerks were all
too frightened to go. But he had been younger then too.

They came to a room. It was a small room for the size
of the palace, but a very large room to a man who lived in
Rose Cottage. The soft crimson carpet of the corridor con-

tinued here, and the candelabra on the walls were ornate gold, with great golden pendant drops made to look like dripping candle wax, and the wallpaper was a weave of red and gold, patterned to look like ripples of fabric bound with golden cords. There was a fire in a fireplace large enough to roast the pony, and a table drawn up beside it, with a place laid for only one person but with enough food for twenty.

The merchant gave a great sigh and unsaddled the pony. She staggered forward and stood, swaying and steaming, in front of the fire; then she turned her head and ate three apples out of a silver-gilt bowl on the table. "I wish there was hay for you," said the merchant, picking up a loaf of bread and breaking it into pieces with his hands and offering it to her; she ate it greedily. But as he held it out to her, something caught at the corner of his eye; he looked over her shoulder and saw . . . a golden heap of hay in a little alcove on the other side of the fireplace, opposite the table. He would have sworn that neither hay nor alcove had been there a minute before. But when the pony had finished the bread, he turned her gently round, and she went to the hay at once, as he sat down at the table.

He did not fall to as quickly as she; he was too worried about his host. But he was tired and hungry almost past bearing, and he tried to comfort himself with the thought that there was plenty of food here for two, should the master of this place appear after all—or perhaps his hydra. He looked again at the amount of food provided, and the single place setting, and worried about the appetite of the creature usually catered for. Finally, and half embarrassed, the merchant moved the single place setting round the edge of the table, so that he was not sitting at the head but only on the master's right hand.

He ate eagerly but hesitantly, looking often towards the mouth of the lit corridor where he had entered, taking great pains to spill nothing on the snowy tablecloth, laying the serving spoons exactly back where he found them, choosing nothing that would by its absence spoil the elegant appearance of the whole. By the time he was no longer hungry, his eyelids seemed to be made of lead; with a tremendous effort of will he stood up from the table, thinking he would lie down in front of the fire to sleep. His knee knocked against something, and he discovered a little bed with many blankets drawn up close behind him where he had sat at the table. He shivered because he knew there had been no bed there earlier and he had heard nothing. But there it was, and he was tired. He stayed awake just enough longer to pull the biggest blanket off the bed and throw it over the now-dozing pony.

He woke to the sound of munching. There was more hay in the alcove, and his pony was going at it busily. There was also a bucket of water and another of the remains of a feed of mixed corn. The blanket was still over her, barely; it hung down to her toes on one side and was halfway up her ribs on the other, and it was caked with mud and pony hair. The merchant pulled it off her—she paused to say good-morning, shoving at his breast with her nose—and laid it in front of the fire, thinking sadly that their ghostly presence here did not extend quite far enough after all, and hoping that perhaps he might be able to brush the worst of the mud and hair off when the blanket was dry.

But he was growing accustomed; when he turned back to his side of the fire, he was not surprised to discover that his bed had disappeared, and the large table replaced with a smaller one, again with a place setting for only one, but enough breakfast for six hungry old merchants. "They are adjusting," he murmured to himself. There was also a single red rose in a silver vase.

When he looked up from his breakfast, his eye was caught by a small door in the wall opposite him, standing a little open. He obediently crossed the room to investigate; within was a bathroom, gloriously appointed, and the bath full of steaming hot water; beyond that was a water-closet. When he had climbed at length from the delightful bath, he found a new suit of clothes waiting for him; when he returned to the main room, the blanket he had laid before the fire was not merely dry but clean, and the pony herself was clean and brushed and saddled with tack as fresh and supple as if it had been oiled every night since the day it was made. The pony's thatch of a forelock had been braided and tucked under the browband, and she looked very pleased with herself.

"Thank you," he said helplessly, standing in the middle of the floor. "Thank you, thank you. You saved our lives." There was no answer. He turned towards the door and then paused, looking back at the breakfast table. The remains of his breakfast were still there, as was the rose in the silver vase. He remembered Beauty's sad, half-joking wish, and plucked the rose out of the vase, and put it into the breast of his coat. Then he took up the pony's rein and went through the archway, down the long crimson-carpeted corridor towards the door, open now on a bright spring day.

But the silence of the palace was shattered by roars as of some enormous wild beast; his quiet pony reared and shrieked and jerked the rein out of his hands. He was knocked winded to the floor; when he struggled to stand up, the bright doorway was blocked by a Beast who stood there.

The merchant's heart almost stopped beating in the first moments of dumb terror. The Beast seemed not merely to blot out the sunlight but to absorb it and grow even larger by its strength. The outside edge of his silhouette was fuzzy and shimmering, as confusing to the eye as the merchant's view of the grey-white palace with its glinting white driveway had been the day before. When the Beast stirred, rays of dazzling light shot in at the merchant like messages from a lost world, but as he moved again, and they were effaced, it was as if the Beast deliberately struck them away from the merchant, as a cruel gaoler might strike at the outstretched hands of his prisoner's beseeching friends.

The merchant's first fumbling thought was that this Beast was rearing on his hind legs, but then he saw that his shape was not unlike a man's—only hugely, grotesquely, bigger than any man—and that he dressed like a man. Grasping at his reason, the merchant hoped it was only fear, and the dazzling, narrow bursts of light, which made the Beast so difficult to see. He lifted his eyes, trying to find this man-shaped Beast's face, to look into his eyes, the better to plead

with him, for would not a man-shaped Beast respond to the
direct look of a man? His gaze travelled up the vast throat,
found the great heavy chin, the jaw of a carnivore, the too-
wide mouth, thin lips curled back in a snarl, the deadly
gleam of teeth— He could raise his eyes no farther; his mind
was disintegrating with terror.

Before he lost himself to madness, he dropped his gaze
to look at the Beast's garments, forced himself to stare at
them, to recognise, and to name to himself, cloth, buttons,
laces, seams, gores, pleats. He saw that the Beast was
dressed entirely in black, and the clothes were themselves
odd, of no fashion the merchant knew. He wore an open,
sleeveless gown, of some kind of stiff heavy material over-
laid with black brocade and trimmed in black braid, which
fell from thick gathers at the shoulders to a great whipping
length of hem which roiled out round him like half-opening
wings as he paced and roared. Beneath this was a long, soft,
but close-fitting waistcoat, embroidered, also in black, but
in a pattern the merchant could not make out. Even the shirt
beneath it, the ruffle at the collar and wrists were unrelieved
black, as were the trunk-hose and the low boots, strapped
tightly round the ankles.

The Beast threw back his head and roared a last time;
then he spoke, and his voice shook the walls. "I have fed
and sheltered you and your creature when you both would
have died in the blizzard else! And you repay my kindness
and hospitality by stealing my rose!"

The merchant opened his mouth, but no words came. He
leant against the wall of the corridor and closed his eyes,
waiting for the blow.

"Speak!"

The merchant opened his eyes. The Beast was standing
still at last, and now the sunlight streamed in round him;
there was a wide channel of light from the doorway to the
merchant's feet, one edge of it sculpted by the shape of the
Beast's shoulder and the fall of his gown. Perhaps that gave
the merchant courage; perhaps it was that as the Beast was
now standing, he was half turned sideways, and with the
wings of the gown collapsed round him, he looked only

huge, no longer big enough to obliterate the sky. The merchant wondered where his pony had got to.

"I—I—" The merchant's voice was a croak, but as he discovered he could again speak, his mind began to race, spilling out frantic excuses. "I am very grateful—I am very grateful—truly I am—I know we would have died—we were nearly dead—I am sorry about the rose—I was not thinking—that is, I was thinking, but your house is so grand—I thought you would not miss it—it is just that my youngest daughter grows roses, but the weather this year meant none of them bloomed, and she was so sad, so sad, her roses are her friends, and she is such a good girl, a kind girl, I thought to bring this one to her. . . ."

As the merchant said, "Her roses are her friends," the Beast gave a little shudder. The merchant saw it in the ripple in the edge of the channel of light, as the Beast's gown swirled and fell still again. The merchant had kept his eyes fixed on that track of sunlight as he spoke, and now both edges of the channel ran suddenly straight, as the Beast moved away from the door. The merchant looked longingly out upon the shimmering white driveway, at the border of smooth lawn he could see, and the dark haze of trees beyond, but he knew there was no point in trying to run. The Beast would snatch him out of the air before he reached the door. He wished again he knew where his pony was.

He glanced towards the Beast, who had his back to him, and the merchant was suddenly, unwelcomely shaken by an unmistakable flare of pity, for the Beast stood with his great shoulders and head bowed in a posture unfathomably sorrowful. If he had been a man, and even if that man had threatened his life but a moment before, the merchant would have put a hand on his shoulder. But he was a Beast, and the merchant remained next to his wall. But he wondered . . . and now, perhaps, he hoped.

The Beast turned back towards the merchant, catching the edge of the sunlight again, halving the bright track that led to the merchant's feet, and fragments of light glanced off the curves and angles of his face as he turned. The merchant's breath caught on a sob, and he turned his own face to the wall. He did not dare close his eyes—were not the Beast's footfalls silent?—but he had, just then, confused by pity and dread and daylight, nearly looked into the Beast's face.

"Your daughter loves roses, does she?" the Beast said at last. Now that he was no longer roaring, his voice was so deep the merchant had to strain to hear the words. "They grow for her, do they?"

"Oh yes," said the merchant eagerly, looking at the Beast's feet. "Everything in the garden grows for her, but the roses most of all. Everyone in the town comments on it." The merchant raised his eyes just to the Beast's breast level; his peripheral vision told him the Beast still stood with his shoulders stooped and his head lowered. The merchant was appalled when he heard his own voice saying: "I—I—may I bring you some this summer, to—to replace what I—I stole? Her—her—her wreaths are very much admired. . . ."

In the silence following his involuntary words, the merchant heard his heart drumming in his ears, and there was a red fog over his vision that was not explained by the crimson carpet. The Beast stood as if considering. "No," he said at last. "No. I want your daughter."

The merchant gasped; a great pain seized his breast, and two tears rolled down his face.

"Stand up, man, and catch your pony, and ride home. I could kill you, you know, and it would be my right, for you have stolen my rose. But I am not going to kill you. Go home and tell your daughter to come to me."

"No—oh no!" cried the merchant. "No—you may as well kill me now, for I will not sacrifice one of my daughters to take my place!"

"Sacrifice?" said the Beast. "I said nothing of killing the girl. She will be safe here, as safe as you were, last night, till you stole my rose. Nothing comes here that is dangerous—save me—and I give you my word she will take no harm of me."

The merchant, far from standing up, had sunk down, as his knees gave way, and now he bowed down till his forehead nearly touched the floor, and covered his face with his hands.

"Nay, you think a Beast's word is not to be trusted?" As the Beast strode towards him, the merchant, in a final spasm of terror, struggled again to his feet and spread his hands, thinking to meet his death as bravely as he could, but all he felt was the sleek thickness of the Beast's fur as he forced his huge clawed hand into the breast of the merchant's coat. He saw the Beast's great hand closing tight round the rose's stem; when he opened it again, the palm had been pierced by one of the thorns, and three drops of blood fell softly to the crimson carpet, making a dark stain like a three-petalled flower or the first unfurling of a rose-bud.

"I am a man in this," said the Beast, staring down at the merchant; the merchant felt that look burning into his scalp. "I keep my promises. By my own blood I swear it.

"I am lonely here—tell your daughter that. She is a kind girl, you say. Just as no fierce creatures come here for fear of me, who am fiercer, so no gentle ones come either. I desire companionship.

"I give you a month; send her to me by then, or, believe this, merchant—I will come and fetch her. Take her this as a token of my oath." And the Beast bowed down low before the merchant's amazed eyes, lower than the merchant would have guessed any Beast of such bulk could bow, till his long mane trailed on the carpet and mixed with the crumpled wings of his black gown, and laid the rose at the merchant's feet.

The Beast sprang up at a bound, turned, and took two steps out of the doorway, turned again, and disappeared. The merchant heard no footfalls, but perhaps that was only because of the ringing in his ears.

He slowly picked up the rose and stood staring at it. As he had fixed his mind on the Beast's garments a little time before, now he fixed his mind on this rose. It seemed to him he had never seen one so dark, in its centre almost as black as the silhouette of the Beast; but the outer petals were of a redness more perfect and pure than he could remember

seeing anywhere in his life, with no hint of blue suggesting
purple, no weakening of its depth of colour towards pink;
and as most of Beauty's roses reminded him of silk, so this
one reminded him of velvet.

He looked up. He seemed quite alone, and his heartbeat
no longer deafened him. He took a cautious step; again his
legs would hold him. He turned away from the sunlight,
walked back down the corridor, and found his pony trembling in the now-empty alcove where she had spent the
night. So glad was she to see him that he led her without
fuss back towards the front door and towards the place
where they had met the Beast, though he felt her neck under
his comforting hand still rigid with fear. He mounted just
over the threshold, and they set out on their journey once
again.

CHAPTER
5

It was hardly noontime when the merchant saw the tiny track to Rose Cottage winding off to the right of the wider track he was on, which he had found almost at once, as soon as the pony had stepped into the trees at the edge of the Beast's garden. He was not fully convinced that he was not still held in some dream-state manipulated by the Beast, and he often reached out and touched the branches of trees, when they passed near enough, to reassure himself of their reality—but what, he said to himself despairingly, was not a sorcerer as great as the Beast capable of?

But then Beauty was running towards him; she had seen him from where she had been in the garden, and she flew to him, and half dragged him off the pony, and embraced him, laughing, and crying Jeweltongue and Lionheart's names. It wasn't till all three sisters—and Tea-cosy—were there, hugging and patting him and saying (or barking) how glad they were to see him (under the astonished gaze of Lydia, who stopped eating to watch), how relieved they were to have him home with them again, that it came to them he was not rejoicing with them.

"Father, what is it?" said Lionheart.

He shook his head. "Let me sit down—let us all sit down,

and I will tell you. Beauty—this is for you." And he took
the rose from the breast of his coat. It should have been
crushed and wilting after several hours in a pocket, but it
was not; it was still a perfectly scrolled, half-open goblet-
shaped bud of richest red, poised delicately on a long stem
armed with the fiercest thorns.

"Oh! What a beauty!" said Beauty. "I have none of that
colour. I wonder if it would strike if I cut the stem?"

Lionheart had turned to the pony. "That's a good little
beast," she said, not noticing how her father shivered at the
word *beast*. "Is she your profit from the city? You could
have done much worse."

Jeweltongue was rubbing one of her father's lapels between her fingers. "That is the most elegant cloth. I wish I
had some of that. Perhaps I can ask the traders to look out
for some for me when they come through again. Father, you
must tell me where you found it. Master Jack would buy a
coat of that faster than his sisters order dresses."

"Father, you have pricked yourself," said Beauty.
"There is blood on the stem."

And then the old merchant shuddered so terribly that he
nearly fell down, and the sisters forgot everything in their
anxiety for him.

He seemed to them to be feverish, and so they drew out
his bed, and pulled off his boots, and tucked him up with
blankets and propped him with pillows, and fed him soup,
and told him not to talk but just to rest. He wanted to resist
them, but he found he had no strength to resist, so he drank
the soup and lay back, murmuring, "I will lie here just a
little while, and then I will tell you," but as he said, "I will
tell you," his face relaxed, and he was asleep.

Once or twice that day he woke and said aloud in distress,
"I must tell you—I must tell you," and each time one of
the sisters went and sat beside him, and took his hand, and
said, "Yes, yes, of course you will tell us, but wait a little
till you're feeling stronger. You have had a very long journey, and you are weary."

Beauty dreamt the dream that night, but the endless corridor was lined with rose-bushes, and while she could see

no roses, their scent was heavy upon the air. But this time the perfume gave her no comfort, and the long thorny branches tore at her as she tried to walk past them, and one caught her cheek. With the sharp suddenness of the pain she almost cried out, only just stopping herself by biting her lips, and when she touched her face, there was blood upon her fingertips. When she woke, she found blood on her pillow; she had bitten her lip in her sleep, and three drops had fallen on the pillow slip, making a shape like a three-petalled flower or a rose-bud just unfurling.

The old merchant slept all the rest of the next day, and that night, and the day following, waking seldom, though sleeping restlessly, and Beauty and Jeweltongue went about their ordinary tasks with heavy hearts and distracted minds, wondering what their father would tell them and wishing both that he might sleep a little longer so they need not hear it quite yet, and that he might wake soon and let them know the worst. Lionheart, much valued as she now was by her employers, had asked and been granted special leave to come home every evening while her father was so ill, at least till she had some notion of whether he grew sicker or would mend. She left before dawn and came home after dark, riding her father's pony, whom she had named Daffodil, and she was tired and short of sleep, but so were all three sisters, for worry.

On the third evening, at last, the old merchant's head cleared, and he called his daughters to him, that he might tell them his story, and he told them all of it, sparing himself nothing. He finished by saying, "I do not wish to lie to you now. But there is no question of Beauty taking my place. As soon as I am strong enough again to walk that far, I will return to the Beast's palace. And then the Beast can deal with me as he sees fit. But I am glad to have had the chance to see you all, my dears, my dearer-than-dears, this final time, to tell you how much I love you and to say goodbye."

Beauty had sat cold and motionless through the last of her father's story, and at these words the tears ran down her cheeks and dropped into her lap. "Ah! That I should have

asked you for a rose! I was selfish in my little, *little* sorrow—and it is I who will take up the fate *I* have earned.
Father, I am going to the Beast's palace.''

He would not hear of it; but she would hear of nothing
else, and they argued. Beauty, always the gentle one, the
peace-maker, was roused to fury at last; she crossed her
arms tightly over her stomach as if she were holding herself
together and roared like Lionheart—or like the Beast. But
the old man's strength came back to him twice over in this,
and for a little while he was again the man he had been just
after the death of his wife, wild with the strength of grief
and loss. And so the old merchant and his youngest daughter
shouted at each other till Tea-cosy fled the house and hid
in the now-crowded shed with the goat, the chickens, and
the pony, Daffodil.

But Jeweltongue and Lionheart, after a little thought,
came in on Beauty's side, saying, ''He says she will take
no harm of him, and he declared he would kill you!''

''I am old, and the little left remaining of my life is worth-
less; you love me, but that is all. The three of you will do
well enough without me.''

But that all three of his daughters should range themselves
against him was too much for him after all, for he was older
now, and the winter had gone very hardly with him, and he
had been near the end of what remained of his bodily
strength before the blizzard and the meeting with the Beast.
His fever came on him again, and he lay half senseless for
many days, rousing himself occasionally to forbid Beauty
to leave him, although he seemed to have forgotten where
she was going. The sisters took a little of what remained of
their thatching money—for they had come through the lean
winter just past with a little to spare, partly on account of
having one less mouth to feed in their father's absence—
and paid the local leech for a tonic, but it had no effect.

''I do not think he will mend till I am gone,'' said Beauty
at last, a fortnight after their father had come home with his
dreadful news. But then her sisters clung to her, and Jeweltongue wept openly, and even Lionheart's face was wet,

although she had twisted her expression into her most ferocious scowl.

"I will—I will surely be able to visit," Beauty said, weeping with them. "This palace must be close at hand—as Father has described it. Or he is so great a sorcerer as to make it seem so, and I do not care the truth of it. I am a quick walker—I will find a way to come here sometime and tell you how I get on. It will—perhaps I will be like Lionheart, who comes home every seven days. I will—I will weed the garden, while Lionheart bakes bread. Remember, he has—he has promised no harm to me. And—can a Beast who loves roses so much be so very terrible?"

Her eyes turned again to the red rose in the vase on the windowsill. It had opened slowly and was now a huge flat cupful of darkest red petals, and its perfume filled the little house. As its colour was like none of her roses, so was its perfume different from them also; this was a deeper, richer, wilder smell, and it seemed almost to follow her round during the day, so that it was in her mouth when she cleaned out the shed or weeded the farthest row in her vegetable garden. And it came to her every night, in the dream, where the rose-bushes now grew thicker and thicker, till they crossed the corridor and tangled with the bushes on the other side, and she could only force her way through them more and more slowly, wrapping her hands awkwardly in her skirts as she handled the dangerous stems. And yet, in her dream, it never occurred to her not to go on; it did not even occur to her to look behind her and see if the way back was clear.

Beauty had cut two bits off the long stem of the dark red rose and thrust them into her cuttings bed, and she spoke to them every day, saying, "Please shoot for me, for my sisters and my father, so that they may think of me when they see you bloom," for she in truth did not believe, in her heart of hearts, that the Beast would keep his promise. But it was equally clear to her that this was her fate, that she had called its name and it had come to her, and she could do nothing now but own it.

And so it was less than three weeks since the old mer-

chant's return when Beauty packed up the few things she
had chosen to take with her and set out. But she had thought
often and long about her father's story: how the Beast had
been roused by the theft of the rose, how he had dwindled
and looked sad, how he had taken particular interest in the
daughter who believed her roses were her friends. And so
she took one more thing with her, secretly, tucked away in
her clothing.

She embraced her sisters on the doorstep in the early
morning. Their father had had a bad night, and Jeweltongue
had sat up with him. There were hollows under her eyes
and heavy lines around her mouth, where there had never
been lines before. Lionheart looked little better, for her late-
and-early hours were telling even on her strength. The three
of them spoke quietly, for their father was finally asleep,
and they hoped that he would not learn that Beauty was
gone till it was too late to stop or to follow her.

Tea-cosy, aware that something had gone wrong with the
old merchant's homecoming, had been shadowing each sister in turn so closely that whoever was chosen for that hour
could not move without tripping over her. In the last few
days she had apparently decided that the wrongness threatened Beauty most and never left her side, generally creeping
up the loft ladder during the night to sleep on her feet and
having to be carried down in the mornings. She was now
leaning against Beauty's shins so heavily she felt like a
boulder instead of a small dog, except that boulders don't
tremble.

"I cannot think the Beast's palace can be found unless
he chooses it be found; surely Father will understand that
searching is useless. . . ." Beauty's voice trailed away. "Do
not forget to water my cuttings bed every day; twice a day,
if the summer grows hot. . . ." Again her voice faltered. It
was difficult to think of what needed to be said when there
was so much and so little to choose from. Finally she stood
silent, gripping her sisters' hands, smelling the warm human
smell of them, the scent of each as precise and individual
as the shape of her face, and she was terribly aware that she
was going to a place where there would be no hands to grasp

nor arms to embrace her, and no friendly human smells.

Jeweltongue loosed her hand from Lionheart's and reached into a pocket in her apron. "This is for you," she said to Beauty. She held out a tiny embroidered heart on a silk rope. "It's to—to—I don't know. It's not to remember us by, because I know you'll remember us, but it's to have something to hold in your hand when you think of us. I—I only thought of it myself a few nights ago; you know it's been so hard to think clearly about anything since Father returned. . . . I would have made you a rose, but I didn't think I could do one well enough in so short a time; hearts I can do in my sleep. As I think I did this one. And—I've used some of Lionheart's hair. You remember you picked up the bits after you finished cutting it, and put them in the old sugar bowl on the mantel? So you have both of us, Lionheart and me. Here. Take it."

Beauty released both hands to take the silk rope and set it round her neck, and then the three sisters embraced, till Beauty broke away and went running down the track, her tears cold on her face in the early-morning breeze, and the desolate howl of Tea-cosy in her ears.

When she came to the end of the little track that led to Rose Cottage and set her feet upon the wider way that came up from the city and wound past Longchance on its way to its end in the wild mountains of the east, she closed her eyes and turned in a circle three times clockwise, and then she walked three steps forward, holding her hand in front of her face just in case she walked into a tree, though she was quite certain she would not. After three steps she opened her eyes and found herself on a track only a little bigger than the one that led off the main way to Rose Cottage, but it was a track she was quite sure she had never seen before.

The wood on either side of her beyond the track looked older and wilder than that around Rose Cottage. The tangle here told her that there would be no frequent glimpses of farmland beyond, as there were everywhere near Longchance, where the undergrowth was regularly cleared and the old trees were felled for firewood and building.

Furthermore, running on either side of her, at just a little distance, as if the track had once been broader, were two rows of beech trees, as if lining a drive. She had seen few beeches since they had left the city, and she had missed them. She left the track for a moment when there was a little suggestion of a gap in the low scrub and put her hands on a beech tree. The feel of the smooth familiar bark gave her courage. She touched Jeweltongue's little embroidered heart and returned to the path.

She wondered if her father had awakened yet, if he had missed her, if Jeweltongue would tell him she was only out in the garden, if Tea-cosy's wretchedness would give them all away immediately. She wondered if she had been right to guess that her father would not mend till she left—and that he would mend when she did. Had the Beast sent his illness? Did he watch them from his palace? What a sorcerer could and could not do could never quite be relied on—not even always by the sorcerer. She could hate him—easily she could hate him—for the misery of it if he had sent it. If he kept his promises like a man, did he suppose that they, mere humans as they were, would keep theirs any less? The price was high for one stolen rose, but they would pay it. If he had sent her father's illness to beat them into acquiescence, she would hate him for it.

The bitterness of her thoughts weighed her down till she had to stop walking. She looked again at the beech trees and, not waiting for a gap this time, fought her way through to the nearest and leant against it, turning her head so that her cheek was against the bark. The Beast is a Beast, even if he keeps his promises; how could she guess how a Beast thinks, especially one who is so great a sorcerer? It was foolish to talk of hating him—foolish and wasteful. What had happened had happened, like anything else might happen, like a bit of paper giving you a new home when you had none finding its way into your hand, like a company of the ugliest, worst-tempered plants you'd ever seen opening their flowers and becoming rose-bushes, the most beautiful, lovable plants you've ever seen. Perhaps it was the Beast's

near presence that made her own roses grow. Did she not
owe him something for that if that were the case? It was a
curious thing, she thought sadly, how one is no longer satisfied with what one was or had if one has discovered something better. She could not now happily live without roses,
although she had never seen a rose before three years ago.

She could not stand here forever, and she had best not go
on standing here at all. If the Beast had been watching them,
if he was watching her now, he would see no good reason
for her stopping, because there was none. And she wanted
no sorcerous prods to send her more swiftly on her way.
Would the Beast tell her, if she asked, that her father had
recovered?

It was clear daylight when she reached the beginning of
the gardens and the white pebble drive. But even Beauty's
young eyes could not see how far either the clearing or the
palace itself extended; the building seemed to run a very
long way in both directions, and a distant dark irregular haze
seemed to suggest that the trees pressed up close just beyond
its corners.

Beauty walked down the drive, staring at the clipped box
and the stark paths and stone pools, thinking forlornly that
there was nothing here for her. Her eyes burnt with unshed
tears, and she walked stiffly, because her legs were trembling. This will not do at all! she said to herself, a little
frantically. I haven't—I haven't even met the Beast yet! But
this was the wrong thing to think of, because then fear and
sorrow broke free of their bounds and seized her.

She turned off the path, and groped her way through the
openings in one of the hedges, and sat down on the edge of
a stone pool. The stone was cool and hard like any stone,
and this served to comfort her a little; she took a deep sigh
and contrived to find some humour in being comforted by
the dull grey coping of an uninteresting round pool. She
looked at the statue in her pool: a blank-faced maiden carrying an urn and wearing what would have been impractical
and highly unstable draperies, except for the fact that they
were made of stone. The maiden was not nearly so graceful

and attractive as the statue in the centre of the garden at
Rose Cottage.

Beauty turned a little where she sat, to look at the palace
again; it seemed to her very bleak, and she wondered if there
was any rose that would climb tall enough to soften its harsh
face. Even the one galumphing over the rear wall of Rose
Cottage (its stems were now appearing on the far side, and
Beauty predicted that in another year or two it would likely
be locked in a battle for precedence with the slightly more
subdued one by the front door) might find this palace too
much for it. Then she thought of window-boxes under all
those gigantic, joyless windows, full of cheerful, untidy
plants like pansies and trailing peas and nasturtiums, in the
vividest colours possible. She was by now genuinely smiling.

I wonder where the Beast's rose garden is, she thought.
For there is no sign of it here.

She stood up and made her way slowly back to the drive
and more slowly yet towards the gaping front door. There
were no candles lit today, and in the bright daylight the open
door looked like the mouth of a cave. Or of a Beast.

She came to within a few steps of the portico, and halted,
and could make herself go no farther. Her heart was beating
so quickly she had to keep swallowing, because it seemed
to be leaping up her throat; her head felt light, and there
was something wrong with her vision, as if everything she
looked at were no more than an elaborate mirage. . . . She
touched Jeweltongue's embroidered heart again. The decision was made; she was here; she would not turn back; she
would not even look back over her shoulder. . . .

She had been standing, staring at the portico and the door
beyond in a kind of half trance. A shadow caught the corner
of her eyes, and she spun round, backing away so quickly
that she blundered against the nearest box hedge; it pricked
her sharply even through her skirts. She stumbled, regained
her balance, and stood staring at the Beast.

She was less lucky than her father, who had never looked
the Beast clearly in the face. The old merchant had had some
little warning of the Beast's approach by hearing him roar

before he appeared and was therefore already frightened enough to have difficulty looking at the threat directly; and the Beast had remained, throughout that interview, with his back to the daylight. Beauty had had the warning of her father's experience, but it was the wrong sort of warning, or she had taken the wrong warning from it. She had thought only that this Beast was a very large, strong, and therefore dangerous Beast, who was the more terrifying because he walked and dressed and spoke like a man.

Had she had the opportunity to choose, she would still have chosen to look immediately into the Beast's face upon meeting, to have the worst borne and past at once. But the worst is not necessarily past and over with thereby. The worst of fighting a dragon is being caught in its fire, but you do not survive dragon encounters by commanding your muscles to withstand dragon fire, because you and they cannot. You survive by avoiding being burnt. Beauty knew no better than to wish to marshal her forces before she met the Beast, though that marshalling would not have saved her. As it was, she was surprised into looking into the Beast's face.

The contrasts she found there were too great: wisdom and despair, power and weakness, man and animal. These made him far more terrible than any hungry lion, any half-tamed hydra, any angry sorcerer, terrible as something that should not exist is terrible, because to recognise that it does exist shakes that faith in the foundations of the natural world which human beings must have to bear the burden of their rationality.

Later Beauty thought of a metaphor to explain the shock of that first sight of the Beast: She felt as if she were melting, like ice in sun. Water is perhaps a kind of ice, but it is not ice, it is water. Whatever—whoever—she was, it was being transformed implacably into something else; *she* was being undone, unmade, annihilated. . . . But that unravelling thought—which she would later put the words to of ice burning in the heat of the sun—made her drowning mind throw up a memory of those last days in the city. And she remembered staring into the eyes of the salamander, into

those two pits of fire whose dangerous heat she had felt,
and she heard the salamander's dry, scratchy voice saying,
I give you a small serenity.

With her last conscious strength, she cupped her hands
and immediately felt the warmth between the palms, as if
she held a small sun; and then the heat surged up her arms
and into her body, reaching into every niche and cranny, till
it had reshaped her flesh into her own precise, familiar, individual contours, and she was neither water nor ice nor
unmaking but again herself. And she opened her mouth and
gasped for air, for since she had raised her eyes to the
Beast's eyes, she had not breathed.

All of this took no more than a minute, as clocks understand time.

She lowered her eyes then, and wishing to regain her
composure and not wishing to appear rude, she dropped a
curtsy, as she would have done to a great lord of the city,
keeping her eyes upon the ground; but the graceful dip of
her curtsy was hampered by the box hedge. She could not
quite bring herself to step away from it, for any step forward
would take her nearer the Beast.

"You need not curtsy to me," said the Beast. "I am the
Beast, and you will call me that, please. Can you not bear
to look at me?"

She looked up at once, pierced to the heart by the sorrow
in his voice and knowing, from the question and the sorrow
together, that he had no notion of what had just happened
to her, nor why. From that she pitied him so greatly that
she cupped her hands again to hold a little of the salamander's heat, not for serenity but for the warmth of friendship.
But as she felt the heat again running through her, she knew
at once it bore a different quality. It had been a welcome
invader the first time, only moments before; but already it
had become a constituent of her blood, intrinsic to the mar-
row of her bones, and she heard again the salamander's last
words to her: *Trust me.* At that moment she knew that this
Beast would not have sent such misery as her father's illness
to harry or to punish, knew too that the Beast would keep
his promise to her, and to herself she made another promise

to him, but of that promise she did not yet herself know. *Trust me* sang in her blood, and she could look in the Beast's face and see only that he looked at her hopefully.

This time it was he who looked away first. "If you will follow me, I will show you to your rooms," he said.

"I—I would rather see your garden. I—I mean, your flower-garden," she said almost shyly, and hesitating to mention roses. She took one, two, three tiny steps away from the box hedge. The Beast was so large! And it would be easier to be near him outdoors, in these first few minutes of—of—in her first attempts to adjust to—to— She did not think she could bear to look at the rooms she was now to live in, that did not have her sisters in them. Roses might comfort her, a little. Or if they could not, nothing could. . . .

She shook herself free of that thought quickly and allowed instead her gardener's passion to be drawn by the prospect of roses which bloomed so far out of their season as the one that had decorated their father's breakfast table, the one which still stood in the window of— No! She would not let herself think of it. Roses; she was thinking of roses, of what a great sorcerer indeed the Beast must be, to have roses blooming in winter.

She might have been frightened of the Beast's silence if she had not been so absorbed by her thoughts, in not thinking the thoughts that most pressed on and plucked at her. She came to herself and noticed his silence and wondered if she had offended him, and a small cold prickle of fear touched her. But then he said: "You will see . . . what remains of my garden." He looked out over the box hedges, the paths, and the stone pools, and she thought that they brought him no pleasure; this was not what he thought of when he thought of his garden. "Later."

He led her into his great house, and Beauty followed timidly, keeping not too near to him, but not—she hoped—too far away. Everything was silent, except when Beauty brushed her hand against a curtain, or a dangling crystal drop from a low sconce—just to hear the sound. The carpet was deep, and neither her footsteps nor the Beast's made any noise at all; nor did he make any further attempt at conversation, and she could think of nothing she wished to say to him.

But there was still—wasn't there?—some odd quality to this silence, a heaviness, as if the air itself were denser here than usual, that it did not carry sound as ordinary air did, that it required a slightly greater effort than usual to walk through. Was this what a sorcerer's house always felt like? She had never been invited indoors at the house of the salamander's master, but he had also been retired, so perhaps that would still have told her nothing. There had been no sense of oppression—of *otherness*—in his front garden, except by what the salamander provided in its own self, and that was all she knew. There was an almost liquid quality to this air, to this unknown ether coiling among the solid objects, herself and the Beast among them. She waved her arm in front of her and fancied that she saw tiny, ghostly ripples of turbulence, like the surface of a troubled pond, following the motion.

But even this occupied only part of her attention. She was so astonished by everything she saw that this oppression—whatever caused it—was not as great as that simpler oppression of spirits she had anticipated when she had followed the Beast indoors. She knew that her weariness of soul and body, after what had already happened to her both today and all the days since her father had returned from his disastrous journey, made her more susceptible to intimidation, but knowing this, she was still oppressed and intimidated and had little power of resistance.

This indoors was so unlike what she had left, so unlike even the very grand house they had had, long ago, in the city when they had been wealthy. It seemed to her that this house was as much grander than their city house as their city house was to Rose Cottage, and it was Rose Cottage that she loved, far more than she had ever loved anything in the city. And the walls were so high and wide, the ceilings so distant that the Beast seemed no larger than an ordinary man, in such a setting, but Beauty felt no bigger than a beetle, creeping after him.

At last they came to an enormous circular room, with an

eight-pointed star inlaid upon the floor, and eight doorways leading out of it, and sunlight through a dome overhead, the dome ringed with an inlay that matched the star. Even here the Beast's footfalls made no sound, but Beauty's more ordinary shoes made a soft tapping on the smooth bare floor. The Beast strode across the star without hesitation, the wings of his gown laying flying shadows over the sparkling tiles, and threw open one of the doors. "I will leave you now," he said. "If there is anything you need, say it aloud, and if it is within this house's power—or mine—it will be brought to you at once." He turned to go the way they had come.

"Oh, but wait," said Beauty. "Please. Your garden—"

"Later," said the Beast, his hand on the door, and he crossed the threshold without pausing.

Beauty looked after him as the door closed behind him, but as soon as she looked away—to the other doors, to the sun lighting up the gilt and coloured enamel tiles in the floor—she no longer knew which door they had entered by. She turned to the one that had remained open, the one the Beast had opened for her.

Inside was an enormous room, or rooms. There were no proper doorways with doors, but a series of large spaces semidivided by half-width walls, their demarcations more clearly indicated by the arrangement of the furnishings. There were jungles of furniture, cities of statuary, and the walls were thick with tapestries and paintings.

The outer rooms of the palace which she had seen had been even larger, more dramatically designed, more spectacularly ornamented; these rooms were almost more humbling by being closer to her own experience of wealth and magnificence. She knew she did not belong in this palace; this recurred to her with every caress of the queer thick air against her skin. But in these rooms . . . It was a little as if a king had decided to reward a farmer, and knowing the farmer would have no use for, nor interest in, silks and velvets and fancy wines, still gave him a phaeton and a team of blood horses when he would rather have had a good pair to pull his plough.

It took her a little while to realise that her sense of the
wrong sort of familiarity—the not merely disorienting, the
distressing pull towards something unsuitable, as the farmer
might have admired, and even longed for, the phaeton
team—was caused by the fact that every decorative pattern,
every carving, every lick of paint and bit of fabric, were of
vines and flowers and trees and fruit. And the commonest
representation was of roses.

The carpet she first stepped on from the mosaic floor of
the chamber of the star was dark green, but it was also thick
with huge pale pink cabbage roses. Towards the first wide
door space these grew darker till in the next room the roses
were all a vivid pink; but they faded again and lost some
of their petals towards the next doorway, till in the next
room the roses Beauty walked on opened flat, their golden
stamens showing in the centre of but a dozen or so gracefully curved petals which were pink-tipped and cream-
hearted . . . and so on.

The wallpaper—what could be seen of it—all bore small
climbing roses in different colours, and the table that stood
in the centre of the first room, so that Beauty had to go
round it to reach the next, had roses carved in relief round
its edge, and inlaid in exquisitely tinted pietra dura across
its surface; the stems of the torchères, standing in slender
elegant clusters in every corner, were wound round with
roses, and tiny rosebuds surrounded each individual candle;
a stone maiden, not unlike the one Beauty had seen in the
pool in the front garden, stood holding a bowl of roses over
her head, whose brim she had tipped, and she was so covered by a cascade of stony roses that all of her that was
visible were an eye, one cheek, a smiling mouth, and the
tips of her toes.

In the second room the panelled walls were almost entirely covered by a series of tapestries portraying a garden
in each of the four seasons. "You're cheating," murmured
Beauty, for there were roses showing in both the spring and
autumn scenes, as well as rioting so profusely across the
summer ones it was almost impossible to ignore them long
enough to see what else was represented. "But perhaps it is

true here," Beauty said; "perhaps this is the garden I have yet to see?" And she heard the hope in her voice, but she also felt the wrench as she averted her mind from recollecting a dark red rose on a cottage windowsill.

She walked over and touched one of the summer tapestries with her hands. A little peacefulness seemed to sink through her skin at the contact, and she realised that the dense air of this palace was lighter in these rooms, in her rooms, and her lungs did not labour here. She felt the tiny pressure of the silk rope round her neck that bore the little embroidered heart; she remembered the comfort of the touch of the beech tree in the middle of the wild wood, remembered the moment before the front door of the palace when she had known the Beast would keep his promise to her . . . and, before she could stop herself, remembered the last moments of her sisters' arms round her and their scent in her throat. It was in the midst of that memory, as she took a deep, steadying breath, that she became aware of another scent.

She dropped her hands and turned round, and on a tall japanned cupboard she found a china bowl full of dried rose petals. She drew her fingers through them—as she had often drawn her fingers through rose petals in smaller cracked or chipped bowls or saucers that stood at various sentinel posts around Rose Cottage—and gloried in the smell released; but at the same time there was a tiny doubt in the back of her mind that this was not quite the same rose smell as—as—When? Just now? Just when? She looked round, puzzled. Perhaps there were other bowls of other sorts of roses' petals scattered about in these rooms, though she had not seen them. What she seemed to be remembering was a deeper, richer, almost wilder smell, a smell that might almost have given her dreams.

She walked on through the rooms, following a wide swathe of sunlight. At last she came to what she recognised as a bedroom, because it contained a bed, although the bed was so tall it required its own short flight of stairs, drawn up against one long side (its wooden surfaces carved with rose-buds, its tread carpeted with pink rose-buds), and its

curtains (patterned with crimson roses) looked too heavy for
her to move by herself. She walked over to it, slid out of
the straps that held her small bundle of belongings to her
back, dropped the bundle at the foot of the bed. It tipped
over and disappeared under the trailing hems of the bed-
curtains.

On the wall nearest the bed there was a fireplace, with a
fire laid but not lit on the clean-swept grate, the tips of
whose uprights and crosspieces were round flat open roses.
Round the corner from it were two doors. She opened the
first and found a tidy water-closet, with a subdued pattern
merely of grapevines on its walls and one tactful candle
sconce dripping golden grape leaves. But the second door
opened upon a bathroom as grand as a ballroom, the walls
gold-veined mirrors, the floor pink marble, and the bathtub
as large as a lake, its taps so complicated by water violets
and yellow flags it was hard to guess how they worked. The
whole effect was so gaudy she took an involuntary step
backwards, and then she laughed aloud. "No, no, I can't
use anything like this; I won't; I should drown in the bath—
supposing I ever made sense of those taps—fall down on
the floor, and be horribly embarrassed by the walls. I'd
rather wash out of a teacup, standing up in front of the fire,
thank you."

She closed the door hastily and continued her exploration.
There was a vast wardrobe suitable for hanging dresses, and
next to it a chest of drawers with matching footstool, so that
you could see into the top drawer when you opened it (both
chest and footstool were festooned with roses twisted among
the delicate stars of virgin's bower). Next to that were a
lower table, with what was probably a jewel-case (painted
over with roses) sitting on it, and a cushioned chair (its
needlework seat pansies and roses). "You are all very handsome, but nothing to do with me," she said, and made no
move to open anything. "All I need is one small—quite
small—shelf, if you please. You do know what *small*
means?"

She turned back towards the bed, and there next to it, in
a corner of the fireplace wall, was a small white-painted

shelf, perfectly plain—she blinked—no, it was not perfectly
plain; almost white roses were dusted all over it, almost
white with the faintest blush of pink, that caught the eye
only after you had been looking at it for a little time—
because of course it must be nonsense to think she had
watched them coming into being. . . . "But what do I know
of housekeeping in enchanted palaces?" she said. She
looked at the edge of her bundle, just visible as a wrinkle
in the bottom of the bed-curtains, and thought, No, I cannot
bear unpacking just now. She looked round again at the
huge, beautiful, crowded room. Not now. Not here.

She walked rather quickly towards the window, which
took up half the wall; curtains were bunched on its either
side, and there was a dignified frill at its head, but the tall
panes reached the floor and were hinged like doors. She
went to them, pushed the centre ones open, and stepped
outside onto a narrow balcony.

The warmth of the sun wrapped round her like the arms
of a friend or of a sister, and her desolation struck her, and
the tears rushed down her face, and she sobbed till she could
not stand and knelt on the balcony, clinging to the rail,
pressing her wet face against the warm stone. She wept until
her throat hurt and her eyes were sore and her head ached,
and then she stopped because she was too tired to weep
anymore. After a little time she stood up and went back into
the bedroom to look for water to wash her face, and there
it was, on a little table near the fireplace, a generous basin
of it, with pink soap and an assortment of ruby-coloured
towels; the outlines of roses were stitched in red thread
along their hems. The water was warm, as warm as the
sunlight, although it stood in shadow; she looked round, to
catch sight of some servant leaving, but saw no one.

How silent the palace was! No rustle and murmur of human life, not even birdsong, the scritch and patter of mice
in the walls, or the creak of beams adjusting their load.
Nothing but the silence, the thick, liquid silence, a silence
that was itself a presence. A listening presence.

This house was quieter even than their city house had
been during the last weeks they had lived there.

Hastily she picked up the soap. It was very fine, smooth soap and made her aware, as she had not been aware for many months, of her rough gardener's hands, and it smelt of roses. Her tears began to flow again, so she set the soap down and made do with the warm water. Then she returned to the balcony.

From where she stood, the palace ran round at least three sides of an immense courtyard. She could see only partway along the long faces to either side of her and could not see at all where the fourth side should run, or whether it was open or not, because her view was blocked by a glasshouse.

The glasshouse was itself big enough to be a palace, and it glittered so tempestuously in the sun she had to find a patch in its own shade for her eyes to rest upon. It was very beautiful, tier upon graceful tier of it rising up in a shining silvery network of curves and straight lines, each join and crossing the excuse for some curlicue or detail, the caval-cades of panes teased into fantastic whorls and swoops of design no glass should have been capable of. Merely looking at it seemed an adventure, as if the onlooker's gaze imme-diately became a part of the enchanted ray which held the whole dazzling, flaring, flaunting array together.

Beauty found that she was holding her breath—in delight; and when she expelled it, a laugh came with it. The glass-house was joyous, exuberant, absurd; immediately she loved it. It was her first friend, here in the Beast's gigantic palace, sunken in its viscous silence.

At the very top of the glasshouse—she blinked against the glare—was a small round cupola and what she guessed was a weather vane, although she could not identify its shape, but she thought she saw it move. The palace was three immense storeys tall, but the glasshouse was taller yet.

She had turned and was making her way quickly back through the long swirl of rose-covered rooms before the idea had finished forming in her mind: There is the Beast's gar-den.

CHAPTER

6

She half ran out upon the round chamber with the star in its floor. She stood in the centre, turning round and round, with the sun pouring down on her, and her feet playing hide-and-seek with the coloured tiles in the centre of the star. "Oh! I shall never find my way! How do I go to the glass-house?" She had spoken aloud only in her private dismay, and had only just noticed that there were ten doors instead of eight, and had begun to tell herself she must have mis-counted the first time when one door swung slowly open. She fled through it before she had time to change her mind, before she had time to be frightened again or to weep for loneliness. The garden would comfort her.

She had only the briefest impression of a portrait of a dauntingly grand lady in an extravagantly furbeloved frame, hanging on the first turn of the corridor beyond the door, before she rushed past it. She was remembering the glass-houses in their garden in the city, which were paltry things compared to this one, nor could they convince their summer flowers to bloom quite all year round—not even the mayor's great glasshouse could do that, with its hot-water pipes, which ran beneath all its benches and floors, and its shifts of human stokers, working night and day, to keep the boiler up to temperature—and the winters there were much milder than in the environs of Longchance and Appleborough. Perhaps this glasshouse was the answer to the question of how the Beast had had a rose with which to ensnare her father. . . . She jerked her thought free of that grim verb *ensnare*. But perhaps it was only a glasshouse, and not sorcery, that was the answer to her question.

Unexpectedly she found herself remembering something Mrs Greendown had said to her: *Roses are for love. Not silly sweethearts' love but the love that makes you and keeps you whole, love that gets you through the worst your life'll give you and that pours out of you when you're given the best instead. . . . There aren't many roses around anymore because they need more love than people have to give 'em, to make 'em flower, and the only thing that'll stand in for love is magic, though it ain't as good, and you have to have a lot of magic, like a sorcerer. . . .*

But the Beast was a sorcerer, wasn't he? Of course. He must be.

The corridor twisted and twisted again, and the sunlight came through windows in what seemed any number of wrong directions, and she began to wonder at the decisiveness of her feet, so briskly stepping along, nearly scampering, like Tea-cosy after a thrown stick. . . . But then the world straightened out, with a lurch she seemed almost to feel, and there was a door to the outside, which opened for her, and she stepped through it and was in the courtyard she had seen from her balcony, and the glasshouse was in front of her.

She approached it slowly after all. It was very splendid and very, very large, and she felt very small, and shy, and shabby—"Well, I am very small and shabby," she said aloud. "But at least my face and hands are clean." And she held up her clean hands like a token for entry. "No, that is the wrong magic to enter even a magic garden," she said, and looked up at the glasshouse towering over her, and all its gorgeous festoonery seemed to be smiling down at her, and again she laughed, both for the smiling and for the ridiculousness of the notion.

"Here," she said, and reached inside the breast of her shirt with one hand, and drew out a small wrapped bundle of the cuttings she had brought, and with her other hand reached into her pocket and drew out a handful of rose-hips. She stepped forward again, holding her gifts to her body, but when she came to the glasshouse door, she held them out, as if beseechingly.

And then she laughed yet again, but a tiny, breathless snort of a laugh, a laugh at her own absurdity, tucked her rose-hips and her cuttings back inside her clothing, set her hand upon the glasshouse door, and stepped inside.

She had been able to see little of what might lie inside the glasshouse from her balcony because the sun was so bright; she had had some impression of shadows cast, but she was unprepared for what she found. The glasshouse's vastness was entirely filled with rose-bushes. The tall walls were woven over with climbers, and the great square centre of the house was divided into quarters, and each quarter was a rose-bed stuffed with shrub roses.

But they were all dead, or dying.

Beauty walked slowly round the edges of the great centre beds, looking to either side of her, looking up, looking down. Occasionally some great skeletal bush had managed to throw up a spindling new shoot bearing a few leaves; she saw no leaves on the climbers, only naked stems, many of them as big around as her wrists. She had thought when she first saw the thorn-bushes massed round the statue in the garden of Rose Cottage that they were dead; but she had not known what sleeping rose-bushes look like. She knew now. The Beast's roses were dying.

In the last corner she came to, her head turned of its own volition, following a breath of rich wild sweetness, and there was the bush that had produced the dark red flower that had sat on her father's breakfast table in the Beast's palace and on Rose Cottage's windowsill. The living part of it was much smaller than the dead, but living it was, in all the sad desert of the magnificent glasshouse; three slender stems were well clothed in dark green glossy leaves, and each stem bore a flower-bud. Two of these were still green, with only their tips showing a faint stain of the crimson to come, but the third was half open, just enough for its perfume to creep out and greet its visitor. Beauty knelt down by the one living bush and slowly drew out and laid her cuttings and her rose-hips in her lap, as if demonstrating or offering them or asking acceptance; and then, as if involuntarily, both hands reached out to touch the bush. The stems nodded at her gently, and the open flower dipped as if in greeting or blessing. "We have our work laid out for us, do we not?" she said softly, as if speaking in the ear of a friend.

She left the rose-hips in a little heap under the living bush but stood up again holding her cuttings, looking round her thoughtfully. "Where shall I put you?" she said aloud. "Shall I make a little bed for you, so that I can watch you, or shall I plant you now and hope you will give hope and strength to your neighbours? You must be brave then, because I cannot spare even one of you." And so she planted them, one each in the four outer corners of the centre beds, four more in the inner corners, sixteen more centred on each side of each square.

Her four cuttings from Rose Cottage's two climbers she placed in the four corners of the glasshouse, beneath the skew-whiff jungle of the old climbing stems. She found a water-butt and watering-can near the door she had entered by, and she watered each of her tiny stems, murmuring to them as she did so, and by then the sun was sinking down the sky, and the glasshouse was growing dim, and she was tired.

She said good-evening to the one living bush and the pile of rose-hips and went to the door; with her hand on the faceted crystal doorknob she turned and said: "I will return tomorrow; I will make a start by pruning—by trying to prune you—all of you— Oh dear. There are so many of you! But I shall attend to you all, I promise. And I must think about where to make my seedbed. Sleep well, my new friends. Sleep well." She went out and closed the door softly behind her.

She had taken little thought of how to go where she wished to go; she had turned automatically in the direction she had come, but brooding about the dying roses, she had only begun to notice that she seemed to be walking into a blank wall . . . when suddenly there was an opening door there. She stopped and blinked at it. She supposed it was the same door she had come out by; all the palace walls looked very much alike. She turned and looked at the glass-house. The glasshouse had only one door; she had looked very carefully while she was inside it. Very well, the glass-house was her compass, and this was the way she had come when she left the palace, and the door was set very cleverly into the palace wall so that it was invisible until you were very near, and an awful lot of these doors did seem to open of themselves, although the Beast had opened doors in the usual way, and the glasshouse had waited (politely, she felt; it was what doors were supposed to do) for her to open its door.

She stared at the palace door, now standing open like any ordinary door having been opened by ordinary means. Very well, she knew she had entered an enchantment as soon as she set foot on the white-pebbled drive leading to the palace; if self-opening doors were the worst of it, she was . . . she could grow accustomed.

She looked up again and could see the weather vane twin-kling in the golden light of the setting sun. She thought for a moment that it twinkled because it was studded with gems—anything seemed possible in this palace, even a jewel-encrusted weather vane—but then she realised that it was carved, or cut out, in such a way that what she was seeing were tiny flashes of sunlight through the gaps as it turned slowly back and forth on its stem. She strained her eyes, but she was no nearer guessing what its shape was. Twinkle. Twinkle. There was no breath of the breeze that the weather vane felt on the ground where she stood.

She went through the open palace door, and some of the candles were now lit in their sconces—even though the sconces lit seemed to be in different locations on the walls from when they had been unlit—and shone brighter than the grey light coming through the tall windows. Just over the threshold she paused and looked round her. There had been

a little square table beside the door to the courtyard, a little
square table of some dark reddish wood, with a slope-
shouldered clock on it, and the clock had a pretty painted
face. She had only caught a glimpse of it, for she had been
in a hurry to go to the glasshouse, but she was quite sure
of the table and the clock. The clock was still there, but it
now had an inadequately clad shepherdess and two lambs
gambolling over its curved housing, and the table was
round.

She followed the lighted corridor till she came to the
chamber of the star—eight doors; she counted and shook
her head—and found the door to her rooms open for her.
She drifted through them till she came to her bedroom, and
she looked at the bed, longing to lie down on it and be lost
in sleep, and her hand reached up and grasped the embroidered heart.

But there was a beautiful scarlet and crimson dress laid
across the bed, and stockings and shoes, and a necklace lay
almost invisible on the ruby towels of the washstand, so
dark were its red stones, and there was fresh warm water in
the basin and a steaming ewer at the foot of the table. "I
am to dress for dinner, am I?" she said wearily; but she
was too tired either to protest or to be afraid of seeing the
Beast again (he is so very large, whispered a little voice in
her mind), and so she washed, and dressed herself, and
clasped the necklace round her neck and the drops in her
ears, and tucked the little embroidered heart at the end of
its long rope into the front of her bodice, and tied up her
hair with the ruby-tipped pins she found under the necklace.

When she went to the chamber of the star, she was too
tired to count the doors, too tired to do anything but concentrate on not listening to the little voice in her head, saying, You will not be able to see him clearly, now, as the
twilight deepens, and the candle flames throw such strange
shadows; he is dark, almost black, and he wears black clothing, and he walks very quietly—noiselessly; you will not
know where he is until he is just beside you. . . .

The chamber of the star itself was dark, the first stars
showing through the dome overhead, but another door was

open for her, and candles gleamed through it, and she went towards the light at once, her shoes pattering like mice. . . . He is so very large, whispered the voice.

She went down the dim candlelit corridor surrounded by darkness, and suddenly she was in her dream.

Her tiredness dropped away, and panic replaced it. Her heart drummed in her ears, and her vision began to fail her; she sat down where she was, in the middle of the corridor, with her cascades of skirts and petticoats flying round her, and she was weeping again, weeping like a child, whole-hearted and despairing, for she was all, all alone, and the monster waited for her—for her—

"Beauty—"

The Beast had approached her as silently as he had done that morning, as silently as the little voice had said he would. She looked up through her tears, snapping her head back so quickly her neck sent a sharp shock of pain up and down her spine, and all she could see was a great dark shape bending over her from the coiling shadows. She shrieked and scrabbled away from him, dragging herself along on all fours, smothered by her skirts. She could not see properly, between tears and darkness; she thudded into the corridor wall and stopped because she had to. The jolt shook the panic's hold on her; she still wept, but less violently, and then she remembered the Beast.

She rubbed her face with her hands and tried to look up at him again, but she could not find him in the shadows. Was he there, in the corner between the tallboy and the wall, or there, where the shadow of that plinth extended the black pool of shadow left by the heavy deep frame of that picture? . . . Fear seized and shook her, as savagely as if cruel hands held her shoulders; but she set her will against it and forced it back, and then another little unhappy fear said to her: What if he had left her before she had a chance to apologise?

Speaking into the darkness, she said: "I—I am sorry— please forgive me—it is a dream—a dream I have had since childhood—that I am lost—walking down a dark corridor, alone, and—and—" She scrambled somehow to her feet, stepping on her skirts, needing to lean against the wall to sort herself out, knocking her hand against the frame of another picture, its subject invisible in the gloom though she stood directly next to it. The Beast had emerged from the shadows by taking a step towards her, his hand outstretched to offer her his aid, but she saw him check himself before the gesture was completed; had she not shrieked at the sight of him but a moment before?

She was ashamed. She would not—she *would not*—be frightened of him; he was what he was, and he had made a promise he would keep. It is only the silly human way of needing to be able to see everything; if Tea-cosy were here, she would know at once everything she needed to know through her nose. . . . The shadows fell across his face, but she could hear him breathing. There was a faint, elusive odor; it reminded her of the scent she had caught—or imagined—in her rooms that afternoon.

"The dream—the dream has frightened me all my life." She moved towards him in such a manner that he must turn to look at her, turn so that the candlelight fell once more on his face. She saw him flinch as it touched him, and she kept her eyes steadily on his face. "I am ashamed of myself."

She heard the rumble of his voice, like a low growl, before he spoke any words: "Do not be ashamed. There is nothing to forgive. This . . . house . . . is large, and it is strange to you. As am I." He paused. "But I know that dream. I have had it too. And you have not told me all of it, have you? There is something that waits for you at the end of the corridor. Something that waits just for you. Something terrible. A monster—or a Beast."

"Yes," said Beauty gravely. "You are right. Something does wait at the end of the corridor. But it is a monster—not a Beast."

They stood still, the shadows curling round them, the little glow of the candlelight on their two faces.

The Beast turned away at last, saying, "I am keeping you from your dinner." He raised his arm, that she might precede him, but she slipped up to him, and put her arm through his, and led him down the corridor, the long train of her skirts rustling behind them, the Beast silent beside her. It was only then that she realised that the corridor was full of a wild rich rose smell, and that the smell came from the Beast himself.

Dinner was laid in a hall so tall and wide that both walls and ceiling were lost in darkness, though there were several many-armed torchères clustered round the end of the table nearest them as they came through the door. The Beast held the chair at the head of the table for Beauty; she settled herself in it reluctantly, and it was not till he had sat down some little distance from her that she realised there was a place setting only for her. "Do you not eat with me?" she said in simple surprise.

He lifted his shoulders and spread his hands—paws. "I am a Beast; I cannot eat like a man. I would not disgust you—in any way I can prevent."

Beauty bowed her head. When she looked up, her plate had been served, though she was quite sure the Beast had not moved. She ate a little, conscious of the Beast's silent presence. (What is he looking at? said the little voice in the back of her mind. Even sitting down, he is—so very large. Look! One of his hands—half curled, there, as it lies—one of his hands is as large as—as large as that bowl of fruit. And see! The nails are as long as your fingers, shining and curved like crescent moons, the tips sharp as poignards. . . .) She finished quickly, saying, "I fear I am not very hungry; it has been a—a long and tiring day. I must ask you to forgive me—again."

The Beast was on his feet at once, his gown eddying round him, briefly blocking the brightness of the gold and silver bowls and dishes on the dark table. "Again I say to you that there is nothing to forgive. If I were to have my will in this, I would ask that there be no talk of 'forgiveness' between us. I have not forgotten—I will not forget—on what terms you are here at all."

Beauty, for all her desire to trust him, to not fear him, to remember her pity for him, could think of no response to this. "I—I will be clearer-headed in the morning," she said faintly. She stood up and turned towards the door.

"Beauty, will you marry me?" said the Beast.

For a moment the panic of the corridor, and of the dream, swelled up in Beauty's mind and heart again, but as she put her hands on her breast, as if to press her heart back into its place, the little wind her hands made blew the smell of roses to her again. She sighed then, and more in sadness than in fear she whispered, meaning the words only for herself, "Oh, what shall I say?"

But the Beast had heard. "Say yes or no without fear," he replied.

She raised her eyes; again he stood in shadow, and she could not see his face. The candlelight made a silhouette of him; she knew he fidgeted with the edge of his robe with one hand because she could see the cloth judder and jerk. She could not see his face. "Oh, no, Beast," she said.

The Beast nodded once and then turned and left her, disappearing into the darkness towards some other way than that by which they had entered, moving perfectly surely into the blackness; her last glimpse was of a shimmer of long hair sliding over one shoulder.

She had no recollection of making her way back to her rooms, undressing, or climbing the little stairs by her bed, but she woke hours later, staring at the canopy, not sure if she was awake or dreaming still, for she had been walking down a dark corridor full of the smell of roses, and she had been hurrying, hurrying, to come to the end of it, to comfort the sadness that hid itself there.

She fell asleep again and dreamt of her sisters.

At first it was a very ordinary sort of dream. She seemed to watch Jeweltongue and their father at Rose Cottage, going about ordinary activities; she was pleased to see that her father seemed fit and well again, although his hair was whiter than it had been, and his face more lined with grief. She thought: Not for me! Oh, Father, not for me! She yearned to be there with them, but she was not; she was an onlooker, and they were unaware of her presence.

But then something changed, and Beauty, dreaming, did not know what it was, only that it made her uneasy. Perhaps it was only that her family looked so—so ordinary without her, and she wished some clear token that they missed her as she missed them—no, that wasn't it, for she could read the careful look on Jeweltongue's face, the look she had always used when she wished to hide something, a look that had often worked on her father and her elder sister, but never on her younger. Beauty knew Jeweltongue was hiding the same grief that lined their father's face, and it struck at her like the blade of a knife. This was not right; she wanted them to *miss* her, to know that she was—not even so very far away—in an enchanted palace, and that she held a small embroidered heart in her hands and loved and missed them. Their apparent grief made her feel more isolated than ever, as if the enchantment were an unbridgeable chasm, as if she would never see them again, never hold them in her arms and be held by theirs. . . . Now Lionheart was with them, whirling round the kitchen, setting dough to rise, rolling out pastry, chopping herbs from Beauty's garden; and Beauty knew too what her blaze of activity meant, just as she could read the look on Jeweltongue's face, and again she felt the blow like the blade of a knife, and her heart shook in her breast.

But the scene changed again, but only a very little, as if a veil had been thrown over it, or a veil taken away; it was almost as if the colour changed or as if the sun went behind a cloud, and Beauty remembered Jeweltongue laying swatches of lace and netting over an underskirt and saying, "This one, do you think? Or this one?"

Jeweltongue's face and manner were now stiff and brittle; Lionheart's gestures seemed informed by an old anger.

"You shouldn't have gone," said Lionheart, and Beauty with a shock seemed to hear her voice as if she were in the room with them.

"I know I shouldn't have gone! But I did go. It's done. I went."

"It was very silly of you. I don't understand how you could have been so silly."

"Don't be so dull! Don't you ever feel . . . lonesome?"

Lionheart set the bowl she was carrying down carefully

and stood still for a moment. Her brows snapped together.
"No," she said forcefully. Her face relaxed again. "But . . .
I'm too busy. I make sure that I am too busy. And there are
always other people around—always—even when none is a
friend."

Jeweltongue nodded, and her voice lost a little of its edge.
"Father is out all day, and Beauty is . . . we don't know
when we'll see Beauty again, and if I am working on something, I may see no one at all but Father in the evenings all
week. Sometimes I go along to market-day just for the company. I have even thought of asking Mrs Bestcloth if she
might let me have the little room over her shop, to work in;
it is only a kind of storeroom, and I don't take up much
space. I'm almost sure she would let me; it is not only that
she knows I am good for business, she has been a friend to
me. But that is why I cannot ask her. We still cannot afford
to pay rent money, even for part use of a room the size of
a small wardrobe.

"I don't miss the city, but I do wish we could live nearer
town. If it weren't for Beauty's garden . . . But I would still
wish to live in town, where you can hear footsteps outside
and voices that aren't always your own, even if you're
working, even if you don't want to talk yourself."

Lionheart shook her head. "No towns for me. But . . . I
don't like wild land, like this. Oh, I know it isn't really
wild—Longchance is too close—but it's wild enough.
Longchance is not a big town, is it? And then there's nothing much till Appleborough, and then there's nothing at all
till Wishington, which is too far away to do anyone in
Longchance any good. Goldfield is the only one who farms
this end of Longchance, you know? There's Goldfield, us,
and . . . more nothing. I want fields, with horses in them, or
growing hay for the horses—like up at the Hall—or wheat
for my bread. If it weren't for Beauty's garden, I wouldn't
want to come back here either." With her most ferocious
scowl: "I keep thinking I see things among the trees."

Jeweltongue tried to laugh. "Maybe they're friendly."

"You see them too, do you? The ones I see are never
friendly."

"Since Beauty . . . I never used to . . . I almost fancy them as a kind of guardian, or I like to think so. . . . Something to do with Beauty, that they watch over her too, or even that the Beast sends them, that Beauty has told him . . . that he isn't . . . that he is . . . I would think I was imagining all of it, except that Lydia sees them too. Silver shadows, among the trees, where the shadows should be lying dark, like shadows do."

Lionheart took a breath to speak, but Jeweltongue cut in quickly: "You're worrying about nothing, you know. His father will prevent anything. Everything. I'm sure poor Miss Trueword has been raked up one side and down the other for inviting me." Jeweltongue was trying to speak lightly and failing. "I only hope my misjudgement doesn't prove disastrous for business."

"But what if the brat does decide to court you? I can tell you the other stable lads think he's smitten. They all want to tell me about it—my friends to warn me, my enemies to gloat about the trouble it will cause."

"The son of the squire court a dressmaker?" Jeweltongue's tone was sharp as needles. " 'But you have such beautiful manners, my dear,' " she said in a cruel imitation of Miss Trueword's fluting voice. "A dressmaker who is so busy saving up to have the thatch replaced on the hut she lives in that she had to keep her hand over the hasty darn on her only half-decent skirt all the evening that the squire's brainless sister had invited her to supper, which she had been brainless enough to accept."

She put her hands up suddenly and covered her face, and her voice through her fingers was muffled. "Oh, Lionheart, what came over me? Miss Trueword is kind and meant to be kind to me, and she genuinely likes my work. I do not believe it is just her vanity; she jokes that she has a figure like a lathe and does not expect me to deck her out in frills like a schoolroom miss. What need has she to be so clever she could cut herself on it? That has always been my great gift. I—I think she just invited me home to meet her family because she likes me, and the young ladies like me, and to the extent that that amiable animated bolster the squire married can stir herself to likes and dislikes, Mrs Trueword likes me, and there is not—there is not much society here, is there? The Oldhouses, and the Cunningmans, and the Tooksomes, and only the Oldhouses are . . . nice to have around. It was not at all a grand supper. . . . Perhaps the darn in my skirt did not matter.

"Lionheart, do you know, it was because I knew I should not be there that I was so bright, so witty, that I talked too much? I wished to draw attention away from the holes in my skirt . . . the holes in my fingers . . . draw attention away from the fact that I am a dressmaker."

There was a little silence as the two sisters looked at each other. "A very fine dressmaker," said Lionheart. "I hated your salons, have I ever told you? Full of people being vicious to each other and using six-syllable words to do it with. Your dresses are beautiful. Jeweltongue, love, it's not that he's the squire's son—which I admit is a little awkward—but you're wrong about old Squire Trueword. The real problem about Master Jack is that he's a coxcomb and a coward. If you want to charm someone, cast your eye over the second son, Aubrey. I grant you he is neither so tall nor so handsome—nor will he have any money—but he is a good man, and kind, and—and—"

Jeweltongue's real laugh rang out, and as Beauty awoke, she just heard her sister say, "What you mean is that you approve of his eye for a horse—"

"It was only a dream," Beauty whispered to herself, "only a dream," she insisted, even as she could not help looking eagerly around her new, strange, overglamorous bedroom for a glimpse of her sisters. Jeweltongue's laugh still sounded in her ears; they must be here, with her, close to her, they must . . . She squeezed the little heart between her palms till her finger joints hurt.

"Oh, I wish I knew what was happening! But I've only been gone a day. It was just a dream."

There was breakfast on a table in front of the balcony as she sat up, shaking herself free of the final shreds of her dream; the smell of food awoke her thoroughly. She had been too distressed yesterday to be hungry; today that dis-

tress on top of two days' unsatisfied hunger made her feel
a little ill. She slid out of bed, forgetting the stairs and land-
ing with a bone-jarring thump on the floor. She put a hand
to the bed-curtains to steady herself. "That is one way of
driving sleep off," she murmured, "but I think I prefer gentler means."

The tea on the breakfast tray was particularly fine; the
third cup was as excellent as the first—enchanted leaves
don't stew. She held up the embroidered heart as she drank
that third cup, turning it so that Lionheart's hair caught the
light, listening to the silence.

She was grateful there was no rose in a silver vase on the
table.

She had been too tired the night before to notice that the
nightgown she put on was not her own. She looked at it
now and admired its fineness, and the roses embroidered
round the bands of the collar and cuffs. It was precisely as
long as and no longer than she could walk in without tread-
ing on the hem. There was a new bodice and skirt hanging
over the back of the chair drawn up near the washstand,
which was once again full of warm water, when she turned
away from the breakfast table. She looked at them thoughtfully while she washed.

"These are a bit too good for the sort of work I have in
mind today," she said to the air, "although I thank you very
much. And I know that you are much too polite and—and
kind to have thrown my shabby old things out, because I
would be so unhappy without them, so I assume I will find
them beautifully pressed and hanging up in the wardrobe—
with all the other things, including my nightgown, that I see
have disappeared, with my knapsack, from under the bed."

She said this in just the tone she would have used in
speaking to a miserable dog, or any of her other rescued
animals, who was refusing to eat. "Now, my sweet, I know
you are a good dog, and good dogs always do what they
are told when it is for their good, and I know the things you
have been told recently have not been for your good, but
you must understand that is all over now. And here is your
supper, and you will of course eat it, you good dog." And

the dog would. Beauty went to the hanging cupboard and opened the doors, and there were all her few clothes, hanging up lugubriously in one corner, as if separated carefully from the other, much grander things in the rest of the wardrobe, and they looked self-conscious, if clothes can look self-conscious, and Beauty laughed.

But when she took down her skirt and shirt, there was a sudden flurry of movement, and a wild wave of butterflies blew out at her, as if from the folds of her dull patched clothing, and she cried out in surprise and pleasure. For a moment the butterflies seemed to fill the room, even that great high ornamented room, with colours and textures all the more glorious for being alive, blues and greens and russets and golds, and then they swirled up like a small whirlwind and rushed out the open doors, over the balcony, and away.

She ran to watch them go and saw them briefly twinkling against the dizzy whiteness of the palace and the dazzle of the glasshouse, and then they disappeared round a corner, and she saw them no more. She dressed slowly; but she was smiling, and when she touched the embroidered heart she wore, she touched it softly, without so piercing a sense of sorrow. And when she stepped into the chamber of the star, she deliberately did not count the number of doors and ignored the glare of the haughty lady in the portrait just beyond the one that opened.

There was a pruning-knife and a small handsaw lying on top of the water-butt inside the door to the glasshouse. She spent most of the morning studying stems and bushes and cut very little. After a while she said, "Gloves. May I please have a good stout pair of gloves?" And turned round and discovered just such a pair of gloves lying at the foot of the water-butt, where she might have overlooked them when she first came in. "Ladder?" she said next, after another little while. "What I would like best is a ladder light enough that I can—that I can handle it on my own," she added, for she was remembering that the last time she had had much to do

with a ladder she had had Lionheart there to help her wrestle
the great awkward object to where they needed it.

There was a ladder behind the door. "Thank you," she
said, "but I don't believe I could have missed that, you
know," she added to the listening silence; but she kept her
eyes on the ladder.

At noon she stopped, and rubbed her forehead, and went
in search of lunch, and there was lunch on the table by her
balcony. She still was not at all certain how she got from
her rooms to the glasshouse or back again; the corridor
never seemed quite the same corridor, and the dislocating
turns seemed to come at different stages of the journey, and
the sun came through windows where the walls should have
been internal, and even at noon there were far too many
shadows everywhere. She was also beginning to feel that
the portrait of the handsome but haughty lady just beyond
the door from the chamber of the star was not just one
haughty lady but several, sisters perhaps, even cousins, in a
family where the likeness is strongly marked; but that did
not seem plausible either, for no such grand family would
allow all its women to be painted wearing nearly identical
dresses, with their arms all bent with no perceptible kindness
round the same sort of browny-fawn lapdog.

The table by the door into the courtyard had reverted to
square, and the slope-shouldered clock now had a shepherd,
more suitably attired for his occupation, keeping company
with the gambolling lambs.

But she did not care, so long as the magic she needed
went on working and allowed her to go where she needed
to go and do what she needed to do. And there were few
shadows in the glasshouse, and the ones there were laid
honestly, by stems and leaves and the house's own glittering
framework—and her ladder.

In the afternoon she took her first experimental cuts, beginning with the climbers, and she was rejoiced to find, as
she cut cautiously back and back, living wood in each. She
nicked dormant buds in gnarled old branches with green
hearts and said, "Grow, you. *Grow.*"

She stopped for tea and a shoulder-easing stretch in the

afternoon, and then she spent the last of the lengthening
spring twilight marking out her seedbed, peeling her rose-
hips, and punching rows of tiny finger-sized holes to bury
the seeds themselves in. ''Grow, you,'' she whispered, and
went indoors.

CHAPTER
7

This evening a sapphire-coloured dress lay across her bed, and a sapphire necklace on the blue towels of the washstand; but though the soap, and the bath oil in the great tin bath (enamelled over with roses) drawn up before the fireplace, again smelt of roses, today it did not make her weep, for she had work to do and felt she knew why she was here.

She did not examine this feeling too closely, for she was too grateful for the possession of it, and even less did she examine the conclusions it might lead her to. But for the moment the roses in the glasshouse demanded her attention and care, and that was enough, for a little while, and she had a little space to nurse a little precarious security in. She lay in the bath while twilight turned to dusk, and she felt the aches slide out of her muscles and dissipate in the warm water, till she found herself falling asleep, and then she flew out and whisked herself dry in such a commotion of haste that she half believed herself assisted with extra towels by invisible hands.

The Beast was waiting for her in the long dim dining-hall, and he bowed to her, and said, "Good evening, Beauty," and she replied, "Good evening, Beast."

The silence and the shadows pressed round them. He

moved to her chair and bowed her into it, poured her two
kinds of wine, and took a chair himself a little distance from
her. She picked up a glass, touched it to her lips, set it down
again untasted, served herself blindly from the nearest plate.
She was hungry—she had worked hard since lunch—but
the silence was heavy, and the Beast, again dressed all in
black, his head bowed so she could not see his eyes, was
almost obscured by the gloom and seemed as ominous as
all the rest of the silence and shadow. She put her fork to
the food on her plate; the click of the tines was too loud in
the stillness; she set it down again. She was hungry, and
could not eat. She sat motionless for a moment, feeling as
if the shadows might seep into her blood, turning her into
a shadow like themselves. . . . Her hand crept to the little
embroidered heart tucked into the front of her bodice.

When the gentle *plonk* came from the darkness at the far
end of the long table, Beauty started in her chair, feeling like
a deer who knows she is tracked by a hunter. There was another *plonk,* and then a *rustle-rustle-rustle,* and Beauty's
heart slowed down to a normal pace, and she began to smile,
because it was a friendly, a silly sort of sound. There was a
third *plonk* and then a quick run of tiny thumps. . . . Whatever
it was, it was coming towards this end of the table.

The Beast stirred. "I believe Fourpaws is coming to introduce herself to her new guest," he said.

She still had to strain to hear his words when he spoke
anything beyond common courtesies such as "good evening"; it was like learning to hear articulate speech in a
rumble of thunder. "Fourpaws?"

But at that moment a small grey and amber cat appeared
from behind one of the wine carafes, tail high, writhing once
round the carafe as if that were her entire purpose at this
end of the table, so supple and sleek in the dimness that it
seemed she would overstep her hind legs and take a second
turn round the narrow vessel. But then with a boneless
flicker like a scarf coming loose from a lady's neck, she
unwound herself again and became a slim short-bodied cat,
with silky fur just enough longer than short to move gently

of its own in response to her motion, and to give her a very wonderful tail.

She stood so that Beauty could admire her for a moment, while she looked off into some chosen distance, and then she turned as if to walk straight past the edge of Beauty's plate. But Beauty was far too charmed by her not to make an effort, and she reached across her plate and offered Fourpaws the tips of her fingers. The fingertips were deemed acceptable, and the base of ears and a small round skull between were presented to be scratched. Beauty scratched. Fourpaws purred. Fourpaws then sat down—at just such a distance that Beauty would be risking the lace on her bodice to the food on her plate if she wished to go on scratching ears, so she stopped.

Fourpaws moved a little towards Beauty and looked at her for the first time, stared at her with vast yellowy-greeny eyes, misleadingly half shut. She curled her tail round her feet—careful not to trail the tip of it in Beauty's plate—and continued to purr. The purr seemed to reflect off the sides of the bowls and dishes and goblets round her. Beauty picked up her knife and fork again and began to eat.

"It is so very quiet here," said Beauty between mouthfuls.

The Beast roused himself. "When I was . . . first here, here as you see it, the silence troubled me very much."

But you are a sorcerer! You cannot have come here against your will—against your will—as I did. . . . Beauty was briefly afraid that she had spoken aloud, so painfully had the words pressed up in her throat; but the shadows were tranquil, and Fourpaws was still purring, and after only the merest pause, the Beast continued: "I had forgotten. It was such a long time ago. I have learnt . . . I have learnt to look at the silence, to listen to the dark. But I was very glad when Fourpaws came. I believe she must be a powerful sorcerer in her own country, which is why I dare not give her any grand name such as she deserves, for fear of disturbing the network of her powers. She comes most evenings and drops a few rolls and bits of cutlery into the darkness, like coins in a wishing well. I am grateful to her."

"As am I," said Beauty fervently, for she was discovering just how hungry she was. She moved a candlestick nearer and peered into various tureens. She recognised little, although everything smelled superb, which was enough recommendation, but when she turned back to her plate, which had been empty but a moment before, it had been served again for her already. "The chef's speciality?" she murmured, thinking of grand dinner parties in the city, but she picked her knife and fork up readily and began.

Fourpaws had moved herself again slightly, so that her bright furry figure slightly overlapped the great shadowy bulk of the Beast from Beauty's point of view. Beauty smiled at her a little wonderingly; Fourpaws' eyes shut almost completely, with only a thin gleam of green left visible, and her purr deepened.

As soon as Beauty laid her knife and fork down for the last time, she felt exhaustion drop over her, shove down her eyelids, force her head forward upon her breast. "I—I am sorry," she said faintly. "I am much more tired, suddenly, than I had any idea . . . If you will excuse me . . ."

The Beast was on his feet again at once, bowing her towards the door. "Beauty, will you marry me?"

Beauty backed two steps away from the table. Her eyes fell upon Fourpaws, who was still sitting where she had been while Beauty ate; but her eyes were now opened wide, her head tipped up, and she was staring at Beauty with an unnervingly steady gaze. "Oh, no, Beast," said Beauty to the cat. Fourpaws leapt off the table and disappeared under it.

"Good night, Beauty," said the Beast very softly.

"Good night, Beast," said Beauty.

She went slowly up to her rooms, the whispering of her skirts the only sound, and stayed awake only long enough to take her elegant dress off carefully, lay the necklace of sapphires back on the washstand, and climb up the stairs to her bed. She almost didn't make it to the top; she woke up to find herself with her head resting on the top stair and pulled herself the rest of the way into bed.

She dreamt again of Rose Cottage.

There was a new rug on the floor by the fireplace at the sitting-room end of the downstairs room, and Tea-cosy, looking unusually well brushed, lay on it in her traditional neat curl. There was a new tablecloth, with a bit of lace at its edge, on the old table—Beauty could still see its splinted feet beneath—and the place settings were as mismatched as ever, although none of the cups or plates was chipped.

The old merchant was talking, and the other two were listening—three, counting Tea-cosy's half-pricked ears—or rather, as Beauty's dream shimmered into being, her father had just stopped talking. Beauty's dream-eyes ranged over the familiar scene and picked out its unfamiliar elements, pausing finally on the person sitting in what had been Beauty's chair. There was a little silence in which Beauty could almost hear the echo of her father's last words—she had a half notion that he had been reciting poetry—but she did not know for sure.

The strange young man spoke first. "That was very moving, sir. Perhaps—perhaps you would come to one of our meetings?"

"Oh, do, Father!" said Jeweltongue. "I had no idea you were—you were—" She stopped, blushed, and laughed.

Her father looked at her, smiling. "You had no idea the old man had any idea of metre and rhyme, you were going to say? I never used to. It seems to have come on me with moving here, to Longchance and Rose Cottage. I would be honoured to come to your meeting, Mr Whitehand, if you think I will not embarrass you."

"Embarrass us! Father! Wait till you hear Mrs Oldhouse, whom we name Mrs Words-Without-End, but we cannot bring ourselves to turn her out, not only because she has the biggest drawing-room and serves the best cakes—"

"Thank you," murmured the young man called Whitehand.

Jeweltongue reached towards him and just touched the back of his hand with the tips of her fingers, but Beauty saw the sweet look that passed between them as Jeweltongue continued. "But she is so genuinely kind, and surprisingly has quite a good ear for other people's work! But we shall

put you at the top of the list for your evening, because if
she reads first, she may frighten you away.''

"Not before I have eaten some of Mr Whitehand's cakes,
at least,'' said her father, and Beauty then remembered
where she had seen Mr Whitehand, for he was the baker in
Longchance. It occurred to her then that for quite some time,
as Jeweltongue divided up the errands when the two of them
went into Longchance together, it was never Beauty who
went to the baker's, though they almost always had lardy-
cake or crumpets for tea on any day Jeweltongue had been
to Longchance. But Beauty had never heard of poetry-
reading evenings.

"To be fair,'' Jeweltongue went on, ''she tells excellent
stories—when she doesn't try to put them into verse first.
She learnt them from her father, who was a scholar, but his
real love was collecting folk-tales. . . .''

Beauty woke to a soft *shush*ing sound. It was a gentle
sound, and her first thought was that there was water running somewhere nearby, and she wondered if she had
missed seeing some fountain, perhaps in the inner courtyard,
perhaps invisible behind the glasshouse. But the rhythm of
the *shush* was wrong for water, she eventually decided, still
half in her dream and wondering about the young man and
the new hearth-rug and wishing to hear her father's poems—
and telling herself it was all only a dream again, just as last
night.

She eventually decided that it could not be water. It
sounded like something flying.

She opened her eyes. After a moment of reorienting herself, she picked out the small shadow hurtling back and forth
across her room which went with the *shush*ing sound. It flew
very near each wall and then wheeled away as if panic-
stricken. It disappeared, while she watched, into the other
rooms through the wide doorless archway, and the *shush*ing
died away; but then it came streaking back into the bedroom, straight towards the clear glass of the closed balcony
doors.

Beauty, still too sleep-dazed to make an attempt at scaring
it onto a safer course, held her breath for the inevitable col-

lision, but it swerved away at the last minute and raced towards her bed. It flew straight under the canopy towards the wall, did another of its last-minute, violent changes of direction before it struck, flew back towards the bed, and collapsed on the counterpane.

When Beauty first saw the small flying figure, she guessed it was a bird, trapped somehow indoors, having fallen down a chimney, or mistakenly crept in through a half-open window. But she had caught a glimpse of furry body and naked wing as it swept just in front of her and was now expecting what she found lying panting in her lap. It was a bat.

Beauty had rescued members of most of the commoner animal species in her life, including a few bats. The last one had been in much worse case than this one, terrified by the housemaid's screaming, beating itself pathetically against a corner of the attic where it had fled. Beauty had trapped it finally by ordering the housemaid to *Go away* and, when it flopped to the floor half stunned, put a wastebasket over it.

After a few days of hanging upside down in Beauty's dressing-room (which she kept locked for the duration, for fear of housemaids, and entering it herself only long enough to change the water in the water-dish and to release the fat house-flies she patiently collected in jars), she ordered the dogcart one evening, drove herself to the outskirts of town, and released it.

She'd heard it whirr just a moment, as it had leapt out of her restraining hands and the scarf she had wrapped it in, and had wanted to believe that the perfectly silent shadow, which had then swept low twice over her head—nowhere near enough to risk any danger of becoming ′ ∧ngled in her hair, because as any sensible person knows, bats only lose their sense of distance and direction under such duress as being screamed at by housemaids—had been it saying thank-you, before it went off to find its friends and family. She hoped it had not, during its convalescence, developed such a taste for house-flies that it would ever risk any more attics.

This one was not quite the length of the palm of her hand. She could feel the quiver of its body through the counterpane as it tried to catch its breath, and could see into its open mouth, the delicate pink tongue, smaller than the first leaf of heartsease to open in spring, and the teeth, finer than embroidery needles. Its dark brown fur looked soft as velvet; its wide pricked ears and half-folded wings were only a shade or two paler than its fur. It stared straight at her with its bright black eyes, and lay in her lap, and panted.

"Well," said Beauty, after a moment. "I have never heard of a tame bat. I suppose you were merely confused, but you are very confused indeed, to be lying in my lap like that and staring at me as if I were a legendary saviour of lost bats whom you have recognised in your extremity. What reputation I had of such is years and miles behind me, little one. The bats at Rose Cottage had—have—the good sense to stay in the garden. . . . Which is to say, I suppose I need something to muffle you with, so you cannot bite me with all those tiny piercing teeth. Not that I would blame you, mind, but I get quite enough of that sort of thing dealing with roses. . . ." She reached slowly behind her, so as not to frighten her visitor further, and began awkwardly to work her top pillow out of its pillow slip.

The bat lay where it had fallen, but it had folded its wings neatly against its body, and closed its mouth, and now looked perfectly content. "If I didn't know that you are supposed to hang upside down—or at least creep into narrow cracks—I would expect you to curl up now, like a very small Tea-cosy, and have a nap. Saints! This is a maddening activity when I cannot see what I am doing!"

But the pillowslip came free at last, and she wrapped it softly round her hands and picked up the bat, keeping its wings closed against its body. It did not even tremble, but it did turn its head a little so it could go on looking at her.

She groped her way out of bed and down the stairs till she stood on the floor, the bat held gently in front of her. "Now, what do I do with you? I cannot lock you in the water-closet, as it is the only one I know where to find in all this mazy hulk of a palace; I would have something to say to the architect about that, if I met him!

"My old dressing-room, where I used to put your sort of

visitor, was quite a narrow closet, with one tiny window
easily blocked off, and I never used it anyway, even bat-
free. But these rooms are full of sunlight, and you know,
none of your brethren that I have met have understood about
keeping the carpets clean, and so I need to, er, leave you
somewhere I can spread something, er, bat-proof beneath
you—''

She thought of the bolt of poachers' jackets material the
sisters had found in the housekeeper's room, and two tears
dropped to the breast of her nightgown; but her voice was
as steady as ever. "What we need, I feel, is—is an empty
wardrobe or even a secret room. I would like that. I would
like a secret room." She spoke half-idly. She had learnt the
use of speaking quietly to all rescued animals; even the wild
ones seemed to find such noises soothing, and she also
wished to fling herself away as quickly as possible from the
sudden memory of her sisters.

She began to walk slowly away from her balcony, and
when she came to the room hung with the tapestries of a
garden in all four seasons, she paused. There came to her
there some strange breath of air, some movement just seen
at the corner of her eye. She turned her head; the edge of
the nearer summer tapestry stirred. She looked down at her
bat; her bat still looked at her and lay calmly in her grasp.
She shifted it, very slowly, in case it should protest after all,
into the crook of one elbow, where it settled, snug and tranquil as a tired kitten. Now she had one hand free and could
lift the edge of the tapestry—and push open the crack of
door revealed there.

There was a good smell in that darkness, of rich earth
and of . . . peace, of the sort of peace she had been used to
find in her garden, and she sighed. "There, little one. This
should do for you—I hope. And I will come and let you
out again just as soon as it is dusk."

She raised the tapestry a little farther, so that she could
duck under it, as she was unwilling to leave any creature
somewhere she had made no attempt to investigate herself
first, and found that she was standing in what appeared to
be an underground chamber.

If she turned to look behind her, she could see the day-light shining across the rosy carpet of her rooms, could see it winking off the corners of furniture and strips of hangings visible to her through the half-open door; but if she turned inwards again, she saw only rough shadows, dimming quickly to blackness, the shapes of earth and stone only varied by what looked very much like the roots of plants.

She raised her hand to feel over her head, having the sense of little trailing things touching her softly, and fearing spiders, as even she was a little hesitant about spiders; and found instead a great net of what felt like tree roots, if she could imagine what tree roots might feel like from under-neath. The trailing things were root hairs. Could anything but root hairs look so like root hairs?

"But we are two storeys above the ground," she said, bewildered, and turned again to look at the sunlight lying on her carpet. She lifted her gaze to the hinges of the door; it seemed to be pegged straight into the rock, and the frame to be made of some impossible mix of stone fragments and woven roots, impossible, but strangely beautiful, as the vein-ing of marble is beautiful.

"Well," she said to the bat, "I guess I do not have to worry about protecting the floor here—wherever here is. And there are lovely, er, tree roots for you to hang from, should you wish to hang, and—and bat droppings are ex-cellent fertilizer. I will need fertilizer for my roses as soon as I finish pruning them. I should wish to find a whole col-ony of you here, I suppose, but—I don't quite think I do. The results might be a bit . . . complex. Good-bye, then, till this evening."

She laid her tiny parcel down in a little hollow in the earth between two roots, loosened the pillow slip so that it could crawl out when it chose, and stepped back, under the summer tapestry, and onto a carpet covered with roses. She closed the door, which from this side was panelled with plain wood, to match the panelling of the wall (plain but for the occasional carving of a rose), and went, very thought-fully, to eat her breakfast.

• • •

She found her gloves with the pruning-knife and the saw
on the water-butt in the glasshouse this morning. "Today
we will be bold," she announced, and she was. She cut and
lopped and hacked and sawed, and then she stopped long
enough to water her cuttings and check her seedbed, and
then her stomach told her it was lunchtime, and she went
back to her bedroom balcony, and lunch was waiting for
her.

When she returned to the glasshouse after lunch, she
looked at the scatter of rubbish she had produced and said,
"I need somewhere to build a bonfire."

She left the glasshouse again and stood in front of its
door, looking down the side of the palace away from her
balcony. The bulk of the glasshouse prevented her from seeing very far, but she knew there was nothing, between the
door to the glasshouse and the door (if it was the same door)
she used to enter the palace and return to her rooms, that
would do for a bonfire.

This area of the inner courtyard was covered with gravel,
gravel just coarse enough not to take footprints, but fine
enough that it was smooth and easy to walk on. It was also
the same eye-confusing glittery grey-white as the palace
and the front drive. Studying it now, Beauty teased herself
with the notion that if she narrowed her eyes to take in none
of the details of where pebbles became walls, she might walk
straight to the end of the courtyard and up the wall without
noticing, like an ant or beetle. . . . She looked up, blinking, at
the bright sky. The scale was about right, she thought. If Rose
Cottage is the right size for human beings, then here I am an
ant or a beetle. A small beetle. Probably an ant. Even if my
feet cannot carry me up walls. How confusing, when one
came to walk on the ceiling, to be abruptly blinded by one's
skirts. . . .

In any event, there was nowhere here to light a bonfire;
it would make a dreadful mess of the whiteness, and even
magical invisible rakers and polishers might resent the effort
to remove the ashes and the heat-sealed stains and the bits

that wouldn't burn no matter how often you poked them back into the hottest heart of the fire. And she didn't want to annoy—any more than she could help—whoever was responsible here . . . the Beast? She was beginning to wonder. She remembered his words last night: *When I was first here . . . I had forgotten . . . I was very glad when Fourpaws came.*

She had never seen any sorcerer who had chosen not to appear human, though she had heard tales of them; her friend the salamander had met one who looked like a centaur. *His familiar pretended to be a lion, and while I knew he was not, still, he kept me busy enough with his great paws and his sense of humour that I could never look long enough at either him or his master to see who—or what— he really was,* the salamander had said, laughing his rustling laugh. *My master was vexed with me, but I told him he should have made me appear to be a panther.*

Beauty thought of the salamander's gift to her—and of her first sight of the Beast. *Can you not bear to look at me?* he had said. Most sorcerers enjoyed making the sort of first impression that would give them the upper hand in any dealings to come; but that first sight had almost . . . and the Beast had taken no advantage as he certainly . . . And then Beauty remembered the story of a sorcerer who looked like the Phoenix, and who had married a human princess because her hair, he said, was the colour of the fire of his birth.

I am no princess, she said to herself.

She turned away from the familiar end of the palace courtyard and began to walk towards the end she could not see. She went on a long way, a very long way, and the way disconcertingly seemed to adjust itself somehow as she walked, like the corridor from the chamber of the star to the door into the courtyard. The sense of mortar and stone fluidly running into and out of each other, like a cat standing up and stretching or curling up into a cat cushion, was much more unsettling out of doors in sunlight.

She glanced to her right; if the palace was adjusting, then so must be her darling glasshouse. She was sure it was not this big from the inside—unless the other end of the palace

was horseshoe-shaped, and she was going clear round it and
would eventually find herself at the opposite corner of the
one square-ended wall that held her balcony. But the glasshouse itself had corners—at least from the inside—and she
had not passed any, and she was not willing to suppose that
her glasshouse was anything other than what she saw—that
it would pretend to be a panther when it was a salamander.

She stopped once and looked up, reassuring herself that
the sky, at least, even here, looked as it had from her garden
at Rose Cottage or from the city. But how was she to know
that? The sky was blue, or it was grey, and it was full of
clouds, or it was not, and the walls of the palace blocked
too much of it. There was no horizon; it was like standing
in the bottom of an immense well. Or of a trap. The sky
was too far away to be of much comfort.

Once she paused because her eye was caught by some
variation in the wall of the palace, a break in the tall ranks
of windows. She peered at the gap, unsure of what she saw
as she would be of shapes found in clouds or fish swimming
in a dappled pond; were they there or not? But she held her
ground and stared and at last could say: Here was an archway, but barred by solid gates, fitting so perfectly into both
the wall itself and the plain formal architecture of the rest
of the facade that they were difficult to see unless searched
for—and she would not have searched had she not wondered (and been grateful for the distraction) at a stretch of
wall that had gone on too long without a window in it.

She stepped up close and laid her hand on the crack between the left-hand door and the wall; closing her eyes, she
could barely find it with her fingertips and could sense no
difference between the texture of the wall and that of the
door. Opening her eyes, she was redazzled by the surface
shimmer and lost both doors entirely; it was not till she
stepped back and looked again that she could pick out the
thin line of the arch, silver as fish scales.

It was all so silent! There was the scuff of her shoes in
the fine gravel, and the occasional whisper of wind, and that
was all. Not even any birds sang. But what was there for
birds here, in this bleak stone wasteland?

She went on; how long she did not know. She began to feel tired and discouraged and, without meaning to, swerved in her course till she could reach out and touch the glass-house. She trailed her fingers idly over the width of one pane, bumped over the tiny ridge of its connecting frame, onto another pane. . . . But then, suddenly, there was a corner of the courtyard after all, and another wall running at right angles to it, and her glasshouse produced a corner of its own to keep parallel pace with it. And very soon after she turned the corner, she found a great dark tunnel running through the palace, like a carriage-way, though she saw nothing to suggest the presence of stables, and the curve of its arch was much the same shape as the nearly invisible doors she had found in the last wall.

She walked through the tunnel, shivering a little, for it was surprisingly cold in its shadow, and the tunnel was surprisingly long. I should stop being surprised by things being very long, she said to herself. When she came out the other side at last, she found herself in a wild wood and halted in astonishment. She took a few cautious steps forward and then whirled to look back through the carriage-way and was reassured by the glint of the glasshouse she could see on the far side.

She remembered her glimpses of something that might have been wild wood at the edges of the formal gardens fronting the palace, but such wilderness still seemed so unlikely a neighbour for a palace. But then, she reminded herself, this was a sorcerer's palace, and sorcerers could surround their palaces with anything they liked. There was a story of one, known to dislike visitors, who had surrounded his with the end of the world. (Whether it was the real end or not was moot; you disappeared into it just the same.)

But the only magic she knew that still connected her to Rose Cottage and her family was on the other side of the dark carriage-way. She did not want to wander into any wild woods and not be able to find her way back.

But here was a splendid site for a bonfire.

The old branches and other bits and pieces had been tidily

swept together and were waiting for her—just inside the
carriage tunnel, just within the edge of its shadow, at the
mouth that led to the wild wood. Beauty shivered again,
thinking that the magic ended there for certain, or that if
this wood was magic too, then it belonged to some other
sorcerer than the one who ruled the Beast's palace. She
would much rather that it was merely a wild wood and not
magic at all, but this was not something she was likely to
learn—at least not until it was too late, when she found
herself dangling from the roc's claws or cornered by the
wild boar, and even then who was to say the wild boar
wasn't a familiar in disguise? Oh dear.

She dragged the branches clear of the tunnel and into the
middle of the ragged little clearing among the trees, and then
she muttered, "Knife, candle, tinder-box, besom," and went
back to an especially deep shadow near the far end of the
tunnel, where she might not have seen them till she was
looking for them. She swept her bonfire into a rough hummock, and while it took a little while for the candle flame
to catch the old leaves and twig shreds she'd made with her
knife, the branches were all dry and brown-hearted and
burned very satisfactorily once they were going.

Beauty stood and watched for a little time, waving away
sparks and wiping smuts out of her eyelashes, turning occasionally to look again at the winking glasshouse, to make
sure it was there, and sweeping the edges towards the centre
of the fire again as it tumbled apart. One did not leave a
bonfire till one was sure of its burning down quietly, even
in a wild wood—perhaps especially in a wild wood.

She went back to the glasshouse, walking near it down
the length of the palace wing, reaching out to touch it occasionally—it was a much shorter journey on the return, she
was sure; she was almost sure—and tidied up, or pretended
to tidy up, since most of it had been done for her already.
"Tomorrow, please, may I have a small rake that I can use
among the rosebushes and a bag or a basket to collect leaves
in? And if you would be kind enough to leave the besom
somewhere I can find it again."

She addressed the water-butt for lack of a better choice

and a dislike for looking up. She tended to feel that magic must *descend,* and she did not want to see it happening. Furthermore, the water-butt was so straightforward a thing to find in a glasshouse. And almost as comforting as a cat in an immense shadowy dining-hall.

By the time she went back to her room, twilight was falling again. There was the tall rose-enamelled bath waiting for her, its water steaming, drawn up by the fireplace. The sapphire towels had been replaced by amethyst ones. She shook them out very carefully so as not to drop the amethyst necklace, ring, and earrings in the bath. She took off her clothes thankfully and stepped into the water; it was per- fumed slightly with roses. But as she sat down, and her arms touched the water, she hissed in sudden pain, for they were covered with thorn scratches. A few thorns had stabbed through her skirt and heavy stockings, and her legs throbbed in short, fiery lines, but the hot water quickly soothed them; her arms were so sore it took her several minutes to slip them under water.

When she stepped out of the bath again, she patted her poor arms very tenderly with the towels and found that the lavender-blue dress laid on the bed for her tonight had slashed sleeves, the material meeting only at the shoulders and wrists and belling out between in a great silken wave. "Thank you," she said aloud. "How glad I am this is not the grand dinner-party this dress is suited to, however; a rose-gardener's battle scars might be embarrassing to ex- plain."

It was nearly full dark now. She had closed the balcony doors while she had her bath; now she opened them again and stood looking out. The headachy glitter of the stone palace and courtyard were quieted by darkness; she sur- prised herself by drawing a deep breath and feeling at peace. One hand crept to the breast of her dress, where the em- broidered heart lay hidden beneath silk and amethysts.

She turned back into her rooms again, leaving the doors wide, and went into the next room, where the four seasons tapestries hung, and lifted a corner of the right-hand summer one and felt for a door frame. She had not wanted to light any candles, and in this inner room there was very little daylight left, merely shadows of varying degrees of blackness. (She had blown out the candles that stood round the bath and the washstand, muttering *Stay,* as one might to a well-meaning but slightly larky dog.) She found the door edge, and ran her hand down till she found a little concavity in the wall, and pressed it, and the lock uttered a muffled *clink,* and the door slid open an inch.

She curled her fingers round it and pulled, calling softly, "Bat! Bat! Are you there? It is nighttime again, and if you fly straight out from my balcony windows, you will soon come to a wild wood which I think should suit you very well."

She heard nothing, but felt a soft puff of air and, between blink and blink, thought she saw a small moving shadow. She turned round to follow it, hoping to see a little dark body fly out the balcony, but saw nothing, and tried not to feel sad. "It was only a little bat, and I meant to set it free," but it did not work; she was sad, and her sense of peace was gone, and she was lonely again.

But then something caught the corner of her eye, out beyond the balcony, some small moving shape darker than the falling night, but it was too quick for her, and by the time she thought she saw it, it had vanished again. But then the flicker of darkness reappeared, curving round the corner of the balcony doors and flying straight at her. She was too astonished to duck, even had she had time to tell her muscles to do so, and the soft puff of air was not air only—she was quite sure—but the tiniest brush of soft fur against her cheek.

The shadow raced back out through the doors but remained near the balcony for a moment, bobbing and zigzagging, as if making sure that her slow, ill-adapted eyes could see it, and then shot away, and she did not see it again. She closed the doors slowly, smiling, and went down to dinner.

CHAPTER
8

She went gaily through the door from her rooms into the chamber of the star, but her eye betrayed her there, rushing into a count round the circumference before she could cancel the impulse. There were twelve doors.

Having counted once, she counted again, and a third time, counterclockwise for a change, beginning each count with the door to her rooms where she still stood, and there were always twelve doors. And, while she did not want to notice, she also noticed that the shape of the star-points themselves had altered, and the colours of the enamelling, and her memory told her, although she tried not to listen, that this was not the first time her eye had marked this inconstancy. A little of her gaiety drained away from her, and she went pensively through the door that opened for her, not quite opposite her rooms' door.

She had not seen the Beast all day. If she was again to dress for dinner, she must be about to see him now. She put out of her mind the dreadful question he had asked her at the end of the last two evenings. She wanted to see him—yes, she positively wanted to see him; she wanted to talk to him. She wanted him to talk to her. Talking to bats and rose-bushes was not the same as talking to someone who could talk back. She wanted someone to speak to her using human words—if not a human voice. She would not think of her sisters; she *would not*. She would think of him; she would think pleasantly of the Beast, of—of her companion, the Beast.

Almost she put out of her mind the size of him, the ease with which he walked through the shadows of his palace, the silence of his footfalls, the terrible irreconcilabilities of his face. She touched the embroidered heart Jeweltongue had given her and, surreptitiously, as if there might be someone watching her, cupped her hands momentarily to feel the salamander's heat. It rolled against her palms, warming her cold fingers. There was nothing to be frightened of. The Beast had given his word, and she believed him. And she was going to make him happy; she was going to bring his rose-bushes to life—and then she could go home. He would release her, as she had released the bat and the butterflies. He would release her to go home again, home to her sisters, her father, home to Rose Cottage, home to her garden.

A thought pulled itself from nowhere in the back of her mind and formed itself into a terrible solidity before she could stop it. She flinched away from it, but it was too late. It was a thought she had often suppressed in the last year and a half, but here, in the Beast's palace, where she was distracted and dismayed by too many things, it had broken free of her prohibition.

What was the curse on three sisters living at Rose Cottage?

She had held to her decision not to ask for more details—nor to make any reference to the little Mrs Greendown had told her of it to her family. Nor had Jeweltongue nor Lionheart ever mentioned any disturbing hint of such a tale to her.

Had Beauty's hopeful guess been correct, that Longchancers, accustomed to their long-standing loss of magic and again disappointed of a greenwitch—and secure in the knowledge of only two sisters living at Rose Cottage—had been content to let the tale lie silent? Could Jeweltongue, who had developed almost as great a gift for gossip as she had for sewing, really never have heard anything of it? Or did she have the same fears of it—and had she made the same decision about it—that Beauty had?

A curse must be a very dreadful thing, but it was unknown, a bogey in the dark, as insubstantial as a bad dream. Her bad dream never had done anything to her, then, had it? It was just a bad dream. But her sisters' happiness was as near to her as her own heart, and as precious. They were happy at Rose Cottage—happy as they had not been when they lived in the city and were great and grand.

It seemed to Beauty that Lionheart's imposture was so fragile and dangerous a thing that even thinking too much about a curse—which might only be a folk-tale—could topple her. And then, if it weren't a folk-tale, destroy them all.

If it weren't a folk-tale, surely it would have caught up with them—or whatever it was that curses did—by now? When they first set foot over the threshold to Rose Cottage, when they first went to Longchance, when they had lived there for a year and a day? And Mrs Greendown had said that the greenwitch had been a good one and that Longchance had been fond of her—the greenwitch who had left Rose Cottage to three sisters.

Well, three sisters did not live at Rose Cottage now.

What had the princess who married the Phoenix felt about her fate?

And using the same force of will that had enabled her to sort through and comprehend her father's papers, when his business failed and his health broke, she thrust all thoughts of the curse away from her again and pretended that her last thoughts had been of bats and butterflies.

The Beast will release me, she repeated to herself. He will release me because . . . because he is a great sorcerer, and I am only a . . . a gardener.

He was waiting for her just inside the doorway of the same hall where she had eaten dinner—and he had not— the two nights previous. For the first time since she had closed her balcony windows and turned away to come to dinner, her heart truly failed her, and an involuntary gesture towards her little embroidered heart did not reassure her.

Her heart had not sunk when she set eyes on the Beast, but when her eyes had moved past him and into that dark hall. She hoped Fourpaws would come again.

She turned back to the Beast and smiled with an effort. "My lor—Beast," she said. My Beast, she thought, and felt a blush rising to her face, but the hall was not well lit enough for him to see. But what did she know of how a Beast's eyes saw? And she remembered, and did not wish to remember, how quickly and surely he had walked into the darkness when he had left her the night before. And the strangeness of him, and of her circumstances, washed over her like a freak wave from a threatening but quiet sea, and she turned away from him and moved towards her seat, grasping at the tall stems of the torchères she passed as if she needed them for balance.

He was at her chair at once, moving it forward as she sat down. She thought of dinner-parties in the city, when some tall black-dressed man would help her with her chair, and of her dislike of making conversation—laboriously with dull, or distressedly with maliciously witty—strangers, and tried to be glad she was here instead. But the effort was only partly successful. The Beast bent to pour her wine, and she wished both to cower away from the looming bulk of him and to reach out and touch him, to know by the contact with solidity and warmth that he was real, even if the knowing would make her fear the greater. She stared at his reaching arm, candlelight winking off the tiny intricacies of black braid, dipping into the miniature pools of shadow in the gathers of his shirt cuff. She folded her hands securely in her lap.

He sat down where he had sat the night before, and the night before that, at some little distance down the table, on her right hand. If she had leant forward and stretched out her arm, she might still have touched his sleeve. She could think of nothing to say after all; distractedly she reached out, took an apple off a silver tray, and began to peel it.

"You have found my poor roses," he said, after a little silence. "That is, you found them on your first evening here and then knew why I did not wish to show them to you. But today—"

"I—oh, I had not thought!" she said, a whole new reading of the day's work she had been so proud of opening before her mind's eye. She dropped her apple and looked up at him, reaching forward after all, and touching his sleeve, but without any awareness that she did so. "I love roses—I wished to do something for you—for them—I did not think—I should have asked—but I cannot bear to have nothing to do. Oh, are you offended? Please forgive—please do not be offended."

"I am not offended," he said, obviously in surprise. "Why would I be offended? I love roses too, and it is one of my greatest sorrows that mine no longer bloom. I honour and thank you for anything you can do for them."

One of my greatest sorrows, she thought, caught away from roses by the phrase. One. What was—were—the others? Why are you here? You would not have killed my father if I had not come. Why did you say you would? "They—they needed tending," she said hesitantly. "Your roses."

"And why have I not done so myself?" He raised his hands again. "I am clumsier than you know. Lifting chairs and pouring decanted wine is the limit of my dexterity. I feared to hurt my darlings worse. . . ." There was another little silence, and then, so low Beauty was not quite sure she heard the words: "And besides, I do not know how."

He paused again, and Beauty thought: Who is it that conjures gloves and ladders out of the air, who is it that hauls my rubbish to the mouth of the carriage-way—the mouth and no farther? When the Beast showed no sign of continuing, Beauty said timidly: "But . . . sir . . . the . . . the Numen of this place is very powerful."

"Yes," said the Beast softly. "It is. But it can touch nothing living."

Silence fell again, but for the first time in this hall, the silence did not oppress her—although she hoped that did not mean Fourpaws would stay away. She thought: I have something to do; I have earned my bread, and I may eat it.

As she was reaching for a platter of hot food, the Beast began: "I thank you again for your . . ." and his hand approached hers as she touched the platter. There was a rack of candles just there, and for a moment their two hands and the platter made a graceful shape, the shadows crisp and elegantly laid out, a bowl of fruit and a decanter adding height and depth. *Still Life, with Candles,* she thought, or perhaps *Portrait of Two Hands.*

"But—" rumbled the Beast, and his face curled terrifyingly into a frown. Beauty snatched her hand back, shrank in her chair. "What?" he said, standing up, making a grab at her hand as she drew back, and then standing still, visibly restraining himself. He sat down again, leant towards her, and held out his hand. Slowly, feeling like a bird fixed by a snake, Beauty extended her own, laid it in his. The palm of his hand was ever so slightly furry, like a warm peach. "You have hurt yourself," he said, in his lowest growl; she felt she heard his words through the soles of her feet rather than in her ears.

"Oh," she said; her arms still stung and throbbed, but she had not thought of them since she counted the doors in the chamber of the star and found twelve. "Oh—it is only thorn scratches." Relief made her voice tremble. "They—they will h-heal."

"You must be more careful," he said.

"Oh—well," she said. "It is very hard not to be scratched, pruning roses."

"You must be more careful," he repeated.

She smiled a little at his earnestness. "Very well. I will be more careful. Perhaps the—the magic that lays out these dresses can come up with a long-sleeved shirt that is thorn-proof but not so stiff and heavy as to prevent me from bending my arms. That will be a very great magic indeed."

The Beast laid her hand on the table again, as gently as he might have set a bubble of blown glass on its pedestal. He turned and walked away so swiftly she thought he must still be angry; she looked down at her arms and touched the scratches with her fingers, wondering on whose behalf he was angry. Hers, his, for his wounded honour as host, by his guest wounding herself on his rose-bushes, for the roses themselves? It was true, her arms did ache, she had been more careless than she should have been, in her eagerness to get on—her eagerness to have something to do that would prevent her from thinking about her family and her own garden, about why she was here. One or two of the deeper cuts were slightly warm to the touch, perhaps turning septic.

She looked up sharply; the Beast had returned, as silently as he always did. In one hand he held a tiny pot, which he set on the table at her elbow, and raised its lid. Because his hands were close under her eyes, she saw for the first time that he was indeed clumsy; she saw the difficulty with which he closed his fingers round the lid of the pot and how the pot nearly slid from his other hand's hold as he pulled the lid off, and she wondered for the first time how much of a Beast he truly was. Perhaps his size and strength were as illusory as his ferocity and cruelty. Then why . . . then what . . . then who . . . ?

The lid popped free, rolled across the table, skittered into the side of a plate, and fell over, thrumming to itself till its motion was exhausted and it lay still. The pungent smell of an herbal salve eddied up and smote her sense of smell, and the Beast's own odour of roses, strong from his nearness, was overwhelmed.

She tried to laugh. "That will cure me, will it?" she said, and looked up at him where he towered over her; he was nothing but a huge black shape against what little light there was. One wing of his robe had fallen on the edge of the table and huddled there like a small creature. As he moved back, and it slid away and disappeared, following his motion, it did not look like the hem of a garment righting itself, but like a small wary lover of darkness regaining sanctuary. He sat down.

"It will. It will cure . . . almost anything."

She looked at him, at his face; she thought she could guess something the ointment could not cure. She touched the cool salve timidly, touched it to the back of one hand, to her wrist, dabbed it on her forearm. The Beast sat in silence, watching her, but she felt his impatience. She stopped and looked at him.

"You are less kind to yourself than you are to my roses," he said. "Like this." Before she had time to think, he had fumbled at the sleeve catch of her nearer wrist, and it fell open, the light material of the sleeve falling away and leaving her arm bare, pale in the candlelight but for the dark lines of blood. He dipped his own fingers in the pot—one at a time, for the pot was small and his fingers were large— put his other hand over the tips of her fingers, and ran the ointment in one long luxurious swathe up her hand to her arm and shoulder and down again. The long dangerous talons did not reach past the deep pads of his fingers; the glittering tips never so much as grazed Beauty's skin. He picked up her hand, turned her arm over, and smoothed more ointment down the tender insides of her wrist and forearm and elbow, to the delicate flesh of her upper arm; then he stroked the arm all over, back and front, again and again, till the ointment disappeared. His fingers and palm felt like suede, and the warmth they left was not wholly that of friction.

"Turn towards me, that I may do the other," he said gruffly. Half in a trance, she turned and held her other arm out towards him, leaving him to unfasten the wrist catch before he drew more ointment deliciously over her skin.

He leant towards her, the shaggy hair of his head falling low over his forehead so that she could no longer see his dark eyes, and pulled her arm gently straight, till he could tuck the hand against his own round shoulder; she felt his warm breath stirring the fine hairs on her forearm; his long mane brushed the back of her hand. How could a Beast smell so sweetly of roses? No, no, it must be the sharp smell of the ointment that was creeping into her eyes, drawing two tears from under the lids to spill down her cheeks.

He saw, and stopped at once, drawing back, holding only her hands in his, holding them against his breast; her knuckles grazed against the embroidery of his waistcoat. "Have I hurt you? The last thing I meant—"

She drew her hands gently out of his, curled them under her chin. "No—no—I do not know what is wrong with me.

I—I think it is only that I am tired." She blinked, looked
at him, smiled a little tremulously; she was shivering, a
deep, deep tremor far inside herself, but she did not wish
him to see, to know or to guess, and she feared what he
might guess. She told herself she did not wish to hurt him
by making him think she was still afraid of him. "It is only
that I am tired. Your ointment is—is wonderfully soothing.
I no longer even feel the scratches."

She turned back to her plate, leaning in her chair as she
had been before the Beast brought the little pot of salve.
The Beast did not return to his customary place, but he had
straightened where he sat. She touched the half-eaten apple.
"I—I think I am not very hungry either," she said, for her
appetite had gone. "I think what I most need is sleep. If
you will excuse me—"

He was on his feet in the instant, drawing back her chair.
She moved away without looking at him, conscious of her
loose sleeves billowing away from her arms, for she had not
refastened the wrist clasps. She had arrived at the doorway
when she heard the Beast's low voice behind her, where he
still stood behind her chair. "Beauty, will you marry me?"

"Oh, no, Beast," she whispered, and fled.

She did not run far. She was as tired as she had told the
Beast she was; she did not know if the corridor had short-
ened itself in sympathy or if she had fallen asleep while she
walked. In her bedroom her dress fell away from her as soon
as she touched the clasps at her shoulders, her fingers as
clumsy as the Beast's. It pooled like water round her feet;
starlight and candlelight made it shimmer, as if it moved to
a secret tide. The little embroidered heart tapped against her
skin in response to her quick breathing. She was again almost too tired to pull her nightgown over her head, and she
crept up the stairs to her bed on all fours.

She dreamt her old dream, but with the change that had
come to it since she had spent her first night in the Beast's
palace; she hurried down a long dim corridor, anxious to
come to its end, for she was needed there. She was wearing
the dress she had worn this evening, and the wrist clasps
had come loose. A small, chilly wind pursued her, snaking

up her open sleeves, making the untended scratches on her legs ache when it crept under her skirts. She must hurry. . . .

She woke weeping. She knew at once it was very late; there was a difference in the stillness even in the Beast's palace that told her the o'clock was inimical to daylight creatures. She remembered nights in the city when they had danced till dawn, both inside and outside lit by lamps that made the dancing floors almost as bright as day. . . . She thought she saw Jeweltongue speaking to a young man with a handsome, intelligent, sulky face, on a tall horse; she thought it was a picture out of her memory till she saw that Jeweltongue was wearing Mandy's old skirt.

There was a small plopping sound from the direction of the bed stairs. She turned her head on the pillow to look and saw a small round mound perched there. "Fourpaws?" she whispered. The mound rose up on four legs and became slender and graceful, and Fourpaws walked delicately onto Beauty's bed, purring in her room-filling way. Beauty fancied she could see streams of purring leaking out through the cracks in the bed-curtains made by the bedposts, pouring out in the wider spaces on either side of her, which she preferred to leave open so she could see out; she thought perhaps it was the strength of the purring that roused the scent from the potpourri in the low dish on top of the japanned cabinet, for as she drifted towards sleep again, slowly stroking Fourpaws' furry side, she could smell roses. Fourpaws' fur was wonderfully sleek and soft, soft as . . . She fell asleep and dreamt she slept on warm fur, and in the dream she slept both deeply and dreamlessly, for she was guarded by a great shaggy shadow that paced back and forth in front of the door of her chamber, and the tiny breeze of his motion brought the smell of roses to her where she lay.

And then the dream changed again, although there was still a cat's fur under her fingers, and she blinked, and there was a black-brindle-and-white cat winding itself round her outstretched hands as she stooped to pet it. There was bright daylight all around them, and she heard the clop of hoofs. "There, Molly has lost her mind at last," said a familiar voice. ''I hope it won't put her off her stroke with the barn mice.''

''She's only enjoying the sunlight,'' said a strange male voice.

''She's not,'' said the familiar voice; ''she's being petted by a ghost. Look at her. She doesn't purr like that for a sunny afternoon.''

The male voice laughed. Beauty thought: I am dreaming. Quite composedly she looked up and saw Lionheart and a young man she did not recognise leading two horses towards a barn a little distance away. The young man was no taller than Lionheart, though he had broad shoulders and big hands and a plain, square, kind face. They paused near Molly, and Beauty looked at their two faces and saw friendship there, the pleasure in each other's company—and something else.

''You are pleased with him, are you not?'' said Lionheart in a suddenly businesslike tone, turning to the horse the young man led. ''I can tell Mr Horsewise you will take him?'' And she held out her hand for the young man's reins.

The young man hesitated, looking at her, and Beauty wondered at the odd way in which Lionheart now avoided meeting his eyes. Her hand, still outstretched, trembled slightly. ''Yes,'' said the young man at last. ''Yes, I do like him, but it was you who saw him, was it not? Mr Horsewise himself said it was you who asked to try him.''

Lionheart dropped her hand and shrugged. ''Yes, I saw him first, but it was only that I was looking in the right direction. Mr Horsewise would have seen him sooner or later.''

''That's not how he tells it. He says he had seen enough horses for the day, and that it was you who insisted on poking round in all the corners where the Gypsies lurk for the unwary, and found Sunbright there, and recognised his worth, and insisted Mr Horsewise come look at him when he sought to put you off. And you—you know me very well. I prefer Sunbright to any of the other horses Mr Horsewise brought back from the fair.''

''Good,'' muttered Lionheart.

"Lionheart, I don't understand you," said the young man, and there was something in his voice other than exasperation, something unhappy, even anguished. "Mr Horsewise thinks the world of you, says he's training you up to be his successor. If you don't want—even if you don't—why won't you at least accept the—the reward you have earned?"

Lionheart smiled a little, but she still would not meet his eyes. "I don't need a reward. My wages are as much as I need. And I love my work here."

"You love it, do you?" said the young man softly.

Lionheart stepped away from him violently; the horse she held threw up its head and sidled away from her. "It's— it's just a manner of speaking!" she said. Clumsily she reached out and tried to snatch Sunbright's reins out of the young man's hands, but the young man was too quick for her and grasped her hand instead.

"Lionheart—"

"Let me go!" said Lionheart. "Please. Just—just let me go."

"You must listen to me," said the young man. "I've known for some time. You know I guessed, don't you? But I've kept your secret. Haven't I? Can't you trust me a little? Because I also know—I—Lionheart—"

But Lionheart had broken free and was running back to the barn, with her puzzled horse trotting obediently behind her.

There was still sunlight in her face, but she was back in her bed in the Beast's palace. She blinked at the canopy for a moment and then turned her head and looked into the room, looked at the queer shape the shadow of the breakfast table threw on the sunlit carpet. The roses there looked so bright and real she wondered if she might be able to pluck them and put them in a vase. "But it can touch nothing living," the Beast said. These roses would be soft and rather furry, like the carpet; touching them would be like stroking a dense-furred cat. But they would have no scent, only a smell of dust and weaving.

She sat up. There were short grey-amber-brown hairs on her pillow. She tried to brush them off, but she found her first attempts only seemed to leave more cat hairs than ever, and some of them now looked black and white. "Nonsense," she said aloud, a little too sharply, and she half flung herself down the bed stairs to the carpeted floor. It was sun-warm on her bare feet, and she felt herself relaxing.

"At least you don't change," she murmured, sitting down where she was, drawing up her knees, and putting her arms round her shins. "I am grateful," she said aloud, "that these rooms—my rooms—don't change. In this palace, where too many things change—where the paintings hanging in the corridors change their faces and their frames, where the candlestands and torchères and sconces are in different places and are higher or lower and have more branches or fewer, and there are different numbers of doors in the chamber of the star, and the enamelwork around the sun window changes colours, and sometimes it's vine leaves and sometimes it's little medallions, and the size of the tiles underfoot is sometimes larger and sometimes smaller, and there are of course different numbers of points on the star because there are different numbers of doors, but that doesn't explain why the points are sometimes straight and sometimes curly—and perhaps it is a different dining-hall every evening too, only it is too dark to see. There is almost nothing here that does not change, except the glasshouse and—and me. And the Beast. And these rooms. The roses on the carpet in the first room are always pale pink cabbages, and the carpet in here is always velvety crimson roses that have opened flat—I suppose the carpet is dyed with a magic dye and will not fade in all this sunlight—and the tall japanned cabinet with the potpourri dish on top is always where I first saw it, and the mountain and the bridge and the trees on its front are always the same picture, and the potpourri bowl is always the same pale green china. And the fire grate always has the same number of bars—eight, I counted—and the bed stairs are the same number of steps, five.

"And the garden tapestries are always there. I particularly love the garden tapestries. I might not realise if some of the other things were changed just a little—things I can't count—but I would see it at once in those tapestries; you, er, you change the tint of one columbine, and I would notice it. I am glad they are all, always there. Even if, er, you have rather odd habits about matching jewelry with bath towels. I am even glad of those gilt console tables, although I think they are hideous, because at least they are always the same hideous."

She was still half asleep as she spoke, her eyes wandering meditatively over what she could see from where she was, and her gaze slowly settled back on the carpet she sat on. Several of the roses really did look surprisingly three-dimensional, although this one close at hand seemed less dark crimson than brown. . . . Her eyes snapped fully open, and she leant towards what was distinctly a small round lump on the carpet. Not Fourpaws, too small. "What . . . you're a hedgehog!"

It stirred at her touch and then curled up tighter. "You're a very small hedgehog. And you shouldn't be wandering round enchanted palaces looking for adventures. How did you get in here? At least bats and butterflies *fly*."

She stood up and began tapping gingerly at other bits of carpet. She found two more hedgehogs. Bemusedly she sat down at her breakfast table and poured herself a cup of tea. "Well. You would be quite useful in the glasshouse if there were any slugs, but at present there's nothing for slugs to eat, so there are no slugs. I daresay by the time there are slugs, you will be full-grown and somewhere else. If I had a compost heap, you could sleep under the compost heap. Oh dear! If only I had something to compost! Grey and white pebbles and stone chips will not do. How am I going to feed my roses?" She put her feet under the table. "Oh!" She raised the edge of the tablecloth to look. Four hedgehogs.

When she came to get dressed, she discovered a canvas tunic with long sleeves folded up on the floor of the wardrobe under her skirt, and behind her skirt on its peg a canvas

overskirt. "Very convenient for the transportation of hedgehogs," she said. There were tough leather boots that laced
to her knees in the way of her searching hand when she
scrabbled under the bed for her shoes. Then she bumped the
curled hedgehogs together with one foot as gently as she
could (even rolled-up hedgehogs do not readily roll) and,
protecting her hands behind her overskirt, bundled them into
her lap. "I hope tomorrow's animal infestation isn't fleas,"
she murmured, and walked towards the chamber of the star,
grateful for the first time for the eerieness of doors that
opened themselves.

The lady, or the lady's cousin, who was usually in the
first painting in the corridor that led to the glasshouse had
changed her hair colour, and her pug dog was now a fan.
She gazed at Beauty with unchanged superciliousness, however. But this morning Beauty, with her arms full of possibly
flea-infested hedgehogs, put her tongue out at her.

She laid her four spiky parcels down at the foot of the
water-butt (having had a brief exciting moment holding her
laden skirt together with one hand and one knee while she
rapidly worked the glasshouse door handle with the other
hand). "These are excellent garments," she said, brushing
her sleeves and her skirt front. "I can even bend my arms.
The shirt reminds me very much of Jeweltongue's first . . .
oh." She squeezed her eyes shut on her tears as one might
hold one's nose against a sneeze; after a little while the
sensation ebbed, and she opened her eyes again and gave
one or two slightly watery sniffs. The hedgehogs had not
moved. "If you stay there a little longer, I will take you to
the wild wood later on. But I have things to do first."

The half-open bud of the red rose was fully open now,
and one of the other two was cracking, and—best of all—
she found a tiny green bump of a new flower-bud peeking
from the joint between another leaf and stem. She took a
deep breath of the open flower's perfume; it was as good as
sleep, or food.

She watered her cuttings. "You are striking, are you
not?" she said to them briskly, like a governess addressing
her students. "You are sending out little white rootlets in

all directions, and soon you will prove it to me by producing your first leaf buds. I want you blooming by the end of this season, do you hear me? You shrubs, at least. You climbers, perhaps I will give you till next year.''

She heard her own voice saying it—by the end of this season, next year—and she stopped where she stood, and the water from the watering-can she carried wavered and stopped too. She looked up towards the cupola several storeys over her head, and her mind went blank, and she felt panic stir in its lair, open its eyes. . . . She opened her mouth and began to sing the first thing that came into her head: ''And from her heart grew a red, red rose, and from his heart a briar. . . .''

She worked all that morning as hard as she had worked the day before. She worked to keep her memories at bay and to keep panic asleep in its den. And as she worked, she sang: ''A knightly dance in the grove they tread, with torches and garlands of roses red.'' She worked until her back and shoulders ached and sweat ran down between her breasts and her shoulder blades, and it was as well for her that she was wearing long canvas sleeves and overskirt, for she would not have noticed if the thorns had cut her, if her pruning-knife or her hand rake had slipped. She worked because there were new memories that troubled her now, not only memories of the sisters and father she missed but memories of kindness and . . . memories of the Beast.

''She had not pulled a rose, a rose, a rose but barely one, when up there starts . . .'' Beauty faltered in her singing, and her stomach took advantage of the break in her concentration and told her loudly that it was lunchtime.

She stopped and looked round almost blankly. The rose beds were now all splendidly tidy. She had pruned away almost as much dead wood as she had the day before; there was tying and staking yet to be done, but the elegant shapes of the bushes themselves were now cleanly revealed. There were rows of little hillocks of leaves down all the paths, and the rather bigger hill she'd automatically collected near the door (though she supposed the magic would once again transport it all for her to the mouth of the carriage tunnel to

her bonfire glen) had four little collapsed-entry leaf-falls on
one side of its circumference. "Oh dear," said Beauty guiltily. "I'd forgotten all about you."

She put her hand on the glasshouse door and thought. She
was a gardener, and she disliked the idea of putting four
perfectly good slug- and insect-eating hedgehogs into a wild
wood—wasting them, to her mind. She went outdoors and
looked up, stretching her back and shoulders as she did so;
the jacket and the overskirt were protecting her skin admi-
rably, but they could do nothing for the ache in her muscles,
or for the weariness of the hand that held the pruning-knife.
It was still early enough in the year that the sun, while
warm, was not yet oppressive. She wondered how hot the
glasshouse became in high summer; was temperature regu-
lation within the magic's purview? Or was the excellent system of vents and of windows that opened and panes that
unlatched, and lacy screens that rolled down, and the han-
dles and levers to work them, invisible till there was need
for it? Maybe it was merely hidden from her dull eyes
amidst all the gorgeous tomfoolery of the glasshouse's design.

She looked up at the weather vane she could barely see
and wondered again what it was; she could just make out a
bulk of shape to one side, a narrower finger of something
on the other.

Just where did the food she ate come from? Conjured out
of the air from dust motes? There were hardly even dust
motes in the Beast's palace; the sunbeam that woke her in
the mornings was washed clean. But even sorcerers had to
negotiate with ordinary merchants for some things; she
knew her father's story about the hydra who answered the
front door. Her friend the salamander preferred real flies to
the magical banquets his master laid out on grand occasions.

Beauty thought of the fourth side of the courtyard she stood
in, which she had not yet explored. There were doors on each
of the other three, even if one only led (at least, led her) to her
rooms, and one was sealed shut. Her curiosity rearoused by
the mysterious weather vane, her conscience pricked by
hedgehogs, and her memory disturbed by dreams, she de-

cided that lunch could wait a few more minutes. She would have a look first at the fourth side of the courtyard.

She walked along the glasshouse wall instead of nearer the palace, half thinking that she should begin looking for vents or vent openings; she was a little worried that just as the glasshouse door opened by putting your hand on the handle and turning it, like all the other doors she had known except the ones in the Beast's palace, and as she had taken on the dying roses as her special care, so perhaps the glasshouse cooling system might be her practical responsibility too.

Perhaps it was studying the shining ridged whorls and scintillant beams and bars—sometimes it was as though they ran up and down for no other reason than to give her pleasure, for she could often make no sense of them architecturally; but she found herself laughing as she looked—that made the time pass so quickly. Almost before she thought of it, she was already rounding the corner of the glasshouse and looking down that fourth side. And there was another open archway, like the one to the wild wood. She went towards it eagerly, teasing herself with ideas of what might lie beyond in the few moments before she could see for herself.

The tunnel felt shorter, perhaps because it was so much brighter. This one did not debouch upon a wild wood; here was an orchard.

It was the wrong time of year for apples and pears—and plums and peaches and apricots—but they were there all the same. She plucked a peach and bit into it, cupping her free hand under her chin for the juice she knew would run down it; when she finished the peach, she lapped the little pool of juice from her palm and then knelt and wiped her hands on the grass and her face on a reasonably clean corner of her skirt. It wasn't lunch, but it would keep her a little longer while she explored.

She didn't see him at first; she saw only another huge old tree at a little distance; his back was to her, and the near black of his hair blended into the unrelieved black of his clothing, and both into their background. Then he turned without seeing her and pulled an apple off the tree he stood next to and ate it, neatly, in two bites, core and all. *I am a Beast; I cannot eat like a man.* She thought of the peach juice running down her chin, but she waited till his hands had dropped to his sides again before she stepped forward.

He saw her but made no move towards her, and so she hesitated, uncertain of her welcome. "It is a lovely day for a picnic," she said, but her voice betrayed her, and *picnic* wavered, ending like a question.

He still said nothing, so she turned to go. "If you are enjoying my orchard, stay," he said.

"I do not wish to disturb you," she said.

He shook his shaggy head. "You do not—" he began, and stopped. "I would be glad of your company," he said.

She came to stand next to him, and then, uncertain again, stepped away, leant against a tree. "You must be very fond of fruit, to have so magnificent an orchard," she said.

He gave a rumble that might have been a laugh. "The magic consents to feed me, to keep me alive," he said.

"Fruit?" she said, astonished. "You—" Her mind flew back over her meals in the Beast's palace. "There is no meat on your table."

The Beast nodded. "I am a Beast, and other beasts fear me. They cannot live here in peace because of my presence, and I cannot give them a merciful death. I sent them away, long ago. No beast—no other beast—comes here now but Fourpaws."

And a few hundred butterflies, a bat, and four hedgehogs, thought Beauty, and ask me again tomorrow morning. But she did not interrupt.

"Fruit sustains me," continued the Beast. "When I was first here, the orchard fruited in the autumn, as orchards do; and sometimes in early summer, no matter how careful I had been about storing my previous year's crop, before the next harvest, I grew very hungry. I ate grass, but it did not agree with me. Over the years the trees have carried their fruit earlier and earlier—and longer and longer.

"I told you last night that the magic here can touch nothing living. Within the walls of the courtyard, it is master; outside those walls it . . . may ask. The front garden answered and obeyed. But here, in this orchard . . . It is the trees who have chosen to carry their fruit early and late; it is not magic that compels them.''

Beauty knew what he was about to say before he said it, and she had her mouth open to protest almost before he spoke: ''But my poor roses—''

''The glasshouse is different,'' said Beauty almost angrily. ''The glasshouse is not like the rest of the palace. It doesn't change. It isn't one thing one minute and something else the next. It is itself.''

''It is the heart of this place,'' said the Beast, ''and it is dying.''

Beauty put her hands over her ears, as if she would not hear him. ''No. *No.* There is something wrong there, but we are putting it right, the roses and I. I do not know what it is that has gone wrong. I think it is only that it has been neglected for too long. Neither you nor the magic can tend it, but I can. It will not die. It *will not.* I will not let it.'' She took her hands away from her ears and took a deep breath. A little breeze curled round her warm face and patted her cheeks, bringing with it a whiff of a deep-scented rose. Her hands were shaking. ''There is cheese on your table— and butter,'' she said abruptly, remembering.

''Yes,'' said the Beast. ''There is cheese and butter.''

''But—'' She looked at him, and he looked at her; but it came to her that she was learning to read his face, and she knew he would answer no questions about the cheese and the butter. But even after she realised this, she went on looking at him, and he at her. The little breeze swerved round her and blew the heavy mane off the Beast's forehead. It was only the strangeness of what he is, she thought. It is as if you looked at a—a hedgehog and expected it to be a rabbit, or looked at a cat while anticipating a phoenix. I wonder what the hydra thought of the first human being it ever saw, and whether it liked answering a front door that always opened on creatures with only one head.

She looked away. "And bread." She thought of Lionheart and added hastily, "And vegetables."

"Vegetables," agreed the Beast, without enthusiasm. "They are all grass, as far as I am concerned, but the vegetable garden is that way, if you are interested."

She laughed at him then, because he sounded like a small boy, not like a very large grown-up Beast with a voice so deep it made the hair on the back of your neck stir when you heard it. "But vegetables are good for you," she said, and added caressingly, "They make you grow up big and strong."

He smiled, showing a great many teeth. "You see why I wish to eat no more vegetables. But I am sure the magic is glad of someone to cook and bake for more capable of being pleased than I."

Beauty thought of the five slices of toast she had eaten that morning, and the half pot of marmalade. She had been very hungry, after no supper the night before. "You speak of—of it—as if it were a person."

"I think of it as such. Or"—he hesitated—"as much of a person as I am. I think—I sometimes think—we are both a bit bewildered by our circumstances. But as with this orchard, we have grown into each other's ways, over the years."

You speak and you move, and the echo in your voice says that you know yourself to be trapped here. As if you and—and the magic are both trapped. But the trees carry their fruit for you, and you sent the other beasts away, that they might not be unhappy. "You have been here a very long time," she said tentatively.

"Yes. I have been here a very long time. And you have been standing talking to me a very long time. Go eat your lunch. Even magic can't keep it hot forever."

Dismissed, she ran off, wishing she dared invite him to accompany her, aware of his gaze on her back, watching her go, wondering if he would still be there by the time she returned after lunch, to smuggle a few hedgehogs into the vegetable garden. He had sent all the other beasts away, long

ago. But the trees had learnt to listen to him, and now the
beasts were returning.

She was both disappointed and relieved that she did not
see the Beast later, with her skirt full of hedgehogs. She
made her way as swiftly as she could through the long path-
less grass in the orchard, keeping the courtyard archway
behind her; her burden made her a little slow and cautious,
both for her sake and for her passengers', and a little
clumsy; nor could she entirely resist the temptation to look
round her, even at the risk of losing her footing or straying
from the shortest route. The grass was spangled with wild-
flowers, and she saw tall bulrushes a little way off, at the
bottom of a gradual slope, suggesting water, but it was too
far away for a diversion.

It was not too long before there rose up before her another
sort of wall, an old brick wall, such as might contain an old
garden. There was a wrought-iron gate in the wall, and the
glimpse she had through it gave her a little warning, but still
the garden was a surprise. "Oh! This is how the glasshouse
should look!" The words burst out of her. She knelt, to let
the hedgehogs roll off her lap, but she was looking round
her all the time.

The paths that ran away from her in three directions were
wide enough to walk along—and to let sunlight in—but no
wider, and in some places the great vegetable forest leant
over them, and in other places it sprawled across plots the
size of banqueting halls. The rhubarb were tall as trees, the
runner bean vines taller than giants; the red-stemmed chard,
brilliant as rubies in the afternoon sun, grew as high as her
waist, though the leaves were still a fresh young green; and
the cabbages, some of them so big around she could not
have circled them with her arms, bore extravagant frills as
elaborate as ball gowns and as exquisitely coloured; and
there were melons nearly the size of Rose Cottage. Did the
Beast eat melons? she thought. I must ask. And figs—for
there were fig trees espaliered against the walls, looking as
if they needed the support of the wires to hold up their
splendid weight of fruit.

She looked down, so as not to step on any hedgehogs,

and saw that they had all uncurled, and were standing up on their legs, and sniffing the air in an interested manner. She thought one of them looked up at her and deliberately met her eyes, as if to say, "Thank you."

"Well," she said, "thank you too. I hope you'll stay here, and eat lots of slugs and things, and be happy. Be happy too, please. You won't be very small hedgehogs here for long, will you? Although I can't say this place looks as if it has ever seen a slug in its life—I guess if there are hedgehogs, there will be slugs too. Oh—and to think I told the bat to fly to the wild wood. Perhaps it already knew better. Perhaps that's why it came, and it only got a little lost and flew through my balcony instead."

She wandered down the paths for a little while, thinking about a rose jungle like this vegetable jungle. All her bushes would be at least as tall as she was, and the climbers would climb right up into the cupola, and there would be so many leaves and flowers everywhere that the overeager gardener wouldn't know where the thorns were lying in wait until it was too late.... She laughed. As she walked, she picked a handful of pods, and shelled them, and ate the peas raw, and they melted on her tongue; and she pulled off handfuls of different lettuces, and every leaf was as sweet and tender as the peas, and she was sorry for the lunch she had had, that she could not eat more.

In her wanderings she came to another wrought-iron gate, and she opened it and went through it, and here were great fields of sweet-corn, with fat green ears trailing golden tassels as long as her arm, and of wheat, and the longer-haired barley. She walked just a little way along the barley, to run her hands through the feathery awns, softer than any birds' down, softer than Fourpaws' flank. "But I must go back," she said, "for I have work to do."

Inside the walled garden again she put her hand out, for one last mouthful of peas, for a fig to eat on her road; but her hand paused in the reaching, and even though the sunlight still shone on her warm and bright, she shivered. The taste of the peas and the lettuce in her mouth was not as sweet as it had been, for it seemed to her suddenly somehow soulless—as if while her tongue could be fooled, her body knew this food would not nourish her. And she thought again of the meals in the Beast's palace—and wondered again about the cheese and the butter.

It was not until that moment that she noticed the silence. She was growing accustomed to silence, to the nearly un-broken silence of the palace and its grounds, the silence that made her talk aloud to herself in a way that would never have occurred to her when she still lived with two sisters and a father (and a dog, a goat, and chickens), and a little town not far away. But she now realised that there had been an uneasiness shadowing her from the moment she had stepped through the first gate, struggling with her hedgehog-filled overskirt. And the uneasiness was that she neither saw nor heard any birds.

In the palace there was some excuse for soundlessness; in the courtyard, perhaps, as well, but in a garden, in any garden, let alone one so magnificent as this one . . . There must be birds in a garden, just as there must be midges and flies and aphids, and slugs and beetles and borers, and spiders and hedgehogs and butterflies. But there were none here, neither flying overhead, nor calling from the branches, nor hopping through the leaves at ground level.

As she went back towards the gate into the orchard, she found herself brushing against the plants for the soughs and swishes and rustles, just as she had brushed her hand against curtains and sconce pendants when she had followed the Beast into the palace for the first time. Before she let herself through the second gate, she looked round for the hedge-hogs, but they had all disappeared.

It was later than she realised; the light was already length-ening towards evening. The long grass in the orchard seemed to drag at her, and by the time she came to the tunnel into the courtyard, she was conscious of how tired she was. She stood for a minute at the edge of the orchard, listening to the wind moving among the grass blades and the trees; it was a comforting sound, but not so comforting as the chirp of a single sparrow would have been. She was thinking about nothing in particular—about the end of day,

about weariness, about the likelihood of a hot bath waiting
for her. But there was a little, itchy, tickling sense of some
thought trying to catch her attention, something about . . .
about strength, about sorrow, about joy; about the joy
of . . . of . . . As soon as she was aware even of so much, it
was gone.

CHAPTER

9

Her dress that evening was dark green, with long close-fitting sleeves buttoned with many tiny buttons, and a high neck, and round it went a wide necklet of great square emeralds, each as large as the palm of a child's hand. There were emerald drops for her ears that were so heavy she was not sure she could wear them all evening; when she had put them on and turned her head, the tiny spray of opals and peridots that hung below the emeralds brushed her shoulders. There were two heavy emerald wristlets whose clasps closed with small substantial snicks like the locks of treasure vaults; her shoes were so stiff with the gems sewn closely all over them she could barely bend her feet. When she leant down to pick up a dark green bath towel and hang it over the back of a chair, she creaked. "All I need is—let's see— a tiara, and perhaps a cape, sewn all over to match the shoes, and I will be too ponderous to move," she said, "and you will have to send a coach and four to transport me to the dining-hall."

There was a sudden wild sibilance from inside the wardrobe, and she started. "That was a joke!" she said hastily; her voice had gone all high and thin. She turned and half ran—tittupping in her unyielding shoes—through her rooms to the chamber of the star; there her shoes made a dramatic, resonant clatter, as if the coach and four were there, waiting for her, invisible but not inaudible.

"Oh dear!" she said. "No more jokes!" She ran across the star and through the door that opened for her, and at once her shoes were muffled by carpeting. "Maybe that is the trouble with this place," she said. "No sense of humour." But her words were muffled even as her shoes were, and she began to feel her spirits muffled too; and she went on silently to the dining-hall, where the Beast silently waited.

She sat down, tasted the wine the Beast had poured for her, and resolutely began to eat. She was not going to miss any more dinners. The shadows that were the Beast caught at the corner of her vision. She only knew he was there because she had seen him sit down; he sat as still as some great predator waiting for his prey. The tinkle of her cutlery hid the sound of his breathing, as the mutter of dry leaves underfoot might hide the hunter's. She tried to recall the mood of the morning. "Do you go every day to the orchard?" she said.

"Yes. I spend much of each day there. Nights I spend on the roof."

Beauty said, astonished, "But when do you sleep? And does not the weather trouble you?"

"I do not sleep much. And the weather troubles me little . . . in this shape. It is harder on my suits of clothing. The magic can turn the weather too, when it chooses. I prefer it to come as it will; mostly I have my way in this." The Beast looked at her. "In the winter, occasionally, sanctuary is provided to some traveller."

Beauty shivered and, because she could not help herself, said, "It has happened more than once then."

"Yes . . . more than once. They run away, of course, when they see me. If they do not see me, they leave for loneliness—or fear of shadows."

Very low, Beauty said: "But none has ever stolen from you before."

The Beast said, "Your father is not a thief. It was my

heart he took, and he could not have known that. Others have stolen." The Beast's voice became indifferent. "They had no joy of what they took, and no one has ever found this place twice."

The silence was all round her again, pressing through even the Beast's words while he was still speaking; with a tiny gasp Beauty made a sudden gesture and knocked the butt of her knife against a copper bowl, which rang like a gong. "Oh! I'm sorry!" she said, but as the echoes died away, there was Fourpaws, winding round the table leg nearest Beauty's chair, twisting the long tail of the heavy dark table runner till the goblet and small saucer near the corner danced in their places. Beauty reached out to steady the goblet just as Fourpaws stopped and looked at her reproachfully.

"Pardon me," said Beauty. "I should have known you never knock anything over unless you mean to do it."

Fourpaws forgave her, and purred, and jumped into her lap, and Beauty began to eat again, but only with one hand, since the other was necessarily occupied with stroking Fourpaws. It is rather awkward, eating with one hand. The Beast had not moved, but he was smiling.

"Not all other beasts fear you," said Beauty, stroking and stroking as Fourpaws purred, and lashed her tail, and purred.

"A cat is a law unto itself," said the Beast gravely, "even one cat from another cat. And Fourpaws, like any cat, is herself. That is the only explanation I have; and while she stays here, as she does, it is enough."

"It is enough," agreed Beauty, and asked another question, as she might ask a friend: "What do you do on the roof at night?"

"Look at the stars, when it is clear enough. I told you that this place and I have grown to each other's shape over the years. I will send no weather away if I know it is coming, but it is often clear at night here."

Beauty thought of the bit of sky she could see from her balcony, and how blocked it was by the hugeness of the palace and even the peak of her beloved glasshouse; and she remembered the trees around Rose Cottage and the great bowl of sky she could see from there; and she thought of what the view must be from the roof of the palace, with no trees, no houses, no city lights. . . . "Oh, might I ever come up? Is there some bit of roof where I would not be disturbing you?"

"I answered a question much like that in the orchard earlier today. I would be glad of your company."

"How shall I know where to find you?"

"Any late night that you wake, look out of your window, and if the sky is clear, come and find me. Any stair up will take you eventually onto the roof." He paused and looked troubled. "You—you will not be frightened? I know you do not like the dark."

Beauty looked at him in surprise, but she realised at once that the surprise must be directed at herself, for while she had loved the soft darkness in the garden at Rose Cottage, she did not like the dark in the Beast's palace, which was silent but not quiet, did not like the shadows thrown by things which changed into other things when she was not looking at them, did not like the shadows containing other things she could not see. . . . "Perhaps I shall be frightened," she said slowly, "but I shall still come and look for you."

"Will you marry me?" said the Beast.

"No, Beast," said Beauty, and the hand stroking Fourpaws stopped and curled its fingers, and Fourpaws leapt from her lap and disappeared into the darkness.

She slept too deeply that night for wakening. She saw her sisters moving round the ground floor of Rose Cottage. Their father was again frowning over bits of paper by the hearth, but his scowl was that of firm concentration, and he bit the end of his pen briskly. She looked into his well-loved face and saw a clarity and serenity there that had never been there before. Even her earliest memories of him, when her mother was still alive, made him out to have been . . . not merely preoccupied with business or by his adoration of his wife, but somehow a little haggard, a little overstretched by life or work, by responsibility or longing. Beauty smiled in her sleep to see him now, even as she wished to put out her hand and smooth the lines from his face and the sorrow from his eyes that had been there only since she had come to the Beast's palace, only since she had begun having these dreams about the home she had left. If this is only a dream—she thought, dreaming—why can I not do this? Why can I not tell my dream-father and my dream-sisters that I am well and whole? Just as I used to touch the wall-paper of that long windowless corridor and feel the rough-ness of the paper and the slickness of the paint and the edges where the lengths joined.

Just as I petted a cat called Molly while Lionheart and her young man looked on.

But she could not.

Jeweltongue was humming to herself as she settled down across from her father and picked up a froth of pink ribbons and net. "I will be glad when Dora outgrows the frou-frou stage. Mrs Trueword never grudges paying my labour, but all this nonsense is simply boring."

Lionheart, at the kitchen table, beating something in a bowl, said, "She may not outgrow it, you know. She may decide she is expressing a unique and exquisite taste. Try considering yourself lucky. Out of six women in one family to sew for, you have only one addicted to frills."

"Hmm," said Jeweltongue, biting off thread and watch-ing her sister through her eyelashes.

Lionheart lost her grip on her bowl with the violence of her mixing, hit herself in the stomach with her spoon gone out of control, and grunted, *"Rats'-nests!"* as batter flew across the room.

"You've been out of sorts for weeks now," said Jewel-tongue. "You come home every seventh day and bang round the house like a djinn in a bottle, and go off again next morning looking like the herald of the end of the world. I say this with the understanding that you may now upend the remains of your bowl over my head."

Lionheart's face relaxed, and she gave a faint and reluc-tant laugh. "I'm sorry. I know I am—I am not at my best,

which is to say that I know you must know that I am not
at my best, and I—I—oh, I can't help it! It's just the way
it is. It won't go on forever. I can't . . .'' But whatever else
she thought of saying remained unsaid.

Jeweltongue laid the net and the ribbons down and came
over to help Lionheart mop up. ''What's wrong, dearest?
Surely it would be a little easier for you if you told us.''

Lionheart, on her knees, leant her forehead against the
edge of the table and closed her eyes. ''No.''

''Well, will you tell me anyway if I ask you?''

Lionheart opened her eyes and began to smile. ''You are
giving me warning you are about to begin plaguing me to
death about it, are you?''

''Yes,'' said Jeweltongue at once. ''I was willing to let
it alone, you know, and wait for you to solve it yourself,
but it's been weeks. It's been—it's been since the week after
you went to the horse fair with Mr Horsewise. Your great
triumph, I thought. Has Mr Horsewise decided his protégé
is just a little too young to be so clever?''

''Your estimation of my abilities is touching but mis-
placed,'' said Lionheart. ''Mr Horsewise knows more than
I'll ever learn. It isn't Mr Horsewise.''

''Then you had better straighten out whatever it is, or it
will be Mr Horsewise,'' said Jeweltongue, ''because I can't
believe you aren't behaving like this at work too. I know
you too well.''

Lionheart rocked back on her heels and stared wide-eyed
at Jeweltongue, and then her face began to twist and crum-
ple, and, savagely as she bit her lips, the tears would come.
Jeweltongue put her arms round her, and Lionheart pressed
her face into her sister's breast and roared, for Lionheart
could never weep quietly.

Their father rose from his place by the sitting-room
hearth, and came to the sink, and began to pump water for
the teakettle, stooping to pat Lionheart's back as he passed
her. He filled a bowl and left it on the table near Jeweltongue, with a towel, and when Lionheart had subsided to
a snuffle, Jeweltongue tenderly wiped her sister's face till
Lionheart snatched the towel away from her with a return

of her usual spirit and muttered, "I'm not a baby, even if I'm behaving like one," and scrubbed at her face till the skin turned a bright blotchy red. "Matches your eyes nicely, dear," said Jeweltongue.

Tea-cosy, judging that emotions were cooling to a safe level, came out from behind the old merchant's armchair, to which haven she had withdrawn after being hit in the eye with some flying batter. She sidled up to Lionheart, put her nose in Lionheart's lap, and when she was not rebuffed, the rest of her followed.

The old merchant made tea and passed cups down to the two sisters still sitting on the floor, murmuring, "Old bones, you must forgive me," and drew up a chair for himself. When he sat down, Lionheart leant back against his legs and sighed, and he stroked the damp hair away from her forehead.

"It's—it's Aubrey," Lionheart said at last. "He's—he's guessed."

"He won't have you turned away!" said Jeweltongue, shocked. "I would not have thought him susceptible to doltish views of propriety. And he has been a good friend to you, has he not?"

"It's worse than that," said Lionheart. "I—I'm in love with him. And I think—I'm pretty sure—he's in love with me."

"But that's not—"

"Isn't it?" said Lionheart swiftly. "Has Master Jack forgiven you for preferring a short, stoop-shouldered flour-monger with hands like boiled puddings to his tall, elegant, noble self, whose white hands have never seen a day's work? D'you want to think about what happens next? This is going to be one too many for Master Jack's vanity, from the occupants of that tatty little witch's cottage beyond the trees at the edge of Farmer Goldfield's lands, where no respectable sort of folk ought to be willing to live in the first place. You must have heard some of the stories that are being told about why Beauty . . . where Beauty . . . why she isn't here just now. Stories with magic in them, here in Longchance, where everyone knows magic never comes."

Her voice faltered, and then she went on. "And surely you've heard that there's a curse on this place if three sisters live in it? The lads like to tease me about it, say I'm pretty enough to be a girl if I wore a dress and learnt to walk right, but they've never told me what exactly the curse is, and I don't like to ask outright, do I?

"Our friends love us, so at present the stories are only stories, even the curse—whatever it is. But . . . the True-words do what their eldest son tells them to, you know; they think he's wonderful; they think he's just too clever and wise and good to bother himself with *doing* anything. And Longchance does what the Truewords tell them."

Beauty felt herself driven out of her own dream, pushed away, as if by a storm wind, and battered and beaten by some force she could not resist—but the sensation was much more sluggish than that. She felt weighed down, dragged, muffled and mauled. She no longer dreamt, but she could not wake, and she tossed in her bed as if her bed-clothes imprisoned her.

Finally she threw herself successfully into wakefulness, and there was sunlight on the carpet, and the teapot steaming through the spout slit in the tea-cosy. All her pillows had fallen to the floor, and the bedclothes, and her own hair, were wound in a great snarl round her. It took her a minute or two to creep free, for she moved languidly, and she had trouble understanding what she was looking at and which way to pull to loosen the snare. She had to think about it to so much as brush her hair out of her mouth in the right direction. Even awake as she was now it was difficult not to feel trapped and to struggle blindly.

She felt her way down the bed stairs and poured herself a cup of tea with an unsteady hand and then sat, staring at the cup while the tea grew cold, holding the embroidered heart in both her hands, and saying to herself, It was only a dream. It was only a dream. Please. It was only a dream.

Finally she drank the cold tea, and poured herself another cup, and drank it hot, and the clouds in her mind and heart began to thin and shred and then to blow away. "I must—I must return soon," she muttered. "I must know what is happening. And—if anything is happening, I must be there to share it with them.'' She kept remembering Lionheart saying, *The stories that are being told about why Beauty isn't here.*

And the curse. *Surely you've heard that there's a curse on this place if three sisters live in it?* The curse was catching up with them at last. *They've never told me what exactly the curse is. . . .*

She knew little of the Longchance baker and less of either of Squire Trueword's sons, but she knew about gossip, about how people talk and how stories grow. She remembered Mrs Greendown saying, *I like to talk.* And she remembered Mrs Greendown telling her about the country greenwitch to whom it mattered so much that Rose Cottage go to a particular family, who lived many miles away in a city that perhaps no one living in Longchance had ever seen, that she went to a lawyer and had papers drawn up to do it. Papers drawn up that left it specifically to the three sisters of that family. And she remembered Mrs Greendown saying, *I ain't prying . . . much; but it's . . . interestin', isn't it? Like you said to begin, you can't help being interested.*

And she remembered saying to Mrs Greendown, *I'd much rather know,* and Mrs Greendown replying, *You may not, dear, but I'm thinking maybe you'd better. . . .*

"I must go home," she said. "The roses must bloom soon, for I must go home." She stood up from the breakfast table and walked out to the balcony, nursing her teacup in one hand and the embroidered heart in the other, and stood staring at the glasshouse, effervescing in the light of the early sun; slowly her face eased into a small smile. "Well," she said in her ordinary voice, "what is it to be today then? Nothing too—too demanding. I'm probably about in a mood for spiders."

As she said *spiders,* there was a twinkle in the corner of her eye, as if the glasshouse had found a mirror to repeat itself in, and she turned to look. The spiderweb hung the entire length of the balcony door frame, and it caught the sunlight just as the glasshouse did, and lit up in tiny fierce lines of fire and crystal.

"Oh," said Beauty, letting out a long breath. "Oh." It was so beautiful she almost touched it, remembering just in time; but even the tiny air current stirred by her fingers made the nearest gossamer thread quiver and wink, and she saw the spider come out of its corner of the door frame and pluck a connecting thread to see if there was anything worth investigating.

"Well, you are a handsome spider," said Beauty bravely, "as spiders go, and I salute you for a most radiant and well-composed web, and I daresay I can bear you as a room-mate—so long as you stay out here. I do not want any of your daughters spinning their homes in my bed-curtains, I hope you understand."

The spider dropped the thread and retreated. A narrow gleam of sunlight, barely thicker than gossamer itself, found an unexpected entry into the spider's corner and touched its back. The spider had curled itself into a little round blob with no legs showing (it immediately became smaller when, with its legs tucked up, it was no longer so mercilessly identifiable as a spider), and under the sunlight's caress it glittered bright as polished jet, and there was some faint gold and russet pattern upon it, which would not have disgraced the bodice of a lady or the shield of a knight.

Beauty had leant closer to look and gave a kind of hiccup, which should have been a laugh, except that she did not want to disturb the spider again with her breath. "I draw the line at discovering spiders to be beautiful too," she said, "but I, er, take your point."

It was not until then that she remembered she had wanted to wake during the night and go onto the roof, and her life in the Beast's palace crept back to her and wrapped itself round her, and she did not notice it or how comfortably it fitted her.

On this, her fourth day, she found the first leafbuds on her cuttings and the first green tips aboveground in her seedbed.

She had a last load of clippings and rubbish to haul to the bonfire glen; she raked and swept till the ground between the bushes was satisfyingly brown and bare, and she went round a last time, looking at everything with her pruning-knife in her hand, and mostly felt her decisions had been good ones. She had found green wood in nearly all her new roses (to herself she called them her roses, as if they were merely an extension of those at Rose Cottage, though she knew she was only rescuing them for the Beast), and even those she had had no success with she was not yet ready to dig up and dispose of; arguing to herself that they might yet shoot from the base if she gave them a little more time.

There was perhaps more tying up she could do, more propping and spreading out—the stakes and string had of course appeared for the purpose, under and around the water-butt—but the glasshouse was nearly as tidy as she could make it. "Barring an infinity of buckets of hot soapy water and a rag on a very long stick," she said, looking up at the thousands and thousands of bright panes round her; "but I'm very—*very*—glad to say you don't look as if you need it."

She leant her tools by the water-butt and bundled up a few handfuls of leaves and twigs in her overskirt with her tinderbox in her pocket, so that she could begin the fire, while she didn't examine too closely her expectation that the magic would bring the rest of the debris. And she might keep her back to the carriage-way, so she need not see it arrive either. Would leaves and twigs tumble suddenly out of nothing? Might she see—*something*—carrying a great bundle of rubbish? No, she would definitely keep her back to the carriage-way.

She put a trowel in another pocket as well. "I might have a look round for heartsease at the edge of the wood," she murmured, "just to have something flowering to frame the paths. But once you're all growing, and I see what shapes you come to, I can plant up the empty spots with pansies." But this time she did not react to the implications of her words, and though she hummed and sometimes sang to herself as she worked, she did not do so to drive fear away from her.

She returned from the bonfire glade with her overskirt

heavy with carefully uprooted heartsease, and spent a little time kneeling by the crosspath at the centre of the glass-house, planting tiny purple faces in small clusters among her cuttings at the four corners.

It was near lunchtime, but for the first time she was not hungry for it. She stood restlessly in the centre of her glass-house, with the transplanted heartsease gleaming velvety and merry in the sunlight, and looked round her. The good work she had done no longer pleased her, because she knew her task was only half accomplished. She had to feed the soil, feed her roses, or nothing would come of all she had done so far, and her cuttings and seedlings would die too. "If I say 'compost,' I don't suppose a compost heap appears by the water-butt, does it?" It didn't.

She walked through the orchard, too preoccupied to look for the Beast—or too ashamed, for how could she face him now, when the job she was here to do she was about to fail at?—and let herself into the walled garden again; but she found no compost heap, nor any of the usual signs of human cultivation, rakes and hoes and spades, trowels and hand forks and pruning knives, seed trays and bell glasses and pots for potting on, odd bits of timber that might do for props but probably won't, twists of paper that used to contain seeds and haven't found their way to the bonfire, broken pots, frayed string, and bits of rusty wire. "Very well," she said. "You are much too—too *organized* for such mortal litter, but if you, you magic, don't need compost to make—to allow—things to grow, why are the Beast's poor roses dying?" *It is the heart of this place, and it is dying.* She looked out again over the too-tidy, too-beautiful vegetable beds and listened to the silence. Where were the birds?

She slunk back through the orchard, looking only at her feet, not even interested in exploring the pond or stream the bulrushes heralded, not stopping to twist a fruit off any of the generously laden trees, because she suddenly felt she did not deserve such a pleasure. She went up to her balcony and stared at her lunch with no appetite.

There was a slab of cheese, and she poked it with her finger. "Where do you come from then? Herbivore dung is exactly what I want. Cow would be splendid—goat, sheep, even horse. I'm not particular. Chicken is also good, although I'm quite sure one cannot produce cheese from chickens. I wish I knew more about cheese." She tried to recollect everything the dairymaid who had married a city man might have told her about cheese varieties, but it was all too long ago. She had not been a good pupil because she had had too much on her mind, and the woman had been careful to give her only the most basic instructions. She thought of her own experiments with goat's cheese and smiled grimly; no help for her there.

She broke off a bit of this cheese and nibbled it, stared at the pattern of crumbs as if they were tea-leaves which could tell her fortune. "This isn't even like any cheese I can remember anywhere else. It's—it's—" She stopped.

She had eaten cheese in the palace before, and no doubt what was happening now was only because she was concentrating so hard that her mind had to leap in some direction, like a horse goaded by spurs. But suddenly she seemed to stand in a forest, and there was an undulating sea of moss underfoot, and the sunlight fell through the green and coppery leaves in patterns as beautiful as those on a spider's back, and there was a smell of roses in her nostrils and in her mouth. But just as she would know Lionheart from Jeweltongue in the dark simply by her smell, just as each of the roses at Rose Cottage possessed a smell as individual as the shape of its stems and leaves and the colour of its flowers, so was this smell of roses different from the rich wild scent that belonged to the Beast. This scent was light and delicate and fine and reminded her of apples after rain, but with a flick, a touch, a tremor of something else, something she could not identify. She drew in a deep breath, and her heart lifted, and then the vision—and the scent—dissolved, and she was back in her rose-decorated room, staring at a plate of cheese and cheese crumbs.

She hardly knew how she got through the afternoon, and she was preoccupied at dinner. When Fourpaws failed to put in an appearance, she found herself playing fretfully with the tails of the ribbons woven into her bodice, fidgeting with the silken cord of her embroidered heart, and twisting the gold chain set with coral that hung round her neck.

"May I ask what troubles you?" said the Beast at last.

Beauty laughed a little. "I am sorry; I am not good company this evening. No, I think I want to worry my problem one more day. It would please me to be able to solve it myself, although at present I admit I am baffled."

"I will help you any way I can," said the Beast. "As I have told you."

Beauty looked at him. He had turned his head so that the candlelight fell on one cheekbone, lit the dark depths of one eye; the tips of his white teeth showed even when his mouth was closed. He always sat so still that when he moved, it was a surprise, like a statue gesturing, or the wolf or chimera's deadly spring from hiding.

"Yes, Beast," she said. "I know . . . you have told me this."

He made his own restless motion, plucking at the edge of his gown, as she had seen him do before. The fabric rippled and glistened in the candlelight, seeming to turn of its own volition to show off its black sheen, like a cat posing for an audience. She repressed the urge to stroke it, to quiet the Beast's hand by placing her own over it.

"It is a little early," he said after a moment, "but I could take you on the roof tonight."

"Oh, yes!" said Beauty. "Please. When I woke up this morning, I was angry, because I usually do wake at least once in the night."

"Do you?" said the Beast, as he stood behind her chair while she folded her napkin and rose to her feet. "Does something disturb you?"

She turned round and looked up at him. He was very near, and the rose scent of him was so heavy she felt she might reach out and seize it, wrap it round herself like a scarf. "I have always woken in the night," she said, "since I was a little child, since—since I first had the dream I told you of, my—my first evening here."

The Beast was silent for a moment. "I have forgotten," he said at last, and the words *I have forgotten* echoed down a dark corridor of years. "I too used to wake most nights, when—before—when I slept more than I do now. I had forgotten."

He turned away, as if still lost in thought, but she skipped round after him and slipped her hand beneath his elbow. His free hand drew her hand through and smoothed it down over his forearm, and his arm pressed hers against his side.

She was aware that he was walking slowly to allow for both her height and her elegant burden of skirts—thank fate my shoes are more reasonable tonight, she thought—but still they made their way swiftly through what seemed to her a maze of corridors and then up a grand swirl of stairs. Magnificent furnishings demanded her attention on every side, but she turned her gaze resolutely away from them, preferring to stare at the fine black needlework on the Beast's sleeve, glimpsed and revealed as they walked through clouds of candlelight and into pools of darkness.

She was tired of looking up at portraits that stared down scornfully at her. She was tired of ormolu cabinets and chinoiserie cupboards that when she first looked bore sprays of leaves and flowers which when she looked again were deer or birds; tired of divans that had eight legs and were covered with brocade but between blink and blink had six legs and were covered with watered silk. She moved her fingers to ·lie lightly on a ridge of braid on the Beast's sleeve; it was the same ridge in or out of candlelight. The rich scent of the crimson rose embraced her.

But as they paced up the stairs, she looked up, for the ceiling was now very far away, and she wondered if she was seeing to the roof of the palace. It seemed much higher than the cupola on her glasshouse, and this puzzled her, and before she could remember not to let anything she seemed to see in this palace puzzle her, her eyes were caught by the painted pattern on the ceiling, which seemed to be of pink and gold—and auburn brown and ebony black, aquamarine blue and willow leaf green—and perhaps had people worked into it, or perhaps only rounded shapes that might be limbs and draperies, but certainly it seemed to reflect the swirling of the staircase—except that it did not, and the spiral overhead began to turn quickly, too quickly, and she lost her sense of where her feet were, and she stumbled because she could not raise her feet fast enough, and she tripped over the risers.

The Beast stooped and picked her up as easily as she might have picked up Fourpaws and continued up the stairs. "Pardon me, please," he said. "Close your eyes, and hold on to me because I am only . . . what I am. And forgive me, for I should have warned you. I went up this stair on all fours more than once before I learnt not to look up. This house—this place—has a strange relationship with the earth it stands upon. If you want to look round you, stop. When you walk, look only where you are walking. And in particular, do not look at the ceiling when you climb a turning stair, and do not look out any windows when you are walking past them. I—I should have said these things to you before; I have never had occasion to explain to—" He stopped. "I do not think the contents of any of the rooms will make you dizzy if you stand still to look at them. They mostly only, er . . ."

"Change their clothing," said Beauty, and the Beast gave a low rumble of laugh.

"Yes," he said. "And please forgive me also for treating you so—"

"Lightly," suggested Beauty, and was gratified by another quick growly laugh.

"—disrespectfully," continued the Beast. "But I have also learnt that it is better not to—not to acknowledge when something here has had the better of you, if you need not."

And at that he reached the top of the stairs, and took two steps into the darkness there, and set her gently down on her feet. Involuntarily she leant against him, listening to the slow thump of his heart, hearing her own heart pattering frantically in her ears in counterpoint as she stirred and put herself away from him, feeling with her hands for the wall. "It is so dark!" she said.

"Yes," said the Beast's voice, and it seemed to come from all round her, as if he still held her in his arms, or as if he had swallowed her up, like an ogre in a nursery tale.

"This hall is always dark; I do not know why. I do not know why this great staircase leads you to something you are not permitted to see; I can tell you that candles will not stay kindled here, though the air is sweet to breathe. But this is the shortest way to the roof. I told you that any stair up will lead you to the roof eventually; it will, but sometimes it is a tedious process. And it is the sky we want."

He leant past her and threw open a door. Starlight flowed in round them, lighting up her pale hands, which she still held out in front of her against the dark of the hallway, playing in the carved surfaces of the cameo rings on her fingers and tweaking glints and gleams from the lace overlay of her skirt. The Beast was a darkness the starlight could not leaven.

She turned, went up a narrow half flight of stairs, and ducked through a low opening. She was on the roof, surrounded by sky. "Directly before you," said the Beast, and she could hear him stooping behind her, so that when he pointed over her shoulder, his arm was low enough for her eyes to follow, "is the Horse and Chariot. There"—his arm moved a little—"is the Ewer, and there"—only his finger moved—"the Throne."

"And there," she said dreamily, "is the Peacock, and the Tinker—how clear his pack is, I have never seen it so clear—and the Sailing Ship."

"Then you are a student of the skies as well," said the Beast.

She laughed, turning to him. "Oh, no—I have told you nearly as many as I know. Our governesses taught us a little—a very little—a very little of anything, I fear, but the night sky was not their fault, for we lived in the centre of a city, where the gas-lamps were lit all night, and in weather fine enough to stand outdoors with your governess, there was probably also a party going on in some house nearby, with its grounds lit as bright as day. Please tell me more. I have never seen so many stars, so much sky. At home"—she faltered—"at . . . outside Longchance, where I lived with my sisters, although there are no gas-lamps, there are trees. I know no stars that stay low to the horizon, and the turning of the seasons always confuses me.''

And so he told her more, and sometimes, with the name of some star shape, he told her the story that went with it. She knew the story of the Peacock, who was so proud of his tail that he was willing to be hung in the sky instead of marrying his true love, and how his true love, both sad and angry, asked that peahens, at least, might be spared having tails so grand that conceit might make them forget necessary things, like looking for supper and raising children.

But she did not know the story that the Tinker was not a tinker at all, but a brave soldier who, having stolen the Brand of War, carried it in his pack till he could come up to the Ewer, which contained the Water of Life, where he could quench it forever. But the Ewer always went before him, and he chased her round and round the earth, because she knew that humanity could not be freed of its burden so easily and, for love of the Tinker, could not bear him to know his courage was in vain. Beauty had never seen the Three Deer, who dipped back and forth above and below the horizon, ever seeking to escape the Tiger, who ran after them; nor the Queen of the Heavenly Mountain, whose realm touched both the earth and the sky, and if you were the right sort of hero and knew exactly the right path, you might visit her, and she would show you the earth constellations spread out at your feet and tell you the stories they held.

Beauty at last sighed and bowed her head. "You are tired," said the Beast. "I am sorry; I have kept you too long. You must go to bed."

"I am not tired—or, that is, only my neck is tired," said Beauty, reaching beneath the gold and coral chain, and the silken rope of the embroidered heart, to rub it. But then she blinked, looking down at her feet, and backed up a step, and backed up another. "But, sir—Beast—what is this we walk on? Why are we walking on anything so lovely?" And she went on backing up and backing up, but the roof was covered with the delicate, glowing paintwork.

She knelt down and touched the arched neck of the fiery

chestnut Horse drawing the red-and-blue-and-gold Chariot, and the face of the Queen of the Heavenly Mountain was so kind and the eyes so welcoming that Beauty almost spoke to her, and, between opening her mouth and, remembering, closing it again, had reached out to brush a lock of hair from where it had fallen across her cheek, as she might have done to one of her sisters. For several minutes after that she was too stunned, too enthralled to speak; at last she said wonderingly, ''There is nothing as splendid as these anywhere inside your palace.

''But—no—splendid is not the right word. They are splendid, but they are—they are so friendly. Oh dear!'' she said, and looked up at him, half laughing, half embarrassed. ''How childish that sounds! But so many of the beautiful things in the rooms beneath us—push you away—tell you to stand back—order you to admire and be abashed. These—these draw you in. These make you want to stay and—and have them for company. Yes, that's right. But I— I am still making them sound like a—like—sort of comfortable, though, am I not? Like a bowl of warm bread and milk and an extra pillow, and that's not it at all. They are not comfortable. Indeed, I feel that if I lived with them for long, I should have to learn to be . . . better, or greater, myself. If this Queen of the Heavenly Mountain looked down at me from my bedroom wall every day, soon I should have to go looking for that path to her domain. I wouldn't be able to help myself.''

The Beast still stood silent.

''Oh—am I still describing it all wrong? I told you our governesses never taught us much. And Jeweltongue is the artistic one of us. Lionheart is the bold one, and I—I—I am the practical one. I don't mind being the practical one, but these—oh, these pictures do not make me feel the least bit practical!'' She took a deep breath and clasped her hands over her heart, as if she felt some stirring in her blood she had not felt before.

''Tell me—please tell me—do you know how they came here—these pictures? It is so odd that they should be here, where they will be rained on and scoured by wind. Do you know how they came here?''

There was a long silence. "Hmm," rumbled the Beast at last. "I drew them."

"You?" she said, amazed. "But—but you told me you are clumsy!"

"My hands are clumsy," said the Beast, "but they are steady. I have had . . . enough time, to learn how to do what I wish to do. I tried . . . different things. Sometimes I use a very long brush, which I hold between my teeth."

"But—you have said you spend the nights here! Do you work in the dark?"

"I see very well in the dark, so long as the sky is clear," said the Beast. "The shadows indoors are much darker."

She crept, feeling foolish but too entranced to care, across the roof, stooping even lower to peer at a particularly fine bit of work: a deer's flank, a peacock's feather, the vine leaves winding up a pole. There were more stars and stories here than she could learn in years of nights. She came at last to the low balustrade which ran along the edge of the roof. There was something painted here too, but it was almost entirely in shadow, and she could not see it.

She looked down the vast length of the roof—for they had walked round only one tiny bit of this wing of the palace—and along its balustrade, and it seemed to her that all the shadows were populated by the Beast's fine, living, vivid painting, but nowhere could she see any bit of balustrade that did not stand so thoroughly in its own shadow that she thought her weak human eyes could make out what was upon it.

"Candles," she said aloud—a little too loud—and went firmly to the low door, which projected into the roof no higher than the balustrade, and looked inside on the top stair. She saw nothing, but she persisted, seeing candles in her mind's eye, insisting on candles, and eventually she found a nook, and in it a candle in a small holder and a tinder-box. She lit the one with the other, and stood up, and went back to the balustrade where she had first noticed the patterns she suspected were painting, and stooped again, and—

somehow she had known this was what she would find—
the Beast had painted roses all along the balustrade, as far
as she walked, stooping for the candle flame to light them
but careful with the candle, that no wax would drip on the
paintings she could not help but walk on.

She walked back to the Beast, who had moved away from
her as soon as she began examining his paintings. She
touched his arm timidly. "They are all so beautiful," she
said.

He looked down at her. "Not half so beautiful as you
are," he said. "Nor do they speak to me, nor touch me.
Even Fourpaws will not touch me. Beauty, will you marry
me?"

She shivered as if she had been struck by winter wind,
but she left her hand on his arm. "Good night, Beast," she
said, and turned away, to go through the little door, and find
her way to her bedroom, and sleep.

"Good night, Beauty," said the Beast behind her. "Do
not forget: Keep your eyes downcast while you are on the
stairs."

"I will not forget," whispered Beauty.

CHAPTER
10

She was not sure when the dream began. She remembered walking down the long vortex of stairs, keeping her eyes on the next tread, and the next, as her feet stepped down, and down, and she remembered how the darkness seemed to rise towards her as she neared the bottom, till when she stood on the floor again, she could see no more than she had at the top, before the Beast had opened the door that let in the starlight, though it had not been dark at the bottom of the stairs when the Beast had been with her. She stood for a moment, her heart again beating in her ears, and this time the Beast did not stand near her; but then a door opened in front of her, and the twinkle of candlelight beckoned to her from the darkness, although the little light seemed to struggle, as if with some fog or miasma.

She did not remember how long she walked through corridors, familiar and unfamiliar—a little familiar, a little less familiar—till she came again to the chamber of the star, eerily lit by its sky dome, and she walked through her rooms, and rather than at once undressing and climbing into her bed, she went to stand upon the balcony. The spider-web glistened in its corner like hoarfrost.

As she stood, leaning against the railing, her mind and

heart still spinning with the images of the Beast's painting, she looked idly out into the starlit courtyard. And she saw a bent old woman carrying a basket walk slowly round the corner of the glasshouse, as if she came from the carriage-way where the wild wood lay, and she walked slowly down the wing of the palace where the closed gates were hidden. Beauty could not see the gates from where she stood, but the old woman set the basket she carried down, in front of where they might be. And then she turned and walked slowly away again.

And now Beauty knew she dreamt, for she saw the old woman turn the far corner of the glasshouse and walk through the carriage-way into the wild wood, and Beauty watched her till her shadow emerged from the darkness of the tunnel to lie briefly against the starlit ground of the bonfire clearing. Beauty could only just make out what she was now seeing, and she thought she saw silver shapes, like four-legged beasts, come out of the woods round the glade and touch the woman with their long slender noses. But this was very far away, and the trees threw confusing shadows, and it was over very quickly, as the woman disappeared beyond the narrow opening of the archway.

But when Beauty turned to run downstairs and into the courtyard, to see what was in the old woman's basket, she found herself turning over in bed, with the sunlight streaming onto the glowing carpet, and Fourpaws purring on the pillow, and breakfast on the table, and the deep wild scent of the crimson rose tangled in her hair.

Her first impulse was to rush downstairs in her nightgown and look for the basket even now, knowing it was too late, even knowing that what she remembered must be a dream. At least, she thought, as she threw back the bedclothes, she could look for any sign that those barred and inimical gates had opened recently.

She paused at the top of the bed stairs. There was something very odd about the carpet this morning. She thought back to the morning before last. More hedgehogs? Many more hedgehogs? Positively a lake of hedgehogs? No. This—these were not hedgehogs.

There was a low forlorn croak from one corner of the
room and a following gruff murmur that ran all round
the floor. "Oh, my lords and ladies," said Beauty. Frogs?
The shore of the lake round the bed stairs rippled and shifted
a little. No—toads. Hundreds of toads.

Fourpaws, still purring, went daintily down the stairs, and
leapt to the floor. Toads scattered before her, pressing themselves under furniture and into walls. She sat down, looked
up at Beauty still paralysed at the edge of the bed, waited
for the duration of three tail-lashings, and then stood up
again and began to walk towards the opposite wall.

Toads hurtled out of her way, tumbling over one another,
making small distressed grunting sounds and a great deal of
scrabbling with their small slapping feet. "Oh, stop!" said
Beauty. "Please. I'm not really afraid of them—really I'm
not—not poor toads—it's just—it's just there are so *many*
of them."

Fourpaws sat down again and began washing a front foot.
The toads quieted, and there was the gentle flickering light
of many blinking yellow and coppery eyes from ankle level
all round the room and in clumps round the legs of furniture.

Beauty came down the stairs and stepped very softly in
the toad-free space in the centre of the carpet. Nothing
moved, except Fourpaws beginning on the other front foot.
"Well," said Beauty, only a little shakily, "there are too
many of you to carry in my skirt, and frankly, my pets, I
don't wish to handle you, for my sake as well as yours; but
how am I to convince you that I will lead you to a wonderful
garden full of—of—well, you'll have to ask the hedgehogs
what it's full of, but I'm sure you will like it. That is, you
will like it if I can get you there."

She stood still a moment longer and then sidled towards
the chair next to the hearth, where her dressing-gown lay.
There was a flurry of toads from that end of the room. She
picked up her dressing-gown very softly and eased herself
into it. "On the whole, I think I would rather try to shift
you first. I don't fancy breakfast by the light of toad blinks."
She paused and added under her breath, "Thank the kind
fates that only one spider was enough."

She walked towards the doorway, paused, and looked back. "This way," she said, not knowing what else to do. Several toads hopped out from under her bed and stopped again. Several from the far corner between the bed and the hearth joined them. Toad eddies drifted out from under the wardrobe and the gilt console tables and pooled near the centre of the room, in front of the breakfast table. Fourpaws stopped washing to watch.

Beauty turned and walked to the door that led into the chamber of the star; as the door swung open, she turned round. There was an army of toads following her, ochre-coloured companies, low brown regiments, yellowy-green battalions, and last of all came Fourpaws, tail high, the tip just switching back and forth, eyes huge and fascinated.

She led them all into the chamber of the star; but the noise their flapping feet made, and the little tapping echoes that ran up into the dome, obviously upset them, and she went on as quickly as she could through the door that opened onto another corridor. The corridor made itself short for them, and it was not long before she saw the courtyard door opening onto sunlight. She paused again on this threshold and addressed her army: "Now you must be brave, because you won't like this bit. It is still quite early, and the sunlight will not be too strong for you, but I am sure you will find it unpleasant, and the pebbles will scratch your bellies. But it will be over quickly—I hope—and then there will be lovely grass for you, and dirt, and an orchard, and a garden."

The toads blinked at her. She turned and walked out into the morning light; and the rustling noise behind her told her that the toads were following, flapping and pattering through the stones. She was so preoccupied with how far they might have to walk that it took her a little while to notice that the rustling noises had increased and somewhat changed their note; and that there was now a humming in the air as well.

She had gone instinctively to her glasshouse and put her hand on it, and as she had done once before, she ran her fingers along it as she walked next to it. And the rustlings increased, and the humming grew louder, and as she came

to the corner of the glasshouse, she heaved a great sigh of
relief, and turned, and saw the tunnel into the orchard only
a short distance farther. At that moment it registered with
her that she had been hearing a humming noise for some
time, and she looked up, and there was a cloud of bumblebees, hovering in the air, as if they were waiting for her and
the toads.

"Oh!" she said. Their black and yellow backs gleamed
bright as armour in the sunlight. "Oh, how I wish I could
let you all into the glasshouse! Perhaps the trouble began
because the roses are lonely! But you, you bees, you must
have been here all along, or how does the fruit grow in the
Beast's orchard? How does the corn swell in the fields? But
why has he not seen you? Why have I never seen nor heard
you till now?"

As she said this, the bumblebee swarm rushed upwards,
trailing a long tail of single bees behind it, and whizzed
along the slope of the glasshouse as if seeking a way in.
There were one or two left behind, buzzing disconcertedly
and making little zigzag lines in the air as if wondering
where the others had gone. One of them very near her bum-
bled against a pane of the glasshouse, near a strut.

And disappeared.

As it disappeared, Beauty's hand, which was resting gently against the next strut supporting the next pane of glass,
felt a sudden faint draught of air, and her third and little
fingers, which had been touching the pane of glass inside
the frame, were resting on nothing at all. She snatched her
hand away as she saw the bumblebee disappear, looked at
what should have been a pane of glass, and was just reaching out to touch it timidly, because the glasshouse panes
were always so shining clear that but for their reflective
sparkle it was hard to say if they were there or not, when
she heard the bee cloud returning.

There were too many things to attend to at once. She
looked up at the windstorm sound of the bees, her hand
hesitating just before touching the pane of glass that should
be there; the bumblebees stopped politely before they flew
into her face; and she saw the bumblebee which had dis-

appeared reappear from behind the strut . . . where it had flown in, and out, of a glasshouse pane.

Beauty touched the glass. It was there, and solid. She touched the pane that the bumblebee had flown through. It was there, and solid.

There was a faint scuttling noise behind her, and her dazed mind flew to the easier recourse of remembering her toads, growing too hot in the sunlight, and worrying about their comfort. She began walking away from the glasshouse, taking the shortest route to the tunnel to the orchard. But her astonishment-heightened senses now reminded her that the susurration of the toad army had changed, and she turned to look, expecting . . . something. And so she was no more astonished than she already was when she saw the grass-snakes, and the slow-worms, and the red mist of ladybirds, so thick it threw a dappled shadow on the backs of the toads, and which made no sound at all. And as she looked, she saw the crickets creeping out, as it seemed, from among the white pebbles of the courtyard, as if they had been sleeping in hollows beneath. They paused, as if surprised by the sunlight, and then they sprang into the air, as if to hurry to catch up with the toads, and the snakes, and the slow-worms, and the ladybirds, and the bees; and then there was not merely the faint clicking of their legs against the small stones, but the soft *tink-tink-tink* as the ones with imperfect aim bounced off the wall of the glasshouse as they leapt.

"Perhaps the—the badgers, and foxes, and deer, and rabbits and hares, and mice and voles and weasels and stoats and squirrels, perhaps they are waiting for us. And the birds. I do so hope the birds come back!"

Beauty led her ever-increasing menagerie into the orchard and on towards the walled garden, and the grass stems rattled almost as loudly as spears as it followed her. She did not quite dare to stop again, but she walked sideways for a few steps to look behind her, and she could no longer see her creatures, but the grasses tossed and rippled like a sea cut by a fleet of ships. She turned to face front again just as there was a small streaking explosion like the path of a

cannonball to one side of her, and something landed with a
heavy thump on her shoulder.

"Oh!" said Beauty, recognizing the bushed-out tail in her
eye as belonging to Fourpaws. "I wondered what had become of you." Even a cat has some difficulty riding on the
shoulder of someone wading through tall grass, and Beauty
put up a hand to steady her and did not protest the faint
prick of several sets of claws through the thick collar of her
dressing-gown. "A few too many of them even for you,
eh?" said Beauty, and added hastily, mindful of Fourpaws'
dignity, "I am myself very grateful for your company—
someone else with warm blood and breath—even if your
tail is still in my eye."

When she came to the walled garden, she threw open the
gate and stood aside, and she looked back as well and saw
little threads of bobbing grass stems leading off in all directions from the main body of her army, assuring her that
everyone was seeking the sort of landscape it liked best.
"There's water at the bottom of the slope," she called
softly. "But you probably knew that already."

When there was a lull in the flow of creatures over the
threshold, she went in and opened the gate on the far side
of the garden, into the fields of corn. She paused again to
stroke the barley and wheat-awns, and as she paused, she
looked round, and her eye was caught by a yellow and white
butterfly. It whirled up in a warm draught, and she saw more
coloured flickers; there were half a dozen deepest ruddy gold
and peacock blue and green butterflies sunning their wings
on a narrow mossy ledge in the garden wall.

At that moment she felt a gentle shove against her foot.
She looked down, and there was a hedgehog, looking up at
her; it was much larger than any of the four she had brought
to the garden in her skirt. "The slugs and snails, and borers
and beetles, they're back too, are they? You would not be
so shiny and plump else."

She went back thoughtfully through the garden, and now,
when she looked, she could see holes and spots on some of
the stems and leaves, and once she saw a snail hastening
across the path in front of her, its shining neck stretched its

fullest length, its tail streaming behind it; she could only see that it was moving at all by the tangential observation that it was now nearer the side of the path it was aiming at than it had been when she first saw it. She also heard the crickets singing, and swirls of butterflies were gleaming over the heads of the ruby chard, and she had to wave her free hand at a little puff of gnats she walked through.

Surely, if all this were happening, she would find a way to save her Beast's roses? *It is the heart of this place, and it is dying.*

Fourpaws leapt down when they reentered the orchard, but she stayed close at Beauty's heels all the way back to the palace and upstairs to the breakfast table laid in front of Beauty's balcony. Beauty set a bowl of bread and milk on the floor for Fourpaws and poured herself her first cup of tea. "When the bluebottles are buzzing repellently in all the corners where one can't get at them, and the mice are chewing holes in the wainscoting and leaving nasty little pellets in the pantry, and the wood borers are eating the furniture and leaving ominous little heaps of dust about, will the tea stew, too, like ordinary tea, instead of tasting fresh-brewed when it has sat half the morning, as this does?" she said; but her eyes were on the pyrotechnics of her glasshouse in the sunlight.

Fourpaws finished her bread and milk and mewed for more. "You're going to have to start catching mice, you know," said Beauty, setting down a fresh bowl. "Instead of shadows. I would have thought you might prefer mice." But when Fourpaws finished the second bowl and mewed for a third, Beauty looked at her in surprise. "Someone your size can't possibly need a third bowl of bread and milk," she said. Fourpaws looked at her enigmatically and, holding her gaze, reached out with one imperious forepaw and patted the empty bowl. Beauty laughed. "Very well. But this is your last. Absolutely."

Beauty was dressing by the time Fourpaws finished her third breakfast, but between the time Beauty dropped her shirt over her head and the time she could see again and was smoothing her hair back, the cat had disappeared. When she had finished brushing and tying up her hair, and lacing her boots, and patting her pockets to check that everything she needed was still there, and had paused to drink a last cup of tea, she realized that through the minor bustle of getting ready for the day (what remained of the day, she thought), she had been hearing furtive noises coming from under her bed. She knelt and lifted the edge of the long curtain. "You aren't tormenting any lost toads, are you?"

Fourpaws sat up and looked at her indignantly. There was just room for a small cat to sit up to her full height under Beauty's bed. Then she threw herself down and rolled over on her back, curving her forepaws invitingly; but Beauty looked at her face and her lashing tail and rather thought she had the mien of a cat who was planning on seizing an arm and disembowelling it with her hind feet while she bit its head off. "I think not," said Beauty.

Fourpaws dropped over onto her side and half lidded her eyes, but the tail was still lashing. "I have no idea what you're up to," said Beauty, "but I will leave you to it." She dropped the curtain hem and rose to her feet.

She knew it was a vain gesture. But once she was out of doors, she could not resist walking down the second side of the palace wall, and looking for the closed gates, and, having found them, looking for any trace of—of anything, any disturbance, any mark of any sort of visitor, but no trace did she find. The pebbles were as flawlessly raked as ever, the grey-white wall as spotless, the doors as perfectly barred.

She walked the rest of that wall, and through the carriage-way in the crosswall, and stood at the mouth of the tunnel and peered out. The trees looked as if they went on a very long way, but perhaps they did not. Perhaps there was a clearing just behind the first rank, where milk-white cows grazed, where an old woman made butter and cheese to bring to the poor imprisoned Beast and his guest. . . .

She sighed deeply, squared her shoulders, and walked into the glen. When she arrived at its edge, she took a bit of gardening string from her pocket and tied it round the trunk of a slender tree that stood opposite the carriage-way, and then she began working her way through the trees beyond, letting the string trail through her fingers behind her. If the old woman came here often, there should be a path, but perhaps the path was magic too, and only appeared on clear nights when the old woman wanted it.

She could find no glade where cows, milk-white or otherwise, grazed, nor any small secret huts where old women might churn their butter and draw off their whey and leave their cheeses to ripen. She followed her string back to the clearing, tied it to another tree, and set out in a slightly different direction, twice that morning and three times in the afternoon. She found nothing and gained only filthy bramble-scratched hands and smudges on her skirt where she had tripped and fallen, and crumbly leaves and sapsticky twigs in her hair and down her collar.

As the sun sank towards twilight, she gave it up, rolled her string into its ball for the last time, and went slowly through the carriage-way and into the courtyard. Slowly she entered her glasshouse for the first time that day, to water her cuttings and her seedbed, but she entered sadly and neither sang nor looked round her as she went about her tasks.

When she said good night to the one blooming rose-bush, she felt like asking it to forgive her. She did not, not because it was a foolish thing to say to a rose-bush but because she felt she could not bear it if the bush seized magic enough to give itself a voice for three words and forgave her as she asked.

Her bath towels this evening were as golden as the sunset on the glasshouse panes, and her dress was as golden as the towels, and her necklace was of great warm rough amber, strung with garnets so dark they looked nearly black till they caught the light and flared deepest crimson, like the heart of a rose.

Her mood lifted a little when she saw the Beast waiting for her, and she made an effort at the conversation over dinner, telling stories of her childhood in the city, of her governesses, of her sisters, of her garden. But when she touched the embroidered heart, as she inevitably did when she spoke her sisters' names, she did so abstractedly, for her mind was on the old woman and on her roses, the Beast's roses, which must be fed or die.

But she did notice that when she fell silent, the Beast offered no tales of his childhood in response to her own.

"Fourpaws does not join us this evening," she said at last, as she sliced a pear; candlelight winked off the blade of her knife and warmed its ivory handle almost to the gold of her sleeve.

"She cannot come every night," said the Beast, "or we would cease to hope for her appearance; I learnt that long ago."

Beauty laid her knife down and took hold of her courage and said, "Why sat you alone in this dark hall, for all those nights, when you will not eat with knife and plate?"

There was a silence, and Beauty looked at her neatly sliced pear but did not move to pick up any bit of it. She folded her hands tightly in her lap and willed herself not to take her words back. She did not fear his anger, and she did fear to do him hurt; but it seemed to her that he held too much to himself as a burden and that if he had chosen— had demanded—had ensorcelled her to be his companion, she would do the best for him that she could. And so, while she waited for his answer, she thought again of the glass-house, and the roses there, and the old woman, and the silver beasts in the wild wood, and did not offer to withdraw her question.

At last he spoke, and each word was like a boulder brought up from the bottom of a mine. "When the change first . . . came upon me, I . . . I lost what humanity remained to me . . . for a time. I still cannot . . . remember that time clearly. When I had learnt to . . . walk like a man again, and had . . . found . . . clothes that would cover me as I now was, and discovered that I could still speak . . . so that a man or woman might understand me, I . . . still wished some daily ritual of humanity to remind me of . . . what I had been and what I no longer was. And I chose . . . to sit in this dining-hall, though I cannot . . . wield knife and fork like a man. There might have been other rituals that would have done.

This is the one which first . . . suited me, and . . . I have looked no further."

When the change first came upon me . . . If his words were boulders, they weighed her down too. Beauty leant towards him, so that she could lay her hand on the back of his nearer hand. Her hand and fingers together could not reach the full width of his palm, and when, after a moment, his other hand was laid over hers, it covered her wrist as well.

He released her and sat back. She ate her pear, and then picked up a nutcracker in the shape of a dragon, and began cracking nuts. "I guess you have not yet solved your dilemma," said the Beast.

"Oh dear," she said, fishing out a walnut half with a nut pick on whose end crouched a tiny silver griffin. "Is it so obvious? I have tried—"

"I have learnt your moods, a little," said the Beast. "I see you are preoccupied."

"I fear I am," she admitted, "but—if you didn't mind—a walk on the roof would be the pleasantest of distractions."

"I would be honoured," said the Beast, and this evening, as they walked up the whirlpool stairs together, Beauty kept her eyes firmly down and on the Beast's black shoes and her soft gold slippers, coruscating with tiny gems. And when she left him, much later, on the roof, and he said to her, gravely, "Beauty, will you marry me?" she answered as she had the night before, "Good night, Beast," only this time she did not shiver.

She kept her forearms crossed against her body as she hurried back to her room and pinched herself every few steps, saying aloud, "I am awake; I am still awake." When she reached her rooms, she took off her dinner dress but put her day clothes back on. She almost thought her nightgown flapped its sleeves in protest; there was some pale flicker caught at the edge of her sight, where it always lay over the back of a chair by the fire, so it would be warm when she put it on. She turned sharply to look at it, but it only lay limply over its chair, as a nightgown should.

"Basket," she said. "I need a basket, and I'm afraid I

need it now, please. And a trowel. A wide one. I should
have asked before, but I hadn't thought of it yet.'' She
turned round looking, but there was no basket. "Never mind
what I need it for,'' she said. ''The Beast did say you would
provide anything in your power. I don't believe you can't
find me a basket.'' But there was still no basket.

''Well,'' she said, and picked up a candle, kindled it at
the edge of the fire, and began walking through her rooms,
peering into dark corners. She found the basket at last,
tucked behind a small ebony table, inlaid with hammered
silver, which sparkled like snow in the candlelight. The glitter was such that she almost didn't see the basket. The
trowel lay in its bottom.

''That was not good-natured of you,'' she said, ''but I
still thank you for the basket.'' She returned to her balcony,
a little anxiously, for she was not sure how much time had
passed. She saw nothing and had to hope she had missed
nothing.

She went quickly to the chamber of the star, but no door
opened for her. She counted the doors: twelve. No, ten.
No—eleven. *Eleven?* Can you make a star of eleven points?
''Stop that,'' she said. ''Or I'll make a rope out of the sheets
on my bed and climb over the balcony.'' A door opened.
''And no nonsense about where this corridor goes,'' she
said. The door closed, and another one opened. She walked
through it, and it closed behind her, but the corridor was
dark. She was still carrying her candle from her basket
search, and so she held it up before her in a hand that trembled only a little; fiercely she recalled her dream to her
mind. . . . But there was the door into the courtyard. It was
a little open; she could see a crack of starlight round it.

She stepped softly outside, and there was the old woman,
already moving back towards the carriage-way, having left
her basket at the palace doors. Beauty had been much longer
in the corridor than she guessed. She flew after her, trying
to make her feet strike the treacherous courtyard pebbles as
quietly as the Beast always walked. The old woman did not
look round, but perhaps it was only because she was old
and deaf.

She disappeared into the shadows of the carriage-way so
completely that Beauty, pausing at the tunnel's edge for fear
of being seen by the waiting silver beasts, thought suddenly
that perhaps she had imagined her, that she had seen no old
woman at all. Frightened and bewildered, she looked back
over her shoulder; the basket by the doors was gone. She
let her breath out on a sob—"Oh"—and moved forward
again, and the old woman was on the far side of the bonfire
clearing, about to disappear finally among the trees, but one
of the milky-pale creatures that followed her turned its head
at the sound of her sob and looked straight into Beauty's
eyes.

She might not have noticed if it had not turned its head.
Its haunches were too round for a deer, its legs too long and
slender for a horse, and the curling tail was like nothing she
had ever seen, for it looked more like a waterfall than anything so solid and rooted as individual hairs, but it was still
a tail. It turned its head to look at her, and so she saw,
shimmering in the starlight, the long pearly horn that rose
from its forehead.

She looked, blinked, and they were gone—old woman
and unicorns. Gone as if they had never been; gone as the
old woman's basket at the palace doors was gone; gone
without sound. The light of the stars still flooded the bonfire
clearing, poured silver and glinting over the remains of
Beauty's bonfires, over the tiny-tempest piles of last year's
leaves, over the scatterings of stones, over the patches of
earth seen among the rest. Over queerly gleaming golden
heaps of . . .

Beauty emerged from the carriage-way in a daze and
stooped at the first golden pile, took out her trowel, and . . .
began to laugh. "Oh dear!" she said. "This is not the way
a maiden is supposed to meet a unicorn. It should be a
romantic and glamorous meeting . . . but if I had not needed
what I need, I would not have been so interested in strange
silvery creatures that met mysterious old women at the edges
of wild woods, certainly not interested enough to dare to
follow them here, in the middle of the night, in this . . . this
place." Her laughter stopped. "But then again . . . what

would either the unicorn or I have done after it laid its head in my lap?''

She looked at her hands, dim in the starlight, at their short, broken nails and roughened skin. Her memory provided other details: the blotches of ingrained dirt, the thorn scabs and scars, the yellowy-grey streaks of bruising across the back of one hand where she'd pulled a ligament in her forefinger. ''I wonder—I wonder, then, is it only that it is unicorn milk and butter and cheese? None of my dreams are my own—none of the animals—not even the spider— they all—they only—they come to a maiden who has drunk the milk of a unicorn? Is that all that matters?'' she whispered, as if the Numen might hear and answer her. ''This is a story like any nursery tale of magic? Where any maiden will do, any—any—monster, any hero, so long as they meet the right mysterious old women and discover the right enchanted doors during the right haunted midnights. . . .''

For a moment she felt as if some hidden spell had reached out and gripped her and turned her to stone. She felt that while her body was held motionless, she was falling away from herself, into some deep chasm. With a tremendous effort she opened her eyes again and spoke aloud, although her voice was not quite steady. ''Well, I cannot know that, can I? I can only do what I can do—what I can guess to try—because I am the one who is here. *I* am the one who is here. Perhaps it will make a good nursery tale someday.''

She let her trowel fall into her lap and cupped her poor hands together, and the quick soft liquid rush of the salamander's heat comforted her. But there was a juddering or a tingling to the warmth that sank through her skin and ran through the rest of her body—like the pinprick thumping of numberless tiny impatient feet. She knew the rhythm of those steps; they were the steps of someone going back to check she'd latched the chicken-house gate, when she knew perfectly well that she had, or those of a nursemaid going to fetch the third clean handkerchief in as many minutes, trying to send her small charge to a party clean and combed and well dressed. ''I am sorry, my friend,'' she said to the salamander in her mind. ''I suppose I am rather like a chicken or a small child—to a salamander." There was a little extra thrill of heat between her palms—the nursemaid saying, *You had better not lose this one*—and then it was gone.

She rose to her feet again, laying down her basket and dropping her trowel, and moved towards the edge of the clearing. She put her hand on a convenient tree and paused, because she did not wish to lose herself in the wood, but she leant beyond her tree, peering into the tangled black wilderness where the starlight could not reach.

She felt almost as if there were gentle fingers rubbing her neck softly, then just touching her temple, to turn her face to look in the right direction. . . . The fingers were gone, if they had ever been, but there was a meadow before her—though the trunk of the tree was still beneath her own hand—and animals grazed there: ponies, horses, cows, and sheep. The meadow was large, larger than she saw at first, for it was dotted with clumps of trees, and she could see narrow bridges of grass through greater stands and thickets that led into other meadows.

She did not see the old woman for a little while, for she was hidden behind the flank of the cow she was milking. She heard her singing first, but since it was a song she often sang herself, she thought she was only hearing its echo in her own mind: "And from her heart grew a red, red rose, and from his heart a briar."

The old woman stood up, her head appearing above the fawn-coloured back of the cow, and as she rounded its tail and the rest of her came into Beauty's view, Beauty saw the pail of milk in one hand and the stool in the other. She walked carefully to the next cow, sat down on the stool, and again began to milk and to sing; she had the voice of a young girl, sweet and joyous.

Now Beauty could see the entire process: the old woman's head half buried in the cow's flank, the slight movement of each wrist in turn, the faint quick twinkle of the streams of milk. It was only then that Beauty began to see what she had assumed to be piles of earth or stones in the long flowery grass were small leggy sleeping heaps of calves and lambs and foals. Two lambs lay on top of their dozing mother not far from Beauty's tree, looking very like the cow-parsley they lay among.

Beauty still stood in starlight, but she looked onto a morning scene and felt the sleepy summer heat of it against her face and against the hand on the cool trunk of the tree. She did not think her feet could be made to move, out of the starlight and into some strange dawn, but there was a great peace held in this meadow, like water in a lake. She wished she had a goblet, or a ewer, and might dip it up, like lake water; she could smell it where she stood, a fresh morning smell, mixed in with the warm smells of grass and grazing animals. She stretched her other hand out and felt something—something—something just brush against her fingertips that was neither sunlight, nor starlight, nor grass, nor tree. She closed her eyes to concentrate, and the sensation became just the tiniest bit like velvet, just the tiniest bit like someone's breath, just the tiniest bit like whiskers. She opened her eyes.

It was a unicorn, of course. She was expecting that. Its eyes were deepest gold-brown-green-blue and held her own. What she was not expecting . . . she could see the meadow through the rest of it. As it bowed its head to settle its muzzle more snugly into her hand—carefully, for its luminous horn stretched past her shoulder—she saw it as she might see leaf shadows moving across the meadow, except that these shadows were dappled silver-white, instead of dappled dark, and the shape of them was not scattered, like tossing leaves on wind-struck branches, but formed quite clearly the long beautiful head, the graceful neck, the wide-chested body, the silken mane and curling tail, the exquisitely slender legs of the unicorn. If it were not for the eyes and the faint whiskery velvet against her hand, she might have thought it was not there at all.

In the back of her mind—in the part of her brain and body still in the bonfire clearing in the middle of the night—a voice said, What makes you think you are seeing anything but the shadows cast by your own fancies? The meadow, the old woman, all the grazing beasts and their little ones,

the serenity, tangible as a warm bath smelling of roses at
the end of a long weary day, all this you think you see is
because you live alone in a huge haunted palace with a huge
haunted Beast, whose secrets you cannot guess. All you see
is only because you miss Rose Cottage, you miss your sisters, your father.

What makes you think any of it is there?

And the silver-dappled shape before her shivered like
smoke, like cloud beginning to uncurl itself into some further metamorphosis of the imagination; perhaps it would
become a lion, a sphinx, a rose-bush. . . .

But a tiny singing voice in another part of her mind answered: *I know* it is all, all there, all as I see it. And the
unicorn raised its nose from her hand and breathed its warm
breath into her face, a breath smelling of roses, but light and
gay and fresh, as exhilarating as spring after winter, but with
a faint sweet tang a little like the smell of apples after rain.
The currents of air touched her skin like rose-petals; it
breathed into her face and vanished.

But her eyes had adjusted now, and she saw the old
woman, moving very carefully indeed with a full pail, walking towards the edge of one of the bigger stands of trees,
and in the dark shadows under their branches, she saw the
silver shadows. The old woman turned, just before she entered the dark-and-silver shadows, and, framed by them,
looked towards where Beauty stood, as if she knew someone
watched there. She was too far away for Beauty to see her
plainly, but Beauty thought she had the face of a friend, and
she was strangely reassured by that brief indistinct glimpse
of the old woman's face, as if some memory of long-ago
comfort had been stirred. Then the old woman turned away
again, and the silver shadows parted to let her through.

Beauty knew that was all. She dropped her head, and her
hand from the trunk of the tree, and there were the wild
woods close round her again, and the only light was from
the stars, and the air was chill. She took the few steps back
to her basket dully, but as she stooped again beside it, it
was already full, full of the darkest, sweetest, richest compost she could imagine; and her unused trowel lay beside

it, its clean blade winking in the starlight. She scooped up
a handful of her basket's contents and crumbled it between
her fingers; it smelt of earth and kept promises. There was
still a wink of gold in it, like no ordinary farmyard fertilizer,
telling her where it had come from, but it was as if two
seasons of weather and earthworms had already sieved and
stirred and transformed it into something she and her rose-
bushes loved much better than gold. She could almost hear
it sing: *And from her heart a red, red rose. . . .*

"I will never be able to shift the basket," she murmured.
"It must weigh more than I do." She put the unused trowel
in her pocket. Then she took a deep breath, and put her
hand under the peak of the basket handle, and stood up. The
basket came up too, as lightly as if it were empty.

She walked slowly through the bonfire glade, the
carriage-way, and went at once to her glasshouse, and ran
her free hand along its framed panes—*slide-bump-slide-
bump*—as she walked between it and the palace wall, because her glasshouse would not change its length to dismay
her. But she went on putting each foot down very carefully
and breathing very gently and regularly, for she was still
half afraid that the midnight magic that was carrying the
basket for her would take fright at her mortal presence so
near it and run off.

When she came to the glasshouse door, she went in at
once and set the basket down with a happy sigh. The starlight seemed brighter in here than it did in the courtyard,
despite the white reflecting walls of the palace and the pale
stones underfoot, despite the black stems of the roses and
the wild labyrinthine structure of the glasshouse itself,
whose shadows fell on her like lace. She walked round her
rose-beds, dropping a handful of her beautiful compost at
the foot of every rose-bush. She smoothed it with her other
hand, so that it formed a little ring at the base of each. After
each handful she returned to the basket for the next; her
trowel remained in her pocket, nor did she touch the hand
fork lying on the water-butt. The last handful went to the
dark red rose blooming in the corner. The basket of compost

went just around, one handful for each, not a thimbleful was left; but that last handful was just as full as the first. There was no room in her heart and mind for words, even for a song; she was brimming over with joy.

She went slowly, baffled by happiness, upstairs to her room, where a bath awaited her; reproachfully, she thought, as her filthy skirt was very nearly whisked out of her hands as she pulled it off. "Now, you stop that," she said, light-headed and blithe. "What am I for if not to rescue the Beast's roses?"

But there was a sudden frantic shimmer in the air as she spoke, as if something almost became visible, and the breath caught in her throat; she opened her eyes very wide and stared straight at it—tried to stare at it—and then screwed her eyes up to stare again, but whatever the something was, was gone.

She shook her head to clear the dizziness, and then lay down in the bath and closed her eyes. When, a little later, she put her hands on its rim, to rearrange her position, she knocked into something with her elbow, opened her eyes, and discovered a tray sitting over the bath, with a little round loaf, a little round cheese, a pot of jam, and a pot of mint tisane upon it. But it reminded her of one of Jeweltongue's peace offerings, and she did not know whether to laugh or cry. Crying won, and her joy was all gone away in a rush, like bathwater down a drain, and even meeting unicorns was nothing in comparison to the absence of her sisters.

"It will all come right soon," she said to herself. "Soon. The roses will grow again, and then I will be able to go home." But this did not comfort her either, and she wept harder than ever, till she frightened herself with the violence of her weeping, and stood up out of the bath, and wrapped herself in several towels, and went to kneel by the little fire. Its heat on her face dried her tears at last, and she returned to the forlorn tray laid across the bath, and lifted it with her own hands, and set it down by the fire.

She began to eat, realised how hungry she was, and ate it all, wiping the last smear of jam from the bottom of its

pot with her finger, because the jam spoon wasn't thorough
enough. She was by then only just awake enough to remember to divest herself of her towels and put on her nightgown
before she crept up the stairs to her bed.

CHAPTER
11

She had no dreams she remembered. She woke, with daylight on her face, to a faint cheeping noise. She lay, still half asleep, her eyes still closed, with the bedclothes wrapped deliciously round her, and thought about things that cheep. It wasn't a bird sound. She knew that immediately. It wasn't exactly familiar, but it wasn't totally strange either. It didn't sound at all dangerous or threatening or—or— It did sound rather near at hand however. Near enough at hand that if it was something she did not want to be sharing her bed with . . .

She opened her eyes. Fourpaws had made a nest in the elbow between two pillows and had scrabbled up a hummock of coverlet to face it. She lay with her back against the pillows, and with the sun behind her—and shining in Beauty's face—and with the hummock of the coverlet in the way as well, it took Beauty a moment to comprehend the tiny stirrings that went with the cheeping noise: kittens. Fourpaws responded to Beauty's eyes opening, followed by her rolling up on an elbow and breathing a long ''Oh!'' by beginning to purr.

There were four of them. They were so small it was impossible to guess very much of what they would become,

but three had vague stripes and looked as if they might take
after their mother's colouring, and the fourth was as black as
the Beast's clothing. Beauty stroked each with a finger down
its tiny back, and Fourpaws' purring redoubled. Their eyes
were still fast closed and their ears infinitesimal soft flaps, and
their legs made vague gestures as if they believed that the air
was water, and they should attempt to swim in it.

Fourpaws leant over them and made a few brisk rear-
rangements, and the cheeping stopped and was replaced by
minuscule sucking noises.

"Oh, Fourpaws, they are beautiful!" said Beauty, knowing what was expected of her, but speaking the truth as well.
"I am so glad that this palace should have kittens in it! I
only wish there were many more of them!"

Fourpaws stopped purring long enough to give Beauty a
look like the edge of a dagger, and Beauty laughed. "You
will produce more kittens if you wish, dear! And not if you
don't wish it. You needn't look at me like that! I always
want more of anything I think good; it is a character fault!"

She almost missed Fourpaws beginning to purr again, because as she said, "I always want more of anything I think
good," she remembered her adventure of the night before.
"Oh—I must see—no—no, not yet. I mustn't go into the
glasshouse today at all— Oh, no, I can't possibly wait all
day! Till this afternoon then. Late this afternoon, when the
light begins to grow long, and the glasshouse is at its most
beautiful anyway, because the light is all gold and dia-
monds." She turned back to Fourpaws and her kittens. "Oh,
but whatever will I do till then? I can think of any number
of things in this palace I should like to see a kitten unravel—
supposing I could find any of them again—but your children
are a little young for it. Well."

She climbed carefully out of bed—Fourpaws' nest was
directly blocking the bed stairs—poured herself a cup of tea,
and came back to the bed to drink it in company. The second
time she maneuvered round the kittens to the bed stairs, once
she was on the floor, she tried to push the stairs over a little;
it was like trying to shift the palace by leaning against one
of its walls. "Here," she said. "If the magic that carried

my basket last night is anywhere in call, I could use a little help.'' As she stood looking at the stairs, there was a faint singing in her mind, and a half sense like a vision approaching, like the odd sensation she'd had just before she saw the meadow with the old woman milking her cows. She put her hand against the side of the stairs, and they moved softly over and settled again. ''Thank you,'' said Beauty very quietly. The singing sensation faded and disappeared.

She spent as long as she could at breakfast—which wasn't very. Fourpaws and her kittens fell asleep, and Beauty couldn't bear her fidgety self near that peaceful scene. She dressed and ran out to the chamber of the star, but then thought again and tried to take her time in the corridor on the way to the courtyard. She curtsied to the painting of the bowl of fruit, which today hung opposite the lady who used to hold a pug dog, and then a fan, and now a bit of needlework in a tambour; Beauty examined her after her impertinent curtsy, and the lady looked stiff and offended, but then she always did.

Beauty opened the doors of a red-lacquered cabinet and closed the doors of a secretaire inlaid with mother-of-pearl. She moved an inkstand from another secretaire to a low marble table, and a tray from one sideboard to another. She set matching chairs facing each other instead of side by side; she turned vases and small statues on their pedestals and plinths; she flicked the noses of caryatids holding up mantelpieces. She twiddled and fiddled, poked and patted. She remembered the Beast's warning to stop when she wished to look round, and the stopping let her fool away a little more time. She thought of having kittens with her.

She thought she noticed, or perhaps it was only her own mood, that the shadows did not seem to lie so thick in the palace rooms as they generally did; even in daylight, darkness tended to hang in the corners like swathes of heavy curtain. She did notice that there was no speck of dust anywhere she looked, no smudges of handling or of use, save what she left herself, and the floors, when she strayed off the carpets, were as impeccably brilliant as if the polisher had only just slipped out of the room as Beauty came into it.

She stepped at last into the courtyard, feeling as if she had bees buzzing in her brain. She scuffed her feet in the pebbles, and then looked up; there were big clouds in the sky today, for the first time; it had been clear every previous day she had been here. She saw shapes in the clouds she did not wish to see: Rose Cottage, her sisters' faces. Lionheart's hair was long again, and the cloud that was Jeweltongue held out her arm, and Beauty saw a great ruched, embroidered sleeve such as she had worn when they lived in the city. She looked back at their faces. She did not want the sisters who had lived in the city, she did not want the person she herself had been when they lived in the city.

But the clouds had shifted and her sisters had disappeared. For a moment longer she saw the door of Rose Cottage, framed with roses, and then it too was pulled apart and became a scud of cloud fragments.

The weather vane glinted when the sun broke through.

Finally Beauty wandered into the orchard to look for the Beast. She did not want to tell him what she had done, and she was afraid her mood would betray her into saying something, but she felt she could bear her own company no longer. She thought again of the Beast's solitude—his solitary imprisonment—here; how had he borne all his own moods, with no one, ever, to talk to?

She found him under a different apple tree. "What is the weather vane that spins at the top of the glasshouse, do you know?" It was the first harmless remark she could think of. She wanted too to tell him of Fourpaws' kittens but felt it was Fourpaws' privilege to make that great announcement, and she did want to know about the weather vane. It had intrigued her since she had first come to this place. Even at the peak of the glasshouse it was not so very far away, nor was it so very small, that she should not be able to make some kind of guess at what it represented. The shape seemed very clear and fine and detailed, and then there were all the small curls and chips delicately cut out of the inside of the silhouette; these should have given it away at once. But they did not.

The Beast turned and looked towards the archway, but from where they were standing they could not see the court-yard. "Would you like to examine it?"

"Oh yes—but how?"

"How is your head for heights?"

"I do not mind heights," said Beauty, remembering her efforts to help Lionheart poke the sitting-room chimney clear from the roof.

"Do you not?" said the Beast thoughtfully. "I dread heights. When I am painting on the roof, I am careful not to let my eyes wander. But if you do not mind them, I think we can find a ladder."

He looked preoccupied for a moment, and then his face cleared, as if he had received the correct answer to a ques-tion, and he led the way back towards the arch but stood aside that she might precede him through it. When they made their way round the side of the glasshouse facing the archway, they found a ladder already in place, braced against the silvery architecture that held the panes, nowhere touching the glass, and it reached to within an arm's length of the distant weather vane.

Beauty set her foot on the lowest rung. Her heart was beating a little quickly, for she had never climbed anything half so tall; Rose Cottage's roof had been her limit. But she did want to see the weather vane. She looked up; white clouds were still scudding merrily overhead, but there was no breeze in the courtyard, surrounded by the palace walls.

"I will hold the base," said the Beast.

"Thank you," she replied, and mounted quickly, before she could have second thoughts.

She was above his head at once and climbing past the slender silver girder that marked what would have been the first storey, had there been any floor or ceiling; climbed on, and then on and on. It was farther—higher—than she'd real-ised, looking up from ground level. She thought of the long, long staircases inside the palace and the fact that her glass-house stood taller yet. And she took a deep breath, ignored the beginnings of rubberiness in her legs, and of ache in her lower back, and climbed on.

She began to feel the wind up here; it tugged at her hair
and teased her skirts, but it was a little, friendly wind, whis-
tling to itself a thin gay tune. Her heart was still beating
quickly, but now from the speed of her climb and with excitement. She paused a moment; her leg muscles were growing stiff and clumsy, and she couldn't risk being clumsy this
far up. This was the final stretch of her journey; the glasshouse was narrowing gracefully towards its little cupola at
the peak of its third storey, and she suddenly didn't want to
hurry to its end. She deliberately looked away from the
weather vane, saving the moment she would see it till she
was at the very top of the ladder, of her adventure. She
looked round her instead.

She was above the flat roof of the palace here and could see
in all directions. First she looked at the roof itself, hoping to
have some provocative glimpse of the Beast's work from this
distance, not knowing if she might see anything at all; perhaps the gorgeous roof was a nighttime enchantment.

Directly in front of her lay an expanse of pure white-grey,
with the same shimmery surface of the walls and the pebbles
in the courtyard. She was facing the front wing, with the
formal gardens beyond; she could just see the farthest edge
of them. To her left was the wing that contained her rooms;
to her right the bonfire glade. She looked closely at the roof
immediately before her—having to look round the final peak
of the glasshouse and the weather vane itself, whose shape
tickled her peripheral vision—till she was satisfied she could
see no glint of any color in its confusingly reflective surface.

Then, her heart sinking a little, she looked to her right,
and there was nothing there either. Very calmly now, like a
polite child who believes no one has remembered its birth-
day, she turned her head to look left. . . . Down the centre
of that wing of roof to about halfway ran a slender stream
of colour, curving precisely round invisible islands that were
only blank spaces to Beauty's eye. It widened at its left-
most end, and Beauty tracked it round that corner, turning
carefully on her rung of the ladder, to look at the final wing
of the palace the one that had lain behind her, the one that
was backed by the orchard.

The buffet to the sense of sight was so powerful that for a moment Beauty felt she was tasting, touching, smelling, and hearing what she looked at as well. Here was something like the coloured version of the wild geometry of the glass-house; she could see the exuberant complexity of shape and design not merely covering the flat roof from edge to edge but splashing up the low balustrade; in places it spilled over the top and made little pools of vividness there.

Wherever she looked, her eyes were drawn both farther on and back the way they had come, as every figure, every contour she saw held its individuality only in relation to every other one. And looking, she wondered, if she looked at the glasshouse more intently, might she see the tales of stars and heroes written in the silver struts and the clear glitter of the panes? Perhaps she had only to learn how to see them. One hand of its own volition loosed its hold on the ladder and slipped off to touch softly the nearest pane of the glasshouse; it was the same caress she used when she touched her little embroidered heart.

The life and vibrancy of the coloured roof were the greater in contrast to the palace it crowned—as if, having risked much to gain entry to the dread presence of the sorcerer, one found his hydra in the kitchen wearing an apron and baking teacakes. Why had she only seen the roof at night? She must ask the Beast to allow her to come up during daylight. She looked back at the single tendril of colour running down the second wing of the palace roof. Suddenly it was easy to see it as a long stem of some wandering rose, easy then to see it arching round a familiar doorway and small leaded windows Lionheart had once thought too small, and now she seemed to make out the two corner bushes, guarding the front face of the house. . . .

She took a tight little breath, and held it, and turned herself round on her ladder till she was facing the wing beyond which lay the bonfire glade, but the glade itself was hidden by the height of the palace. She climbed a few more rungs and turned again; she hooked her left arm through the ladder and leant against it. She still could not see the glade, and the forest seemed to begin immediately outside the wall. She

shivered a little and looked again towards the front gardens,
but there was the wild wood pressing against its boundary;
it sprang up just behind the wing containing her rooms, as
it did behind the wing opposite.

She craned her head to look again over the orchard wing,
ignoring the painted roof. There she could see the farther
trees in the long grass of the meadow, kindly spreading fruit
and nut trees, not the dark menacing trees of the forest;
beyond them she could see the wall of the vegetable garden,
and a slip of the beds inside, visible beyond the wall, and
beyond the far wall, the fields of corn . . . and beyond that,
the horizon beginning to blur with distance, so she could
not be sure, but it seemed to her that there too the wood
held the outer margin.

There was no sign of human habitation anywhere, no thin
wisps of smoke as if from chimneys, no landscape muddled
with little boxy shapes that might be farm buildings or
houses; nothing but fields and the tangle of close-growing
trees. She shivered again and turned a sigh into a reviving
gulp of wild air. The breeze was kicking up a little more
strongly, perhaps because she was now so high; she found
she wished to cling to the ladder with both hands against
its pestering.

She turned to face front again to make the clinging easier—still looking carefully round the weather vane—and
stared at that far edge of the front gardens, the forest edge.
This was also the wing that contained the gates closed
against any courtyard entry: the gates that were so profoundly closed Beauty could barely find the cracks between
door and frame with her fingertips in daylight, when she
was awake and alert and looking for them, where at night,
half asleep or half ensorcelled by the magic of this place, her
head full of the Beast's painting and the stories it told, she had
thought she had seen an old woman leave a basket . . . had
thought she had seen her walk down the length of the courtyard to be welcomed at the edge of the wild wood by shapes
of silver shadow. . . .

Stop that! Beauty said to herself crossly. Do you expect
an enchanted palace to take its place in ordinary human

geography, that I should be able to track its location by finding Longchance a morning's brisk walk away just to the north and east, and Appleborough just visible, because I know where to look, in the northwest?

But the roses, said a little unhappy voice in her mind. If— if you did not see the old woman—if you did not see the unicorns—what about the roses?

Beauty remembered the walk back from the glade last night, carrying or not-carrying, the heavy basket; the crumbly, sweet-smelling stuff in her hands, spreading it carefully round her hopeful bushes, her decision not to go in the glasshouse this morning, to let the magic work.

If anything since Father came back from his journey to the city has happened, she replied to the voice, then that has happened. But her hands, clutching the rung of the ladder, trembled, and she involuntarily looked down, trying to peer through the slope of the glasshouse beneath her ladder, looking for new leaves, for new green stems, even for snippets and hints of flower colours. . . . But she turned her eyes away again almost at once. I will not look, she said. I have done what I could. I have worked hard, I have done my best, and it is now up to . . . to . . . to the magic. *It can touch nothing living.* But the unicorn had breathed into her face, breathed the breath of a living creature.

Still her heart was heavy, and she tried to find the path through the wood that had led her to the parterre, the grand front facade of the Beast's palace; but she could not. I should be able to find the double row of beeches, even in the wild wood! she thought. No, no, it is not like that here, just as I cannot see Longchance, though it must be near at hand. It is only the way this place is. And the tears that crept down her face were only the result of the wind.

She turned finally to the weather vane. She was a few rungs from it still, and these she climbed, and sat sideways on the topmost one, so that she would look at it level, the two uprights of the ladder enclosing her and giving her a little protection from the still-freshening wind. She and the weather vane were the two tallest points for as far as she

might see, but she was no longer looking out; she was gaz-
ing at what she had come to see.

It was the profile of a woman, with a great sweep of hair
behind her, as if belled out by the wind, and in her hands
she held the stem of a rose, whose head pointed away from
her; this was the narrow finger Beauty had glimpsed looking
up from the ground. The rose was half open and cut so
carefully that the smith had let little lines of light peep
through where the edges of the petals would curve round
the heart of the flower, as the woman's hair had been cut
so that light gleamed through the windblown strands. The
woman held the stem against her breast, as if it were growing from her heart.

Beauty reached out and touched it.

There was a great ringing gust of wind from somewhere
which nearly knocked her off her precarious perch. In her
delight at the weather vane, she had let go with both her
hands; the hand that had not reached out to touch the vane
was laid flat against the short roof of the cupola. As the
wind grasped at her and pulled and shook her, she seized
the vane, first with one hand and then the other, and then
she was lying facedown over the square pyramidal peak of
the glasshouse, her arms wrapped round the base of the
vane, her cheek flat against the glass and her forehead
against her upper arm, while the wind shrieked and pried at
her fingers, levered itself under her body like human hands
plucking at a cloth doll, and rattled the heavy ladder where
it stood.

The sky darkened, and the wind swelled further, and its
shriek became a roar, and she felt the first drops of rain on
her back, huge, heavy drops, striking her like stones. She
clung where she was, the vane turning this way and that
above her head; she felt the vibration through the pole she
held. She was weeping now, her sobs lost in the sudden
storm; even if the wind died away as abruptly as it had
begun, she would not have been able to move, and knowing
this, she was even more frightened. And now she could feel
the ladder jolting under her hip, with a slow, regular jolt;
she supposed the wind would have it off altogether soon.

She must have lost consciousness. The wind's roar dulled, though she still heard it, and it still shook her where she lay, but not so strongly. But she no longer seemed to be lying down, but sitting, sitting in a straight-backed chair; she was in a small, comfortable room, with a great many other people. . . . As she looked round, she reordered her labouring thoughts and realised that it was a small room only in comparison to the rooms of the Beast's palace and crowded only in comparison with their emptiness; there were about twenty people in it, which would have been a small intimate group when the sisters had given parties in the city.

I am dreaming, she thought, as I have dreamt before. And then she saw her father standing at the front of the room, one hand on the mantelpiece, the other holding a little clutch of papers, and he was reading aloud:

> *"Yours while I live, and yours still, though I die*
> *I sign, and seal this letter with a sigh. . . ."*

The wind hurled itself down the chimney, and a little puff of sparks and ash fell onto the hearth-rug; it flung itself at the windows till they rattled in their frames, and the curtains moved uneasily in the draughts. But the audience never stirred, listening to the reader with all their attention; only Beauty jumped in her chair, feeling the rain beating her down, the wind clawing at her. . . . She seemed to be at the end of the second row, on the centre aisle. When she started, a cat, which had been lying on the hearth-rug just out of range of any misbehaviour on the part of the fire, sat up and stared at her. This was an orange marmalade cat, with great amber eyes almost the colour of its coat.

> *"While Reason hesitated, Love obeyed.*
> *No foe withstood him, nor no friendship stayed. . . ."*

Beauty had difficulty attending to every word; her hearing was full of wind and rain; she seemed to drop in and out of the story, as the young man faced the cruel father and the

wealthy baron to save his true love, and it was the lady
herself who, ignored in the ensuing mêlée, slipped between
the men, pulled the dagger from its sheath at the baron's
thigh, and, as he turned to shout at her, sweeping his sword
round to menace her, ducked, and thrust it between his ribs.

The wind howled like a pack coursing a tiring stag;
Beauty could hear nothing else. But the lovers had escaped.

> *"Their hoofs, so quietly the horses strode,*
> *Scarce stirred the pale dust of the moonlit road."*

Everyone applauded. It was a friendly noise, and for a
few moments it drowned out the sound of the storm outside.
Beauty saw Jeweltongue stand up and go to embrace her
father, and then everyone applauded again, and there was
Mr Whitehand, the baker, standing up beside the place
where Jeweltongue had been sitting, and then everyone was
standing up and applauding, except Beauty herself, who
seemed to be bound where she sat, and the marmalade cat,
still perched on the hearth-rug staring at her.

The applause tapered off but was replaced by excited conversation. Beauty could follow little of it—there was an animated discussion going on to one side of her about what
sort of dagger the bad baron was likely to have been carrying in an exposed thigh sheath—but she thought she recognised the woman who was their hostess by her proprietorial
manner; and by the dazed but good-humoured look of those
listening to her, and the size of her parlour, she guessed this
was Mrs Oldhouse, the woman Jeweltongue had described
as Mrs Words-Without-End.

There was a lull, and Beauty heard a single voice clearly:
Mrs Words-Without-End was saying that there was a small
supper laid out in the next room. As she turned to indicate
the way, her glance fell on her marmalade cat. "Oh!" she
said. "Our ghost must have joined us; how very interesting;
usually she is very shy. It must be the weather; it makes me
feel quite odd myself. How the wind bays! Did anyone sit
on the end chair of the second row?"

There was a general negative murmur.

"Well Becky," said Mrs Words-Without-End to the cat, "do try to make her feel at home, since you are the only one who can see her this evening, and I cannot believe your unwinking stare is the best way to go about it." There was a blast of wind that Beauty felt might almost drive the rain through her skin; Mrs Words-Without-End gave a little "Oh!" and clutched distractedly at her collar, fidgeting with a brooch and the lace spilling round it.

"Supper can wait a little," suggested someone behind Beauty.

"It's the perfect night for a ghost story," someone else said cajolingly.

"Yes—yes, I suppose it is," said Mrs Words-Without-End, still fidgeting and looking at the rain sluicing down the nearest window. "It is a very romantic story . . . although I daresay it may have improved over time and telling. My grandmother said this happened before her grandmother's grandmother's time, when there were still greenwitches living all about here, and at least one sorcerer. Well, you all know that part of the story, do you not? There are a good many versions of it about, and many of them do not agree about what the—the definition of the problem was, but they all agree that the beginning of it was a sorcerer.

"So many problems do start with a sorcerer. My grandmother said that this one was even more vain, and unfortunately more powerful, than usual, and he grew very jealous of a certain young man who also lived in this neighbourhood and who was himself a very great—a very great philosopher. That is, that is what he chose to call himself, a philosopher, although in fact he too was a sorcerer, but a very unlikely one. Do you remember that my father collected folk-tales? He was particularly interested in this one, because it was in his own family. My grandmother told me the story, but it was my father who told me that he had never read nor heard of any other sorcerer who did not care for magic in itself at all, who declared—as this sorcerer who called himself a philosopher did—that it was a false discipline which led only to disaster."

Mrs Words-Without-End's voice had steadied and grown

stronger as she went on with her tale, but she still stared at the rain. "Well! The sorcerer wasn't having any of that from some young upstart, especially a young upstart who was far too admired by people who should be admiring the sorcerer— the sorcerer who gloried in his sorcery—and so the sorcerer began to plague the young man's days, in little ways to begin. But the young philosopher was such a scholar that he barely noticed, and this made the sorcerer mad with rage, because he hated above all things to be overlooked, and he hated the idea that he would have to exert himself over this dreadful young man, instead of throwing off a few tricks carelessly, as one might set a few mouse-traps. This was worse than being told that magic was a false discipline.

"Now, the philosopher's servants were quite aware that the sorcerer was to blame for a variety of the little things that had gone persistently wrong in their household of late and began to talk among themselves as to what they might do about it, because an angry sorcerer would shortly make all their lives a misery, if indeed he left them their lives, which he might not, because angry, vain sorcerers are capable of almost anything.

"They decided to ask a greenwitch for advice. A greenwitch of course hasn't nearly the power of a sorcerer, but a good one is often very wise or at least very clever, and this one was a good one, and she liked the young philosopher herself, because he loved roses, just as she did.

"The greenwitch might have done what she did out of friendship's sake only, but there were other things about the sorcerer which disturbed her. The first one was merely— what was he doing here at all? Sorcerers—even sorcerers— have a place—something like a place—in a city or at a mayor's or general's elbow, but there is nothing for them in a small town in the middle of nowhere, unless the sorcerer has a fancy to enslave the inhabitants without any interference from someone who might be able to stop him. And the second one had to do with her friend the philosopher. She had an idea that he was pursuing some course of study that an ordinary sorcerer might find very valuable, did he find out about it, and she was very much afraid that this sorcerer

would find out about it and that her friend would be able to
do nothing to stop him exploiting it, any more than a country scholar could stop an army from using his notes on the
forging of steel for hoes and rakes on the forging of swords
and cannon.

"And so, when her friend's servants came to her with
their story, she was almost ready for them.

"I have told you the sorcerer was very vain. One of the
ways he was vain was that he thought himself very handsome—which he was—and that he was irresistible to
women, which he was not, because women surprisingly often have minds of their own, and besides, sorcerers are a bit
scary for lovers, aren't they? You never know when one
might tire of you and turn you into a fish-pond, or a toasting-
fork, or something. So the sorcerer often found himself short
of mistresses since, like many vain men, he grew bored with
everyone but himself rather quickly.

"The greenwitch outdid herself. She made a woman—a
simulacrum, of course, not a real woman—she made her out
of"—and here, for the first time, Mrs Words-Without-End
hesitated—"rose-petals. She was of course very beautiful—
the simulacrum, I mean. She had to be, because the sorcerer
would only look at her if she were beautiful, but she was
beautiful in a way that was . . . not human, because she was
not human, of course, but that made her beauty unique. The
sorcerer enjoyed possessing unique things. . . ." Mrs Words-
Without-End's voice sank. "It is only an old tale, and I'm
a foolish old woman to be repeating it."

"No go on," came several voices, and after a pause Mrs
Words-Without-End continued: "Well, at first all was well.
The sorcerer fell passionately in love with the simulacrum,
and the simulacrum declared she was bored in the country
and wished to live in the city, and such was the binding that
the greenwitch . . . somehow . . . laid on her that he agreed
to the change, and indeed, he did very well in the city, which
was full of people eager to be impressed by him, even if he
did sometimes have to share them with other sorcerers.

"But the simulacrum, the poor simulacrum . . . The
greenwitch had put no end to the spell; she could not, for

she was doing something she could not do, and it had done
itself. She was not human, the simulacrum, so she could not
love and hate and wonder and worry as humans can, but
she had lived for a long time with the sorcerer and had come
to see that as human beings went, he was not a good one;
and she grew lonely without understanding what loneliness
was. The sorcerer had had many mistresses since they came
to the city, of course, because that was the sort of man he
was, but he retained a sort of fondness for the simulacrum
and never turned her into a fish-pond or a toasting-fork, but
gave her fine rooms, and clothing, and jewels, and maidservants, and everything he felt a woman should want, and
left her alone.

"But one day he came into her rooms without warning,
after he had not visited her for years, and he found her
weeping for loneliness. He had never seen her weep. But
she was not weeping tears; she was weeping rose-petals.

"He was a sorcerer; if he had not been blinded by her
beauty and his vanity, he might have seen what she was
long ago. As it was, he suddenly understood everything, and
then his rage was . . . beyond anything.

"Her he blasted where she sat, and there was no woman-
shape there anymore, but only a pile of rose-petals. It was
enough that he destroy her; he knew the trick played was
none of hers. He struck her, and he left. He left the city and
went north, where he had a vengeance to pay."

Mrs Words-Without-End paused again, and again eager
voices urged her on: "This is a tremendous story! Why have
we never heard it before? You have been holding out on us!
Go on, go on!" But when Mrs Words-Without-End took up
her story again, she spoke very quickly, as if she wished to
be done with it.

"The simulacrum was not dead, for she had never been
alive, except as petals on a rose-bush. And the petals she
became were just as fresh as the petals the greenwitch had
gathered many years ago to work her spell. Rose-petals do
not necessarily die when they fall from their flower; they
may lie dreaming in the sunlight for days and days. These
particular petals had been a woman—or something like a

woman—for very many years, and the dreams they had, lying in beautiful rooms in a grand house in a city, were quite different from the dreams they might have had, had they fallen off their rose-bush in the greenwitch's garden and lain there in the summer sun, and wind, and rain.

"Perhaps it is easiest to say that they were no longer rose-petals. Somehow they warned the greenwitch what had happened. Perhaps they spoke to her in a dream. But the result was she had warning—not enough, not much, but a little. The greenwitch had known—had to have known—what she risked by deceiving a sorcerer. And she had to have known that if—when—he discovered the truth about the simulacrum, his rage would be very terrible, and more terrible still if he understood that a mere greenwitch was responsible. But his rage was even greater than that which is to say that in the moment of revelation, when he saw what he had carelessly believed to be a woman weeping rose-petals, he guessed as well that the philosopher he had despised—had hated—had indeed been pursuing some course of study that the sorcerer would have found very useful, that he would yet find very useful, just as soon as he had his revenge.

"Quickly the greenwitch threw up what defenses she could, and they were little enough; but she was still clever, if perhaps not as wise as she had thought she was on the day she had gathered rose-petals to make a simulacrum. She had not time to send word to the young philosopher, who was now nearly a middle-aged philosopher, but she had time to throw some kind of spell over him and his house. . . ." Mrs Words-Without-End faltered to a halt and looked round at her audience.

"You see the story does not have a proper ending. The sorcerer meant to blast both the greenwitch and the philosopher off the face of the earth, which he would certainly have been able to do had he come down on them without warning. But blasting people leaves traces. There were no traces. The philosopher disappeared. His servants woke up one morning and found themselves lying in a field. Their master and his fine house were gone. It took a little longer to discover that the greenwitch had disappeared too—and not merely gone off on one of her collecting expeditions, to return when she chose. But the sorcerer had also disappeared. My grandmother said he's the reason no magic will settle here—but there are many tales told about that; why should this one be the right one?—that it was what he did that has left this place so troubled that no good magic can rest here. She said that it's only the rose-bushes the greenwitch planted at Rose Cottage that have held Longchance safe from worse—even though they'll only bloom when a greenwitch lives there."

CHAPTER
12

Mrs Words-Without-End went to Jeweltongue, who was standing, looking stricken, and seized her hands. Her father gripped Jeweltongue's shoulder; Mr Whitehand stood close at her side. Mrs Words-Without-End said: "It is only a silly tale, the silliest of tales. I forgot myself in the pleasure of your father's reading of his most romantic poem. It is all nonsense, of course, as silly tales are—"

Jeweltongue said, stiffly, as if she were very cold: "And the ghost? You never told us who the ghost is."

"Yes!" said several voices at once. "Who is the ghost?"

Mrs Words-Without-End said to Jeweltongue: "The ghost is the ghost of the simulacrum. Sometimes she is nothing but a breath of the scent of a rose on the air, especially in winter. Sometimes you can just see her, but often only as a kind of shadow, a silhouette, of a woman with long hair, holding a rose to her breast, as if its stem grew from her heart. I saw her often when I was a little girl—I had seen her several times before my grandmother told me the story— and then it was as if she went away, oh, for twenty years or more. But then she came back, about ten years ago now. . . ."

"But why does she come to you?" said a voice.

Mrs Words-Without-End said to Jeweltongue: "My father was a kind of cousin to the philosopher who disappeared. My father's great-great-great-great-great-great-grandfather inherited the philosopher's other properties, including this house. I've always lived in this house. I made my poor husband come here when I married him. I might have made him change his name, except that he is a cousin too, and already had it. I—I have been afraid that if one of our family no longer lives here, perhaps the ghost will no longer have a home; and if she needs a home, I wish her to have it. I—I don't know what possessed me to tell the story tonight. I do believe the storm has crept into my head and disarranged all my thinking. I have never told it to anyone but my husband and my daughters, once they were grown, when our ghost returned after her long absence. Except that . . . it has seemed to me lately that she is around much more than she ever used to be. Even my husband has seen her several times, in the last several months, and he had never seen her before. And she seems to be restless in some way; I have even felt that she has been asking me to do something, and the only thing I can think of to do for her is to tell her story."

Beauty heard the rain pounding against the windows and the wind thundering as if it would have the house off its foundations, and she felt as if the wind and the rain were dragging and drumming at her, and wished she could hold on to her chair for comfort; but she could not move her hands. She seemed only able to move her eyes, and she stared at Mrs Words-Without-End, stared as the marmalade cat stared at herself, as if she could not look away. A gust against the wall of the house made her quiver, and she had to blink, and blink and blink again, as if rain were running into her eyes. I am dreaming, she told herself again. There is nothing to be frightened of; it is only a dream; I will wake in my bed, I will wake in my bed in . . .

As Mrs Words-Without-End fell silent, the sound of the storm seemed to swell; the lash of rain against the house struck like a blow from something solid as a bludgeon, and it poured down the windows with a heavy splash like a bucket overturned on a doorstep. Everyone in the room had moved slowly towards the front, to be near Mrs Words-Without-End as she told her story, as if attracted by some irresistible force, and now seemed fixed on the sight of Mrs Words-Without-End with her hand holding Jeweltongue's, staring into her eyes, and the dumb, amazed look on Jeweltongue's face; and with the muffling of all other sound by the bellow of the storm, everyone started and looked round in alarm when someone threw back the half-closed doors at the rear of the room.

Beauty still could not stir. She turned her eyes, and her neck consented to move slowly, slowly, slowly, but still not so far that she could look over her shoulder and see who—or what—had arrived. Mrs Words-Without-End seemed to shrink away from whoever it was; she put her arm round Jeweltongue's shoulders, but whether she wished to comfort Jeweltongue or herself it was impossible to say.

Beauty felt a tap on her shin and looked down; there was the marmalade cat, patting at her leg, as if asking to jump into her lap. Beauty's lips slowly shaped the words *Oh, yes, please,* though she had no voice to utter them, nor could she have made herself heard now over the storm bar shouting; but the cat understood, and leapt up, and trod her skirts into a shape it liked, and lay down. Beauty gave up trying to look over her shoulder and, automatically trying to bend her arm to cradle the cat, discovered that she could, and with the first touch of warm fur on her skin a little life seemed to come to her, as if she were in this room in truth instead of only in dream. And as the intruder strode down the aisle towards Mrs Words-Without-End and the little group on the hearth-rug, she was able to turn her head easily and watch.

''The weather has held me up, or I would have been here sooner,'' he said, speaking in an authoritative, carrying voice, which rode over the storm like a practised actor's over hecklers. He took off his wide-brimmed hat and gave it a shake, sending water fanning out over the empty chairs on the side of the aisle away from Beauty. Beauty saw Mr Whitehand's fists clench at his sides.

"I was delighted when I heard of your little literary occasion, and I planned to come—I know you would have sent me an invitation had you known I was interested—because I have a story to tell too."

Beauty had recognised the man now: Jack Trueword, the squire's eldest son. She had only seen him once or twice, in Longchance, riding his glossy highbred horse, looking faintly amused or faintly bored, staring over everyone's heads, perfectly certain that everyone was looking at him, because he was the squire's elder and handsomer son. Beauty remembered him chiefly for that conviction of his own fascination, which he wore like a suit of clothes; to her eye he had never been more than a good-looking, spoilt, idle young man. But tonight she looked at him and was afraid, as if the spirit of the storm had entered the room in the person of Jack Trueword. His face was animated, but his smile was so wide as to be a grimace, his eyes were too bright, and his sharp glance moved jerkily round the room. He walked and turned and made his gestures with a barely restrained energy, as if with every motion he had to remember not to knock people down and hurl the furniture through the windows or into the fire.

He tossed back his hair, held his wet hat delicately in one hand, and shrugged out of his cape, deftly catching it with his other hand. He gave the cape a spin, and this time Beauty was spattered by the wet, though she did not feel it. The cat on her lap did and interrupted her purring with little bass notes like growls. If anyone looked at me, thought Beauty, and I am a ghost, where is the cat sitting? Is she floating a handsbreadth in the air?

But no one did look at her; everyone was looking at Jack Trueword. He laid the cape over the back of a chair, and the hat upon it, with a flourish worthy of the villain in a penny pantomime.

"I think I heard the rather interesting end of a story Mrs Oldhouse was telling, as I was entering. Something about a ghost—a woman made of rose-petals—and a sorcerer. Quite a flamboyant mix, perhaps—just the thing for a literary company." He strolled up the rest of the aisle and turned on the hearth-rug. "My story has perhaps some elements in common with it." The marmalade cat stopped purring.

"Mrs Oldhouse," said Jack Trueword solicitously, "you look tired. Indeed, if you were to ask my opinion, I would say you look . . . drained. As if some . . . involuntary magic—eh?—had been called out of you. Perhaps something to do with that very interesting story you just told, that you have so rarely told? Magic takes care of itself, you know. I would wonder a little myself about a story of magic that so wishes not to be told. Especially here, you know, in Long-chance . . ."

Mrs Words-Without-End, and Jeweltongue and her father, and Mr Whitehand stared at Jack Trueword as if fascinated. The others in the room began to stir and murmur, as if coming out of a trance, as if waking from some spell that had held them. They looked at one another a little uneasily and started as another particularly fierce blast of wind shook the house.

"Even the storm itself seems a bit . . . extreme, does it not?" Jack Trueword went on thoughtfully. "As though something were trying to get in. Or perhaps out. The storm is most powerful just here, by the way. When I set out from the Hall, it was merely raining. Even at the other end of Longchance the wind is no more than brisk. But when I turned through your gates, Mrs Oldhouse, I thought the wind would knock my horse off its legs.

"I am very sorry I did not hear more of your story, Mrs Oldhouse. Perhaps if I had, I would have understood it better. Sorcerers don't disappear, you know. That bit of your story doesn't make any sense—pardon me, Mrs Oldhouse. But sorcerers can be driven away or even ensorcelled themselves. You have to be very strong indeed to ensorcel a sorcerer, but it can be done. There are stories about it.

"I'm afraid I also don't accept the idea that any sorcerer would for a moment fail to recognise a simulacrum as a simulacrum—however beautiful she was—especially a sim-ulacrum made by a greenwitch. No, I'm afraid that doesn't make sense either. I'm very sorry, Mrs Oldhouse, I seem to be ruining your story. But truth is important, don't you think?

"My story begins . . . once upon a time and very long ago, but perhaps not so very far away, there were three sorcerers. I think, really, the first sorcerer was only a magician, but little the less dangerous for that, because she was so very ambitious. The second sorcerer had been distracted from the usual paths of power by his interest in immaterial philosophies. He spent his days discussing, with various citizens of various ethereal planes, how many hippogriffs can dance on the head of a pin, and such airy matters.

"The third sorcerer was a practical fellow. He too was ambitious, and his ambition had once betrayed him into carelessness: He had made the mistake of demonstrating that he was a little too clever for his own good a little too soon— and to the wrong man. He decided to move well away from the city where he had made his little mistake, and to stay away, till his name, in people's minds, and especially in that one wrong man's mind, should have lost some of its prominence.

"He had heard of a town—let us call it Longchance— quite a small town to have two sorcerers in it already, but it was attractively far away from the city he wished to leave, and rather isolated, and he did prefer to go somewhere that contained at least one or two of his colleagues, because he wished to go on studying and knew that studying in a vacuum always leads to carelessness, sooner or later. He was not going to be careless again, if he could help it.

"And so he moved to this town we are calling Longchance, and was apparently welcomed by both the sorcerers—or the sorcerer and the magician—already in residence, and all went well for some time.

"But sorcerers still have to eat, and unsurprisingly, they most often earn their bread by their sorceries. It so happens that the philosopher-sorcerer was the last of a wealthy family, which is no doubt why he could permit himself the luxury of philosophy in the first place. But the woman, sorcerer as she called herself, needed people to pay for her services, as did the third sorcerer. And after the third sorcerer had been living for some little time in his new home, she began to notice that when people wanted sorcery, they more and more often went to him; her they were only asking the littlest, meanest charms, love philtres, counterspells against the souring of milk by ill-natured persons known or unknown, herbs to take warts off or soothe croup. Green-witch sorts of things that no sorcerer should be expected to perform.

"Do I begin to see some doubtful recognition on some of your faces? We all know there is some reason no magic has settled here in a very long time. And we think we know it has something to do with some great conflict between sorcerers.

"The greenwitch—for perhaps she was only ever a green-witch—grew terribly jealous of the third sorcerer, or perhaps she fell in love with him. That she brewed a beauty potion of rose-petals is true, but she made no simulacrum. She could not have done so much. She brewed the potion for herself and arrayed herself in an irresistible beauty.

"No one recognised her, for she had been a plain woman, and both the sorcerers fell in love with her, and each wanted her for himself. But the philosopher had been a philosopher too long, and his sprites were of no use to him here. The third sorcerer won her, as she meant for him to win her. And she convinced him, for her false beauty was the stu-pefying sort which throws a shadow over its lover, that she too was a powerful sorcerer and that together they could do anything. Perhaps she even believed it herself.

"I do not know everything about what happened next. I have been researching the story, you see; something that has occurred recently brought the old nursery tale to my mind again, something I will tell you . . . a little later. But there are gaps in the story I cannot fill. I have even stolen a look at Mrs Oldhouse's father's notes—I'm sure you will forgive me, Mrs Oldhouse, as I was only seeking the truth—but I found nothing about anyone weeping rose-petals. That must be a part of the story you had from your grandmother. Women are such romancers. Well, I believe that the third sorcerer and his new mistress went off to that city the third

sorcerer had left, to confront the man who had made it necessary for him to leave it.

"The third sorcerer lost that confrontation, of course. But
he lost far more than he had over his initial mistake. He
was dying, I believe, and, in dying, was half mad with the
too-late understanding that he had been betrayed. The
woman's beauty was stripped from her, and he saw it go
and knew who she was and what she had done. In order to
save her own wretched life—for she had taken little part in
the disastrous meeting with her lover's old nemesis—she
told him that it had been the philosopher who had bewitched
her—how she lied!—that she herself had only known what
had happened to her when the spell was torn away. She said
that the philosopher had bewitched her because it had been
he who was jealous of the third sorcerer who had come and
settled on his territory, as he had long been jealous of her,
and he saw this means to be rid of them both. . . .

"And with his last strength, the dying sorcerer put a curse
on the philosopher, a curse as great as he could make it.
Perhaps he still loved the woman . . . a little, even with her
beauty gone from her. Perhaps he remembered that the philosopher had not fought so very hard for possession of the
woman; perhaps he, being otherwise made and desiring material successes, underestimated the attractions of philosophy. He wanted what the woman had said to be true.

"And he had been nearly a very great sorcerer, before he
was cut down, and the end of his strength was considerable.
He meant only to seize the philosopher, but he was dying,
in pain, and he did not manage very well. His curse blasted
not merely his supposed enemy—who, with his house, disappeared overnight, and his servants awoke the next morning in a field, just as in Mrs Oldhouse's story—but his curse
fell on Longchance as well, like shards from an exploding
cannon.

"Those shards remain. Their substance seeps into the
ground, hangs like scent in the air we breathe; our noses are
too dull for the work, but as a man will not build his house
near a stagnant bog, no magical practitioner will come to a
place that stinks of an old curse. This is perhaps inconven-

ient, you may say, but little more; Appleborough is not so far away, and there are greenwitches there, and a magician, and what use has Longchance for sorcery anyway? And you might be right—except that is not quite the end of the story.

"If everywhere that had ever had a curse thrown over it became antipathetic to magic, there would be no handsbreadth of earth left where any magical practitioner might stand. The question you must ask is, What became of the woman?

"She was caught by the edge of her lover's dying spell, like dust by the hem of a curtain, and she was swept along by it, back to Longchance, and spilled there . . . somewhere. I think, as in Mrs Oldhouse's story, she is in some sense a ghost, but in some sense she is not a ghost.

"I want you now to think back—only about thirty years. I cannot remember quite so far myself; I was in the cradle when it happened. But we came into a greenwitch again— after years, generations—without one. A greenwitch in Longchance. Rather a good one, I believe. I first remember her for her tolerance of small boys and small boys' games. I saw less of her later on, for rose wreaths do not interest me . . . and I have never needed any of a greenwitch's charms.

"She had an adopted daughter, or there was a girl who lived with her, who grew up to be a very beautiful woman. Very beautiful indeed—eerily beautiful, some said. There were stories that there was something not quite right about her. Stories that went against her. These stories persisted until she decided to leave Longchance. There is a story that she made a very grand marriage in a city to the south, but I do not know if it is true.

"Our greenwitch was never the same again after the girl left, was she? I remember my parents and aunt talking of it. She seemed to fade and to dwindle after the loss of her daughter, and she never recovered. She disappeared herself not so many years later, and greenwitches, you know, generally live a long time, and she was not a very old woman.

"There was a bit of stir created after she disappeared, was there not? When we found out that our greenwitch had

gone to a lawyer to tie up what happened to her cottage.
The cottage that legend has it had been the cottage of the
greenwitch, or magician, or sorcerer, of whom I have just
been telling you, though it had been abandoned to ruin many
years ago, till our recent greenwitch rescued it. Does anyone
know who helped her set brick on brick, lay the rafters, dig
the cesspit, thatch the roof? I have not been able to find
anyone who does. House-building is not the usual run for a
greenwitch's magic, is it?''

The room was silent. Even the sound of the storm had
dropped during Jack Trueword's story; the rain still fell
against the windows, but it made a timid, mournful sound;
the wind wept distantly like a lost child. No one inside Mrs
Oldhouse's best parlour stirred; there were no cries of ''Go
·on, go on!'' Beauty suddenly realised that the slow mea-
sured beat she heard was the tall cabinet clock in the corner.
Be Ware, it said. *Be. Ware. Tick. Tock.* She moved her cold
hands on the marmalade cat's back.

''And then,'' Jack Trueword said, his voice very low and
smooth, ''and then . . . a few years ago three beautiful girls
and their father moved into Rose Cottage. Three girls so
beautiful that Longchance was dazzled by them—were you
not?

''But wait, you are saying, Was it not two daughters and
a son? Very reassuring, that son, was he not, for all that he
was also remarkably beautiful? For by his presence we have
not needed to worry about that foolish fortune-telling rhyme,
the one that describes the final working out of the curse on
Longchance.

''You remember I told you that something had happened
recently to put me in mind of the old stories? Discretion
should forbid me to tell this part of the story, but I began
by saying that truth is important, and thus I cannot spare
myself. I found myself falling in love with . . . one of these
beautiful sisters. It was a curious experience; it was quite
like falling under a spell. Oh, you will say, love is always
like that. Perhaps it is, but was never quite like this before,
in my small experience.

''Well, I recovered; I would have thought no more about

it, except . . . very recently I found that my brother has fallen
in love with another of the sisters. But the second sister, you
will say, disappeared, rather mysteriously, some while ago
now—some story about a relative in the city, which is curious, when you think about it, that we had never heard of
any relatives in the city before; indeed the family has
seemed to have rather ill memories of their life in the city.
Well, that is the second sister. The third child, a son, works
for our master of horses at the Hall. But that son is not a
son; she is a daughter.''

Be Ware, ticked the clock. *Be Ware.* The rain tapped and
pattered; the wind moaned.

Jeweltongue took a step forward, shaking off Mrs Oldhouse's hand and her father's. "Curse? What curse? I don't
believe you.'' Tears began to stream down her face. "Lionheart mentioned a curse; I didn't believe her either. Yes,
Lionheart is my sister, not my brother. It has nothing to do
with your horrid curse; it is that she wanted to work with
horses, and she is good at that, is she not? I know she is
good at that, and she knew no one would take her on if she
were a woman, so she went as a man. What is this curse?
Your curse has cursed us, more like, for it is true—although
not as Jack Trueword says—that Beauty has not returned to
the city. What is this curse! Has it an enchanted palace, and
a Beast, and a rose?''

Mrs Oldhouse said: "A Beast? I have never heard of any
Beast. Jack, you are a bad man. I do not believe this has
anything to do with our friends''—her voice quavered—
"even if Lionheart is their sister.''

Jeweltongue said wildly: "Tell me this curse!''

Mrs. Oldhouse recited hastily: " 'Three in a bower / And
a rose in flower / Until that hour / Stand wall and tower.'
It's only a child's nursery rhyme. We used to skip rope to
it. It was our favourite skipping-rhyme because it was ours,
you know how children are.

"The three in a bower were three beautiful sisters, we
knew that, but the cur—the rhyme doesn't say anything
about their being beautiful, that's just to make it a better
story, that's what happens to stories that are told over and

over. When I was a child, and grew old enough to understand that my favourite skipping-rhyme meant something, it
was all the more delicious, do you see? Not having magic
is just . . . not having something . . . but a curse . . . Of
course the sisters had to be beautiful. And the bower, that
had to be Rose Cottage, because of the rose, even though
when I was a girl, no one lived there, and the wall and tower
were Longchance, although Longchance doesn't have any
towers, but you have to have it for the rhyme, do you see?
It's like the sisters being beautiful. And it was all to do with
some great magic that had gone terribly wrong many years
ago, and it explained why there was no magic in Longchance now, although it didn't explain it very well, but then
foretellings never do, do they? I never knew a seer who
would give you a plain answer.

"And I don't see why—really, now that I think about it—
why our old skipping-rhyme is necessarily a curse. Perhaps
it is only a prediction of how—of how it will all be resolved.
Maybe that's why it says tower—not for the rhyme but because Longchance doesn't have any, do you see? But I have
to say I don't like the sound of your Beast. What Beast? Is
it fierce?"

"Look at the cat!" shouted Jack Trueword, pointing at
Beauty and looking frightened half out of his wits, but as
he did so, the marmalade cat leapt off Beauty's lap straight
at Jack, as if it meant to do him a mischief; he threw up his
arms; Beauty said, "Oh, no!" and made a snatch at the cat
as it leapt, falling half off her chair as she did so; and Jeweltongue shrieked, *"Beauty!"*—

—and Beauty found herself falling off the top of a ladder,
struck down by wind and rain; she screamed, drowning even
the cacophony of wind in her ears, scrabbling for purchase
against the rain-slick panes of her glasshouse; her finger-
ends found eight strange little hollows in the leading of one
frame and dug themselves in, but she would not be able to
hold herself there long, sprawled against the slope, and the
wind blowing so brutally she hadn't a chance of regaining
the ladder, where her useless feet remained, just touching
the rungs—

And then there was a hand on her shoulder, and she was dragged inexorably back the way she had fallen, and her weight was on her feet again, and the wind was partially blocked by something very large bending over her, and a voice she could just hear below the infuriated wind spoke in her ear: "Beauty. I have you. Set your feet firmly on the rungs again; I will shield you. I am too heavy even for this wind to shift. You are quite safe. Listen to me, Beauty. You must come down now."

But the shock of what had almost happened still gripped her, as mercilessly as the storm itself, and she was too panic-stricken to move. When she opened her mouth to breathe, the wind stuffed it with rain and her own sodden hair. She began to shiver, and she realised she was wet to the skin and cold to the bone, and her shivering redoubled, and her hands seemed to have frozen to the tops of the ladder up-rights, she could not make the fingers move.

She whimpered, but he could not hear her, so it did not matter. And she wanted—so terribly wanted—to be off this nightmare ladder and down on the ground again. The rain and wind billowed over her, and the Beast waited, and she thought of what he had said, and she turned her head a little, and looked up; the Beast was only a blackness to her eye, but he must have seen her looking, because one great hand moved from its place below hers on the ladder uprights and wrapped itself gently round her nearer one, and with that touch some feeling and possibility of motion returned to her fingers.

He released her hand, and she stiffly brought it down to the first rung; the finger joints ached with cold and dread. She straightened her body slowly, moved her other hand to the first rung, unsealed one foot from its resting place, and stepped down to the next rung. Now she felt the Beast's arms round her, outside hers, and his waistcoat buttons brushed her back, and she felt him take a step down, to keep pace with hers.

They went down together very slowly. She still shivered, and felt as exhausted as if she had run a great race, and sometimes fumbled for her hand- or foothold, and sometimes had to stop to rest. But she watched his hands following hers, so that she did not have to look up or down, and she never stopped again any longer than she needed to catch her breath. It was a much longer journey down than it had been going up, and the wind still sang in her ears, but the words it sang were the wrong verse: *Lord Goodman died for me today, I'll die for him tomorrow.*

As her feet touched the rung below the first silver girder, the wind slammed in under the Beast's arm, like a clever swordsman finding a weakness in his opponent's guard, and seized her and flung her down, and her feet slid off the rungs, one forward and one back, and there was a sharp hard blow to one of her knees and another to her other ankle, and for a moment she did not know which was up and which down, and the wind would have had her off then had the Beast not caught her in his other arm. The wind screamed and hammered at the ladder, and Beauty stared up at the glasshouse and the tumultuous sky, and there was a cracking noise, and the top of one of the uprights was torn off, the rungs broken, and the pieces hurled down on them.

Beauty felt rather than saw one strike the Beast's back and felt him wince, but he still held her, and he still stood firm upon the ladder. Again he spoke in her ear, calmly, as if he were addressing her across the dinner table: "I fear I need both my hands to climb. But I do not think that will happen again." She nodded against his breast and put her hands and feet on the rungs again, and he released her, and they started down the last part of their journey.

The last few rungs were even harder than the first ones had been; she was sick and dizzy with the after-effects of the dream-vision of Jeweltongue, and Mrs Oldhouse, and Jack Trueword, and the marmalade cat; and she could not believe she and the Beast could reach the bottom of the ladder safely. He stepped off it first and had his hands round her waist to steady her as her feet touched the wet pebbles of the courtyard, but she slipped and slithered on the suddenly treacherous surface, and her ankles twisted and her knees would not hold her, and she was so tired her mind played tricks on her, and she was not sure but what she was still alone on the top of the ladder and feeling it shifting under her as the wind prepared to throw it down. But no, the Beast was here; he held her still.

He pointed along the glasshouse wall, and she remembered they were still standing in flooding rain, and the wind, even on the ground, was nearly strong enough to lift her off her feet; the pebbles of the courtyard scudded before it like crests torn from the tops of waves. And so they made their way together along the wall and round the corner of the glasshouse, and then at last there was a familiar handle under her hand, and she turned it and pushed, and they were both inside the glasshouse.

The storm dropped away at once, as if it had never been, as if the closing of the glasshouse door were a charm against it, or the end of a spell, and with the silence, and the sunlight now streaming through the panes, and the astonishing sight that met their eyes—and the clatter of too many thoughts and fears in Beauty's mind—Beauty forgot climbing the ladder, forgot the weather vane, forgot Mrs Oldhouse's story, and Jack Trueword's, and Jeweltongue shouting *Beauty!,* forgot the storm and the fall that would have killed her, forgot everything but what she and the Beast saw—and smelt.

For the glasshouse had come back to life indeed. There were roses everywhere she looked, red roses, white roses, and pink roses, and every shade among them, in great flat platters and round fat orbs of petals, roses shaped like goblets and roses shaped like cups, roses that displayed stamens as fine as a lady's eyelashes, roses that were full up to the brim with a muddle of petals, roses with tiny green button centres. There were red-tipped white roses, and white-tipped red ones, bright pink ones and soft pink ones that were darker at their hearts and some that were nearly white-centred; white ones that were snowy all through, and white ones just touched with ivory and cream, or the sunset-cloud tints of pink and gold; and the reds were all the tones of that most mysterious and allusive of rose colours, from the warm rosy reds like ripening cherries to the darkest black-

reds of velvet seen in shadow; and the purples were finer
than any coronation mantle.

And the smell, everywhere, was so rich and wonderful
Beauty wanted to cup her hands to it and drink it, and yet it
was not one smell, but all the rose scents discernible and individual as all the colours of roses: the spicy ones, and the
ones that smelt of apples or grapes or of oranges and lemons,
and the ones that smelt of almonds or of fine tea, and most
particularly the ones that smelt only as certain roses smell,
and they were the most varied and seductive of all.

The foliage was so thick, glossy-green or matte-, hunter
green and olive and grey-green and nearly blue, that it
should have shut out every wink of sunshine, but it did not;
the light was so bright Beauty blinked against it, and the
white roses glittered like constellations on a clear night.

"Oh," said Beauty. "Oh."

The Beast, as if in a dream, said, "I have not been here
in . . . I do not know how long. It has been a long time. I
have not come since the roses started dying."

Beauty ran forward suddenly, toward the farthest corner
of the glasshouse, and there knelt—or would have knelt—
by the one rose-bush that had still been in flower when she
had first entered here; but it was tall and strong now, as tall
as she was, and covered with flowers. She could not count
them, there were so many, or rather, she did not wish to
spend the time counting them when she could smell and
look at and touch them. She turned to examine her cuttings,
and all the little bushes were knee-high, and all had flower-
buds, and the first of these were cracking open, and at their
feet an exuberance of heartsease foamed green and purple.
She looked at her seedbed, where the seedlings were only
a little smaller than the bushes from the cuttings, and these
too bore the first tiny green bumps that would become flowers, not leaves. One precocious seedling had its very first
bud just unscrolling, and she wondered what it would be,
for while she knew the mothers of all her seeds, she did not
know the fathers. She touched it softly, and a whiff of rose
scent came to her even among all the perfumed richness

around her, and this scent was new, and not quite like any other, and while it reminded her of a scent she had once breathed standing by a meadow watching a woman milk her cows, a fine, wild, pure, magical smell, it was also unmistakably that of a rose.

She looked up, and the Beast stood near her, looking at the dark red rose-bush which had been the only one alive and blooming the day before. "I remember you," he murmured, as if to himself. "I remember . . ."

And as he said, "I remember," suddenly she remembered sitting as a ghost with a marmalade cat in her lap, and she remembered all those other dreams she had had while she was asleep in her grand high bed in the palace and had told herself in the mornings were only dreams, and she remembered Jeweltongue's voice, as the marmalade cat made its spring, saying *Beauty!* And Beauty herself did not know if she now believed that the dreams had been more than dreams or if it was only that she was frightened to think that they might be more. And, a very little, she remembered the dream she had once had so often, about a long dark corridor and a monster that waited for her—only for her— and remembered too, so faintly that it was barely a memory at all, how that dream had changed when she came to this place, and how she had hurried along that corridor to comfort the lost unhappy creature there. . . .

But the look on Jack Trueword's face was what dazzled her mind's eye now, the look on his face, and the stricken look on Jeweltongue's. Jeweltongue, who had never been overset by anything, not their mother's death, not their father's ruin, not her broken engagement; Jeweltongue, who had found Rose Cottage welcoming even on that first grey, depressing day, who had found her own skill as a dressmaker and chosen it finally over any chance of being what she had been before. Jeweltongue, who loved the life she had made in Long-chance, just as Lionheart loved her life, as their father loved his life, a life, Beauty thought suddenly with a pain like a mortal wound, that they might all lose. . . . *Has Master Jack forgiven you for preferring a short, stoop-shouldered flour-monger with hands like boiled puddings to his tall, elegant,*

*noble self . . . ? D'you want to think about what happens
next? . . . Surely you've heard that there's a curse on this
place if three sisters live in it?* She remembered Mrs Greendown saying: *The tally calls for three sisters, and there's only
the two of you.*

What if Jack's story were true?

They could not be driven out of another town, another
life. They could not do it again. It would break them, and
they would die of it, die as certainly as Beauty would have
died if the Beast had not caught her when she fell off the
ladder.

"Beast—"

He turned to her at once. "What is it? What troubles you?
Can you not be pleased with what you have done here?"
And he sank to his knees beside her and would have taken
the hem of her still-soaking skirt in his hands, except that
she twitched it out of his reach. "No, no! I will not have
you on your knees! Stand up, stand up!"

But he did not want to stand up, and she could not make
him. He rocked back on his heels and looked up at her (not
very far, for he was tall even kneeling); he was smiling,
although there were tears in his eyes, and she noticed that
he was not wearing the long black sleeveless gown she had
never seen him without. *Then we would have taken flight
indeed,* she thought, remembering the wind. But his remaining clothing was plastered to him by the rain, and she suddenly thought how much he looked like the round-limbed,
handsome Beast who stood on a pedestal in the middle of
the garden at Rose Cottage.

She almost could not ask what she needed to ask. Timidly
she moved forward again and set her hands on his shoulders.
"Will you tell me—because I believe I need to know—
what—what brought you to this place, and this—this
shape?"

His smile faded, but he remained looking up at her. "Oh,
please stand up!" she said again, plucking uselessly at his
shoulder. "If you will not stand up, I will sit down," and
she did, and drew her knees up under her wet skirts, and

put her cheek against them, and told herself the damp was only rain and nothing to do with fresh tears.

There was silence for a few heartbeats and the roses, and the sunlight, and the scent were still round them, and Beauty felt like a starving beggar looking through a window at a feast. And then the Beast said: "I told a sorcerer I believed magic to be a false discipline, leading only to disaster. It was a foolish thing to say, if not always untrue, or—I would not be as I am."

Beauty whispered, "Is that all?"

The Beast sighed, and the roses fluttered, and the sunlight came and went among the leaves. "Is it ever all? Do you want the full story of my ruin? For I will tell you, if you ask."

"No . . . yes . . . no. I do not know what I am asking." Her thoughts scrambled among fragments of truth and hope and love and fear, looking for a place to begin: There is a curse on my family—on our coming to Longchance—and it has found us out at last. Then is there not a curse on my coming here?

Why did you ensorcell me to come to this place? Or if not you, who? Who put the rose on my father's breakfast table?

If you are a prisoner here, who ensorcelled you? Who tends your garden? Who is the old woman who leaves a basket in the night in front of doors that do not open?

Why have the bats and butterflies and toads and hedgehogs returned and not the birds?

Why do you ask me to marry you when you will not tell me who you are?

Again she saw Jeweltongue's pale desperate face, heard Lionheart saying: *The Truewords do what their eldest son tells them to. . . . And Longchance does what the Truewords tell them.*

Her heart ached from the absence—the loss—of her sisters, whom she loved and trusted and *knew,* whose blood and bone were the same as her own, and to whom for that reason her first loyalty must lie. Her floundering thoughts seized on this as security: Here must her first loyalty lie.

Here. She put her fingers to her temples, feeling the blood
beating frantically there. "Oh, Beast," she said, but she
could not look at him, and her voice caught in her throat.
"Beast, you must let me go."

He stood up then. "I—"

She scrambled to her feet again too, staggering as her
head swam, but when he would catch her elbow to steady
her, she backed away from him. "You must let me go. See,
your roses bloom again. That is what you called me here
for, is it not?" she said wildly, and now the tears were
running freely down her face, but she told herself she was
only thinking of her sisters. "I have done what you brought
me here to do; you must let me go. Please." Perhaps I can
do nothing, but what comes to them must come to me too.
If we are the three named, let us at least be together for . . .
whatever happens. And . . . I must go away from this place.
If I carry this curse, let me . . . at least let me carry it away
from . . . from this place.

The Beast said, as if each word were a blow from a dagger: "I can deny you nothing. If you will go, then I give
you leave to go. I have never been able to hold you here
against your will."

"I will come back to visit you," said Beauty—the words
burst out of her. "If I can. I will come back."

"Will you?" said the Beast. "Will you?"

"Oh—yes," said Beauty, and put her hand over her
mouth to force the sobs back, but perhaps the Beast saw the
gesture as for some other purpose.

He turned away from her and snapped the stem of a dark
red rose from the bush he had spoken to only a few minutes
before. "Then take this rose. As long as it is blooming, as
it is now, all is well with me. When the petals begin to fall,
then take thought of your promise, for I will be dying."

"Dying?" said Beauty. "Oh—no—"

"Yes," said the Beast, as gently as he had said, You are
quite safe. "I cannot live without you anymore, Beauty. Not
now, not when I have had you here, not now that I have
learnt how lonely I was, and am—was—for a little while—

no longer. But as I brought you here by a lie, it is only just that I should lose you again.''

''Beast—''

Now he put his hand over her mouth, or just his fingertips. ''Listen. Pull one petal of this rose and set it in your mouth, and you will be at home—in Rose Cottage—at once. If you decide you do wish to see me again, pull another petal and set it again in your mouth, and you will at once be here. But if you wait till all the petals have dropped, it will be too late; once they have loosed themselves from the flower, they can no longer return you here, and besides, when the last of them falls, I will die.''

She put her hands over his hand, pulled it away. ''No, I cannot bear it—oh—this cannot be happening. Not like this. Not like this.''

The Beast said, ''You belong with your family. And I have forgotten too much—too much of what it is to be a man. And I had never learnt what it is to love a woman. It is too late now.

''Go.'' He pulled a petal from the rose he held, then handed her the rose. Dumbly she took it. ''Open your mouth.''

''I—''

He slipped the rose-petal between her lips. She just touched his hand again—''Oh, Beast''—but he was gone, and the glasshouse was gone, and all that was left was the feeling of the thorns of the rose he had given her stinging the palm of her hand, and the taste of the rose-petal in her mouth.

CHAPTER
13

Jeweltongue had flung herself on her knees by the chair where Beauty had sat with the marmalade cat. "Oh, she was here, she was here, I saw her, did you not see her? I cannot bear the not knowing what has become of her! I would pull Longchance down with my own hands to know that she was well!" Her head ached, and she was aware that her nose was running and that she was behaving badly, and for the first time in her life, she did not care. Beauty! She *had* been here, hadn't she? Or was it merely that worrying about her had finally begun producing phantoms of her? The ghost of a simulacrum made of rose-petals!

Jeweltongue couldn't remember ever having felt so helpless; even those last terrible weeks in the city, they had at least had one another—something neither she nor Lionheart had ever been aware they wanted or needed. And it had been Beauty then who had done what needed to be done, while all she and Lionheart could see was that their pride and arrogance had shattered like glass, and the shards lay all round them, and it was as if they cut themselves to the bone with every move they made. And so they had moved slowly, had been able to see no farther than across the room, across the present minute. They owed their lives to Beauty, and she and Lionheart both knew it.

Mrs Oldhouse, bending over her from one side, and Mr Whitehand from the other: "My dear, I did not know, why did you not tell us?" "My darling, I did not know, why did you not tell me?" And Jeweltongue weeping, weeping passionately, uncontrollably, as Jeweltongue never wept, as Jeweltongue never did anything.

A sudden sharp heavy sound, a cry, and a clatter of furniture, including the unmistakable *crack* of splintering wood, and Jeweltongue's father stood over the prostrate Jack Trueword, grimacing and cradling one hand with the other. Jack lay still. Someone in the audience laughed. "Well struck, Mr Poet!" said a voice.

Jeweltongue slowly, dazedly, turned her head. Jack Trueword lay sprawled and ungainly across Mrs Oldhouse's hearth-rug; she blinked. Her thoughts were confused by all that had happened; her chief thought now was how grateful she was that he had stopped telling his terrible story. . . . How small he looked, lying there, silent and still. It was the first time, she thought, she had ever seen him ungraceful. Jack had always had the gift of grace, even of charm, however spoilt and selfish you knew he might be in the next moment, but she had been accustomed to believe that she could ignore his bad temper. She closed her eyes. But if his story was more than just bad temper . . .

She opened her eyes and looked at him again. It was suddenly very hard to remember how frightening he had been, just a few minutes ago, telling his story. Lying in the splintered remains of Mrs Oldhouse's chair, he looked like something the storm had picked up and indifferently tossed away.

"I suppose we had best move him," said another voice, without enthusiasm, after a little, startled, general pause.

"Let him come round on his own," said a third voice promptly. "Have you hurt your hand badly, sir?"

"I, er, I fear I may have. I must . . . apologize very profoundly. It was a stupid and a wicked thing to have done. I cannot think what came over me."

"Whatever it is, I'm glad it did," said Mrs Oldhouse, half straightening, but still patting a bit of Jeweltongue's shoulder not covered by Mr Whitehand's arm, and addressing the top of her head. "If someone had done that to him years ago, he might not have turned out so mean-spirited. I could easily have done the same myself to Miss Trueword— who is one of my dearest friends, and after all, she introduced you to me—when I heard of that result of her invitation to supper. My dear, you must learn not to be so clever, it will attract the wrong sort of person—at least until you are as old as I am—but then, you will be safely married soon, so that is all right," she said, and patted Mr Whitehand's shoulder instead. "Have you really damaged your hand, Mr . . . Poet? I shall call you that hereafter, I think, it is so much more suitable than your own name. Should we call for the surgeon? The storm seems to have abated at last."

"I think that might be wise," said a man who had been examining the old merchant's hand, and Mrs Oldhouse rang for a servant.

"At last!" she said, turning back to her friends. "I am free of Great-Aunt Maude's hideous chair! How clever of you, Mr Poet, to strike him in just that direction. I suppose we might put a blanket over him. Or his cape—*oh.*" And she snatched it up off the chair. "How could I not have noticed? I will have his *skin* if that chair is ruined.

"Now, Jeweltongue, listen to me." She knelt by the young woman's side and put her hand earnestly on her arm. Jeweltongue's arms were still stretched across the seat of the chair, her head again resting upon them, but her sobs had ceased. "My dear, why did you not tell anyone? About what had become of your sister? Beauty, that is. How very astonishing that Lionheart is another girl! Then—she must be soon to be married also, I gather? Aubrey is nothing like his brother. If he's fallen in love with her, he'll mean to marry her."

"Yes," said Jeweltongue. "But Lionheart was afraid— afraid of something like what Jack did here tonight."

Mrs Oldhouse gave a very thorough and contemptuous

snort. "The storm had drowned all our intelligence, or we would never have let him go on like that. What piffle. Bringing up that old nursery rhyme and brandishing it like—like—like a little boy bringing a dead snake to scare his governess. One may very well shriek, for who likes dead snakes? . . . Except little boys. But my dear, you can't have thought . . ." She hesitated and looked genuinely troubled for the first time. "Jeweltongue, my very dear young friend . . . Lionheart was afraid, you say? But we all know what Jack is. Just as—why did you not tell anyone about—about whatever it is that has happened to Beauty? Because I gather from Mr Whitehand's response that even he did not know."

"I fear that is more my fault than my daughters'," said the old merchant. "It is I who—"

"Father, we all agreed," said Jeweltongue. "And . . . it was not only your ban, Father dear. Our life here has seemed . . . it is so different from anything we could have imagined when we still lived in the city. . . . But we have been *happy* here, do you understand? And when you are happy, when you have never been happy before, when you hadn't even known you weren't happy, it is hard to believe that it won't all go away again, isn't it? The curse seemed so . . . likely, somehow. I did not quite *not* believe it, if you understand.

"I had overheard a conversation Beauty had with Mrs Greendown—two years ago now—she had said something about a curse, and I saw how Beauty looked afterwards. And I noticed most particularly later, when Beauty told me about what she had said, and she never spoke a word about a curse."

Everyone else in the room was trying to drift close enough to the little party clustered round the end chair of the second row to hear what was being said, without being obvious enough about it to risk being sent away. Jeweltongue looked up and round at them and laughed, a laugh more like her real one, although with a catch in it. "Very well. We are caught out. I will tell you everything—anything you want to know. I am sorry to . . . not to have trusted you. But it seemed like the right thing to do at the time. We have not been here so very long, only a few, few years. Our name isn't a Longchance name—like Oldhouse, or True-word, or Whitehand. And magic—once we learnt there was none here, it seemed—it seemed rude to discuss magic with you, rather like—like—"

"Discussing hairdressing with the bald, or rare vintages with those overfond of their wine?" said Mrs Oldhouse. "Yes, I understand that. We are all used to it, of course, and quite proof against the occasional persons who wish to pretend they are superior to us for—for their perfect sobriety, and full heads of hair. I think you might have—but never mind. I do see."

"And it suited us," said the old merchant. "It suited us that there was no magic here. I have been . . . rather unreasonable about magic since my wife died. It made us—it made me, at least—feel as if we had come to the right place, this town that had no magic."

"Yes, that's right," said Jeweltongue. "And then—it seemed—Jack is right enough that our memories of our life in the city are not very good ones—and why we left—oh dear. I don't want to go into all that—"

"That is none of our business, dear," said Mrs Oldhouse. "But you are here now, not in your nasty old city."

"Yes. But you see, that's part—you have been so very good to us. We have been so happy here!" And Jeweltongue reached up to put her hand over Mr Whitehand's. "Oh, I can't explain! It seemed ungrateful, somehow, to tell you. And it meant—perhaps it meant—that we did not belong here after all."

Her voice went squeaky on her last words, and she clutched her baker's hand rather hard, but he laughed a little and bent down to say something privately in her ear, as Mrs Oldhouse said briskly: "We will go up to Appleborough tomorrow and hire the very best of the seers—I know just the one, Fareye, she doesn't meddle in looking for the future, but she can find anything—and ask her to tell us where your sister is."

Jeweltongue said, "Father? Please."

"Yes, of course," he said. "I should have thought of it myself. I don't care if it's magic. I don't think I've cared about magic one way or the other since Beauty's roses first bloomed. But I am accustomed to doing without it. And here in Longchance . . . and when you feel in your heart there is nothing you can do about something, you do not think clearly about it. And I—it was my fault in the beginning."

"No," said Jeweltongue. "To seek to save your life in a snowstorm? And enchantments are like that. You cannot know which step will spring the trip wire."

Her father smiled faintly. "I just want your sister back— as you do—or at least to know what's become of her. It's been so long."

"Seven months," said Jeweltongue. "Seven endless months. Seven months today."

"But the Beast," said someone. "Won't you tell us about the Beast?"

The marmalade cat, reappearing from nowhere, sprang into Jeweltongue's lap with a thump. "Oh!" said Jeweltongue. "Well, hello yourself!" She raised a hand to stroke it, but it leapt down again at once and trotted off towards the door. It paused there and looked back. "Do you know where Beauty is then?" said Jeweltongue, only half teasing.

The cat flicked her tail, went through the door, turned round, and just poked her head back through, staring at Jeweltongue as she had earlier stared at the empty aisle chair of the second row.

"It's only a cat," said someone.

"Hmph," said Mrs Oldhouse. "*You* have never been the intimate friend of any cat. And you do not know my Becky."

Becky stood on her hind legs to twiddle the handle of the open door with one forepaw and then sank back to the ground again, still staring at Jeweltongue. "I—I think, if you don't mind," said Jeweltongue apologetically, "I would quite like to see what she seems to want to show me."

She rose to her feet, and Mr Whitehand rose too. "I'll come with you," he said.

She looked up and smiled. "No. You stay here and wait till the surgeon comes. I want someone besides my father to tell me what he says—and someone my father will have felt obliged to listen to too, if what he says is unwelcome. Besides, I—I think perhaps—"

"If it is magic," said Mrs Oldhouse, "you will be much better off by yourself than with some dull Longchancer befogging all the—the—whatever magic does. Even you, Mr Whitehand. Go on then." She added to the cat: "Take care of her, mind. Or no more warm evenings by the fire for you."

Becky disappeared.

Jeweltongue took her cloak from the rack by the door and let herself out, Becky winding dangerously through her ankles. The night was clear after the rain, and there were stars overhead; the storm had left as quickly as it had come. Magic? Had the storm brought Beauty, taken her away again? *Where was she?* "I've never seen the stars so bright," she said to Becky. "Have you? There's the Ewer . . . and the Tinker . . . and the Peacock." She took a deep breath, trying to regain her self-possession; it seemed to have gone with the storm and the ghost of her sister. "Oh!" The night air smelt of roses, strongly of roses.

Her nose was not so good for the variations of rose scent as was Beauty's, but this odour put her immediately in mind of the dark red rose their father had brought home from the Beast's palace, which had sat for weeks on their windowsill, whose petals had at last fallen when the roses in the garden—she could not help but think of them as Beauty's roses—had bloomed in midsummer. She turned her head one way and then another, sniffing like an animal searching for water, or for danger, or for safety, and saw Becky trotting purposefully away from her. "Becky!" she called.

The cat stopped, turned her head, and looked at her. Curious how the starlight fell! The marmalade cat looked suddenly grey, and yet she stood next to a stand of black-eyed Susans, whose colour even in this faint light clearly showed orange. The cat turned away again and trotted on.

"Oh dear," said Jeweltongue, but with her first step following, the smell of roses grew stronger still, and Jeweltongue broke into a trot herself. "I hope you are not leading me into any thickets," she muttered under her breath. "I

am a good deal higher up from the ground than you are,
you know, and you are leading me directly into the middle
of nowhere,'' for the cat had gone straight across Mrs Oldhouse's gardens and into the meadow beyond, easily picking
her way across the stepping-stones in the stream at its bottom, while Jeweltongue, confused by the shadow dapples,
splashed less skilfully in her wake. Jeweltongue was jerked
to a sudden halt, and there was a sound of tearing cloth.
''Oh, bother!'' she said. ''I liked these sleeves! I should
have let Miss Trueword have this bodice after all.''

The cat trotted on, and Jeweltongue followed, her sense
of urgency increasing. In her mind there was a picture of
the dark red rose: Only a moment ago it had seemed to be
little more than a bud; now it was full open; now she saw
its petals curling back, drooping; now the first one fell. . . .

She battled her way through a thin hedgerow, and suddenly she knew where she was; this was the end of Farmer
Goldfield's land, and Rose Cottage was only a few steps
that way and through the stand of trees. ''I don't know how
you did that,'' said Jeweltongue to the cat. ''I was supposed
to stay the night with Mrs Oldhouse, you know—do you
know?—because it is much too long a walk home. Much
longer than this. Oh—'' A terrible thought struck her.
''She's not ill, is she? That isn't why you have brought me
in such a hurry—''

She began to run, but the cat was purring round her ankles, and she would not risk kicking her, and then it seemed
rude not to thank her properly. So she stooped and petted
her, and the cat purred, and rubbed her small round skull
against Jeweltongue's chin, and put her forepaws on Jeweltongue's knees, and licked her once with her raspy tongue.
Jeweltongue, looking into her face, said, ''You're not Becky
at all, you're some other cat,'' at the moment that her hands,
stroking the cat's sides, felt the soft swellings of her breasts
hidden by her silky fur. ''Ah! You're only in a hurry to go
home to your kittens. Are you Beauty's cat then?''

But the cat jumped down and ran off, and Jeweltongue
hastened the last few steps to Rose Cottage, and at that mo-

ment she heard a heartrending wail from Tea-cosy, exiled for the night in the goat shed.

At the door of the cottage she met Lionheart, with her hand out to lift the latch; she turned at the sound of Jeweltongue's approach. "You too! Tonight's your literary party, isn't it? You shouldn't be home at all—especially not walking alone at this time of night. Listen to poor Tea-cosy! What's wrong with us? I had to come."

"I don't know," said Jeweltongue. "Something about—"

"—Beauty," finished Lionheart, and pushed open the door.

She was asleep, lying as if flung on the hearth-rug, in front of the banked fire; her arms and legs were sprawled, and her hair lay across her face as if blown there by a strong wind. One hand seemed only just to have dropped a dark red rose, its petals blowsily open and near to falling, and she was as wet as if she had been out in the storm.

"Beauty," breathed Jeweltongue.

"Oh, Beauty!" said Lionheart.

Jeweltongue dropped to her knees beside her sleeping sister and picked up one cold hand and began to chafe it. Lionheart bent over them just long enough to brush the hair from Beauty's face, tenderly, murmuring, "We're like a three-legged stool with one leg gone, without you," and then knelt by the fire and began to dig through the ashes for embers worth blowing on. She said between exhalations: "I couldn't believe . . . any harm . . . had come to her . . . even though . . . I had no real reason . . ."

"But the roses," said Jeweltongue.

"Yes," said Lionheart, feeding kindling chips into her tiny flame flickers. They both glanced at the window over the back garden; even in the darkness, the ruffled· and scalloped edges of a few late roses that framed it were visible. A little wind stirred, and several of the roses tapped their heads against the panes; it was a reassuring sound. "If Beauty's roses were blooming, then so was Beauty."

Jeweltongue rose abruptly and fetched an empty jam jar, upside down next to the washing-up bowl, filled it with clean water from the ewer, and put Beauty's rose in it. "This is another one like the one Father brought, isn't it? I remember the smell. Only it's nearly gone over. I wonder what—" She hesitated.

"—adventures Beauty has had since she plucked it? Yes," said Lionheart. "But her adventure will have been nothing like Father's." She tried to speak firmly, but her voice trailed away.

"The first one lasted and lasted, as if the rose itself were enchanted. . . . Help me get her out of her wet things, and then if you'll go let Tea-cosy in before she brings the wild hunt's hounds down on us."

Tea-cosy rushed out of the goat shed and hurled herself against the closed door of the cottage. At the *thump,* Beauty stirred for the first time. Jeweltongue had been tying her dressing-gown round her. It was a new one; Jeweltongue had only just finished making it last winter, to replace the rag of overcoat Beauty had been using in the absence of anything better. She had refused to take it with her to the Beast's palace, as it was now the nicest of their three: "An enchanted palace must have dressing-gowns and to spare, or if not, I will make a velvet curtain serve." Neither Jeweltongue nor Lionheart had had the heart to use it, however, and it had hung untouched on its peg for seven months. It had been such a long time! She stopped what she was doing and stroked Beauty's cheek. "Beauty? Please, darling . . ."

The door opened to the sound of Lionheart's expostulations, and Tea-cosy launched herself at Beauty and began frantically licking her face, making little squeaking whimpers and wagging her short tail so hard her body vibrated down its full length, and between the counter-impulsions of wagging and licking, her ears seemed to spin out almost sideways, in a blur like hummingbirds' wings.

"Saints!" said Jeweltongue, trying to lift her away, but the dog, usually immediately amenable to anything any of the sisters suggested, struggled in her grip and began to burrow under Beauty's arm and side.

"Tea-cosy," murmured Beauty, trying to sit up. "I'd know that frenzy anywhere . . . you're much worse than

Fourpaws, I'd forgotten . . . don't eat me, please.''

And then there were several minutes while the sisters simply wept in one another's arms, and several more minutes
when no one could say anything in particular, and then
Lionheart got up to make tea, and Jeweltongue, Beauty, and
Tea-cosy remained in front of the now enthusiastically burning fire, and Jeweltongue's arms were round her sister, and
Beauty's head was on her shoulder, and Tea-cosy was
stretched across both their laps.

''Are you ready to talk?'' said Lionheart, returning with
the tray.

Beauty sighed and shook her head—gingerly, because it
felt so odd. She felt odd all over: Her skin was overtender
and faintly prickly, like the end, or the beginning, of fever,
and her thoughts spun stupidly in place and would not con-
nect with one another. She had a strange savour in her
mouth, as if she had been eating rose-petals. Why could she
not remember the journey here? What had happened? She
had a sense of something, of some doom near at hand, but
she could not remember what it was. She did not want to
remember. ''Why is it so dark? Is it the middle of the night?
Where is Father?''

''It is the middle of the night—when did you arrive, my
love?—and Father is in Longchance, at the—the remains of
a literary party. He read his own poem; he was very grand!
And they called him Mr Poet after! But there was, er, a tiny
accident—he's really perfectly all right—and I came on
alone.''

''In the middle of the night,'' murmured Lionheart.
''How did you know to come?''

Jeweltongue felt herself blush, but the firelight was warm
on all their faces, and none of them wanted to disturb their
own little family magic by lighting a lamp. ''Well . . . there
was this cat—''

Lionheart sat bolt upright. ''But that is precisely what
happened to me!''

Jeweltongue tightened her arm round Beauty, and Beauty
looped her arms round the front end of Tea-cosy and hugged
her, and the dog sighed hugely on a long low note of utter

contentment and fell asleep, muttering faintly in her dreams.

The sisters found in themselves a great reluctance to discuss anything at all. They were home in Rose Cottage, all together again, and it was the middle of the night. They had no responsibilities; responsibilities returned with daylight. The fire crackled; Tea-cosy kicked as she ran after a dream rabbit; the roses round the kitchen window tapped against the glass; peace pooled around them like water.

Lionheart sighed, and put her teacup down. "I will have to go back to the Hall soon. I'm sorry. Would that I had known to bring Daffodil! That's something you don't know, Beauty; when we tried to send her back with the traders, they had a note from the captain saying we were to keep her, that she was a country pony, not a city pony. So we sent half a fair purchase price south and will send the other half in the spring. She's a great favourite at the Hall. It's the first time anyone has ever seen Dora happy on horseback, riding Daffodil, which is a great thing for poor Dora, in that family.

"Beauty, please, can you bear it? Can you bear to tell us what happened? Even a little of it? Mostly—really—only— are you home—home—home for—" Her courage failed her, and she could not finish her sentence.

But Beauty, to her sisters' alarm, turned in Jeweltongue's arms and began to weep against her sister's breast. "I do not know what to do! It is all too impossible! He is very kind—and—and—oh—but his roses are blooming again, I am sure that is what he wanted of me—" Why had she a picture in her mind of the Beast saying, *Beauty, will you marry me?* Why would someone so great and grand, like the Beast, want to marry her? She was beautiful, but that would fade, unlike Jeweltongue's skill with her needle and Lionheart's horse sense. She had always been the least of the sisters, called Beauty because she had no other, better characteristic to name her as herself. She could make roses bloom—but that was the unicorns and the old woman. There was a little gap in the magic, that was all, and she had mended it, merely by being there, as if she were a bit of string.

"I am sure that is what he wanted of me, and I cannot possibly live without you and Father, but I have begun to wonder if I cannot live without—" And here her tears overcame her, and she sobbed without speaking. Tea-cosy woke up and began to lick her wrist.

Jeweltongue stroked her hair, and eventually Beauty sat up again, drawing her hand away from the dog. "You will wear a hole in the skin soon, little one," she said, and took the dog's head between both her hands, and smoothed the fur back over her skull and down her neck and ears. "Your hair is so thick and curly, after Fourpaws! I wonder if Fourpaws—" She almost said, "misses me," but stopped before the dangerous words were out. Dangerous, why? she thought; but she had no answer, only the sick, torn, unhappy feeling she'd had since—since . . . She could not remember. How had she come here? Why could she not remember the Beast's last words to her? Why then was she so sure that those last words had been important?

"Who is Fourpaws?" said Jeweltongue.

"Fourpaws is a cat I—who lives where I have been staying. She has just had kittens. She is very pretty—rather small, grey with amber flecks and huge green-gold eyes."

"But that must be the cat that I—" "But that is the cat—" Jeweltongue and Lionheart spoke simultaneously.

"I didn't finish telling you," said Lionheart. "I've been horribly restless all evening, but I thought—I told myself—it was just the storm. Molly came in and wouldn't go out again—usually she sleeps in the barn, and indeed, Mr Horsewise doesn't like her in the house; he says she has to earn her keep—but she wouldn't settle down either and kept winding through my legs and making this fretful, irritating, hoarse little mewing till I thought—with the wind and the rain and her going *grrup grrup* in anything resembling a lull—I would go mad with it.

"The storm cleared off from the east, you know; you would have had it longer in Longchance, I think. As soon as the wind dropped, I opened the door and pretty well threw her out, but when I tried to close the door again, she was standing on the threshold. If I hadn't seen her in time, I think I'd've closed it on her, because she really wasn't moving.

"But I was in a state myself by then. I had this *craving* to go back to Rose Cottage. I don't know how else to describe it. I was convinced I'd find Beauty there, you know? Only I knew that was ridiculous. But I thought a walk might calm me down a little, so I came out. Everyone else was asleep. We get up early, you know, we fall asleep early. We all have our own tiny cubbies, upstairs from the common room, so even if it's not allowed, and it isn't, if you want to slip out, it's not hard.

"Molly was thrilled, and gambolled and played like a kitten, always coming back to me and then dashing off somewhere, and I was so preoccupied with fighting my longing to come home I just followed her for something to do . . . and then discovered I was out in the middle of the woods and had no idea where I was. I would have said I know every foot of woodland around here, not just the bridle paths but the deer trails—the rabbit trails, for pity's sake!— but I was completely lost. And then I followed Molly because I didn't know what else to do.

"And then about the time I spilled out on a track I did know—the one that runs along the length of Goldfield's farm—and I saw Molly in fairly bright starlight after all the shadows under the trees, I saw it wasn't Molly. All cats are grey in the dark, but Molly is brindle-black and *white,* and the white shows. You see her white front twinkle in the dark of the barn when you're up before dawn."

"And she came up to you to say good-bye, and when you petted her, you noticed she was nursing kittens," said Jeweltongue.

"Yes," said Lionheart. "And we'd covered far more distance than we should have been able to. One of the reasons I was so cross about being lost is that we hadn't been walking long—not long enough to get really lost in. When I came out on the farm road, I was only about half an hour from here, and on foot in the dark, from the Hall, it's at least three hours. Which is why I need to leave soon. I don't suppose your Fourpaws will be hanging round waiting to take me back.''

"Half an hour," said Jeweltongue. "I guess she, Fourpaws, had to dash off to relieve Becky, who was bringing me."

They both turned to Beauty, who was staring out the window at her roses. "I can't remember," she said softly. "I remember this morning . . . and Fourpaws' kittens . . . and the night before . . . the unicorns—oh, I remember the unicorns!—and so I didn't want to go into the glasshouse this morning. There is something I cannot remember. I went to find the Beast. . . . Oh!" She sat up again, and leant forward to grasp Jeweltongue's hands. "I remember Jack Trueword—the story he told—I was afraid—have I ruined it for all of us?—Do we have to leave Longchance? I had to come back to see if you were all right—"

"If we were all right!" exploded Lionheart. "You've been gone seven months with never a word, and now suddenly you reappear because of something that conceited little fop said, and you want to know if *we're* all right? You wretched, thoughtless brute, why didn't you ever send *us* word about *you?*"

"Seven months?" Beauty said slowly. "Seven months? But it's only been seven days. The butterflies were the first morning, the day after I arrived, and then the bat, and the hedgehogs, and the spider, and the toads, and this morning was Fourpaws' kittens—seven days."

"Dear," said Jeweltongue, "it's been seven months for us."

There was a silence. "I'm so sorry," said Beauty.

Lionheart slid to her knees beside Beauty, and took her hands away from Jeweltongue, and held them tight. "I'm sorry—sorrier. I'm sorry I shouted. You would have sent word if you could—even if it had been only seven days. It's just . . . it's been so long, and we knew nothing."

"It's been so long," agreed Jeweltongue in a low voice. "And we can't let Father know how it troubles us. . . ."

"Hardest for you," said Lionheart to Jeweltongue, though she still held Beauty's hands. "We've had to pretend that we know you're all right—we're sisters, our hearts beat in each other's breasts, we *know*—and also, it's Father who has the aversion to magic. If it comes up at all, then he berates himself, and he's still not strong, you know; he's never really been strong since we left the city. So it's all been up to us. And Jeweltongue is here, day after day, every day.''

"I've dreamt of you," said Beauty. "I dreamt of Mr Whitehand—''

"Yes," said Jeweltongue. "We became engaged late in the spring.''

"And of Aubrey Trueword—''

Lionheart said suddenly: "That day Molly was behaving like a lunatic, as if she could see someone who wasn't there, was that you? When Aubrey first told me he knew I—''

"Yes," said Beauty. "And tonight—was it tonight?—I—''

"I saw you," said Jeweltongue. "I *saw* you, sitting in Mrs Oldhouse's parlour.''

"But what about Jack's story? He means us harm, if—Lionheart, I dreamt of a day when you told Jeweltongue and Father about Aubrey, but that you didn't dare, because of the curse, because of the stories people were telling about my going away . . . because of Jack—''

It was Lionheart's turn to blush. She stood up abruptly and went to refill the kettle. "I—I'm brave enough about some things. Not about others. When we had to leave the city, I thought I'd die. Not for grief, or even anger, but more from a kind of . . . amazement that the world could be so unlike what I had thought. And then . . . fear. Fear for all those things I didn't know. I would get up in the morning and look at my petticoats, and my stockings, and my shoes, and my dress, and I didn't know which one to put on first, or whether my shoes went on my feet or my head. I would decide they went on my feet from the shape. How could I live when I knew nothing?''

"Darling heart, we all felt like that," said Jeweltongue.

"And people like Jack . . . terrify me," continued Lionheart, as if she had not heard. "It's why I hated your salons so much, Jeweltongue. I'd rather face a rogue horse any day. Horses are honest. You know where you are with horses."

"You know where you are with people like Jack Trueword," said Jeweltongue. "You are in the presence of form without substance, sound without meaning, clatter without articulation."

"Stop it," said Lionheart. "If you mean dog droppings and green slime, say it."

"Wait," said Beauty. "Jeweltongue, you were frightened tonight. I saw it."

"Was I? Yes, I suppose I was," said Jeweltongue. "You see, since you went away . . . anything to do with magic, I cannot help wondering if it has anything to do with you. I keep wanting to know more about spells and enchantments, but I don't want to know, for fear what I learn will be worse than not knowing. But there is no magic in Longchance; there is no way to ask tactfully, there is no way to ask for comfort . . . and what made it worse, although not the way you mean, is that it's true Longchance has been whispering little tales about your going away, dear, but they're hopeful—and embarrassed—little tales. You see, Longchance has never quite given up the idea you're a greenwitch, because the roses bloomed for you, and while the last greenwitch disappeared mysteriously too, the roses stopped blooming when she went, and we've made no secret of it that we've had a garden full of roses this year too.

"And then, as Lionheart says, we've been so determinedly bright and sunny about your absence, everyone positively has to squint from the glare when they look at us, although I know my poor Whitehand had guessed there was something about something I wasn't telling him. . . . And meanwhile I have kept looking at your roses, and they look so—so happy, if one can say that about flowers, I've wanted so to believe they were telling me—"

"Us," said Lionheart.

"—what we wanted—badly wanted—to know. But then Mrs Oldhouse's story, out of nowhere, and with the storm pounding away at us like a monster yelling for our lives, and then Jack coming in, wet as a water spirit, and threatening us with that curse I've been worrying about for years—"

"Then you did know," said Beauty.

"After all the talking-to you gave me the day I told you about Aubrey!" interrupted Lionheart in high dudgeon, and then began to laugh. "So much for no secrets between sisters!"

She had paused, tea-kettle in hand, beside the jam jar containing the dark red rose. Its first petal had already fallen; she picked it up, rubbing it gently between her fingers for the deliciously silken feel, as she hung the kettle over the fire again. "Oh, Beauty, won't you please tell us what has been happening to you? I really must go off again—as it is, I'll be back after dawn and will have to tell Mr Horsewise something—and I will explode of curiosity if you don't. Start with Fourpaws. Why is she called Fourpaws?"

"The Beast named her. She is the only creature—was the only creature—who would live in the palace with him, and he said she must be a sorcerer in her own country, and he would not imbalance the delicate network of her powers by giving her a powerful name when she has done him the great kindness of breaking the loneliness of his house." And there rose up in her the memory of the evenings they sat together in the great dark dining-hall, and she did not remember the pressing shadows, the imprisoning silence, but the companionship of the Beast, and Fourpaws, purring, on her lap.

There was a silence, as Jeweltongue and Lionheart tried to adjust to this other sort of Beast than the one they had heard about from their father. There was tremendous relief in this new idea of a thoughtful, wistful Beast, but there was tremendous bewilderment too. "Will you tell us about the Beast?" said Jeweltongue timidly. "Surely he is a sorcerer too?"

"Oh no," Beauty heard herself saying immediately. "I—I don't know why I said that. I had assumed that he was, as you did, but lately, as I have grown to know him better . . ."

She fell silent, and in the silence Lionheart watched the second petal fall from the dark red rose.

Jeweltongue said: "Surely there is some boundary to the magic—how long to pay the debt of one blooming rose in the middle of winter? Isn't seven months enough?"

Again Beauty heard her own voice answer, speaking almost as quietly as a rose-petal falling: "He told me he cannot—that he never could—hold me against my will." She knew the words were true as soon as they were out of her mouth, but where had they come from? And why could she not remember?

Why couldn't she remember how she had left the Beast's palace and come to Rose Cottage?

Jeweltongue laughed, a laugh like a child's bubbling up from somewhere beneath her heart. "But then you can stay with us! I can finally give poor Whitehand a day! He has been very good, although—since I had not told him the truth—he has been puzzled at why my sister is quite so unspecific about when she might be able to return, only long enough to attend a wedding. I know it has occurred to him that I have not meant to marry him at all, but I do! Oh, I do! But I *could* not be married without your being here, Beauty, or, at the very, very, very least, knowing that you were well. There now, Lionheart, you can put Aubrey out of his misery too."

"We were planning on a double wedding, just like—not at all like—we were going to do in the city many years ago," said Lionheart.

"*Not* at all like," said Jeweltongue quickly, with a touch of her old acidity. "Once you finally overcame your peculiar terrors—rogue horses, indeed! It is as well I do not know the daily facts of your life, or I should not sleep for worrying!—and gave your hand to poor Aubrey."

Beauty leant over to touch Lionheart's knee. "Then you have told him yes? And that is all well? What of Mr Horsewise?"

Lionheart smiled reminiscently. "Mr Horsewise was appalled for about two and a half heartbeats, and then it occurred to him that he's been fighting off a suspicion about me almost since I'd come to work for him, and he hadn't wanted to know because if he knew the wrong thing, he might lose me, and . . . well . . .''

"Go on," said Jeweltongue. Lionheart muttered something inaudible, and Jeweltongue laughed her merry, bubbling laugh again. "Mr Horsewise dotes on her! She is the finest 'lad' he's ever had, you see, and now he not only won't lose her but is positively obliged to promote her, because Aubrey is going to take the horse end of affairs at the Hall on and run it as a business, which is deeply offensive to Jack, of course, but Aubrey worked it out with his father so that Jack can't touch it, although—''

"Although we're going to have to work like slaves to make a success of it," finished Lionheart.

"As soon as the sun is up, I'll measure you for your wedding-dress," said Jeweltongue, "that is, the dress you will wear to our wedding." Her happiness faltered for a moment, for she would have liked it to be a triple wedding, but now that Beauty was home again, surely . . . "You won't be nearly as hard to please as Lionheart, I'm sure. Oh, I'm so glad! What colour, do you think? Gold? Green? Blue? Darling, what is it?''

"Oh—my Beast. He is my friend, you see—''

"Your *friend?*" bellowed Lionheart. "Your gaoler, your kidnapper, and you have told us that he has admitted he could not keep you in the first place, so he is a liar and a trickster as well—''

"Oh no, no," said Beauty in great distress. "You do not understand at all. I will go back to visit him. I take care of his roses!''

"You have roses enough to care for here!" said Lionheart.

Jeweltongue laid her hand on Beauty's. "If the Beast is your friend, then we must—we must learn that. But it is hard for us, just now, at the beginning, especially when we haven't—haven't quite known if we had lost you entirely.''

"He never—" began Beauty. "He always—''

Jeweltongue smiled. "I believe you. Go on. We're listening." She flicked a quelling look at the more volatile Lionheart, but Lionheart was dreamily watching something

behind her and Beauty's heads. She turned to see; another
petal wavered and fell from the dark red rose, and then, after
the merest breath of a pause, a whole gust of petals.

"He is—he is—oh, I don't know how to describe him!"
said Beauty. "He is very tall, and very wide, and very hairy;
he is a Beast, just as he is named. He eats apples in two
bites, including the cores. But he is—that is not what he is
like."

"What is he like then?" Jeweltongue prompted.

"He is gentle and kind. He loves roses. He loves roses
best of all, but his were dying; the only one still blooming
was the one from Father's breakfast table. Of course, when
I knew—when I found—I had to rescue him—help them—
rescue them—him. He walks on the roof every night, looking at the stars. On the roof he has drawn the most beautiful
map of the sky. . . ." Beauty was weeping as she talked.

"My dear," said Jeweltongue, gently turning her sister's
face towards her. "Why do you weep?"

"Every night, after supper, he asks me to marry him,"
said Beauty, and she knew she spoke the truth, that it was
no mirage of memory, and then she was weeping so passionately she could speak no more.

Jeweltongue put her arms round her and rocked her back
and forth as if she were a little child. "Well—and do you
wish to marry him?"

Beauty wept a little longer, and slowly her tears stopped,
and she looked up. Jeweltongue looked gravely back at her.
"He is—he is very great, and grand, and . . . he is a Beast."

"Yes, very large, very hairy, you said. Great and grand—
foo. Are you afraid of him?"

"Afraid of him? Oh, no!"

"Well then, if he were an ordinary man, instead of a
Beast, and my darling younger sister burst into tears immediately after telling me he had asked her to marry him, I
would advise her that it is perfectly obvious that she should
say yes."

"But—"

"He is very large and very hairy, and your introduction
to each other was . . . awkward, and first impressions are so

important. Very well. What is it you dislike? That he eats apples in two bites, including the cores?''

Beauty laughed through the last of her tears. ''No, no! Although in an ordinary garden, I should want the cores for my compost heap.''

Lionheart groaned. ''You only ever think of one thing! Your roses!''

Beauty flashed back: ''You only ever think of one thing! Your horses!''

Jeweltongue said, ''Do you remember Pansy's story— many years ago, when we were still quite little, before Mamma died—of the princess who married the Phoenix?''

''Yes,'' murmured Beauty. ''I remember.''

''It is very odd,'' said Lionheart. ''Jeweltongue, d'you remember the way the rose Father brought lasted what seemed like nearly forever? It wasn't just that it was the middle of winter, was it? Look, the last petal is already falling from the rose Beauty brought with her.''

If you decide you do wish to see me again, pull another petal and set it again in your mouth, and you will at once be here. But if you wait till all the petals have dropped, it will be too late; once they have loosed themselves from the flower, they can no longer return you here, and besides, when the last of them falls, I will die.

''The last petal!'' cried Beauty, her last conversation with the Beast suddenly and terribly recalled to her mind, and she threw herself to her feet, knocking painfully into Jeweltongue, spilling Tea-cosy, who gave a little yip of surprise, to the floor, spinning in the direction Lionheart was looking, reaching for the forgotten rose there in its humble jam jar, reaching for the last petal, her hand darting out faster than her mind could direct it, but that last petal fell from its flower head before her fingers touched it, dropping softly into her palm, and she stared at it in horror. ''Oh no,'' she whispered. ''Oh no.''

''Darling, what is it?'' said Jeweltongue.

''What is it about the last petal?'' said Lionheart. ''What enchantment does it hold that frightens you so?''

But Beauty did not hear them. She looked up from the

last petal in her hand, sightlessly staring at her sisters. *When
the last of them falls, I will die.* "Do you remember," she
said, "when Father brought that first rose home, I cut two
pieces from its stem and planted them, hoping they would
strike. Did they? Did they? Oh, please tell me at least one
of them did!"

Jeweltongue put a hand to her face. "I—I'm not sure. I
don't remember. I—I am not much of a gardener, dear, dear
Beauty. Please try to forgive me."

Beauty turned and fled into the rear garden. She was so
distraught by terror and grief she could not remember where
she had put the two stem cuttings; she cursed herself for not
telling Jeweltongue to tend them particularly, for cuttings
are very vulnerable as they struggle to produce their first
roots, but she cursed herself more for not remembering—
until it was too late—for not watching her rose, the Beast's
rose, that he had given her last of all. And she looked at the
petal in the palm of her hand and saw the smear of blood
there, from clasping the stem of that rose too tightly. How
could she not have remembered?

She thought of the endless wall of the palace, the first
time she had tried to follow it to the corner of the courtyard,
to see what lay behind the glasshouse. She thought of the
first evening she mounted the spiral staircase, the basket she
had almost not found, and the storm that had come from
nowhere, as soon as she touched the weather vane.

But she had turned the corner, arrived at the top of the
staircase, found the basket, and descended from the ladder.
The Beast had carried her up the stair and guarded her down
the ladder. He would not be dead; she would not allow it.
She had sent butterflies and bats and hedgehogs and toads
into the palace gardens, she had welcomed kittens (and one
spider) into the palace when the Beast himself had said no
creature would live on his lands. The unicorn had come to
her, and the roses bloomed. She would not let him die.

She would not let him die. Her resolution faltered. As
soon as her sisters had told her she had been seven months
away, she should have remembered, she should have
thought at once to look at the rose. It did not matter what

her father's rose had done; she knew the enchantment that held her Beast and his roses had changed, for she had changed it. And now she was destroying everything when the Beast had trusted her. When the Beast had loved her.

Blindly she went down the centre path of the garden towards the great riotous tangle at its heart; the roses there had gone over from their full midsummer flush, but there were still a few heavy flower heads bowing their branches with their weight. She was vaguely aware, as her eyes began to focus on what lay round her, that the night's darkness was greying towards morning. Her gaze settled on the statue within that centre bed, the statue of a beast she had never been able to name; and it was a beast like her Beast, and she remembered him on his knees in the glasshouse, drenched by rain, looking up at her, smiling. But the statue was no longer standing, as it had when she last stood in Rose Cottage's garden. It was lying, curled up on its side, one forelimb over its head, looking lost, and hopeless, and as if it only waited to die. "You cannot die," said Beauty.

She heard the first bird heralding the dawn; two notes, then silence. "Tell me," she said to the poor lost Beast, held close by the thorny tangled weave of rose stems, where he could not have stirred even had he wanted to. "Tell me where your rose grows! It must have struck! I say it must have struck! I am coming back to you, do you hear me? Help me! As you made a mistake when you brought me to you, so I have made a mistake now! And as I released you from yours, release me now from mine!" *Lord Goodman died for me today, I'll die for him tomorrow.*

A second bird called. Beauty took a deep breath, trying not to begin crying yet again. I have done nothing but weep this evening, she thought. If I had wept less and thought more, I would not be—and then the tears came very close indeed, and she had to hold her breath altogether to keep them in.

She let her breath out finally and stood quietly, feeling her shoulders slump, listening to a third and fourth and fifth bird. I must bring the birds back to the Beast's garden too, she thought idly; I want to hear them singing when we stand

in the orchard together. . . . And then there was a scent on
the air she remembered, a scent unique to itself, threading
its way through all the other rose scents, heavy in the dew
of predawn, and she turned and walked down the crosspath
to the edge of a little side bed, still half invisible in the
tentative light of early dawn. And there were two tiny, rather
weakly bushes, but they were both alive, and by next season
they would be growing strongly. One of them was wisely
conserving all its strength for growing roots and leaves; the
other one held one black-red bud, much smaller than the
buds of its parent bush and barely open, open just enough
for its first wisp of perfume to have escaped. She knelt by
it slowly and touched it with the hand that still held the last
petal from the dead flower, and as she knelt, she heard her
sisters come up behind her.

She did not rise, but she turned her head to look at them.
"Give me your blessing, please," she said, "and know that
I will come back to you when I can. But I must go back to
my Beast just now, for he needs me most. Jeweltongue, give
your Mr Whitehand his day, and let Aubrey Trueword and
Lionheart share it, and have your wedding, and know that I
bless you in it, wherever I am. Tell Father I love him, and
I am sorry to have missed this meeting with him.

"And—and most especially know that I love you and that
it is true that our hearts beat in one another's breasts." And
for the first time in what felt like years, her hand touched
the little embroidered heart that Jeweltongue had made her,
on her leaving for the Beast's palace the first time, but she
did not draw it out from beneath her shift, and it was only
then that she realised she was wearing the dressing-gown
Jeweltongue had made for her, only last winter, that she had
refused to take with her last spring. It smelt of washing day
and faintly of dust, and she knew, even as she had known
at her leaving, that neither of her sisters would have used it
for the sorrow of her going.

She turned back to look at the little rose; it was half open
now, and one of its outermost petals was trying to curl back,
free from its sisters. "And . . . feed these two little bushes!
Give them a few of the oldest, rottenest, shrivelledest scrap-

ings from the back of the manure heap, just a few, not too many—that is what they like. Even if you haven't time to build a compost heap, you can do that. Cuttings are very tender. They must be encouraged, not bullied, into growing.'' She seized the petal that was separating itself from the others and gave it a gentle tug; it came free in her hand, and she set it in her mouth.

CHAPTER
14

She had remembered nothing of her earlier journey from the Beast's glasshouse to the hearth-rug in Rose Cottage, but after she finished speaking to her sisters and set another rose-petal in her mouth, she seemed to fall into a dream, or rather into her old nightmare dream, when she was walking down a series of long dark corridors with a monster waiting for her at the end of all. And sometimes she hurried, for pity of the poor monster, and sometimes she tarried, for fear of it; but as she walked, and ran, and walked again, her anxiety rose and rose and rose till she no longer knew if she felt frightened or pitying and compassionate, only that there was this great humming something possessing her mind and her body and her spirit. And she felt less and less able to defy it, to think her own thoughts, to wrench her own will free of it, to set down one foot after another to her own direction, and not because she was driven to do so.

"My Beast," she murmured, but her voice made no sound. She put her hands to her throat and spoke again: "My Beast. I seek for my Beast, and I know him, and he is no monster." But though she felt her throat vibrate with her voice, she could not hear her words; and then she touched one hand to its opposite forearm, and there too was a vibration such as she had felt in her throat; and now she felt it through the soles of her bare feet, an itchy, fretful, maddening sensation.

She ran again, and this time she ran for a long way, till she had to stop for weariness. But when she stopped, she stood restlessly, lifting first one foot and then the other, disliking the contact with the thrumming floor; and she could no longer say if the darkness in her eyes was from exhaustion or the dimness of the corridors she ran down.

This will not do, she thought, and she sat down on the floor with her back against one wall, and closed her eyes, and tucked her feet under the hem of her dressing-gown, and wrapped the dressing-gown as close as she could round all of her, and she tried to think. Her legs were trembling from the long run they had just had, but she could feel the humming through her seat bones, though there was no audible sound in her ears, only the drumming of blood and fear. She thought of trying to speak aloud again, but then she thought: No. I have tried that experiment, and I know its result. I will not repeat it, over and over, to frighten myself again and again, till I am too frightened to do anything at all. I must find my Beast and tell him . . . tell him . . . I must find him.

She opened her eyes and looked both ways up and down the corridor, and all she could see in either direction was more corridor, the dull figures of its wallpaper, the occasional loom of furniture or ornament, and the driblets of light from the sconces. There were no windows and no doors. The hum she felt through her seat bones, through her back, through her entire body seemed suddenly both fiendish and triumphant, and she got to her feet again abruptly. "No," she said, or rather, her mouth shaped the word, but she gave no voice to it that she would not be able to hear. "No." And silently in her mind she said: You will not have me so easily, nor will you have him.

She turned round and started to walk back down the corridor she had come up. No! No! No! shrieked . . . something. Some soundless subvibration of the hum that filled the corridor demanded that she turn round; but she had made her

choice, and now she put one slow, heavy foot down after
the other by her own will and of her own choice, and while
each footstep was very hard, dragged as it was in the opposite direction, it was also a victory for her, and the hum
changed its inaudible note and became fury.

She closed her eyes against it. She could not see it any
more than she could hear it, but in this darkness of her own
choosing she could hug herself round with her own
thoughts, her own being, her own knowledge of her self and
of her existence, as she hugged herself round with the
dressing-gown her sister had made for her. She had none of
her outer senses left: Blindness she had chosen, hearing and
touch were deadened by the noiseless vibration, and her
mouth was full of the flavour and scent of the rose-petal.
She put one hand to her lips, touched the fingers with her
tongue; here she felt no alien vibration, only the faint stir
of her breath against her own skin.

She walked forward, expecting at any moment to bump
into a wall, but she did not. And as she walked, hearing
nothing but the silent pressure of not-hearing, she thought
she began to hear some faint echo, as of wind, or footsteps
in a cavern; and she listened, hopefully, and as she listened,
she caught a faint smell—like that of damp earth—and her
toes struck against something that was neither planed wood
nor tile nor carpet fibre, and in astonishment she opened her
eyes.

She stood in complete darkness. When her eyes opened,
and she still could not see, she had stopped automatically.
She blinked several times, waiting for her sight to clear, but
the darkness remained. She held a hand up before her face
and could see it no more than she had been able to hear her
voice a little while before, and a little "Oh!" escaped her
lips without her meaning it to and . . . she heard it. I am
returned one while another is taken from me, she thought.
Well.

She put her hands out on either side of her and felt rough
crumbly wall with her right; she moved a little to her left
and found a similar wall there. She faced left and ran her
hands over the wall, and a few little earth crumbs fell away

from her touch, and she realised she was walking on bare earth, and there was grit between her toes. Her feet were still half numb from the thrum of the corridor, and inclined to curl involuntarily away from what they stood on, without recognising that the irritation was gone. She let her hands climb upwards and found the earth corridor was quite low, and over her head she felt twining, irregularly hairy surfaces that she thought—and suddenly hoped—might be the roots of trees.

She began to walk forward again, in the direction she had been going, with her hands held out in front of her. She was walking much more slowly now, not from the effort of struggling against the intangible will that had wished her to turn round but from a simpler fear of the dark, of blindness without choice. She closed her eyes again, because she was making her head ache by straining to see when she could not; the darkness seemed a little less oppressive with her eyes shut, as the hum had been a little more bearable when she did not try to speak.

But her heart had risen with that first smell of earth, and it beat more strongly now that there was no foreign vibration trying to force it to follow some other rhythm; and in her mind she was trying not to let a certain idea form itself too clearly, in dread of disappointment.

Her outstretched hands touched a smooth surface. She stopped, both because she had to and because that hopeful idea would no longer be suppressed. She ran her hands quickly over the surface that blocked her way, found its squared edges, like a door strangely set in the end of this corridor of raw earth, and her heart beat very quickly indeed. Very well, it was a door, but could she open it? And where would she be if she could and did?

A tiny depression halfway down the left-hand edge, only about the size of a fingertip, with a tiny finger-curved latch or peg within it, as if the hole were a keyhole and a finger the key; and there was a small click, and she felt the door give. She pushed it and saw sunlight outlining the crack of its opening, and a few tears fell from her dark-strained eyes,

and she stepped out from behind the summer tapestry into
her rooms in the Beast's palace.

Her strength returned to her in a rush at the sight of her
rooms; but she hesitated, and turned away from her first
impulse, and instead allowed herself a moment to stand on
her little balcony and look round her. The glasshouse twinkled in the late-afternoon sun; but for the first time the sight
of it could not lift her heart, and her only thought was to
wonder what day it was and how long she had been gone.

Then she ran out into the chamber of the star and found
all the doors open, and she chose one and ran through it,
running down the twisting corridor towards the door into
the courtyard, to the glasshouse, where she had left the
Beast.

But the corridor did not lead her there. It led her to other
corridors, to rooms, halls, staircases, antechambers, and
more corridors, more and more doors to choose, one over
another, always in hopes that the door she sought lay just
beyond. All the doors she saw were already open, but she
would not have trusted any that chose themselves for her.

Late afternoon gave way to twilight; it would be full dark
soon. She plodded on. She began to wonder if she were
merely going round and round the huge palace square, if
the occasional apparently pointless half flights of stairs up
or down were carrying her unaware over the carriage-ways
to the wild wood and the orchard, though these came at no
regular intervals; nor did any stairs seem to hold any relationship to any other stairs. She was increasingly oppressed
by the vastness of the palace and the slightness of her own
presence in it, and she recalled the evil hum of the dream
corridor changing to a note of triumph; but she was near the
end of her final strength now and of her hopes. One knee
and one ankle throbbed as if bruised, and vaguely she remembered, as if it had happened in another life, that she
had banged herself painfully against the ladder when the
wind had seized her from beneath the Beast's sheltering
arm.

Once she paused in a corridor that seemed familiar—but
so many of them seemed familiar—paused by what ap-

peared to be a stain on the carpet. There were never stains
on the carpet in the Beast's palace, any more than there were
marks on the wallpaper, smudges on the furniture, or chips
off the statues. The carpet here was crimson, solid crimson,
and unfigured, which was perhaps how the stain had caught
her eye; it was not very large, much nearer one edge of the
carpet than the other, and looked a little like a three-petalled
flower or the first unfurling of a rose-bud. The stain was
brown, perhaps a rusty brown, but difficult to tell against
the crimson of the carpet. It might have been blood. She
knelt and touched it gently, not knowing why she did so,
and opened her right palm and looked again at the three
small scratches there left by the Beast's rose.

She was now standing in a huge room with windows on
opposite walls. She had been mindful heretofore of the
Beast's advice not to look directly out any windows, and
the wearier she became, the more careful she had been not
to look round her unless she was standing still. She thought
now that she would risk looking out a window—because
she could think of nothing else to try. At least she could
discover on which side lay the courtyard, after the palace's
maze of corridors and smaller rooms which threw windows
at her from unexpected directions. The courtyard had to be
on one side or the other, whether the outer wall faced garden, orchard, or wild wood, and perhaps, at least before the
palace confused her utterly again, she could concentrate on
that courtyard wall. Perhaps the door to it now lay hidden
behind some drapery or arras, like the door to the earth
corridor in her rooms, invisible behind the summer tapestry.
Perhaps, before the palace lost her again, she would be able
to turn round, and cling to that courtyard wall, and search
every finger's-breadth till she found what she was looking
for.

She stood still, and spread her feet a little, and put her
hand on a torchère to steady herself, and looked towards a
window. But her eyes shied away from looking out and
paused on the curtain instead. Her gaze traced the sweep of
drapery, which led back towards the wall, away from the

dangerous window. There was a small square table tucked against the curtain's outer edge.

Hadn't she just seen—in the room before this one, or the room before that, or perhaps even the room before that one, which had been, hadn't it, tucked in what should have been a niche between the angled walls of two other rooms, except that there was not space enough for it to have existed at all—hadn't she just seen that little end table, that very table, with its checkerboard of marble squares of different colours inlaid in its ebony surface? And hadn't it, in that room that could not have been where it was, stood next to just that same painting of that handsome, haughty young man? He was wearing a deep blue robe and a large soft hat, that hung down towards his shoulder, with a feather that curved from its crown elegantly beneath his chin, and over his other shoulder a bird face stared with angry, intelligent eyes above its great curved beak. She did not like the young man's face. It was not the face of a man who would help you if you were in trouble.

She turned her eyes with a jerk and looked directly out the window next to him and saw the wild wood just beyond the panes, a wind blew, and the branches nodded to her like bony flapping hands.

She let go her torchère and walked across the room to be nearer the windows on the other side. She found another torchère and planted herself beside it, holding on its stem rather too tightly with one hand. There was another familiar painting near this window, of a lady who held a pug dog in one hand and a fan in the other, and her discarded needle-work lay on the arm of her chair.

She was smiling. It was not at all a nice smile.

The wild wood pressed against this window too.

Beauty closed her eyes. She thrust her tongue against the roof of her mouth, but the rose-petal had dissolved long ago. She opened her eyes again and gave a brief glance to the torchère she still clung to. It had been brass, with six curving arms when she had first touched it; the upright where her hand rested was smooth, but the six arms each held three candles, and each candle rose from a waterlily, and each arm was made as of three waterlily stems wound together, and its base, below the upright, was wide and shallow, like waterlily leaves floating in a small pond. The smooth brass upright remained, but she now clutched a torchère whose crown held eight plain upright candlesticks bound in silver, and whose base was a solid conic pedestal of brass laid round with silver bands.

She let go of it as if it had produced teeth and bitten her. She took a step away from it, and turned, and looked behind her, towards the portrait of the young man in blue. He looked older now, and his posture, proud and haughty before, was now magisterial, the supple pose of known and proven power. His fingers were slightly curled, and the palms shimmered, as if he held sorcery there. His eyes were staring into hers, and for a moment she felt a thrum in the floor beneath her feet, felt her memory beginning to grow dark, like a landscape under a storm cloud. She jerked her eyes free of his and saw that the bird that stood behind his shoulder had half spread its wings and that it was as tall as a man.

Beauty walked to the nearest window, which lay beside the lady with the pug dog, threw up its sash, climbed through the narrow gap, and slid down the outside wall. Even the palace's ground floor, where she had been, was built up high above the real ground, and she had to hang by her fingers and finally let go without knowing where her feet would strike. She landed heavily, her injured knee buckled, and because she was so tired, she fell.

She lay still for a moment, almost tempted not to move. But the ground was cold and hard, and her urgency was still on her. She stirred, with an effort came to her elbows, and looked round. A great tangle of wild wood rose all round her. She looked up, at the building she had just fled; she had no way back. The white stone gleamed vaguely in the light of the rising moon, scattered by leaf shadow. She could not feel the wind from where she lay upon the ground, but she could hear it singing through the trees. She refused to hear if it sang words; she was sure she would not like them.

Momentarily she put her head down on her forearms and

felt despair waiting outside the weakening barrier of her resolve. She was tireder than she could ever remember being, tireder even than she had been during the first days of their father's business ruin, before she found the paper telling them of Rose Cottage, and giving them something— whatever it would prove to be—to make their way towards.

She looked up again. She had fallen in a gap between trees; there was not so much of it even to be called a small clearing. Her dressing-gown had been wrenched open by her fall, and small sharp edges of forest floor clutter dug at her through her thin shift. She sat up and crept a little way to lean her back against a tree; she was curiously loth to touch the palace wall again. She did not sit long; she did not dare, for she was too tired—and she did not like the sound the wind made. It no longer sounded like singing; it sounded like the far-off baying of wolves. She pulled herself to her feet, hand over hand, up the bole of the tree, faced away from the palace, and began to force herself through the low prickly branches of the trees.

There was no path. She was lost again as soon as she had pushed her way through the first trees, as soon as she could no longer see the white wall of the Beast's palace behind her.

She probably did not go very far. She was too tired to go very much farther, and even driving herself to expend her last strength was only barely keeping her moving through this harsh, intractable undergrowth. Slender, whippy twigs slashed at her face, hooked the collar of her dressing-gown, and snatched at the silk cord round her neck. She stumbled again and pitched forward into an unexpected clearing. As she turned her head, protecting her face from the ground that had struck up at her with such alarming speed, she caught a gleam of motion in the corner of her eye.

On all fours, her foot still trapped by the root which had thrown her, she looked in that direction. She just saw the unicorn turning away from the heap on the ground it had been guarding; she just saw the iridescent gleam of its long horn before it disappeared into the trees on the far side of the bonfire glade. She could see, now, beyond the heap on the ground, a glitter of moonlight telling her where the carriage-way was.

She worked her ankle loose but had no strength to rise. She crept forward towards the heap on the ground, half knowing what she would find. It was the Beast.

He lay quietly on his side, one arm flung straight out above his head, and his head rested on it. The fingers were softly curled; his face, as much as she could see of it, was peaceful. His other hand held something to his breast. His beautiful clothes were gone as if torn from him; he wore only some still-damp shreds of his shirt, the rags of his trunk-hose, and one shoe.

She crept slowly round him, came to a halt just by that hand against his breast; his knees were slightly drawn up, so his body was curved like the crescent moon overhead. She reached out to touch his hand, and a rose, so dark in moon- and starlight as to look black, fell to the ground, the flower head disintegrating into a scatter of petals flung across the little space between the Beast and Beauty; the outliers rode up the edge of Beauty's dressing-gown skirts, like the crest of a breaking wave. She took his hand, and for a moment she thought he was already dead, for it lay heavy and motionless in hers, although it was still warm. And then, as she held and stroked it, she felt the fingers move and take hold of hers, and she heard him sigh.

"Oh, Beast," she said, and her voice was rough and husky, as if her throat were sore from all the gasping breaths she had taken over all this long day and all the tears she had shed. "Oh, Beast, my Beast, don't die. I have come back to you. I love you, and I want to marry you."

There was a noise like a thunderclap, and the ground shook, as if the lightning bolt it heralded had struck within the glen where they lay. She shrank back against the Beast's body, and his arm reached up and drew her down next to him, and they both pressed themselves against the earth as the storm broke over their heads, and yet an instant before the sky had been clear. There was a crying in Beauty's ears as of wind and wolves and birds of prey.

But the Beast's arms were round her, and they were both

alive, and she would not be afraid. She thought, This is the baying of wicked magic, but we have won. I know we have won. It can do nothing to us now but howl. And she slid her arm under the Beast's neck and held him close. It will be over soon, and I will tell the Beast again that I wish to marry him, for I am not sure that he heard.

A voice in her ear, or in her mind, for surely the wind-wolves' howling was too loud for any real voice to be heard, said to her: "That is not quite the truth, my dear, that you—we—have won. I would that it were, but I—I have had my hands full, even keeping a few little doors open—I and my moon- and starlight friends—and that is as much as we have done, and it has grown harder, over the years, for the Beast's poor heart was dying, till you came. . . . I have put a single red rose on every lost traveller's breakfast table here, since your Beast's exile began, but it was your father who was first moved to pity his great and terrible host. Ah! Strix would hate it if he knew how his cleverness—and his hatred— had worked out at last! But I am afraid that enough of him remains in the sorceries that still hold and hobble us that it is your very words now of victory, and, more dangerous yet, of love, that bring the final cataclysm towards us.

"Beauty, you must choose for the both of you, you and the Beast, and he cannot help you, and I can only help you a very little. I am only an old woman with dirt on my hands, and I will tell you, my dear, I am glad to be laying this re-sponsibility down at last, for it has been a long and weary one, though it is much of my own doing that has made it so.

"So, my dear, listen to me now. You may return your Beast to what he was before, if you wish. He was a good and a wise man then, and he will have you with him, and you will keep him mindful of the world outside his studies. He had great wealth and influence, you know, and you will have that wealth and influence again, and you will be able to do great good with it, and your names will be spoken in many lands, and you may raise your sisters and your father to greatness with you. And—have I told you that your Beast was beautiful? He was the most beautiful man I have ever seen, and I have seen many men.

"Or . . . you may take him back to Longchance, and be the sister of the baker and the squire's horse-coper son, and daughter of the man who tots up sums for anyone who hires him, and make your Beast the same.

"You choose."

Beauty was silent, her face pressed against the Beast's shaggy throat, and the wind pouring over them like a river in flood. "I think you are not telling me all of this story," she said at last, tentatively, and the voice laughed.

"You are right, but I am constrained by the . . . the strength of Strix's ancient malice, that entangles us all here. My dear, you may ask me questions, and I will answer what I may, but you have . . . released some great energies when you turned and walked the wrong way down that corridor, and even my moon- and starlight friends will not be able to maze the wind-wolves for long, and you must be gone from here before they come.

"Ask, then."

Beauty struggled with her weariness for questions to ask; but her thoughts and suspicions were as vague as smoke, and as inarticulate. She grasped at her memories of Mrs Oldhouse's tale, and Jack Trueword's; but they wove themselves together like reed straw in a caner's hands, and she could no longer tell one from the other, nor what of either she believed. "How—how is it that we are all held by this magic?"

The voice seemed to sigh. "It is your right that you know what I can tell you, and yet little of what I can tell you is what you would wish to know, and what I can tell you most of I wish not to speak of at all. . . ." The voice laughed again, but it was a sad laugh. "That sounds like a spell itself, does it not?

"There is some truth in both the stories you heard about the three sorcerers. Young Jack was right, by the way: The woman was only a greenwitch, and no sorcerer, but she never called herself anything other than what she was." The voice went on more slowly, the words shaping themselves reluctantly, hazy as images in a low grey bank of cloud;

Beauty had to listen with all her attention, half afraid the voice might become merely something she imagined. "I have earned, as I say, my place in this magic, and that I have found more peace in it than has our Beast is perhaps only that . . . well, I was old long ago, when he was still young, and I have my moon- and starlight friends, and he— he had sought perfection. He knew he would not attain it, but the striving towards it was exhilarating, and he thought he might view it and know it existed. He did not know that the viewing itself would bring him such trouble, and he has not been able to forgive himself that he was not wise enough to handle mere mortal trouble.

"There were three of us—that is true. And the man who became your Beast was my very good friend.

"He was a great sorcerer. But he was not interested in the usual sorts of power, and he called himself a philosopher. But it is not for any human to learn the first and last secrets of the universe, as other men have discovered before your Beast—before he was a Beast—did. You have heard the legends, I imagine. But your Beast was a different sort of man, and the Guardians of those first and last secrets whom he awoke were confused by him. They, who were set there when the world began, had come to believe that any man who came near enough to disturb their solitude can have got so far only through greed and pride, and they therefore are free to eat him up, hair, toenails, and all. But your Beast was not only greedy and prideful; he was also kind and painstaking and responsible, and he knew that his weaknesses were mortal and never pretended they were not.

"The Guardians did not know what to do, and when they reached out merely to block his way into the fortress they protected, and not knowing that anything would come of it but that he could come no farther into their domain, they touched him with their paws. And he, who had been a man, became a Beast—though his heart remained a man's heart. And there, I guess, is where all the trouble came.

"I believe the transformation was very painful. I did not see him till after it was done. He knew what he had become, and he was, as I said, a great sorcerer. He it was who hurled himself into this exile, before any ordinary human saw him, and I fear he was right to believe that the sight of him . . . would be very difficult to bear. But when there is too much going on at once, it is impossible to get one's spells exactly right. His exile from the human world was not absolute. Other sorcerers could still visit him. As, I admit, could one greenwitch, though this had less to do with my magical skill than with my friendship for him.

"The story of the philosopher-sorcerer who had become a Beast was soon told among all the magical practitioners at this end of the great world, and perhaps at all the other ends too. And I . . . grew alarmed at the series of sorcerers who found ways to have speech with him, for it was not merely speech they desired. They saw his transformation as a useful step on the road—their road—to power, an alternative to being eaten up, hair, toenails, and all. To be made into a Beast in exchange for power, power greater than any sorcerer had yet possessed—it was a price they were eager to pay. I think some of them felt that to be a Beast the sight of whom drove other men mad might not be a price at all.

"He would not tell them anything they wished to know, of course. And the change had . . . changed him, for he studied his philosophy no more, and what he knows, or does not know, or knows no longer, he has said to no one, not even me. And his life became a burden to him, for philosophy had filled his heart. When the sorcerers grew angry and began to plot among themselves, he could not be made to care; he would not listen to me when I told him that they believed him to have won more, in that meeting with the Guardians, than he had told, and was working some great magic in secret to ensnare them all."

Again the voice broke off. "And then . . . one sorcerer came to the Beast who was different from the others. The Beast was polite to him, as he had been polite to them all, but this one was clever enough not to ask what he wished to know, but to wait, and to watch, and . . . I knew what he was. I knew well enough. But I fell in love with him anyway. I was old even then, and I have always been plain.

"The story from this point is much like what you have heard. There was a simulacrum, except I took my own heart to beat in her breast, for I am only a greenwitch and could not do what I had done, and besides, I loved him. And it is not true that the dying sorcerer struck at the Beast for his betrayal; he struck at the Beast in fury, for vengeance; he had forgotten the simulacrum entirely, had forgotten me. . . .

"The Beast had not used his sorcery, I believe, for many years, and sorcery, like any other skill, must be often used, if a skill it is to remain. That too may help to explain why certain things came about as they did. Well, he had little enough warning, but he wished to save Longchance, if he could, and he threw his own strength into the destruction Strix had brought down upon him. Longchance survived, in the shape you know, where the earth and air and water are too restless for any magic to take root. And the weather vane—and Mrs Oldhouse's ghost—are what is left of my poor simulacrum, for she had lived too long with a human heart to return herself completely to rose-petals. And yet I think it may be she, with her half connections to both worlds and to neither, who is the heart of the magic that let you enter here.

"And the Beast himself survived. But he survived in what had become a dungeon of solitude, where no living creature could come. The simulacrum is a wisp and a weather vane and a breath of rose scent where there are no roses, and I, now, could not visit him as I had done."

"Not solitude," whispered Beauty. "For you are here, and so is Fourpaws."

"He does not know about me," the voice said, and there was great sorrow in it. "He does not know, for he would have tried to stop me, and in the beginning he would still have been strong enough to do so, like a man blocking up mouse-holes. His strength has waned—it was only the last rose, was it not?—for no human being can thrive in such solitude, not even with a cat such as Fourpaws, and I have told you his heart is still a man's. It is only because he is what he is that he has lived so long—the man he was who became the Beast he is."

"But my father—the other travellers—the butter and milk from your cows, and from—and—and the orchard that chooses to bear its fruit all year—"

The voice tried to laugh. "His dungeon is not perfect, for it is still mortal. There have always been gaps. He does not know I have widened them, pegged them open, thrust stones in their frames so they cannot blow shut. . . . I am an enterprising mouse.

"And the orchard . . . Trees feel kindness just as animals do, but they live slowly, and it takes longer than most humans live for a tree to feel human kindness and respond to it. Trees think we humans are mostly little, flashy creatures, rather the way we think of butterflies. But the Beast has lived here long enough for the trees to learn to know him."

The voice paused and then went on, sadly, reluctantly. "Your Beast also does not know that I . . . for a second time, nearly I—"

The voice stopped, and began again: "I had once hoped for a child, but I was not pretty enough, and my simulacrum could make love like a woman, but she could not bear a child. Your mother looked as if she could have been Strix's daughter—or his great-granddaughter—I do not know. Perhaps she was. It would explain why she was so interested in . . . but I would not tell her; it was then she reminded me too much of the man who had never been my lover.

"When she ran away from me, I never imagined she would marry and have children, and I almost learnt of you too late. The dream you have had since you were very small . . . I am sorry, my dear. I would have spared you it if I could have done."

"It was you, not my mother, the first night of my dream," said Beauty, with a sudden, grieving certainty, and the voice in answer sounded sad and weary: "Yes—it was I, and not your mother."

"It was you who gave us Rose Cottage," said Beauty.

"Yes—yes—that was I also. But listen to me, my dear. Listen. It was none of my doing that a blizzard brought your father to this palace; I am no weathercaster. That is sorcerer's work, and I am only a greenwitch. And still less was it I who stirred your father's heart to pity, nor was it I who gave him words to speak to the Beast which would bring you here. Nor have I anything to do with your own decision to come and then to stay. Nor, indeed, could I have saved you from your first look into the Beast's face, that first, ordinary human glance since he had ceased to be an ordinary man. You had to withstand that yourself. Bless your friend the salamander! But you see, what little I could do, I have done, and I have told you all of it.

"Your Beast's heart came to you, my dear, to you and no other, just as the animals have come to you, because you are what you are. Nor would I ever ask—nor tell—my moon- and starlight friends whom to greet. Do you not know what the breath of a unicorn is worth?"

In a gentler tone the voice continued: "I had been wandering a long time when I came back to Longchance; my old cottage was very nearly a ruin. But after your mother left—and especially when I discovered your dreaming—I began to feel that there were too many sorrows in this world that were by cause of my meddling and that I would be better off not in this world. And I have grown very old; the moon- and starlight shines through me now almost as it shines through my friends."

The voice fell silent, and Beauty thought the howling was nearer. "And the curse?" she said, or thought, for she did not put the question into words, but only felt it lying painfully in her mind.

The voice laughed, and it was a grandmother's laugh, amazed and indulgent at the antics of the young. "It is no curse! It has never been a curse! Children are more sensible than adults about many things; can you suppose that generations of children would have used it as a skipping-rhyme if it were a curse?"

Slowly Beauty found the words for her final question: "You said that if I chose that my Beast keep his wealth and influence, we should use it for good and that our names should be spoken in many lands. How will our names be spoken?"

"Ah!" said the voice, and it sounded as light and merry

as a little girl's. "That is the right question. Your names shall be spoken in fear and in dread, for no single human being, nor even the wisest married pair, can see the best way to dispense justice for people beyond their own ken."

"Then I choose Longchance, and the little goodnesses among the people we know," said Beauty.

At that moment she opened her eyes, and she saw three unicorns leap into the bonfire glade and turn, as if at bay, and she saw the wild wolves leaping after them. And there was another shock and crash of thunder, but the thunder seemed to crack into a thousand sharp echoes, and each of the echoes was the scream of a falcon or of some great owl.

But the lightning bolt was a bright blue, blue as sky on a summer's day, and it shattered as it struck, and the fragments whirled up and became blue butterflies. The butterflies converged in great shimmering, radiant clouds, and their wings flickered as they crowded together, and it was as if they were tiny fractured prisms, instead of butterflies, throwing off sparks of all the colours of the rainbow.

But then they became butterflies again, and now there were other colours among them, greens as well as blues, russets and golds and scarlets, and they flew in great billows round the wolves. The wolves recoiled, and shook their heads, and tried to duck under them, or dodge round them, and some of the wolves stood on their hind legs and clawed at them with their forefeet; but the butterflies danced round them, zealous as bees defending their honey from a marauding bear. The wolves could not shake free of them, nor see where the unicorns stood, and so the unicorns drove them from the clearing, smacking them with the sides of their resplendent horns as a fencing-master might smack an inattentive pupil with the side of his sword, pricking them occasionally as a cowherd might prod his cows, but now prancing and bouncing as if this were no more than a game, and so drove the wolves from the clearing, trailing blue and green and russet and gold ribbons of butterflies.

"Quickly," gasped Beauty, and tugged at the Beast, but he sat up slowly and groggily, moving like one who has long been ill. They would dash through the carriage-way,

Beauty thought, run for the glasshouse; she did not believe
any wolves would dare cross that threshold. But as she
thought this, more wolves leapt into the clearing, but they
came from the carriage-way, and Beauty's hands froze on
the Beast's shoulder, as she stooped beside him, trying to
steady his attempts to rise to his feet.

There was a brief soundless whirr just past her face, and
a soft plop against her bent thighs. "Oh, bat, bat, do you
know where we can go?" she said, and knelt, to give it a
lap. The bat folded its wings together and made a funny
awkward hop-hop-hop, and then it was in the air, and she
looked up, and there were many bats, more and more bats,
streaming through the trees like wind, and she saw which
way they flew. The Beast was on his feet at last, and she
held his arm, felt him sway and check himself, sway and
check again. "This way," she said, and drew him gently
after her.

There were so many bats now, they surged past them like
a river of darkness, and she could no longer see the wolves
or the unicorns or the trees round the clearing. And then
there was a smell of earth in her nostrils, and she put out
her free hand, and felt the crumbly earth wall of the tunnel,
and put her hand over her head, but could find no tree roots.
It is very kind that they should make the corridor this time
tall enough for the Beast to walk comfortably upright, she
thought, and put her hand out to the side again so she could
guide them by touching the wall. But the wall was no longer
there, and the smell of earth was mixed with the smell of
roses, and she could tell by the movement of air that they
were no longer in a tunnel.

There was a faint light like the beginning of dawn round
them, and they were standing in the middle of the crosspath
in the centre of the glasshouse, and the little wild pansies
Beauty had planted there spilt over the corners of the beds
at their feet, and the roses bloomed everywhere round them,
silhouetted in the faint light, and the white roses were shim-
mers in the gloom.

They waited, listening, clinging to each other. There was
the faint, angry baying of a fading storm—or of a pack of

wolves whose prey has eluded it, mixed with the occasional
hoarse cry of a hunting bird that has missed its strike. But
there was some other noise with it, a noise Beauty could
not identify, a noise as relentless as wind and rain, as if feet
as numerous as raindrops were marching towards them.

They looked round them, and near the door to the glasshouse there was a shape, like that of a bent old woman,
except that the pale light shone through her, and she glowed
like the horn of a unicorn, and Beauty heard the Beast give
a little grunt of surprise and delight, and she thought there
was a name in it, but she could not hear what it was. Her
attention was caught then by other lucent shapes, standing
on the square path that led round the inside of the glasshouse, and these were the unicorns themselves, waiting,
watching, poised and alert, lustrous as pearls.

And standing near the rear of the glasshouse were two
other Beasts, looking much like her own Beast, huge and
shaggy and kind, but as much bigger than her Beast as her
Beast was bigger than she. Nor were they terrifying to look
upon, but were shaped into a wholeness, a unity, a clarity,
and a tranquillity that no mortal creature may possess, and
Beauty felt a strange, shivery joy at being so fortunate as to
see them with her own eyes. Behind them, instead of the
fourth wall of the glasshouse, there seemed to stand the
facade of some immense dark fortress.

The sound of the approaching footsteps grew nearer, and
Beauty thought calmly: I cannot bear any more. I cannot.
She turned her face against the Beast's body and closed her
eyes, but she saw them anyway, the massed sorcerous army,
the winged bulls, the manticores and chimeras, the sphinxes,
not the small semidomesticated ones of her childhood, but
the great wild ones, big as the bulls they marched alongside,
who, like the bronze-winged harpies that raged overhead,
had wicked human faces, and hair of hissing asps; the stony-
eyed basilisks, the loathly worms, the cerberi, the wyverns,
like vast, deadly versions of her mother's pet dragon; and
many more creatures she could not, or would not, name.

She had pressed herself against the Beast, and the little
embroidered heart made a tiny hole just beneath her breast-

bone, guarded by her lower ribs. With every breath it seemed to dig itself a little deeper. And she lay against her beloved's heart and . . . began to feel angry. We have come through so much, she thought. Is it for nothing after all? I want to attend my sisters' wedding, I want to attend *my* wedding. If all the hordes of sorcery are here gathered to grind us to nothing, is this the way we shall be denied the small homely pleasures we desire, that we have earned? And she remembered a dry sorcerous little voice once saying to her: *I give you a small serenity. . . .*

She shook herself free of the Beast so quickly he had no time to react, shook herself free so quickly indeed that her one hand did not unclench itself in time and carried a little of the remains of the Beast's black shirt away with her, and ran to the door of the glasshouse. She ran at such speed that she had the sensation of running *through* the shining figure of the old woman. She threw the door open and stood there, facing not the palace but all the worst-omened creatures of the inner and outer worlds, and she clutched the rag of shirt in one hand and her embroidered heart in the other and shook her fists over her head and shouted: "Go away! Can you not see you have already lost? *There is nothing for you here!*"

There was another clap of thunder as if all the thunder in the ether between the worlds had clapped itself at once, and Beauty had a dazzling glimpse of what had been the sorcerous army rolling about on the ground in confusion and sorting itself out into baffled hedgehogs and bewildered toads, confused spiders, flustered crickets, bumbling bees, disoriented ladybirds and muddled grass-snakes, and hosts of other ordinary and innocent creatures.

And the air all round her was full of birdsong.

She heard the laughter of the old woman behind her and heard her voice for the last time, saying, "To think you told poor Mrs Greendown that there was no magic in your family! Bless you, my dear, and your Beast, and bless Rose Cottage, for it is yours now. I am happy with my moon-and starlight friends, and my cows, and my wild wood, and besides, I am too old now to make any more changes. . . .''

And then Beauty lost consciousness and knew no more.

She woke to gentle hands putting cool cloths on her forehead, and she opened her eyes and smiled. It was Jeweltongue who bent over her and stroked her forehead, but
there was someone else sitting at her side and holding one
of her hands, with Tea-cosy in his lap, looking there as small
as a day-old puppy.

"Your exits and entrances are so dramatic," said Jeweltongue composedly. "This time you brought with you the
most exquisite small glasshouse—it looks as if it were entirely made of spun sugar—although it has rather disrupted
the centre of the garden, where it has chosen to root itself.
But it will make the most enchanting—if I dare use that
term?—wedding pavilion, next week."

Then she looked at the person who sat at Beauty's side
and said, "I shall have my work cut out for me, finishing
your wedding-suit in time. I do not think I have a tape that
will reach round you. Fortunately I've almost finished with
Beauty's dress; we have rather been expecting you, if you
want to know. Call me if you need help keeping her lying
down. I am sure she should not get up today, but as you
may have noticed, she is a bit impetuous and wilful. And I
suspect *you* of being overindulgent." And she left them.

They were upstairs in Rose Cottage, and he sat next to
her on the floor by the wide lumpy mattress. By her feet lay
Fourpaws, her eyes half lidded and a half-grown black kitten
playing with her tail. "The first thing I will do is build you
a bed frame," he said. "It is one of the drawbacks of living
too deep-sunk in magic, that the homely tasks are all taken
away from you."

"Dishwashing," said Beauty. "I should be glad of never
doing the washing-up again."

"Then I shall do it," he replied. "But my second task
will be to restuff that mattress."

"No," said Beauty. "The first thing you will do is marry
me, and the second thing you will do is come with me to

Longchance, where we shall scour the town for painting things, for you shall not waste any more of your time on roofs, and if Longchance does not have what we want, we will go directly to Appleborough, and if Appleborough does not have what we want, then we will mount an expedition and go on a quest, and perhaps we will find the Queen of the Heavenly Mountain too. Everything else can wait a little." She sat up gingerly. "How did we come here?"

"I carried you the last way, but it was not far. When my head stopped spinning on my shoulders, and my eyes cleared of the stars that whirled round and round in them, I found us at the beginning of a little track leading through the woods from the main way, and I thought we must be there for a reason. So I picked you up and carried you here, and I understand there is to be a wedding here in a few days and that there are more people about than there generally are in preparation for it.

"But everyone rushed up to me as if we were what they were waiting for—your sisters call me Mr Beast—and welcomed me, even your father. Then I carried you up here— after I have finished with the bed frame and the mattress, I will build a set of proper stairs—to be out of the bustle below. Not, you know, that I am entirely clear about where here is, but I am sure you will tell me in time."

"This is Rose Cottage, of course," said Beauty, "where my family and I moved from the city, when our father's business failed and we were too poor to do anything else. Here Jeweltongue learnt to sew dresses that made people happy to wear them, and Lionheart learnt the language of horses and how to speak to them instead of merely to rule them, and *I* learnt to grow roses. And one sister and our father are going to live with her husband, the baker, because they do not love the country so much as they love the town, and my other sister is going to live with her husband, the horse-coper, who is also the squire's second son, and I hope we are going to live here with lots and lots and *lots* of roses."

Beauty fell silent, looking at him, and her mind and heart were so full of love for him she could at first think of nothing else. But then she remembered the first time she had looked into his face and remembered how she had needed the salamander's gift to do so, and she wondered where that terribleness had gone. Perhaps it had dropped away when he had stood once again in his glasshouse and seen his roses blooming; perhaps it had been torn from him with his fine, sombre clothing—he was presently awkwardly wrapped in a spare quilt, which made a kind of half stole over his shoulders, and it was radiant with pinks and crimsons and purples and sunset colours, for Jeweltongue had made it from bits left over from the Trueword women's frocks, and the bright colours woke unexpected ruddy highlights in the Beast's dark hair. Perhaps, said a tiny, almost inaudible voice in the very back of Beauty's mind, perhaps it left forever when you told him you loved him and wished to marry him.

But then she remembered something else she had done, and her heart smote her. "I—I had to choose for both of us—where I found you, in the bonfire glade. I—I tried to make the best choice I could. Did I—can you—are you unhappy with it?"

Her beloved shook his head. "I am content past my ability to describe. But . . ." And he hesitated.

"But what?" said Beauty, fearing the answer.

"But . . . the husband you would have had, had you made the other choice, would have been handsome—as handsome as you are beautiful. I do not know if—"

But Beauty was laughing and would not hear what he might have said. She put her hands over his mouth and, when he had stopped trying to speak through them, took them away only to kiss him. "I would not change a—a hair on your head, except possibly to plait a few of them together, so as not wholly to obscure the collar and front of the wedding-suit Jeweltongue designs. But I—I think I will choose to believe that you would miss being able to see in the dark, and to be careless of the weather, and to walk as silently as sunlight. Because I love my Beast, and I would miss him very much if he went away from me and left me with some handsome stranger."

"Then everything is exactly as it should be," said the Beast.

AUTHOR'S NOTE

My first novel was called *Beauty: A Retelling of the Story of Beauty and the Beast*. It was published almost twenty years ago.

Beauty and the Beast has been my favourite fairy-tale since I was a little girl, but I wrote *Beauty* almost by accident, because the story I was trying to write was too difficult for me. *Beauty* was just a sort of writing exercise—at first. I very nearly didn't have the nerve to send it to a publisher when I was done. Everyone knows the fairy-tale, I thought. Everyone knows how it ends; no one—certainly no publisher—will care.

But a publisher did take it, and a lot of people have told me they like it. And that was that. Of course I wasn't going to tell Beauty and the Beast again, even if it was my favourite fairy-tale. Even if it has been retold hundreds of times by different storytellers, in different cultures and different centuries. Even though I knew it had resonances as deep as human nature, as the best fairy- and folk-tales do, including a lot that I couldn't reach, though I could feel they were there.

Five years ago I moved to England to marry the writer

Peter Dickinson. I was happy in Maine, where I had been living, with my typewriter, one whippet, and several thousand books, in my little lilac-covered cottage on the coast. And then I found myself three thousand miles away, in another country, living in an enormous, ramshackle house surrounded by flower-beds and covered in wisteria and clematis and ancient climbing roses whose names no one remembered.

Gardening in Maine is an epic struggle, where you can have frosts as late as June and as early as August, where a spade thrust anywhere in the so-called soil will hit granite bedrock a few inches down and rattle your teeth in your skull, and where roses are called annuals only half-jokingly. In England garden-visiting is the top item on the list of tourist attractions—before any of the cathedrals or any of the museums, before Stonehenge or the Tower of London. I didn't plan to become a gardener, but I don't think I could help it. Peter says that the disease had obviously been lying dormant in my blood, and southern England and a gardening husband have been a most effective catalyst.

It occurred to me, now and then, as I planted more rose-bushes—because while I am a passionate gardener, I am a rose fanatic—that it's almost a pity I'd said all I had to say about Beauty and the Beast. There was so much about roses I'd left out, because I didn't know any better.

Last winter I sold my house in Maine. I still loved it, even though I knew I would never live there again, and I knew it would be a tremendous wrench to cut myself loose from that last major attachment of owning property in the country where I was born. I was not expecting, when Peter and I returned to Maine to close up, sign papers, and say good-bye, that everything I have missed about life in America as an American—which I had ordered myself to ignore while I put down roots over here—would rush out of hiding and start hammering me flat, like some of Tolkien's dwarves having a go at a recalcitrant bit of gold leaf. It wasn't just a wrench; it felt like being drawn and quartered.

We came home to southern England in a late, bleak, cold spring, and I sat at my desk and stared into space, feeling as if I were barely convalescent after a long illness.

A friend of mine who runs an art gallery in SoHo (New York, not London) asked me if I would consider writing him a short-story version of Beauty and the Beast for one of his artists to illustrate. I said no, I can't; I've said all I have to say about that story.

But as I sat at my typewriter—or looked over my shoulder at the black clouds and sleet—I didn't feel up to anything too demanding, like the novel I was supposed to be working on. I thought, I'll have a go at this short story. Something might come of it. I can do a little more with roses; that'll be fun.

Rose Daughter shot out onto the page in about six months. I've never had a story burst so fully and extravagantly straight onto the page, like Athena from the head of Zeus.

I've long said my books "happen" to me. They tend to blast in from nowhere, seize me by the throat, and howl, Write me! Write me *now!* But they rarely stand still long enough for me to see what and who they are, before they hurtle away again, and so I spend a lot of my time running after them, like a thrown rider after an escaped horse, saying, Wait for me! Wait for me!, and waving my notebook in the air. *Rose Daughter* happened, but it bolted *with* me. Writing it was quite like riding a not-quite-runaway horse, who is willing to listen to you, so long as you let it run.

If you're a storyteller, your own life streams through you, onto the page, mixed up with the life the story itself brings; you cannot, in any useful or genuine way, separate the two. The thing that tells me when one of the pictures in my head or phrases in my ear is a story, and not a mere afternoon's distraction, is its life, its strength, its vitality. If you were picking up stones in the dark, you would know when you picked up a puppy instead. It's warm; it wriggles; it's *alive.* But the association between my inner (storytelling) life and my outer (everything else) life is unusually close in this book. I don't know why the story came to me in the first place, but I know that what fueled the whirlwind of getting it down on paper was my grief for my little lilac-covered

cottage and for a way of life I had loved, even if I love my
new life better.

I think every writer fears doing the same thing again—
and thus boring her readers. But what "the same thing" is
may be tricky to define. I almost didn't write *Beauty;* having
written it, I had absolutely no intention of reusing that plot.
I read somewhere, a long time ago, a French writer, I think,
saying that each writer has only one story to tell; it's
whether or not they find interesting ways to retell it that is
important. The idea has stuck with me because I suspect it's
true. Maybe I shouldn't be surprised that my favourite fairy-
tale came back to me, dressed in a new story, after twenty
more years in the back of my mind and the bottom of my
heart—and the odd major life crisis to break it loose and
urge it into my consciousness.

Maybe it'll come to me again in another twenty years.

Hampshire, England
October 1996